CLOSING COSTS

A H E N R Y H O L T M Y S T E R Y

ALSO BY THOMAS BUNN

Worse Than Death
Closet Bones

A HENRY HOLT MYSTERY

Thomas Bunn

CLOSING COSTS

HENRY HOLT AND COMPANY
NEW YORK

Copyright © 1990 by Thomas Bunn
All rights reserved, including the right to reproduce
this book or portions thereof in any form.
Published by Henry Holt and Company, Inc.,
115 West 18th Street, New York, New York 10011.
Published in Canada by Fitzhenry & Whiteside Limited,
195 Allstate Parkway, Markham, Ontario L3R 4T8.

Library of Congress Cataloging-in-Publication Data
Bunn, Thomas, 1944–
Closing costs / Thomas Bunn. — 1st ed.
p.   cm. — (A Henry Holt mystery)
ISBN 0-8050-1073-4
I. Title.
PS3552.U472C5   1990
813'.54—dc20   90-30875
                                        CIP

Henry Holt books are available at special discounts
for bulk purchases for sales promotions, premiums,
fund-raising, or educational use. Special editions
or book excerpts can also be created to specification.
For details contact:
Special Sales Director, Henry Holt and Company, Inc.,
115 West 18th Street, New York, New York 10011

First Edition

Designed by Lucy Albanese
Printed in the United States of America
Recognizing the importance of preserving the written word,
Henry Holt and Company, Inc., by policy, prints all of its
first editions on acid-free paper. ∞

1   3   5   7   9   10   8   6   4   2

FOR MY SISTER, BARBARA BUNN

CLOSING COSTS

A H E N R Y H O L T M Y S T E R Y

1

I got my first look at him when he pushed open the rear door of the motel lobby and stepped out into the parking lot. He had a pair of Cokes in one hand and a bucket of ice in the other. As he walked to his room he held the Cokes away from his white shirt, and watched that the ice didn't drip on his shiny shoes. It had been dark for over an hour, but I could see him well enough in the nervous flicker of the motel's neon sign, and what I noticed—beyond the fact that he stood five-ten, weighed a solid 170, and wasn't packing—was the way he moved, his stride martial, his back straight, as if he were a soldier in uniform. When he saw me, though, he shifted to a street strut, displaying his cool; no big deal that a big white man was angling toward him across a shadowy parking lot on the ghetto outskirts of Washington, D.C.

"Excuse me," I said.

My man came to a stop, gave me a lazy once-over and the hint of a smirk. "What you done?" he said.

"Everything but time," I said.

He gave me another look, one that wasn't quite so sure of itself. He said, "What you want?"

I nodded at the motel. "A word with Ed Quinn."

"Say who?"

"The old guy in room 133, the one you're pumping full of heroin when you're not changing his bladder bag. Or maybe your sidekick does it. He's a little younger than you, wears a leather jacket and white New Balance court shoes." This was the description Harry Gibbs and Tim Cooney had given me. I'd connected with them only a few minutes ago, so I was having to take Harry's hurried word for what my man's associate looked like . . . and for everything else that had been breaking the past couple days.

"You po-lice?" My man's cool, like the ice in his bucket, was beginning to melt.

I shook my head. "Quinn's partner."

"How do I know that?" he said, squaring his shoulders and raising his chin.

His dialect had turned white as his shirt, which looked professionally starched. The creases in his wool slacks were as sharp as knives. His plain-toed shoes were buffed to a mirrorlike finish, and his cheeks were shaved smooth as an eggplant. He reminded me of a Marine gunnery sergeant. I said, "And how do I know Ed Quinn wants you feeding him from a needle?

"Quinn told us we didn't have to worry about his partner. Said you'd understand."

The gunny was stalling, thinking over his options, wondering if I could be suckered with a plea or a punch. He had the Cokes and the ice, so I wasn't worried about a punch. If he tried a plea, though, he could probably talk me out of disturbing Ed more easily than Harry Gibbs had talked me into it. "Ed's right," I said. "I do understand. But that gentleman over there doesn't get it at all." I pointed across the parking lot at Harry Gibbs. He was in the shadows, standing next to my car, Tim Cooney beside him.

"That bald guy who I think it is?" said the gunny.

"Ed's lawyer," I said. "The kid's Ed's gofer. The two of them followed you here from the motel outside Lansing where you stashed Ed after you snatched him from the veterans hospital."

The gunny groaned disgustedly, shaking his head. "I already explained to Baldy we're only doing what Quinn wants us to do. He's not our prisoner or anything. I told him that yesterday."

"But then you skipped town."

"Quinn said to."

"His lawyer doesn't think Ed knows what's in his own best interest."

"Quinn's interest is in being left alone. He's dying."

"You a doctor?" I asked.

"Don't have to be a doctor to know he's finished."

"His lawyer still wants a word with him."

"About what?"

"He says he's talked to an oncologist here in Washington who's developed some new techniques for handling pain, methods that weren't available to Ed at the V.A. in Michigan."

"Quinn can't afford no hotshot specialist."

"His lawyer also talked to some other people in D.C. and found out Ed owns a sizable asset. He wants Ed to give him power of attorney so he can sell the asset to pay for proper medical treatment."

"Asset? What asset?"

"I don't know. Being a fiduciary, the lawyer won't say, not without Ed's permission."

The gunny gave this a moment's thought, shoulders back, chest out. Then he said, "Yesterday morning, after we snuck Quinn out of the hospital, we stopped by his house, picked up some of his things before we went looking for a motel. You ever been to his place?"

Ed Quinn lived in a shingle-shedding bungalow that exhibited evidence of human habitation, but little else. I said, "Sure."

"Then you know the man hasn't got any assets."

"That's what I always figured," I said, "but according to his attorney, the asset's here, not in Michigan. Also, he's sure Ed doesn't know what it's worth, says he's being juked out of it: the heroin in exchange for the asset. The lawyer mentioned fraud."

"I don't know anything about that," the gunny said. "I'm just doing this." He nodded at the motel.

I glanced at the paint that was peeling off the cinder blocks, and took in the venetian blinds that were hanging at odd angles. It was Ed's kind of place. "Then maybe you should hear what his attorney has to say," I said, "because certain people might consider 'doing this' a lot more serious than fraud. They might consider it murder."

The gunny shook his head. "No way."

"What do you call it?" I said. "Death by default?"

The gunny's gaze fell. Then he sighed and drew back his shoulders again. "Thing is, it's what Quinn wants, and we promised we'd see him through."

The gunny's tone made this seem less a threat than an appeal to reason. I said, "Does the heroin do the job?"

"Seems to."

I thought it over. "Maybe it's murder," I said, "or maybe it's mercy. Either way, the law calls it a crime."

"It'd be a worse crime *not* to," the gunny said. "Worse than murder."

Out front of the motel there was a lull in traffic, and in the sudden silence I could hear the neon sign buzzing. I thought I could hear Harry Gibbs urging me to get on with it, too. "Tell you what," I said to the gunny, "if Ed Quinn convinces me he's happy with the heroin and doesn't want to return to a hospital, I'll see to it his lawyer leaves him alone. I guarantee it. But let's give the legal beagle a chance to make his case."

The gunny worked on it, jiggling the ice in the bucket as he mulled my proposition. He looked once at the motel as if seeking advice or approval from the blistered bricks, then sighed aloud and said, "Okay."

I sighed, too, but not so he could hear me.

2

I followed the gunny to room 133 and motioned for Harry and
Tim to join us. The gunny, his hands full of Coke and ice,
thumped the door with the toe of his shoe. I tried the knob, but
it was locked. "Open up," the gunny called through the door.
"It's me."

We waited.

Harry and Tim scuffed to a halt a few paces behind us. Harry
Gibbs was in his fifties, a short, small-boned man with a large
head and a perpetually flushed face. He'd lost most of his blond,
very fine hair, and what was left of it was cut so short you needed
a magnifying glass to know it was there. Ed once said Harry
looked like Truman Capote, and this was a fair comparison. Ed
also said Harry liked to tag along with him on cases involving
domestic surveillance because it gave the little lawyer a chance to
study "tits instead of torts." In light of Ed's Capote remark, this
was a compliment. Harry had been accompanying Ed on
stakeouts for a number of years now, so it didn't seem all that
peculiar anymore, and Ed had caged a lot of free legal advice for
himself and his clients.

Ed's relationship with his nineteen-year-old gofer, Tim
Cooney, made less sense than his connection to Harry Gibbs, at

least on the surface. Tim was a helpless, gangling kid, nearly as blond as Harry, and almost as tall as me. He had a narrow face with a jutting chin that didn't look strong, just prominent and fragile. Now that it was October, Tim was wearing his trench coat again. He bought it six or seven months ago, just after Ed hired him. Ed said the boy told him he spent four hundred dollars on the coat, but that it was worth it because it made him feel like a real private eye. Ed Quinn, the quintessential P.I., wouldn't have been caught dead in a trench coat. Even so, he was as proud of Tim Cooney and his London Fog as a father whose son was showing every sign of following him step for step through life. Ed wasn't married and didn't have any kids that he knew of, but he had a paternal instinct as strong as mine, and as long as I've known him, he always had a gofer around, a kid to bring along, teach the ropes to. All his surrogate sons had gone on to other things, though, college or the army. Florida. Even jail. But when I first met Tim Cooney, I knew he was different, the type to end up in a seminary. Or graduate school. Then again, maybe it was Ed who was different. Changed. I think he knew he had something wrong with him when he hired Tim. The way he devoted himself to the boy, I couldn't help wondering if he saw Tim as his last chance at fatherhood. After I got to know Tim a little better, it was clear he saw Ed as a last chance, too.

The knob rattled and the gunny's sidekick opened the door. He looked a little like the gunny, but was several years younger and a shade lighter. He was a sportier dresser, too, wearing a glossy short-waisted fawn-colored leather jacket, pleated jeans, and white leather court shoes with a silver N, just as Tim had said. His hair stood up a good two inches and was mowed as level as my lawn. With a pair of sunglasses propped on his flat top, he looked quite pleased with his appearance, a real sport. When he saw it wasn't just the gunny at the door, though, his expression took a turn, his slightly protruding eyes darting at Harry, Tim, and me, the whites showing like a startled stallion's.

"They aren't police," the gunny said.

The sport looked us over again, altering his stance. He didn't appear to be relaxing . . . more like pumping himself up to take on three gray boys who weren't cops. He seemed to want to start with Harry, who was shifting his weight from foot to foot as if he had to go to the bathroom.

From inside the motel someone said, "Who is it?" The voice was Ed Quinn's, and I could feel the pain the question had cost him.

The sport turned and spoke over his shoulder at Ed. "It the same baldhead' dude I tossed out that motel in Michigan." As he spoke, I noticed that the sport had a hypodermic in his hand.

"Excuse me," I said, motioning for the sport to move aside.

"What you done?" he said.

I glanced at the gunny. "Too bad he doesn't plagiarize your manners, too."

"This is Quinn's partner," the gunny said, thumbing his natty apprentice out of the doorway. "Let him in."

The sport didn't seem to think my partnership with Ed counted for much, but he moved aside anyway, and I pushed past him into the room. It was seedier than a moldy fig, but it had the requisite color TV sitting on a low dresser facing a pair of double beds, a nightstand between them. Ed was in the nearest bed. I went up to the side of it and leaned over him. His eyes were sunken and his odor was bad. He looked as if he'd spent three years in Auschwitz.

He gaped at me. His eyes, normally a metallic, vaguely iridescent blue, had turned the same cloudy-gray a steelhead fades to as it dies. "Jack?" he said, his voice grainy with phlegm.

"Sorry to bust in on you," I said.

Harry Gibbs leaned over Ed from the other side of the bed, then glanced up at me. Harry hadn't seen Ed in a couple weeks and was unprepared for what the disease had done to Ed in such a short time. He looked at Ed again, nervously fingering the pocket flaps of his barrister-blue topcoat, trying to find words

7

adequate to the situation. When none came, his eyes played over the room with an angry impatience, as if he were looking for something to blame. He caught sight of the paraphernalia on the nightstand—a flame-blackened teaspoon, a glass of water, a butane lighter, and a wax-paper packet of white powder—and said, "Look at that. My God, Ed, you're making a terrible mistake dabbling with this trash. You don't—"

"Get the fuck outta here, Harry."

Despite the things he sometimes muttered behind Harry's back, I never heard Ed say anything short or crude to Harry's face. Occasionally Harry would venture an obscenity in Ed's presence, but Ed always refused to follow suit. He seemed to want to keep Harry at a distance, not so far away as to make Harry feel unappreciated, but not so close that Harry could ever form the idea that he was truly tight with Ed Quinn. Of course, Harry counted Ed as his best friend. Nothing Ed could do about that. Nothing Harry could do about it, either. Like most men, Harry aspired to a toughness beyond his genetic means, which was probably why he sat those all-night stakeouts with Ed, a man who'd served in two wars and had come home with six medals. In a courtroom, in defense of a client, Harry Gibbs went to war wielding his bayonetlike brain with the guts of three men. But that wasn't enough for Harry. He craved the approval of someone who had bayoneted three men in the guts and had been rewarded by his country for the effort. Seeing his hero laid out in a rundown motel room, surrendering to a cowardly disease, frightened Harry. He gave me a look of shock mingled with anguish and panic.

I glanced away. Tim was standing with his back to the door, squinting as if it pained him to look at Ed. The boy's trench coat seemed to be the only thing holding him up.

The gunny, having set the ice bucket and the sweating Cokes next to the TV, was wiping his damp hands on his slacks. He was wearing a pair of thin brown-leather businessman's gloves, though, and wasn't drying his hands, but was forcing them deeper into the gloves. Latex would have been a better choice of gloves, but leather was all right, and attracted less attention out of doors, as long as the weather remained cool.

The sport was wearing gloves, too, but they looked as if they deserved to be wrapped around the wheel of a Porsche. He'd dropped his Ferrari sunglasses over his eyes and was slumped in a chair at the far end of the dresser, the hypodermic scissored between the lambskin fourchettes of his gloves like a high-tech cigarette.

"Please listen to me," Harry said to Ed. "Today, while Tim kept an eye on the room, I inquired about the devisee in your codicil, that Kinfolk outfit? I talked to someone who understands the local situation, and I don't think you're aware of the true value of what you've traded for *this.*" Harry gestured angrily at the packet of heroin.

"What the hell's a 'devisee'?" Ed said.

"Do I have your permission to speak freely?"

"Harry, I just want my shot."

Harry nodded at the gunny and the sport. "And they want you to die."

Ed's eyes pinched shut and he caught his lip between his teeth.

My heart was pounding.

Harry said, "Ed, are you all right? What's the matter?"

When the pain eased, Ed looked at Harry with eyes that seemed to have sunk another millimeter into his skull. "The will's kosher, ain't it?"

"Of course," said Harry. "I drew it up."

"I mean the change I made in it."

"A holographic codicil could cause problems. It would be best to do it right, but at least you had the document Tim delivered to me signed and witnessed, and I've placed it with your papers on the assumption it will suffice. But I sugg—"

"Then you've done your job," Ed groaned. "Leave me do mine."

"But it's not necessary for you to be hiding here in this dump like some dope addict. I talked with an oncologist today and he told me about a drug called Dilaudid-HP." Harry made a frantic search of his breast pocket, came out with a spiral note pad and tilted it toward the light from the bedside lamp. "It's soluble, stronger than heroin, works quicker, and lasts longer per dose. The physician I spoke to has an alcohol treatment, too. It's effective in a large percentage of cases. Somehow the alcohol extinguishes the pain but leaves the patient perfectly lucid."

"Booze makes me throw up."

"You don't drink it," Harry said patiently. "They inject it into your pituitary gland through your nose."

I took a deep breath, or tried to.

"Are you listening to me?" Harry said.

Ed was looking beyond Harry, his hollow gaze searching out Tim Cooney. "I'm not going back to any hospital, Timmy," he said. "I thought you gathered that." Beneath the pain, Ed's tone was full of tender bafflement, as if he didn't understand how Tim could have spent all those days and nights at his bedside without having divined the motives behind his decision to bail out.

Tim tried to reply, but explanations failed him.

Ed looked away and squeezed his eyes shut again. "I need my shot!" He was making a feeble commotion beneath the covers, as if he were trying to ward off something with sharp teeth that had got loose between the sheets. After a moment he looked up at me. "Don't let them take me to a hospital, Jack. I'm done with all that."

"All that" had been plenty, starting with the exploratory, which had confirmed the cancer in his bladder. But Ed was sixty-six, and the exploratory had been so hard on him that they made him rest a month so he'd have the strength to endure the main event, the removal of the bladder itself. They were seven hours cutting the diseased organ out of him. When they were done, they clamped his stomach, shutting down his digestive system. For three days he went without food or water, just a little

10

lemon peel to moisten his lips. Then they opened his stomach and started him on the liquid tray: spinach drippings, soup broth, juice, water. They had him scheduled for solid food on the eighth day, but complications set in and he didn't get his mush till the eleventh day. He'd lost another fifteen pounds by then, and a week later they discovered that the cancer had spread to his lymph nodes and elsewhere. It wasn't long afterward that the pain set in for good. Every so often they gave him a "cocktail" brewed of chloroform, morphine, scopolamine, cocaine, and cherry juice, but all it gave Ed was a dry throat and a galloping heart. Before long he was talking about heroin, having convinced himself it was the answer to his agony.

Harry Gibbs gave me a pleading look. "Reason with him," he said, mouthing his words.

Ed Quinn was mouthing words, too, something about forgiving those who trespassed against him. I glanced at the gunny, then cocked my finger at the sport, who was still slouched in the chair by the dresser, watching with amusement the emotions that were naked on my face. I said, "Give Mr. Quinn his shot."

The sport smiled, slithered out of the chair and glided across the room, his white court shoes silent on the rust-colored carpet, the needle nasty in his hand.

Harry glared at me. "Jack, this isn't right."

Ed was uttering breathless cries of gratitude.

The sport edged between the beds, pushed in front of Harry, and drew back the blankets, exposing Ed's wasted arm.

"This is a terrible mistake," Harry cried.

"We'll talk about it after Ed gets his shot," I said.

The sport reached for the telephone on the nightstand and looped the receiver cord around Ed's arm.

"I won't permit this," Harry said.

I said, "Give him some room."

As the sport aimed the hypodermic, Harry clamped his small hand onto the exposed three inches of the sport's thick wrist. The sport dug his elbow into Harry's belly. Harry grunted and doubled over, but wouldn't let go of the sport's wrist. The sport spread the fingers of his left hand, placed them over Harry's face and ran him backward into the TV. The tube imploded with a burst of gray gas and the tinkle of glass. I rounded the corner of the bed as Harry thudded to the carpet, out cold. I knelt down beside him, raised his head, and examined the gash above his ear. Rivulets of blood gushed from the wound.

The gunny leaned over Harry. "He's got to get sewed up," he said. "The hell you do that for?" he snapped at the sport.

"Ain't no white man break bad on me," the sport said.

"Beat it," I said, "before I break not only bad, but your neck, too."

"Sucker grab me, and I got to walk?"

I said, "Do a pig have knuckles?"

The sport seemed to comprehend this. He clattered the syringe onto the night table and sauntered around the foot of the bed, his face full of sly contempt for the tensions of the moment. Tim Cooney, looking as pale as the cloth of his coat and nowhere near as durable, skittered away from the door. The sport yanked it open, took one look back, and melted into the evening.

The gunny helped me lift Harry onto the second bed. I loosened Harry's tie and looked over at Tim again. He was still standing next to the open door, leaning his head against the wall. His eyes were closed and his mouth was working strangely, as if he were trying to swallow something sour. I said, "Close the door, Timmy, and bring me a damp washcloth."

Tim closed the door, then bolted for the bathroom.

Ed Quinn was still praying.

3

I followed Tim into the bathroom and found him hunched over the commode, hawking into the bowl. Cold water hissed from the faucet and puddled in the folds of a washcloth heaped in the center of the sink. I turned the water off, wrung out the cloth, and stepped over the splayed tails of Tim's trench coat. In the main room the gunny was dabbing at Harry's wound with the corner of the bedspread. I lobbed the wadded-up washcloth to him, turned back to Tim and patted his shoulder. "Feeling better?"

The boy coughed and spat into the bowl. His nose was running and his eyelashes were glistening. A bead of saliva swung from his lower lip. He wiped it on the sleeve of his coat and glanced over his shoulder at Harry Gibbs. "I never saw so much blood," he said.

The bathroom was dingy but typical: two tumblers wrapped in paper, a tissue dispenser mounted in the wall, a miniature bar of soap on the lavatory. Ed's ostomy bags were lying next to his shaving kit. I said, "Scalp wounds always seem to squirt."

"It's my fault," Tim said. He was still on his knees, staring down at the mess in the bowl.

I flushed the toilet. "Why do you say that?"

13

"When Mr. Quinn gave me that envelope with the piece of paper in it to take to Mr. Gibbs, that . . . what's it called again?"

I knelt down beside the boy. "Codicil."

"See, I sort of guessed Mr. Quinn was going to do something, you know, like leave the hospital. I thought about telling you right away, but I knew you were out of town and . . . so I didn't do anything." Tim glanced down at the toilet and watched the swirl as if his future were being sucked down the tubes.

"How did you guess Ed was intending to pull out?"

"He said there was a note inside the envelope telling Mr. Gibbs where he could reach him if there was a problem with the codicil."

"Did you open the envelope?"

"No, sir. It was sealed. You can ask Mr. Gibbs. It's just that I figured he already knew he could reach Mr. Quinn at the hospital, so why would Mr. Quinn make a point of mentioning it if he wasn't going someplace different? I didn't ask him about it, though. I just said I'd deliver the envelope. When I left the room he said good-bye in a different way, too, like . . . I don't know, like I wouldn't be seeing him again. You know the rest from what Mr. Gibbs said in the car."

"You gave Harry the envelope and he called the hospital and they said Ed was gone?"

"Yes."

"Why did Harry get you involved in this in the first place?"

"Well, he knew I was sort of close to Mr. Quinn, so he asked me to come with him to the motel out west of Lansing where they'd taken Mr. Quinn. He wanted me to talk him into going back to the hospital, but we never got in to see him. They wouldn't let us, those two black men." Tim shrugged. "Maybe I should have been more, you know . . . aggressive, but—"

"Don't worry about that." I stood. "Your job now is to get Harry to a hospital."

Tim got to his feet and glanced out into the main room at Ed. "What about Mr. Quinn?"

"You think we should take Ed to a doctor?"

Tim frowned, then shook his head. "At first I was really worried about Mr. Quinn leaving the hospital, but now I'm with you."

"Meaning what?"

"I want whatever Mr. Quinn wants."

"Why?"

"I hate to see him in pain."

"He's been in pain for the last month. What changed your mind?"

"I don't know. I guess after he refused to talk to Mr. Gibbs at the motel in Michigan, I just started having second thoughts about following him. I asked Mr. Gibbs if we shouldn't let him go, but he said no, we had to try to save him no matter what."

"Harry means well," I said.

"When he came back to the car tonight he said he was glad we made the effort."

"Did he tell you what he'd found out?"

"No more than he told you outside. He just said there were people here in Washington who were cheating Mr. Quinn. He was really angry. He wanted to barge in on the black men who were taking care of Mr. Quinn, but after what happened the first time, I talked him into waiting for you."

"Did you ever hear of this 'Kinfolk outfit' he mentioned a minute ago?"

Tim shook his head and spat into the bowl again. "I'm sorry, Mr. Bodine."

"Come on. We'll get Ed squared away, then I'll give you a hand with Harry." I turned toward the door.

Tim hesitated. "Mr. Bodine, there's something I've been meaning to talk to you about."

"What?"

"I think . . ." Tim paused as if he'd changed his mind. His gaze dropped and he shoved his hands into the pockets of his trench coat. "I . . ."

"We're in a hurry, son."

"I just wanted to say I hope you're not angry at me because Mr. Quinn changed his will. I'm not talking about this codicil business, but the change he made last month? I didn't try to talk him into it, or anything, and he said he told you about it, and that it was okay with you, but I still feel bad. The things he left to you, now they go to me. Everything."

Everything. Ed's beat-up house, his rusted-out car, and his file cabinet full of old divorce cases. And, of course, the mystery asset, which he never mentioned to me when he said he was making Tim his primary beneficiary. I said to Tim, "Are you sure it isn't the codicil that's bothering you?"

"No, Mr. Bodine. I mean, sure it is. It's costing everyone a lot of trouble, but what I'm getting at is . . . I'm worried you don't want me to be your partner."

"Strictly speaking, you and I won't be partners. But then, Ed and I have never been partners, either, at least not in any legal sense. We just subcontract one another the way a carpenter will subcontract a plumber. The only documents that have both our names on them are the business cards we share. I thought you knew that."

"I did. I just . . . well, Mr. Quinn said you'd sort of help me, um, get a start."

"You mean let you work under my license until you've got your three years in?"

"Yes."

"I told Ed I'd do that for you, and I will."

Tim glanced down at the toilet as if he weren't so sure he could live up to the terms of his vassalage. "Thanks, Mr. Bodine."

"Sure. Now let's see that Ed gets his shot. Then you take Harry to a hospital. Okay?"

"Okay." Tim stepped out of the bathroom ahead of me, his trench coat sagging off his shoulders.

The gunny was sitting on the edge of Harry's bed, pressing the folded-up washcloth to Harry's gash while murmuring encouragement to Ed in the adjacent bed. Ed's eyes were clamped shut again and he was chewing on his lip. I kept thinking about this "asset" of his, but the only physical possession I knew of that he truly valued was his collection of medals. There were four awards, and two purple hearts. A German potato masher had peppered his behind, and a round from a North Korean rifle had opened him up front and back, an "abdominal through-and-through." The heart for the bullet looked the same as the one for the masher even though, according to Ed, the Korean bullet had been a lot less funny and a lot more painful than the German grenade. When it came to pain, Ed knew what he was talking about. Lying on that motel bed, though, he looked as if pain was something he'd never heard of till tonight. I said to the gunny, "You know how to give him his shot?"

The gunny nodded. "You better watch how I do it, too, because I'm clearing out." The gunny had pearl-sized droplets of perspiration on his brow.

"Don't panic," I said. "We'll keep the cops out of this."

"Maybe," said the gunny, "but the Fifth District station's just up the road. All anyone's got to do is step out the door and shout, and the guy on the desk could have me collared and booked before his seat got cold."

Listening to him, I knew I'd been close. The gunny wasn't a Marine, he was a cop. I knew Ed had spent a couple years on the D.C. force just after the Second World War, but I always had the impression he hadn't kept up with friends from those days . . . although the gunny hardly looked old enough to have known Ed back then. Of course, as far as I knew, Ed didn't have any assets, either. I handed the damp compress to Tim and told him to press it tight to Harry's wound. Tim swallowed hard, but accepted the washcloth and laid it on the gash in Harry's head.

I turned to the gunny and leaned down over his shoulder. "All right," I said, "I'm watching."

"You start this way," said the gunny, snugging the telephone cord around Ed's bony arm. The needle-pocked vein in the crook of Ed's elbow swelled gradually, and the gunny, aiming carefully, jabbed the hypodermic into the vein and drew back on the plunger, aspirating a bright bubble of blood into the foot of the syringe. "You suck in a little blood to make sure you're in the vein," he said, "then you slack off on the cord and feed him the stuff. Do it slow, otherwise you'll kill him. When you've squeezed off half a load, you pull back on the plunger, draw some more blood into the syringe to dilute the hit. You don't want him to go into shock. Keep an eye on him so you can gauge the rush."

Years ago, not long before my first wife and I broke up, we spent a week near the Platte River on the same spot we'd camped the summer we got married. On the last day of our vacation we drove down to the beach where the Platte empties into Lake Michigan, and walked far enough to get away from the fishermen who were casting for salmon. It was warm for that time of year, and we stretched out in the sun. After a while I turned to her to tell her what was on my mind, and I saw that she had tears on her cheeks. She was staring into the sky, eyes wide open, her pupils having shrunk to pinpoints. Ed Quinn's pupils looked like that now, just specks. And there were tears on his cheeks.

The gunny slid the needle out of Ed's arm. "He'll be okay for a while. Depends on how much you give him. I use a quarter gram or less, about this much." The gunny raised a gloved hand and touched his thumb to the first joint of his little finger. "If it's not enough, he'll let you know. Too much and he's dead. Just go slow. When he gets like he is now, he's had his max. It'll last a couple hours, maybe five or six. Depends. Just like feeding a baby, he'll let you know when he's hungry for more. You want to, you can talk to him. Myself, I just leave him be."

The gunny peeked beneath the cotton ball he'd thumbed against Ed's punctured vein, then flipped the ball into a wastebasket under the bedside table. "Here's how you set up a hit," he said. "You tap the dope into this spoon, add a couple cc's of water. You measure it with the syringe. It's marked, see? Then you heat the spoon with the lighter. When the stuff melts, you suck it into the needle through one of these little cotton filters. That's all there is to being a junkie. Just don't be filthy like one. Wash out the syringe after you're done, then suck some alcohol through it. There's a bottle of witch hazel in the bathroom cabinet. Or go out and buy a new set of syringes if you want, tell the druggist you're a diabetic. But that's risky. He might make you later on if something goes wrong. Better to do the witch-hazel routine . . . at least till the needle gets dull."

Even though he was wearing gloves, the gunny wiped the phone and the syringe and the disposable butane lighter with his handkerchief. He said in a whisper, "When it's all over, you get out and make an anonymous phone call to the desk. Or let the maids find him. The evidence techs will dust the main spots, the phone, the doorknob, the flush lever on the toilet, so be sure you wipe the place before you leave. And like I said, don't kill him with the dope. The M.E. decides he was overdosed, it'll be murder instead of 'death by default.' I'm going. Those bladder pouches you can figure out yourself."

"What's he eat?" I said.

The gunny nodded at the Cokes on the dresser. He noticed the room key, wiped it, and dropped it next to the Cokes. Then he put on his jacket—a hound's tooth with a necktie stuffed into the pocket—and started out the door, wiping the knob. He stopped, leaned back in and said, "For Baldy there I suggest George Washington University Hospital. D.C. General's closer, but it's Saturday night and us black people be packed in, bleeding and shot. At G.W. he'll go right to the head of the line, up front of all the tennis elbows. Oh, yeah. When you run low on dope, try the 1700 block of Harvard Street, Northwest. Fourteenth and U's good, too. 'Bye." He closed the door.

I glanced over at Tim Cooney. "Think you can find the hospital he mentioned, drive Harry there?"

"Yes, sir, I . . . I've got a map."

19

"Okay. Let me talk to Harry."

Tim got up. I sat down next to Harry and checked his wound. It had stopped gushing. I refolded the washcloth and cleaned Harry up, wiping the dried blood off the side of his face. As I did so, his eyes opened. They were glassy, the pupils huge. I glanced over at Ed. He was still staring at the ceiling, his pupils no larger than microdots. I was glad the dope worked for Ed, but I hated seeing him like that. I didn't like seeing Harry down for the count, either, the two of them laid out like a pair of post-ops in a recovery room. Or corpses on slabs. Ed had been as hale as a Viking all his life, and Harry, despite his apparent frailty, had never missed a court date because of illness. He said of himself that he moved too fast for viruses to catch him. His courtroom colleagues called him Hyper Harry. The first time I met him I could almost hear him crackling with energy, as if he'd just pulled on a sweater and the static charge was still snapping . . . tapping his toes as he talked, wriggling his fingers, telling me how he and Ed had just come from a stakeout where they'd crashed the husband of one of Harry's clients, had caught "the creep" in bed with his own daughter . . . Harry telling me how he'd held up the window while Ed had held down the shutter on the Ricoh point-and-shoot, the two of them racing to the car afterward, Ed explaining how Harry had climbed in and clutched his chest in mock anticipation of the "big one." Harry chuckled over the scare he'd given Ed, clearly proud of himself for having had the guts to put Ed on like that, reeling off one joke after another as the empty bottles of Bud accumulated between them on the table, Harry's repertoire consisting mostly of self-deprecating lawyer gags ("A rooster's the exact opposite of a lawyer because a rooster clucks defiance, whereas a lawyer—"), snickering at his own punch lines, Harry wanting desperately for Ed to like him, but trying a little too hard . . . then as now.

I sighed and nudged Harry. He opened his eyes again and blinked. "Harry," I said, "Tim's going to drive you to a hospital."

Harry's lids fluttered shut.

"Did you hear me, Harry?"

"I heard you."

"Come on."

I got him to sit up and to hold the washcloth to his head. The blood on his dark blue cashmere coat looked muddy-brown. He said thickly, "Ed's the one who should be going to a hospital."

"I'll stay here with him," I said. "You get yourself stitched up, then come back and we'll work something out. Fair enough?"

Harry didn't argue the idea, just nodded dazedly. I helped him up. His legs were rubbery, and I motioned to Tim for help. He was standing to one side watching us, his hands opening and closing as if he were trying to get a grip on a situation that, like his trench coat, was a size too large for him.

"Come here, Timmy."

Tim edged up to us.

I slung Harry's arm around the boy's slim shoulders and walked them to the door. I opened it and they left together, scuffing across the parking lot toward Harry's Olds '88. I closed the door, locked it, and checked Ed. He was still giving the ceiling that faraway look.

I went into the bathroom, turned on the water, and flushed out the syringe.

4

I was several minutes cleaning out the syringe. I expected Ed to drift off, but when I returned to the main room he rolled his head toward me and said thickly, "Sorry you're messed up in this, partner."

"Mixed up, maybe, but not messed up. " I stepped between the beds, eased open the nightstand drawer and nudged aside a match book and a good book. I spread out a hand towel in the space I'd created and arranged the sterilized syringe, the spoon, the filters, the lighter, and the dope on the towel. Then I slid the drawer shut, wondering if the gunny had canceled maid service. I'd have to ring the desk and make sure . . . if I decided to keep Ed here.

"Harry got you into it, didn't he?" Ed asked.

I was certain Harry wouldn't call the blues, but holed up here with a dime bag of heroin not only helped me see things from the gunny's point of view, it gave me a touch of pearly brow as well. Granted, a bust for possession might mean no more than a slap on the wrist. Then again, it could result in a trip to the local lockup, depending on the judge. One thing for sure, Michigan would wad up my license. "Harry's only doing what he thinks is right," I said.

"He hurt bad?"

"No."

"He coming back?"

"Yes."

"Make him leave me alone, will you, Jack?"

"He wants to talk to you about your will."

"None of his business."

"He thinks you're being cheated out of whatever you're trading for the heroin."

"Nobody's cheating me."

"Harry says otherwise."

"Hell, you know how Harry is. You go for a sandwich and a beer, the barkeep's your buddy, you owe him for three months, but Harry tallies the tab anyway."

"He's worried about you."

Ed's voice softened from a rasp to a whisper. "I know. But my tab's added up, Jack, and the bottom line stays. Don't let Harry dick with it. He's just getting his kicks playing P.I."

"That's not what he's doing, not this time."

Ed closed his eyes and rolled his head from side to side. It looked like the pain was giving him a squeeze, but he let out a sigh and said, "Sometimes I think he's queer."

"No," I said.

"He's got a nice wife," Ed said.

"And he loves her."

"Then why don't he leave me alone, huh? Why isn't he home with her?"

"Because . . . he's going to miss you, Ed."

"Hell, we all end up missing somebody sooner or later. People croak."

"But Harry thinks he can save your life—"

"He can't! Nobody can."

"But he sees himself doing it, rescuing you, setting you up with this oncologist he talked to, getting you healthy—"

"No way."

23

"And if he can pull it off, then there'll come a day when you'll say 'Harry, you're a great guy, and a real man, as good as me.' "

"What are you talking about?"

"He wants your respect."

"Aw, Christ."

We were silent a moment.

Finally Ed said, "I guess I'm gonna disappoint him."

"I know you don't want to."

"I don't want him bugging me. Please, Jack, make him leave me alone."

"All right."

"Thanks, partner. Hey, don't look so glum."

"I've got to explain it to Harry."

"Just . . . hey?" Ed scanned the room. "Where'd they go?"

"The guys who were taking care of you? They punched out."

Ed glanced with alarm at the nightstand. "They took the shit?"

"I put it in the drawer."

Ed let out a sigh of relief and eased back onto the pillow. Then he frowned, studying me. "You're staying?"

"Sure."

He moved his head from side to side. "I don't want you involved, Jack."

"Already am. I'm your new needle man." I nodded at the small bulge his bladder bag made beneath the blanket. "I guess that makes me your bag man, too."

Ed managed a shallow laugh. "You been a good partner."

I tried to think of something to say in reply—thanks, Ed, you've been as important to me as my own father, maybe more so, and I love you—but in all our years together, Ed Quinn and I had never exchanged a sentimental syllable, and I didn't see any point in making him more uncomfortable than he already was. I said, "You think I ought to run for office while I'm here in Washington?"

"Hell, I'd vote you president if I could." Ed's smile faded and

24

he gave me a guilty look. "I wanted to show Timmy how a man should die, Jack, but this damn thing just wore me down."

I nodded.

"Maybe you could explain it to him, why I bugged out?"

"Maybe you should."

"I don't want him to see me again. Not like this."

"All right. I'll tell him."

"It's bad enough putting you through it," Ed said.

"I'll manage."

"See, I wanted to tell you what I was planning, but you would have tried to help, and I didn't want you messed up in this. Anyway, I was going to call and let you know after I got set, so you wouldn't think it was a repeat of your old man, me disappearing like that, without saying anything."

"Just for the record," I said, "were you paying attention to what Harry told you about these new painkillers they've got?"

"Later for that. I better sleep while I can, okay?"

"Okay." A lump like a hot coal was lodged in my throat. I tried to swallow it, but it hurt so bad I reached for the lamp and turned down the three-way bulb before Ed got a look at me. I sat down on the bed, flipped the pillow—the one stained with Harry's blood—and lay down.

I wanted to sleep, too. Except for a brief pause in Towson to get a room, I'd been on the road all day and I needed a nap. I would have taken one in Towson, but I'd called Joyce and she'd given me Harry's message to meet him in D.C. I felt like calling her again, not to unload my grief, just to talk. It was part of my routine, to call her whenever I was on the road and settled in for the night. I usually talked to Eddie, too, if he was still awake. It always gave me a peculiar pleasure to hear his voice over the phone . . . something akin to what Alexander Graham Bell must have felt the first time he spoke to Watson over his creation. Speaking to Eddie, I was hearing my own creation talk to me over Bell's invention, and it never failed to seem miraculous.

I rolled over and looked at Ed. He was breathing heavily. I

watched him a moment more, and he began to snore. I sat up and reached for the phone, dialed, and lay down again. My home phone rang seven or eight times before a small voice said, "Bodine residence."

"Eddie?"

"Hello?"

"Eddie, it's Dad."

"What?"

"It's me, Dad."

"Why are you whispering?"

"Because I'm in a motel and someone's trying to sleep in the next bed."

"Who?"

"Mr. Quinn."

"Who?"

"Your godfather, Mr. Quinn."

"I can't hear you, Dad."

"I can hear the TV. How about turning it down?"

"What?"

"Turn down the TV."

"Okay."

I heard a clunk as Eddie set down the receiver. Ed groaned once as I waited for Eddie to come back. I could hear screams echoing from my living room 650 miles distant, then the roar of an engine and the howl of tires churning furiously. More than a minute later Eddie returned to the phone. "Dad?"

"Where have you been?" This was a rhetorical inquiry, but I couldn't resist.

"There was this sweet car chase on TV," Eddie said. "These guys capture Rico so they can addict him to drugs, but Sonny's after them, and this truck gets in the way—"

"What's so sweet about that?" I said.

Something in my tone made Eddie hesitate. "It's just a TV show, Dad. It's not real."

"It's not very original, either. I'll bet you've seen a truck get in the way a thousand times already. That's not sweet, that's sour."

"Yeah, but this was a tanker."

"Just last week we saw a tanker get in the way in *North by Northwest*. Hitchcock made that movie over thirty years ago."

"Yeah, but Dad, the guys who got Rico were driving a Lamborghini."

"Three guys in a Lamborghini?"

"They stuffed Rico in the back."

"And a tanker pulls in front of Sonny?"

"No, in front of the bad guys, but they go right under it."

"Couldn't Sonny squeak through in his Maserati?"

"It's not a Maserati."

"I thought they canceled that program."

"It's a rerun."

"Did your mother say it was all right to watch it?"

"She's taking a nap. She worked all day writing on her computer. You want me to wake her up?"

"No. I'll call back later."

"Okay. 'Bye."

"Wait a minute."

"What?"

I tried to think of something to say that would make me feel like Alexander Graham Bell. "You been a good kid today?"

"Yeah."

From Eddie's tone, it didn't sound like it was worth asking for details. Anyway, it wasn't a question worthy of Alexander Graham Bell. I said, "I'm sorry I didn't get a chance to say good-bye to you before I left town."

"You coming home soon?"

"Not tonight, anyway."

"Where are you?"

"In Washington, D.C. Didn't Mom tell you?"

"Yeah, but I forgot. Oh, Dad?"

"What?"

"I just remembered something you could get me."

"I don't think I'll have time to do any shopping."

Ed groaned and stirred. His hands were ranging beneath the blanket again, and his mouth was moving as if he had something more serious than a hot lump of grief caught in his throat.

"But it's real easy to find, Dad."

"I think I'd better hang up."

"But Dad—"

"You can tell me about it later. I'll phone back in an hour or so."

"What if I'm in bed when you call?"

"You tell Mom about it before you go to bed, then she can tell me, all right?"

"Uh . . . okay."

"I've got to stop talking, Eddie, or I'll wake Mr. Quinn."

" 'Bye."

"It was nice to hear your voice."

"Yeah. 'Bye."

"Good-bye."

As soon as I hung up I wanted to call Eddie back, but Ed was either choking or in the grip of a wrenching dream. As I debated what to do, he cleared his throat and settled down, or seemed to. I waited, watching him. He began to snore again, and I decided to let him go.

I lay back down and closed my eyes, letting myself go, too, thinking as I drifted off that I ought to call the desk and find out about the room, see how the gunny had paid for it, what name he'd given the clerk, and whether he put down a license number or an address. I slipped into a dream, though, in which I couldn't seem to justify the room bill to Harry Gibbs, who kept shaking his head as he added up the numbers, ignoring my explanations. He wouldn't stop even to answer the phone. He just kept adding and the phone kept pealing. It was the phone on the nightstand, of course, and I woke with my heart going BONG! BONG! against my ribs. I sat up and grabbed the receiver.

"Yes?"

A black man's voice said, "This the desk."

"Yes?"

"Mr. Smith say he check out the room."

I glanced at Ed and frowned at the blown-out TV, trying to remember what I was doing here. "Who?"

"Mr. Smith. Say the room s'posed to be in your name now."

I wished my heart would slow down or my head would speed up. The desk clerk repeated himself and finally I caught on. "That's right," I said. "I'll be taking the room from Mr. Smith. They called him away on an emergency and they've got me filling in for him."

An awkward silence.

"Is there a problem with that?" I said.

"See, Mr. Smith, he pay by the day, cash, and he owe us for today, but he say you takin' the room, so you s'posed to pay."

"Is Mr. Smith there now?"

"Yeah, but I ain't lettin' him leave till I hear who it is going to pay."

It was twenty to eight. I'd been asleep for fifteen minutes at most, but it felt like three in the morning. "I'll be glad to pay for the room," I told the clerk. "I'll come down to the desk first thing in the morning, okay? And, by the way, would you hold maid service till further notice?"

The clerk said, "The business you and Mr. Smith into, maybe you ain't mess up the place and don't need no maid, but understand, you come to the lobby here, pay for the room, or the po-lice, they be down there collecting soon's I hang up."

Ed let out a long, weird groan followed by a cry of angry dismay.

The clerk said, "What that sound?"

"The TV."

"Don't sound like no TV."

"It's *The McLaughlin Group.*"

"Say what?"

"How much do I owe for the room?"

Another long pause, then the clerk said, "Rate for a double, thirty-six."

"Give me a minute and I'll be down," I said. I settled the receiver onto the cradle and checked Ed. His eyeballs were rolling from side to side beneath his lids. He looked as if he were watching a tennis match. Suddenly his eyes popped open and he gave me a stricken look. I said, "Having a dream?"

"Yeah."

"Was Harry adding up the room bill, by any chance?"

"Huh? No, there was artillery, and then . . . I forget."

"You hurting again?"

"Not much."

"Ed, I've got to go down to the lobby about the room. I'll be right back."

Something crossed Ed's mind, and a deep crease appeared between his eyes. "I thought you were on a case," he said.

"I was."

"You finish it?"

"I figured it could wait a couple days."

"Bad for business, putting a case on hold."

"Since Joyce got her promotion I've been putting a lot of things on hold."

"Spending more time with the family?"

"Sure."

"That's good. Me, I've always been a loner. Always wanted to do things my way, no dickering."

"It's never too late to change your ways." I raised my eyebrows and stared at him, making it plain I was making a point.

"I almost got married once," Ed said.

"I didn't know that."

"Lost her. Figured I'd never find anyone like her again, so I just gave up looking."

"Looking's no fun."

"You never liked being single, did you, Jack?"

"No. That's why I kept looking."

"How's fourth grade treating my namesake, by the way?"

"Eddie came home with a certificate of recognition from the State Board of Education the other day. It's signed by the governor."

"Yeah? What'd the kid do?"

"He scored a hundred percent on his math and reading skills in the Michigan Educational Assessment Program."

"That's great. You know, you got a hell of a family."

"I consider you part of it."

It was getting too thick for Ed. He glanced around the room. "Where's Harry? He back yet?"

"No. And don't worry about him."

"It's not him I'm worried about, Jack. You could lose your license—"

"Go back to sleep."

"It galls me, him tailing us here from Lansing. I told him to leave me alone, but he don't listen. And then he pulls you off a case—"

"No, Ed. I dropped it when I went to visit you at the hospital and found out you'd disappeared. I talked to a kitchen worker who said she saw a black man carrying you out a service door. She said she thought he had someone outside holding the door, but she didn't get a look at who it was. I checked around town and ended up bracing Emory at the yard. He said he heard the Harpoles mention your name a couple days earlier."

"You thought it was Bonnie and Clyde?"

Beed and Lula Harpole, also known as Bonnie and Clyde, ran a junkyard which was a distribution point for a chain of chop shops in Michigan, Ohio, and Pennsylvania. Bonnie kept the books. She also kept a dozen women busy in the rambling old house at the rear of their auto-parts store retailing what Clyde called private parts. Ed did business with Clyde because his '72 Monte Carlo was always in need of a new carburetor, fuel pump, or radiator. He dealt with Bonnie because he had a Lamborghini for a libido. I said, "Emory told me they'd left town to visit relatives in Toledo."

"It wasn't them took me."

"That's what I found out, but I didn't start suspecting it till I'd driven to Cleveland and was told they were on their way to Pittsburgh. It was a five-hour wait for a flight, so I drove to Pittsburgh, too. By the time I caught up with them, I'd been to Breezewood, Harrisburg, and Baltimore. Towson, actually."

With mock credulity, Ed said, "I didn't know they had relatives in Maryland."

"You'd be surprised what I found out about Bonnie and Clyde. Thing is, you weren't with them, and they didn't have the slightest idea what happened to you."

"Dead end, huh?"

Under better circumstances, Ed would have been enjoying this. "I didn't plan on driving back till tomorrow," I said, "so I took a room in Towson and called home to check in, see if anybody had heard from you. Joyce said Harry Gibbs trailed you here to D.C. and wanted me to fly down, help him out. I was already close enough I just got back in the car and drove. An hour later Harry's telling me about a last-minute change you made in your will, how it's a bad idea, but he won't say what it is till he talks to you."

Ed shook his head wearily. "Burned a lot of gas for nothing, Jack."

"Harry said it's definitely a scam."

Ed expelled a dismissive burst of air. "Harry's nothing but a buff. You know that."

"I know he's a good lawyer. I know he cares about you. What I don't know is this Kinfolk outfit he mentioned."

"Jack, don't let him start bugging me about that."

"You want to change motels? I'll drive you up to my room in Towson."

Ed thought about this. "I don't think I can handle a move tonight. This thing comes and goes, the pain. I'll feel better in the morning."

"All right. But I'll have to let Harry in when he gets back from the hospital."

"I know. Just don't let him take me to one, okay?"

"However you want it, I'll back you up. Meantime, I've got to talk to the desk clerk, straighten out a problem with the room."

"I'll be okay."

I went over to the dresser, slipped the room key into my pocket, stepped out into the cool fall evening and closed the door behind me. I checked the knob to make sure the door was locked, then started for the motel lobby, glancing casually at the windows of the rooms as I passed them by. No one was watching me . . . which was probably what the gunny had thought when he'd gone for the Cokes. I scanned the cars in the lot, but it was too dark to see into them. My Chrysler was tucked in between a red Ford Escort and a black customized van. Harry's Olds was gone.

I had to hand it to Harry Gibbs. With only Tim Cooney for a spotter, he'd managed to follow the gunny and the sport from Lansing all the way to Washington. It's hard enough just to follow a car across town in broad daylight, but Harry'd done it at night, Michigan to D.C., a twelve-hour trip. After which, with Tim staking out the motel, he'd investigated the change Ed had made in his will, had even managed to interview an oncologist. It was more than impressive, Harry's effort. It was an act of devotion.

Now it was my turn. I slowed my stride and concentrated, deciding I'd give the desk clerk a phony name and a false tag number, then park my Chrysler in the used-car lot across the street from the motel. Or maybe I'd tell the clerk I'd taken a cab from the airport. If he asked.

Outside the rear door to the lobby, the one the gunny had used, I paused, pulled out my wallet and fingered my funds. I wanted to use my MasterCard and save my cash to buy more dope, but I couldn't give the card to the clerk because my name was on it. I'd have to pay cash for the room and have Joyce wire more money. Unless the dope dealers in D.C. took Master-Card.

I pushed through the door. There was a Coke machine just inside, and an ice machine throbbing noisily next to it. I headed down a short passageway and turned into the lobby, which was furnished with dirty plastic chairs and dusty plastic plants. A bank of plate-glass windows faced the street. One of the panes had been replaced with a sheet of plywood.

I headed for the desk. The clerk, a small black man, reed thin, maybe sixty-five, was behind it. He had bags like prunes beneath his eyes. He was wearing a cotton jacket that was either a cheap blazer or a fancy smock. There was a name tag pinned to the lapel that said OTHMAN MAPES. Mr. Mapes was on the telephone, talking guardedly. The door behind him was open. It led to a small office. A TV was on in the office, a cop show, maybe the same one Eddie was watching. Michigan was on EST, after all. I noticed a rack of picked-over travel brochures on the wall next to the counter, and found a map of Washington among them. I looked up Harvard Street. It was about a mile from the motel, which was indeed only a short distance from a police station.

The clerk put the phone down and started scribbling on a pad. I tucked the map into my breast pocket and said, "I'm Mr. Smith's associate."

The clerk looked up but said nothing. He seemed to be giving me a chance to change my story.

"I'd like to continue on in Mr. Smith's room," I said. "Where is he?"

The clerk slid a pen and a form pad at me. "He gone. Fill this out."

I used my own pen and printed a false name, residence, and tag number in the boxes of the registration form. Something was bothering me. I glanced at the clerk, but he projected a surly, suspicious authority that rang true. I had the key to the room, and no one had driven in or out of the parking lot. I turned the form pad around and pushed it back toward the clerk.

He scanned the information skeptically, an eyebrow raised. "See some ID, Mr. Jackson?"

I produced my wallet, fished out three twenties, and slid the bills across the Formica-topped counter.

The clerk stared at the money, then at me.

"Three pieces of ID," I said, "all bearing my picture and my name. Keep one of them for yourself."

The clerk blinked, looked down at the money again, and said, "How long you want the room for, Mr. Jackson?"

"Tonight, then we'll see. And I don't want to be disturbed again. No maids tomorrow morning, either."

The clerk nodded, his dark fingers gathering in the twenties as though they were prodigal sons. He said, "Checkout time twelve noon. You don't check out, be sure you showed some ID to the day clerk." He folded one of the bills and stuffed it into his pocket. Then he entered the cost of the room on a calculator, fed the other two twenties into a cash drawer and closed it.

"Let's see," I said, "that was twenty for your trouble, and thirty-six for the room. I believe you owe me some change."

"Hotel tax in D.C. eight percent." He tore the tape off the calculator and handed it to me.

I glanced at the figures. "Says here I've got a dollar and twelve cents coming."

The clerk pointed at my breast pocket. "Them map a dollar twelve, each."

"And a bargain."

I left the desk, headed down the hallway past the ice machine and the Coke machine, stepped out into the parking lot and paused. I heard a siren in the distance. It was coming nearer. I edged over to the corner of the building and watched the traffic on New York Avenue, waiting as the siren drew closer. A tour bus roared by, heading into D.C., and at the same instant an ambulance smeared past in the opposite direction, shrieking, its flashers jabbing the night.

I continued to Ed's room, digging in my pocket for the key. I paused outside 133, gave the parking lot a last look, and slid the key into the knob, easing the door open quietly in case Ed had fallen back to sleep.

There wasn't any need for silence, though. Ed Quinn was gone.

5

The blankets had been thrown back toward the foot of the bed, exposing a yellow stain on the sheet. I tossed the blankets over the stain and checked the nightstand. The needle and the dope were missing. Ed's ostomy bags weren't in the bathroom, either, nor was his shaving kit.

Out in the parking lot everything looked just as it had before I'd entered the motel lobby . . . except that my car was listing toward the black customized van. I crunched across the lot, dug my penlight out of my breast pocket and checked the damage. The port-side tires had been slashed, both of them. As I stuffed the light back into my pocket, I saw the desk clerk, Mapes, duck back into the rear door of the lobby. I crossed the parking lot and went into the lobby and found Mr. Mapes, his arms folded, leaning against the office doorjamb. He was pretending to watch a TV detective knuckle his way through a case. I waited, not saying anything, not tapping my foot, either.

Finally Mapes whirled around, his mouth drawn down, fists hard at his sides. "Made me," he shouted. "Say they stick me, I don't. What the hell I s'posed do?"

"Where are they?"

"Gone."

I realized as he said this that I hadn't heard anyone drive in or out of the motel parking lot since I left Ed's room the first time. He had to be somewhere in the motel. As if this thought were a cue, I heard the grind of a starter and the roar of an engine. Two engines.

I burst into the parking lot and saw the black customized van and the red Escort squeal left onto New York Avenue toward downtown Washington. I turned toward my car, but that was just a reflex. The Chrysler wasn't going anywhere on two flat tires. I thought about calling the cops, but that was a reflex, too. I'd missed making the tags. Even if I hadn't, there wasn't any way I could explain to the law what had been going on tonight without jeopardizing Ed's last days. And incriminating myself. So I just stood there, staring after the van and the Escort, watching their taillights recede in the night. I imagined Ed bouncing around in the back of the van, and I cringed.

"Man say he do me, I don't foo' you to the desk." Mr. Mapes had followed me out into the parking lot. "Shank this big!" Mapes was holding his hands far enough apart to fit a cavalry saber between them.

"Did you give Mr. Smith a pass key?" I said.

"Took it."

"When he checked in he must have filled out a registration form. Where is it?"

"Took that, too."

"You remember what name he put down on the form?"

"Why you askin' me? The man your 'sociate."

"Have you called the police?"

"Nigger say he cut me, I do."

I turned away and stalked over to Ed's room, locked myself inside, popped a Coke and knocked back half of it, the carbonation scalding my throat. I began pacing the room, grinding shards of picture tube into the carpet. On the one hand, Ed was with the guys who had the dope, and the dope was all he wanted out of what little life he had left to live. On the other hand, the guys giving it to him were working for an "outfit" named Kinfolk, which, according to Harry Gibbs, was defrauding Ed.

Fraud's a lot like cancer. Usually it's quite advanced before its victims realize they have a problem. And once they do, their chances of a cure are only fair. Preventive measures are few: watch for the warning signs and see a private eye for regular checkups. P.I.'s make a living off fraud, but we don't like it any better than doctors like cancer.

There was an open cabinet under the nightstand drawer. It was filled with telephone books, six volumes of yellow pages, two each for Maryland, Virginia, and D.C., and three volumes of white pages, one for Maryland, one for Virginia, and another for D.C. I felt briefly daunted. Back home the white pages and the yellow pages are neatly combined in a two-inch-thick book which includes listings not only for Lansing and East Lansing, but for seven or eight outlying villages as well.

I sat down on Harry's bed. The D.C. white pages looked thinnest, so I started with them, thumbing through the Ks in the business listings. The only "Kinfolk" I found was an enterprise named Kinfolk Realty. I jotted the name and number in my note pad and reached for the phone.

My call was answered by a woman who said, "Kinfolk, Benedict." The woman's tone implied she was a good deal more than a functionary.

I said, "This is Ms. Benedict?"

"Yes." Ms. Benedict sounded more than a little irritated at having to repeat herself. There was a fullness and depth to her voice that suggested she was in her late forties, early fifties. I pictured her wearing a white blouse under a business suit. I was sure her hair was tied back and that she had a pen in her hand and was tapping it impatiently on a spray of papers, trying to figure a way to unload a "charming" brick bi-level on a couple of wide-eyed clucks from Runfast, Mississippi.

"Ms. Benedict," I said, "my name is Jack Bodine. I'm calling long distance from the Coast on a rather urgent matter."

Ms. Benedict asked how she could help me in a tone of voice that implied she'd prefer to get rid of me and would if I didn't get to the point, toot sweet.

I said, "I represent the wife of a party recently deceased. His papers were not well kept, so there is some confusion on this end as to whether he had any property listed with you folks there in Washington. His name is Edward Quinn, no middle initial. I'm wondering if you'd be so kind as to—"

"I'm really quite busy, Mr. Bodine. Perhaps you could—"

I made a quick modulation, lowering my voice and taking Ms. Benedict into my confidence. "I'm very sorry to trouble you, but Mrs. Quinn's here now. The poor woman's in tears. She has no way to make ends meet, it was so sudden. If Mr. Quinn owns property in the D.C. area and has it listed with you or with one of the other prominent realtors in town, well, it would mean a great deal to his widow if I could give her some good news this afternoon. We'd want to sell the property right away, and any courtesy you could extend to us would mean a bonus for you over and above your commission."

Ms. Benedict, sounding deeply touched by the mention of a bonus and a commission, stuck me on hold while she checked her computer. As I waited, I thumbed through the Virginia and Maryland white pages. The only "outfits" named Kinfolk were Kinfolk Realty branch offices. This had to be it. If only Ms. Benedict—

She came back on the line and told me she was sorry, but she couldn't find any properties listed under the name Edward Quinn. She didn't sound sorry. She sounded disappointed to have missed the commission and the bonus, so I decided to believe her.

"I certainly appreciate your help, Ms. Benedict. I'm wondering, though, is there anyone else in the office this afternoon who might know something about Mr. Quinn?"

"It's going on eight-thirty here, Mr. Bodine. Everyone's gone for the night."

"How egocentric of me," I said. "But Santa Barbara has that effect on one."

"Yes. Well, I can't help you."

"Ms. Benedict, is it possible one of your agents is handling Mr. Quinn's affairs on a confidential basis?"

"If so, I wouldn't know about it, would I?"

"No, but someone might. The owner of the agency, perhaps?"

"Perhaps, but Craig won't be in till Monday morning."

"Craig? Craig who?"

"Kinney. Craig Kinney." Ms. Benedict said this as if I'd said, "Jesus? Jesus who?"

"Do you have any idea where I might reach Mr. Kinney tonight?" I asked.

"I'm sure he would not wish to be disturbed."

"Maybe if you were to explain to him the urgency of—"

"I'm sorry, Mr. Bodine. Good night." Click.

"Good afternoon, Ms. Benedict."

I cradled the receiver and waded back into the D.C. white pages—the residential section this time—and found a Kinney, Craig, living on Connecticut Avenue, Northwest. I dialed his number and another brusque-voiced female answered. Assuming she was Mrs. Kinney, I addressed her as such, and was frostily informed that she was the *ex*–Mrs. Kinney, and that she had no idea of her estranged husband's whereabouts. The ex–Mrs. Kinney sounded a lot like Ms. Benedict, but, being too well-bred to hang up on me, she suggested I try locating her estranged husband through his brother, Nicholas. She gave me Nicholas's number, and wished me good evening in a tone that plainly conveyed how much she was enjoying her estrangement.

A teenage girl answered my call to brother Nick, and told me I had reached the Kinney residence. I told her I wanted to talk to Mr. Nicholas Kinney, and she told me Mr. Kinney wasn't at home, that she was the baby-sitter. I asked her if she knew where Mr. Kinney might be reached. She gave me a number, but that was all, couldn't recall exactly where Mr. and Mrs. Kinney had

41

gone for the evening. She said this huffily. I'd never had a baby-sitter get huffy with me before, and I couldn't help wondering if Ms. Benedict was calling ahead, cuing people. Or maybe huffiness was all a midwestern guy had a right to expect from the movers and shakers in the nation's capital, baby-sitters included.

I cut the kid off, dialed the number she'd given me, and waited. The phone was picked up after four rings. A black female said, "Kinney residence."

"Nicholas Kinney, please."

"Mr. Kinney at the table."

Which probably meant he was eating supper, although maybe he was shooting craps. "It's important."

"Who is it calling?" No huffiness in this voice, just a guarded distrustfulness.

"The name's Jack Bodine."

"I'll tell him."

"Thank you."

A full minute later I heard a rustling sound on the other end of the line, then the medium-deep voice of a man in his early thirties. He sounded as if he'd just downed a mouthful of food. He said, "Yes?"

"Nicholas Kinney?"

"Yes?"

"Jack Bodine. I'm with Century 21 and there's a little problem with agents and commissions I'd like to talk over with your brother Craig. I'm wondering if you could help me get in touch with him tonight?"

"I'm sorry, but Craig left on a business matter about twenty minutes ago."

"I see. Do you have any idea when he'll be back?"

"No, I don't."

"Do you happen to know where he went? Maybe I could arrange to bump into him there."

"I'm sorry, I can't help you."

42

"I see. Does the name 'Quinn' mean anything to you? Ed Quinn?"

"Quinn?"

"Right."

"My father's brother?"

Ed had never discussed his family with me. For all I knew, he'd sprung fully formed from the salt of the earth, but I didn't miss a beat. "That's correct, his brother, Ed Quinn."

"I'm sorry, I have no idea what this is about." A half-tone of huff had edged into Nick Kinney's voice.

I tuned my tone a little, too, sliding into a mood of cynical amusement, as if I were a leg breaker who enjoyed his work and was eager to put in a little overtime tonight. "You can't guess where I'm going with this, Nicky?"

"No. I haven't any idea—"

"Tell you what, maybe your old man can help me. Where can I reach him?"

"Well, he's here. This is his house, but—"

"What's the address there, Nicky?"

"Wait, I don't think my father would care to talk to you. I mean, if it concerns his brother, I'm sure he wouldn't be interested."

"I'm sorry to hear that, because I'm interested in you Kinneys, especially your brother, Craig. When I met with Mr. Quinn tonight I got the impression Craig's realty outfit was pulling a fast one on him. I want Craig to straighten things out before it's too late. Do I make myself clear?"

"I'm sorry. I'm not going to continue this conversation. And don't bother calling back because I will instruct the maid not to put you through. Good night." *Click.*

Fair enough. I fanned through the residence section of the phone book again and looked up Kinney. I knew I was on to something. It was almost too easy. I found the number Nicholas Kinney's baby-sitter had given me. It belonged to a Douglas Kinney. He was on P Street, Northwest. I pulled out my map of the District of Columbia and determined that Douglas Kinney lived in a section of Washington known as Georgetown. Everyone's heard of Georgetown, even us plain guys from Michigan. I wrote down Douglas Kinney's name and address in my note pad, then looked up "Taxicabs" in the D.C. yellow pages, volume two, L through Z, and called the cab company with the biggest ad.

Five minutes after I'd cradled the phone, someone pounded on the door. "Open up. Police."

I felt reasonably certain it wasn't the cabbie having a little fun with me.

6

I made a quick mental inventory of the evidence against me, and concluded that I was okay unless the gunny had stashed the dope in the room in order to set me up for a possession bust.

"Open up! Police!"

I opened up, and the door was filled with cop, just one. He was wearing plainclothes under a trench coat that Tim Cooney would have eyed with envy, an ancient piece of work that looked as if it had toured the western front when all had not been quiet there. The dick pushed his badge in my face, and I managed to catch his name and unit before he snapped his wallet shut: Detective Henry Sweetser, Homicide. I also caught his bourbon breath.

I backed away from his bad breezes and he stepped in, leaving the door open behind him while gazing around the room as though it might be suitable for something he had yet to think of. Then he gazed at me. His eyes were as flat as his feet. He had to have flat feet because he looked every inch a cop, the way they looked to me when I was a kid, meeting my father's partners, big fleshy guys, pale from all that night work, men who were worn-out but too wrapped up in their jobs to know it. Sweetser had to know it. He looked ten years over the maximum age for a cop on a big city force.

"We got a report on some trouble here," he said, not looking at me, his voice a robust rotgut rasp.

A homicide dick responding to a disturbance complaint was a new one on me. But this was the nation's capital, and my understanding of how things worked had been acquired in a capital far less grand than the District of Columbia. With round-eyed innocence I said, "What kind of trouble, Detective?"

Sweetser nodded at the shattered TV. "That kind."

I glanced at the television as if its destruction had somehow slipped my mind. "Oh, that. See, they were showing a rerun of *Brideshead Revisited* and the young lady I was with threw a tantrum at missing *Pro Wrestling*. I had to ask her to leave."

"Name?"

"Hers or mine?"

"Let's see some ID, pal." Detective Sweetser did not seem to be enjoying my flustered flake routine.

I eased out my wallet and spread my plastic on the dresser.

Sweetser gazed at my driver's license, my credit cards, and my investigator's license, yawning. "Hired fuzz from Lansing, Michigan, huh?"

"I'm on the job, actually."

"So am I. Empty your pockets."

I did, wondering if it was the gunny, Harry, or Mapes the desk clerk who'd called in the heavy guns.

Sweetser poked through my change with glassy-eyed indifference, flicking my keys with his fingernail. "Jacket, too."

I laid out my pen, penlight, note pad, and the map of Washington, D.C.

Detective Sweetser flipped through the pages of the pad and frowned. "Douglas Kinney?"

I didn't nod. I didn't break out in a cold sweat, either.

Still frowning, Sweetser dropped the pad onto the dresser and began casing the place, paying no more attention to the shards of glass on the carpet than to the art on the walls or the melting ice in the white plastic bucket. He ended up in the bathroom, and while he was in there he took a leak. Over the roar of his flow he said, "That your Chrysler with the Michigan plates?"

"Yes, it is."

"Somebody slashed your tires."

"Seemed like a nice neighborhood, too."

Sweetser eased out of the bathroom, zipping himself. The bloodstained corner of the bedspread caught his eye, but not his interest, as he made a casual inspection of the nightstand, then glanced into the closets. He turned toward me and propped his fists on his hips, having drawn back his trench coat to expose his massive chest. He said, "How about you and me taking a drive to the station so you can tell me what brings you to Washington?"

If it had been the desk clerk, Mapes, the cops would have dispatched a scout car, not a homicide dick. Same if Harry'd called. It had to be the gunny, the man who knew there was a police station just up the road. He'd keyed one of his colleagues on to me so he'd have time to set up Ed somewhere else. Or maybe Sweetser was an old friend of Ed's from his D.C. days. I said, "I'll be glad to talk here, Detective, save you the trip."

"Place depresses me."

"Whereas the station features Wayne Newton nightly, six bars, and an indoor pool?"

Sweetser looked momentarily entranced by the possibilities of such a precinct. Then he said, "Naw, all we got's a cold place for bad guys. Pick up your stuff."

Through the open door I saw headlights flare on the trunk of Sweetser's unmarked cruiser. A cab pulled up behind it and honked, the driver peering into the room.

Sweetser glanced at me. "Going somewhere?"

"I'm in the market for a pair of tires."

Sweetser turned to the cabbie, who looked more like one of the Afghan *mudjaheddin* than a hack. "Hey, Mohammed, dispatch say where your fare's headed?"

The Afghan replied.

"What?" hollered Sweetser.

The Afghan said it again.

"Where?"

He said it a third time. Sweetser waved and told him to beat it. As the cab turned around, Sweetser said to me, "You taking a cab all the way to Georgetown for tires, Mr. Bodine?"

"Where else does one purchase a pair of Pirellis on a Saturday night?"

Sweetser's expression changed, as if deep in the pickled folds of his brain a connection had been made, one that held promise. I was about to tuck my note pad away when he snatched it out of my hand and opened it to the page on which I'd written Douglas Kinney's name. He cocked his head to one side and said, "This address on P Street's in a Georgetown residential neighborhood. You were on your way to see this Douglas Kinney at his home, right?"

"You pros take my breath away."

"What's your interest in Kinney? And cut the shit."

I shrugged. "I've been hired to background him."

Sweetser's gaze made another circuit of the room. "I guess I could hack this dump another minute. Let's hear what you're up to."

I shrugged. "A man named Quinn wishes to bequeath something—I don't know what—to an outfit here in Washington called Kinfolk Realty. Mr. Quinn's lawyer retained me to investigate Kinfolk, make sure they're worthy of the gift. I don't know why."

"This Quinn guy from Lansing, too?"

I nodded.

"What've you turned up so far?"

"Just got into town."

Sweetser eyed the room yet again, then gave me a tired smile. It was as if the scene, so lush with evidence of violence, and my story, so stripped of explanatory detail, reaffirmed some privately held theorem of his. Glancing once more at the name and address I'd written in my note pad, something else entered

Sweetser's expression. His flat gray eyes had come alive with a skeptical glitter, as if he'd just figured out where he could scrounge a free case of Beam's Choice but could hardly believe his good fortune. He said, "Tell you what, Mr. Bodine, pick up the rest of your stuff, and let's you and me grab a cup of coffee."

And just like that I found myself in Sweetser's unmarked car, the air rank with the residuals of the job: smoke, sweat, and vomit. As a bonus, there was Detective Sweetser's breath. I cranked down my window and glanced at the motel lobby as we bounced out of the parking lot. Inside, bathed in fluorescent light, stood a coiffured yup wearing aviator glasses, a turtleneck, and a leather sport coat. He was having an intense conversation with Mr. Mapes. Outside, parked on the narrow asphalt apron in front of the lobby, was a Baltic-blue Porsche, its engine idling, its flashers lighting up the weathered sheet of plywood window filler.

I looked over at Sweetser. He had his eye on the lobby, too. I said, "The very picture of decadence, huh, Detective Sweetser?"

"Naw," he replied, yawning with boredom. "It's just D.C."

7

Sweetser drove a couple blocks and pulled into an Amy Joy doughnut joint and slurped down a cup of coffee. I had a cup, too, being careful not to pick up any bad manners.

Eventually he asked me the name of the lawyer who'd hired me to check out Kinfolk Realty. I gave him Harry's name.

"Gibbs work out of Lansing or Washington?"

"Lansing. East Lansing, to be precise."

"How come he didn't mention what the problem was with Kinfolk?"

"I don't know. All he wanted was a background investigation, check out the corporate officers, that kind of thing."

Sweetser nodded.

I decided once again not to ask him who'd called in the "complaint" against me. He wouldn't have told me anyway, and there wasn't any sense betraying an interest in something that would only provide him with a fresh angle from which to question me. The rule of thumb on finding yourself in the company of cops is not to speak unless spoken to. This applies to ex-wives as well.

On our way out of the Amy Joy, Sweetser knocked back a half dozen Venetian mints, little black breath candies, crunching them while running a comb through his graying hair, primping in the plate glass as if he had a date with destiny.

Back in the car, heading toward downtown D.C., he probed my story in the same desultory way he'd fingered the contents of my pockets on the dresser back at the motel. I was cooperative but vague. He knew I wasn't telling all, but he didn't seem to care. He didn't appear to be conducting me to the Fifth District station, either, so I had a good idea where we were headed, and it didn't conflict with my plans in the least . . . although I'd rather have visited the Kinneys unaccompanied by the local law, lax as it seemed to be. I rather liked Sweetser's attitude, though, liked it enough I was about to violate my rule of thumb and ask him to confirm my theory of our destination. But we came to a roadblock.

Sweetser stopped and rolled down his window. There were two Metropolitan Police scout cars parked nose to nose in front of a rundown row house, and a half dozen more scout cars parked across the street along with a police van and an ambulance. The officers at the scene were leaning against their cars. They looked bored. One of them had a riot gun propped on his hip. Another was shouting something incomprehensible through a bullhorn. I'd heard the story on the news as I was driving into town: an out-of-work bricklayer, wielding a shotgun, was resisting eviction.

"The guy's got his family in there," Sweetser said. "Six, eight kids. Got a line to the media and the mayor, says the yuppies are pushing him out, white blight. But that's crap. Not here on New York Avenue." Sweetser waved his hand at the neighborhood . . . the plywood windows, the weeds, and the winos.

A uniformed officer seemed to think Sweetser had waved at him. He trotted up to the cruiser. "You in on this, too, Sweety?"

Sweetser laughed gently, the annoying sweep of the emergency flashers strobing his placid face. "Naw. I got something heavy going down." He nodded at me.

I turned to watch a WJLA camera crew work its way up the street, the reporter looking to interview neighbors who were huddled on their stoops. When the police bullhorn fell silent I could hear the sharp, excited cries of children.

Sweetser and the uniformed cop talked a minute more, then Sweetser levered the cruiser into gear and followed the flow of diverted traffic onto L Street, cruising past a half-dozen black men who were sharing a four-liter jug of wine while lounging in front of a street-level billboard that said TEACHER'S SCOTCH. RICH IS BETTER. On the next block a white Seville was stopped in the middle of the street. The driver's door was wide open, and in front of the car two black women were engaging in a fist fight. A crowd cheered them on. Sweetser made another detour, and said, "I live in Virginia."

Driving around the block, we passed whores in white boots, pimps in pink boots, derelicts in no boots. Sweetser, his voice full of wonder mingled with disgust, said, "Damn near every day for more years than I care to remember I've rode across the Fourteenth Street Bridge down here to Chocolate City."

A figure darted across the street. For a moment I thought it was the sport from the District Line Motel. Sweetser seemed not to notice the runner or the three men streaking after him. He said, "Fourteenth Street Bridge is the longest bridge in the world, by the way."

I glanced at him.

"True," he grinned. "Runs all the way from Virginia to Africa."

Sweetser's laughter trailed off as he turned onto Massachusetts Avenue. Wasn't anything to laugh at here. The restaurants had long, colorful awnings leading out to the curb. The condos did, too. There were boutiques and limousines. The assertion on the Teacher's Scotch billboard seemed true enough. I was sure the guys passing the jug would have agreed.

A mile or two of this and Sweetser accelerated onto a bridge that was flanked by statues of bison. On the pedestrian railing—a low stone wall—someone had spray-painted: RICH PIGS WILL FALL.

Sweetser chuckled again. "Ol' LBJ was in the White House

when we had the riots back in 'sixty-seven. Someone tells him a mob's going to march on Georgetown and burn it. 'Hot damn,' he says, 'I been waiting fifteen years.' "

"This is Georgetown?" I asked.

"Don't look like much, does it?"

I peered out the window. Even though it was late October, the trees that arched over the narrow streets were still mostly green. The light from the nineteenth-century lamp posts gave the leaves a cozy glow, like the lamplit baize of a billiards table. Just beyond the reach of the streetlights, narrow row houses, each painted a different pastel color—blue, cream, yellow, rose—leaned shoulder to shoulder. I gestured back at the graffito we'd seen on the bridge. "Spray paint hardly seemed dry."

Sweetser nodded. "Blacks ever sober up and stop killing each other, the spiffies are going to wish they'd read their bridges."

"Spiffies?"

"Yuppies don't live in Georgetown. Spiffies do. Like that guy with the Porsche we saw back there at the motel? Hey, I used to work Georgetown. Second District. Nailed a spiff once, chopped his au pair girl into eighteen pieces. Maybe it was only sixteen. Anyway, I caught the spiff in blood up to his elbows, flashed my shield, asked him why he did it. I was young then, used to ask why. You know what he said? Said it was his business what he did with his au pair girl. Those were the good old days. They tell me it's weird now. Another block or two that way, over on Wisconsin, you got the fags and the spiffs and the Marines from Quantico, all mixing it up on Saturday nights. High school kids from Woodbridge and Warrenton and God knows where else. College kids from G.W., Georgetown, and American. Punks, kids with green hair. Summer there's thousands of them, orange hair, Marines with no hair, faggots wanting to suck them off, traffic backed all the way to Rosslyn. You go into a place to eat, they got plants tickling your ears and the walls are painted mauve, whatever that is. Out front you got Rolls-Royces parked in puke. Lot of the guys don't like it, the Second District, but I could hack it again, just once before I retire. Only got six more months, Bodine. Going to buy me a horse farm in Upperville, do some fox hunting with the Mellons, sip them mint juleps in the evening, sniff the wisteria, honeysuckle, whatever." Sweetser laughed as if he astonished himself. "Fact is," he said wistfully, "I got a little mistake to put through college. I got a sick mother, too. And I'm talking diabetes, stroke, asthma, round-the-clock nurses. It's going to be me and D.C. till death do us part. I'll be ninety-five, standing security in a Safeway somewhere, one of those twenty-four-hour joints in the Northeast, the ones the bad guys use to brush up on their armed robbery." Sweetser leaned forward. "There it is."

He was squinting up at a three-story free-standing house that was lighted by exterior spots. I had a client once, a pedant, from whom I'd learned everything I never wanted to know about architectural "idioms." The Kinney place was Federalist, which meant it didn't look like anything in particular, squarish with a bit of an eaves, a slight pitch to the roof, a couple dormers. It was on a corner lot, though, and had a large yard, something that probably went for a premium among all the row houses. The yard was bordered by a spiked wrought-iron fence. The front door was red.

"Thing about Georgetown," Sweetser grumbled, "there's never a place to park." He circled the block twice, then said to hell with it and pulled into the driveway of the house with the red door, snapping on his emergency flashers. The door to the two-car garage was up, and inside I saw a silver Mercedes SEL. Sweetser's amber sidelights winked off the Mercedes's paintwork like the bright ideas of a millionaire.

We climbed out of the cruiser, and Sweetser ambled over to the Mercedes and ran his hand along the fender as if he were stroking a woman. "The good life."

"It's supposed to be better," I said.

"Than what?"

I shrugged. "The bad life."

We walked down to the corner. Sweetser paused and dug out his tin of Venetian mints and popped a dozen. As he was tucking the tin away a scrawny, bearded jogger in satin running shorts with a flashlight strapped to his biceps trotted past, gasping, his shoes silent on the cement. Sweetser said, "Is that the good life or the bad life?"

"I think it's the good life."

"Don't know if I could hack it."

I was beginning to like the detective. I nodded at the jogger. "I suppose you could hire someone to handle that part of it for you."

Sweetser laughed—a kind of honking gasp—and we headed up the brick steps toward the house with the red door. The understated portico was flanked by brass carriage lamps. Behind the beveled lenses small blue flames flickered drowsily. The red door sported a hefty brass knocker with a lion's-head escutcheon. Sweetser rapped the lion on the nose and waited, chewing his mints. He smelled great.

8

A large black woman answered the door to the Kinney house. She wore a dark blue uniform dress and a frilly white apron. Despite the maid outfit, she looked as stern and as suspicious as she'd sounded over the phone when I called from the motel. Like the spiked wrought-iron fence that bordered the Kinney house, she stood eye level with Sweetser and me. She looked as sturdy as the fence, too, with a sharp spikelike gaze that promised impalement if you didn't have a good reason to be standing on her stoop.

That's how she looked at me, anyway. When her gaze shifted to Sweetser her expression dulled, as if Sweetser's presence had blunted her sense of authority. "Well," she said, fingering the ruffled hem of her little apron, "if it ain't Sweety hisself." She gave the detective a weak, fast-fading smile.

Sweetser said, "Willie," staring at her. "It's Willie!" He said this several times more until he finally managed to convince himself that Willie was here in the flesh, standing before him. Then he told her what a coincidence it was to see her again and how they should get together one of these days and talk over old times and by the way, could he see Mr. Douglas Kinney for a minute, please?

Willie stepped back from the door, and Sweetser and I fit ourselves into the narrow foyer. Saying she'd tell Mr. Kinney we were here, Willie hurried off to find him, glancing back over her shoulder as if we might be shadowing her.

When she was gone I expressed to "Sweety" my wonder at the smallness of our world.

"I used to work with her old man outta the Second District," Sweetser said perfunctorily. "Retired a couple years ago."

He spoke over the sounds of a dinner party. I could hear the music of crystal accompanying what sounded like a toast, then more laughter. I caught the maid's voice, a kettle drum among piccolos, and thought again about the way she'd greeted Sweetser, as if he were a twist of fate's knife. I said to Sweetser, "She didn't seem too happy to see you."

"She was never crazy about her old man being a cop."

I nodded. I could understand that. A cop never had coworkers a decent woman would approve of. A cop never had a foyer like this one, either . . . in which there was much to admire, particularly the glittering cone chandelier, the pier mirror with matching table, and the set of expensively framed Renaissance cartography leading up the stairway wall.

While Sweetser admired himself in the pier mirror, I wandered through a set of open French doors and took in the sitting room. It was decked out with a Persian rug and a French ceiling. An English fire flickered tastefully behind a monogrammed brass-framed fireplace screen. Two Chippendale shin-toaster wing chairs sat in front of the fire. They were upholstered in cotton chintz with a ribbon-interrupted patchwork pattern. My first wife had wanted chairs like those, with just that fabric. We were going to have a grandfather clock in a corner of our den, too, with triple brass chimes . . . and English-oak lamp tables and fruitwood tea tables and brass lamps by Stiffel. And above the fireplace we didn't have in a den we couldn't afford, she wanted to hang a lithographic transfer of *The Reverend Robert Walker Skating On Duddingston Loch*. I still remember the description of the Reverend Walker in her prized catalogue, something about his exuberant stride belying his dour expression, a man who became more fascinating as he was studied. My wife said I reminded her of the good reverend. I never knew whether that was a compliment, which is probably why I remember it still. Each time it comes back to me, I promise myself I'll look up the meaning of dour. But I never seem to have the exuberance.

There certainly wasn't anything exuberant about Kinney's sitting room. Restfulness reigned. Even the glass case stuffed with World War Two German military artifacts—shoulder patches, black-and-white photographs, faded news clippings overlaid with potato-masher hand grenades, bayonets, and various sidearms, including a nine-millimeter Luger—seemed to cozy up the place. I wandered over to a triptych of photo portraits displayed on a Chippendale side table. One of the photos was of a young Marine, a full-length shot in which the fresh-faced private stood as glossily erect as Kinney's staircase newel post. Something about him looked familiar, or maybe it was just his resemblance to the young man in the middle photograph. Both of them were athletic-looking youngsters. Both had the same wide-set eyes and high cheekbones. Brothers, obviously. The Marine had the squarer jaw and the thicker neck, though, a fullback's neck. He had a glint I'd seen in the eyes of many Marines, too, a look that said, "I could kill you with a well-placed thumb, but you aren't worth the effort." His brother appeared to be posing for a graduation portrait. His look was business school cool. It was hard to guess either photo's vintage. The Marine Corps hadn't changed the look of its dress uniforms in years, and the B-school kid's three-piece was conservatively cut and perpetually in fashion.

More tinkling from the dining room, this time of silverware on china. Sweetser was craning for a view of the festivities, nervously snapping his wallet open and shut, his badge gleaming.

I turned the third photograph toward me and immediately recognized the young face in the frame. Hard to mistake that jutting chin and those timid eyes, eyes so earnest you knew they'd nicknamed this kid "Pooky." For the past six months or so, Ed Quinn had been calling him Tim Cooney.

Detective Sweetser cleared his throat as a tall silver-haired gentleman in a gray suit and maroon tie stepped into the foyer and identified himself as Douglas Kinney. He was in his late sixties, a well-preserved, gauntly intellectual type with a prominent chin and a thin hollow-cheeked face. Even if I hadn't just stumbled onto the photograph of Tim Cooney, I was sure I would have noticed the striking similarities between Tim and Douglas Kinney. The two of them resembled each other so closely they had to be father and son, though Douglas Kinney looked old enough to be Tim's grandfather.

Kinney thrust his hand at Sweetser and said, "Hank, isn't it?"

Sweetser pushed his shield into his back pocket and shook hands with Kinney, the two of them pumping each other with the aggressive masculine enthusiasm characteristic of successful businessmen. Intellectuals never shook hands that way. Neither did cops, but Sweetser and Kinney seemed to enjoy the exchange. When they let go of each other, Sweetser looked ten years younger, as if Kinney's handshake had the power of rejuvenation.

They went on from there, Kinney making a stab at recollecting where he'd met "Hank." He got it wrong, and Sweetser corrected him with a touch of humorous self-deprecation.

"Yes, of course," said Kinney, "I remember now." He looked genuinely glad to have placed Sweetser and equally interested to learn from Sweetser that the two of them had a mutual acquaintance, a retired cop who now worked for Kinney at an outfit called "Kintell." "You say his name is Caparelli?" Kinney asked.

"Right," said Sweetser. "He's mentioned some really great things about Kintell, Mr. Kinney. Cappy says Kintell's top notch."

"I'm glad to know that," Kinney said. "I'm glad to know I have a friend in the department, too."

Sweetser accepted this with a trace of fawning gratitude that did nothing to mar his mask of servile toadyism. "Thank you, sir. You can count on me any time."

Having managed not to vomit in the fireplace, I left the sitting room and stepped into the foyer. I nodded at Douglas Kinney, who, despite the austerity of his features, had a pair of very rosy cheeks. It was almost as if he were wearing makeup, or blushing in embarrassment at my having discovered Tim's photograph . . . about which I decided to say nothing for now.

Kinney frowned at me and said to Sweetser, "My boy, Craig, was called away from the table a short time ago. He hasn't had an accident, has he, Hank?"

"No sir, nothing like that. I'm sorry to bother you this time of night, but something's come to my attention that I thought you might want to know about." It was tough for Sweetser to share the spotlight, but he hooked his thumb at me and said, "The state of Michigan's seen fit to issue Mr. Bodine here a private investigator's license." Sweetser paused for effect.

Kinney raised an eyebrow at me. His look suggested that while he was not about to rush to judgment against the Water Wonderland, neither was he ruling out the possibility of bureaucratic error. "Is there some way I can help you, Mr. Bodine?"

Sweetser said quickly, "Bodine's here because he was hired by a lawyer named Gibbs to investigate Kinfolk Realty, find out what he could about you and your operation for a man named Quinn. I thought you might want to know what Bodine's been up to." Sweetser had somehow managed to sidle up to Kinney. The two of them were standing shoulder to shoulder, facing me. Kinney's shoulders were a lot narrower than Sweetser's, and at the mention of Ed Quinn, they began to sag.

"What's this all about?" Kinney said to me.

"I'm surprised your son didn't tell you about the phone conversation I had with him," I said.

"You're speaking of Craig?"

"Nick."

The maid was watching us from the end of the hall, a silver coffeepot in hand. Kinney turned toward her. "Wilma, ask Nick to step out here, please." She nodded, and Kinney turned in my direction again, eyeing me speculatively. "Where in Michigan are you based, Mr. Bodine?"

"Lansing."

"This fellow, Quinn, is from Lansing, too?"

"You don't know him?"

"I haven't any idea who he is."

"I got the impression he was your brother."

The spots of color drained from Kinney's cheeks as abruptly as if someone had fiddled with a brightness knob on the back of his head. "Who told you that?" he said.

"Yes, Dad?" This from a thirtyish fellow who'd just stepped into the foyer, a solid citizen with a healthy, almost ruddy complexion and wavy bottle-brown hair. He had on a three-piece suit just like the one he'd been wearing when the B-school photograph had been snapped. He was wearing the same serious, sensible expression, too, a look that said, "I'm a guy you can trust to manage your portfolio even though its rate of return is four percent below what I told you it would be, just don't panic, I'm in control." Nick Kinney had gained a pound or two in the years since he'd posed for the picture, but it was hard to tell how much time had passed, he looked so much like himself. He didn't look like Douglas Kinney in the least, however. He stood a good four inches shorter than his father, and was wider through the face and shoulders, and had bright blue eyes, which, when they registered the stricken expression on his father's face, darted accusingly at Sweetser, then at me. "What's the matter here?" he said. He turned to his father. "Are you all right, Dad?"

"I'm fine," Kinney said irritably.

Sweetser seemed suddenly to regret having let me out of his cruiser and into Kinney's foyer. "If this is a bad time, Mr. Kinney, I can hold Bodine. You can question him tomorrow morning."

"Where did you get this 'brother' business?" Kinney said to me. There still wasn't any color in his cheeks. There didn't seem to be any in his eyes, either, which looked as darkly menacing as the muzzle of the Luger I'd seen in the sitting room.

"It came up as I was talking to Nick on the phone a short time ago," I said.

Douglas Kinney shot a look at his son.

Nick Kinney quailed, then attempted by turns to appear confused and indignant. "I don't know what he's talking about, Dad."

Douglas Kinney looked skeptical.

Detective Sweetser looked as if Nick's denial was one of the most compelling expressions of truth he'd encountered in all his years on the force. He made an effort to put this into words, but Douglas Kinney held up one of his bony white hands and said, "Give me a moment alone with Nick, will you, Hank?"

"Sure, Mr. Kinney. No problem." Sweetser looked ready to give Douglas Kinney an arm and a leg as well. If Kinney had blown his nose in Hank's tie, Hank would have thought it was a feather in his cap.

Kinney drew his son into the sitting room. Towering over him, he appeared to be giving him the third degree. I couldn't hear what they were saying because Sweetser and I were having our own little tête-à-tête.

"What," Sweetser growled, "is this shit about Quinn being Kinney's brother?"

There was something in Sweetser's tone and posture that gave me an inkling of what it would be like to have a truncheon make sharp contact with my cranium. "Ask Nick Kinney," I said. "Better yet, ask his old man."

"I'm asking you."

"All I know is what Nick said over the phone."

"What'd he say?"

I repeated the conversation I'd had with Nick.

Sweetser said, "Shit, why didn't you tell me?"

"You're only just winning my confidence."

Nick Kinney, nodding at the instructions his father was communicating at the point of an index finger, turned and marched into the foyer. He said to Sweetser, "My father would like a word with you."

Sweetser looked as though he'd just been invited into the unit-two containment building at Three Mile Island. He took a deep breath and held it momentarily, as if waiting for oxygen to clear his brain. Then he trudged into the sitting room, leaving Nick and me behind.

Nick adjusted his tie, gave me a look of lobotomized indifference, and turned away. He headed down the hall and pushed through a swinging door that looked like it opened into the kitchen.

I gave an ear to the conversation between Sweetser and Kinney, but the bright chatter from the dining room made for poor eavesdropping. After a moment Sweetser and Kinney emerged from the sitting room. Kinney insisted it had been good to meet me, but I would understand if he couldn't get to know me better. He had guests to entertain.

I motioned toward the sitting room and asked him if the photographs on the side table were of his sons.

Kinney, exuding forbearance, said that they were.

"Craig's the Marine and Nick's the one in the suit, right?"

"That's correct. Now, if you'll—"

"And the other boy," I said, "the one who bears such a strong resemblance to you, what's his name?"

"His name," said Douglas Kinney, his voice tight with impatience and pique, "is Timothy. Now, good-bye, Mr. Bodine."

Sweetser reached for my elbow. They have a way with an elbow, cops do. A cop escorting his daughter down the aisle looks as if he's got her in custody. Leaving Douglas Kinney's house, it was everything I could do to keep my elbow out of Hank's hard hand.

63

9

Detective Sweetser backed out of Douglas Kinney's driveway and stomped on the gas. When he hit fifteen miles an hour he eased up on the accelerator and we dogged it a half block to a stop sign, where he stomped on the brakes. When traffic cleared he stomped on the gas again and we loafed along as before, averaging twenty miles an hour at most, crawling and stomping out of Georgetown. The car following us had large streamlined halogen headlamps and no trouble at all keeping up with us. It was like chopping wood for Sweetser, though, taking out his anger on his cruiser while making sure he didn't lose his tail. He was breathing hard, and not a word out of him except to check in with the dispatcher.

There was a mirror on my side of the cruiser, and it wasn't long before I made the tail car as it turned a well-lit corner: a tan Ford Taurus. I didn't say anything about it to Sweetser, not wanting to break my rule of thumb. All Sweetser broke was wind, although he obviously wanted to break my neck for not forewarning him of the fraternal link between Ed Quinn and Douglas Kinney, doubtful as that now seemed. To my eye, Douglas Kinney looked less like Ed Quinn than Harry Gibbs, but there had to be something to it, because Kinney had got Sweetser to do everything but hitch the tan Taurus to his bumper.

My guess it was Nick Kinney back there, and Sweetser was dogging it so Nick could . . . what? Drill me in the back when Sweetser forced me out into some alley? Nick hardly looked like one for wet work. Maybe it was Kinney's maid in the Taurus.

I thought about it another two miles and decided Sweetser would simply drop me at the motel so Nick could stop by for a chat. Or maybe the idea was for Nick to follow me till I led him to Ed Quinn. Which would mean the Kinneys didn't know where Ed was. Unless they wanted me to think they didn't. Or maybe they wanted to be sure I'd never find him, which led back to wet work. Either way, they'd have done better to have Nick drive on ahead to the motel and wait for Sweetser to drop me off there. But on the spur of the moment it's hard to think of everything.

With Sweetser in a slow-motion funk, I had plenty of time to think of everything, but I couldn't come up with much that Ed Quinn had said about his days in Washington other than he'd been on the force for a short while just after the war. He hadn't enjoyed police work, said he disliked wearing a uniform and hated the pseudomilitary "chickenshit" of daily inspections. So he'd quit and become a P.I., ending up in Michigan.

Why Michigan?

I remember him shrugging, giving me a cryptic smile, saying something about Washington being full of chickenshits and hot as hell, telling me he just started west, angling north as he drove, trying to find someplace cool in August, pausing in Lansing not because we had a cold spell, but because he lost his stake shooting craps with some welders from Diamond REO. As he looked around for work he realized he'd landed in a town without a whole lot going for it but politics, Lansing being the capital of the state of Michigan. He knew that where you had politicians you had corruption, nothing like D.C., of course, but enough rot to support a private dick of modest ambitions. Just two hours northwest of Detroit, Lansing was virgin territory. Plenty of divorce cases, too, when political corruption waned as it periodically did after a change of administrations. It was 1954, not long after the close of the Korean war, and Ed, thirty-one years old, stayed on through '55 and '56. Eventually he gave up the idea of leaving, even though mid-Michigan's Augusts were sometimes as hot as Washington's. If limes were scarce in the heartland, there was always ice for your gin.

And that, even though I'd known Ed for a fair portion of his career as a professional P.I., was all I knew about his past. He was as protective of it as he was of his case files. P.I.'s, like priests, learn to keep secrets secret if they want to stay in business. I suppose he would have told me more about his early years if I'd pressed him, but I never did. I knew he wasn't crooked because he couldn't have got a license with a criminal record. He simply didn't want to talk about what he'd left in Washington, anymore than I wanted to talk about what was behind me. We were like a pair of icebergs, Ed and I, four-fifths of us underwater . . . me with four-fifths of a quart under my belt when I met him, sloshed as an iceberg and about as useful as one, too . . . but that was history now, and not for talking about, not with Ed, not with anyone. Those days didn't bear thinking about, even if I could remember them.

What did warrant reflection, however, was Tim Cooney's connection to Ed Quinn. Not Cooney, *Kinney*, Tim Kinney, son of Douglas, brother of Nick. It couldn't be a coincidence he'd ended up in Lansing, working for Ed. It was hard to see it as a callous conspiracy, either. Tim was simply too heartfelt in his concern for Ed to have been faking it, sitting at Ed's bedside during the past month, hours on end, chewing his cheeks and biting his nails as Ed wasted away, despairing as genuinely as I had when my own father got sick. I knew it when I saw it, and Tim's grief was real. If Ed and I were icebergs, then Tim Kinney and I—at least during our visitations with Ed—were reflections of one another, two sons sitting it out, waiting for their old man's end.

"Hey, Bodine, how long you been a P.I.?"

I glanced at Sweetser. He seemed to have calmed down enough to speed up a little. We were hitting thirty-five, cruising along New York Avenue, having got well past the scene of the eviction standoff. Sweetser's knuckles were no longer white on the wheel and he was leaning back in his seat, driving with one hand while using the other to suck on a cigarette. He was the epitome of copness now: jaded, cynical, self-satisfied, suspicious, wised-up, loyal, crafty, unflappable, unhealthy, unrested, unappreciated, and not unequipped with a sense of humor. It didn't seem like an aura he'd have to put much effort into projecting, but there was something false in his manner, a kind of disinterested curiosity, as if it had suddenly occurred to him that I might catch sight of the tail car in the sideview mirror and ought to be distracted with small talk. I said, "Long enough to know better."

Sweetser chuckled. "I only met one other guy who's in the business. Moonlights as a minister in a revival church here in D.C. Straight-up guy. Only time he ever got cute with the law, he was with his family on a camping trip to Mexico. They're out in the boonies and this scruffy little dog starts sniffing around the campsite. The dick's kids feed it, and this dog keeps coming back for more. Before long they've named it Scruffy. They're letting it eat out of their hands, picking it up, hugging it, loving this little mutt. But then it's time to break camp and they can't stand to leave Mexico without Scruffy. So they hide him in the camper and it's touch and go at the border, but they get through. Back home they start making it up to Scruffy for the dog's life he's led south of the border, feeding it leftovers, Christ, he's chowing down at the table with them. But the damn dog goes and gets sick. Now this private dick, he's practically an officer of the court, not to mention an ordained minister, and he's never quit feeling guilty about sneaking the dog past the border authorities. He can't help but think Scruffy getting sick is some kind of punishment. You listening? So he takes Scruffy to a vet. The vet says, 'Hey, where'd you get this dog?' The dick breaks down and tells the vet all about it. The vet says to take it easy, he's not going

67

to report him or anything, it's just that he's never seen a dog like Scruffy before. So he hollers into the back room for his flunky, this Chicano from Gallup, maybe the kid knows what kind of dog it is. The Mex bops into the examining room, takes one look at Scruffy and starts backing out the door. The vet says, 'What's the matter, José?' The kid looks at him and says 'Seenyore, eez a Mexican long-hair rat.' "

Sweetser laughed so hard he almost ran a light . . . wiping tears from his eyes while checking his mirror. Then he glanced over at me. "Hey, no offense, Bodine. I mean, not all P.I.'s are assholes, right?"

"About the same percentage as homicide dicks."

"Hey, hey, come on . . ." Sweetser's laughter trailed off. "I mean, I ain't taking it hard you didn't tell me this Quinn character's Kinney's brother."

"You wouldn't be telling me jokes otherwise, right?"

" 'Course, I'd like to know why you didn't. You knew where I was taking you."

"I guess it didn't seem funny enough at the time."

Sweetser continued to grin, but I knew if it hadn't been for the tail car, he would have whipped into an alley and showed me how funny he could get with the grips of his service revolver.

We were silent a moment, waiting for the light to change. When it did, Sweetser said, "So, how about the line on Quinn? What's the beef between him and Mr. Kinney?"

Sweetser's tone had taken a confidential turn and was oozing with assurances that whatever I revealed about Ed Quinn's relationship with Douglas Kinney would be strictly between the two of us, no reason for "Mister" Kinney to know about it. "There's nothing I can tell you," I said. "I never met Douglas Kinney till tonight. I never heard of that 'Kintell' outfit you mentioned to him, either."

Sweetser said helpfully, "That's Mr. Kinney's investigation agency. It's like a private CIA. Guys that work there are all ex-Justice, FBI, DEA, NSA, DIA, you name it. Pure Brooks

Brothers, too. Hell, compared to Kintell, Pinkertons are just another K mart."

"No divorce work?"

"You don't afford a home like Mr. Kinney's doing divorce work, my friend. Not in Georgetown, anyway."

From what Sweetser had told me about Georgetown, I'd bet he was wrong about that. I didn't say anything, though. The District Line Motel's flickering sign was just ahead, and Sweetser was braking, his foot light on the pedal this time, having warmed up to me again. I said, "I appreciate the lift, Detective. Sorry it didn't work out with Douglas Kinney."

Sweetser came to a stop just outside my room. He turned toward me and said, "Call me Hank. And, hey, don't feel you got to be close-mouthed. You're working on a case, and it can't hurt to have the resources of the department at your disposal . . . if you know what I mean."

"Life's a two-way street, right?"

"Exactly."

"I'll keep in touch."

"I hope so. No hard feelings about me laying you open to Kinney like that?"

"None at all."

"Just seemed the sensible thing to do at the time. See, if I'd known your client was Kinney's brother . . ." Sweetser paused, and said, "Wait a minute. If they're brothers, how come they got different last names?"

"Don't ask me," I said. "I only hit town a half hour before you pulled a bed check on me."

Sweetser glanced over at Ed's motel room as if the blood on the bedspread and the shattered TV tube were caught in the glare of his headlights. Then he looked back at me, nodding as if he were as dumb as he was pretending to be, as if everything were going to work out for the best, even his decision to do as Douglas Kinney had asked him to. After a long moment, nodding the whole time, Sweetser said, "You heard the one about the two gumshoes watching a dog lick its pecker? One of them says, 'Gee, I wish I could do that.' Other one says, 'Mean-looking dog. You better pet it first.' Ha, ha, ha. Ha, ha."

I got out of Sweetser's car. "Nice to have met you, Detective."

Sweetser—his laughter subsiding, but not his obvious urge to slam me against his cruiser and stick his piece in my ear—said softly, "Be seeing you around, Jack."

I *chunk*ed the door shut, and Sweetser swerved out of the motel parking lot and into the heavy flow of traffic, his tires complaining as he stomped on the gas. He passed the tan Taurus as it pulled into the lot of the used-car dealership across the street . . . the driver notching the Taurus into a slot as I darted through traffic and came up behind him. He'd killed his engine and was craning over the steering wheel, wondering if I'd entered the room. The driver was Nick Kinney, of course, and his window was rolled up. I popped the glass with the heel of my hand and the impact made him jump. "You're a liar, Nick," I shouted, "but you're better at that than at tailing people. No offense intended."

The power locks on the Taurus snapped down and Nick Kinney stared at me in frozen-faced humiliation . . . nothing more embarrassing than being made by your mark.

I cut back across the street and headed for the motel, intending to talk with Othman Mapes. In the moments following Ed's disappearance, Mapes had reeked of complicity, but I hadn't aired him out because I'd been half convinced it was for the best that the sport and the gunny had made off with Ed. Afterward, thinking about it, I decided I didn't like the fraud angle. And now there was the knowledge that Douglas Kinney's boy, Tim—innocent as he seemed—was involved. I didn't intend to hurt Ed with what I'd learned about Tim—maybe he already knew—but I wasn't going to let the Kinney clan manipulate my partner without looking under a few rocks first.

I entered the motel lobby under a full head of steam and went up to the desk . . . but Othman Mapes wasn't behind it. I banged on the counter and a moment later a sullen black kid of about eighteen—a cruddy watch cap pulled down over his ears—shambled out of the office. He was wearing Othman Mapes's smock. I said, "Where's the clerk who was on the desk earlier tonight?"

"Ain't here."

"How long has he been gone?"

"Hour."

"You expect him back soon?"

Shrug.

I gave the kid a knowing gaze. "Did they come back for him?"

"Huh?"

"Did they snatch him, too?"

"Ain't nobody *snatch* him." The boy said this defiantly, as if Othman Mapes would have been too much for "them" to handle.

I stepped behind the desk.

The boy said, "Hey."

"Yo?"

"What you doin', man?"

"Looking for Mr. Mapes." I leaned into the office.

"Ain't here," said the boy.

The same crime show was still on the tube, the good guy squeezing off nine-millimeter ammo at a bad guy fishtailing down a narrow palm-lined street in an Italian sports car. Being from Michigan, tropical crime held a secret fascination for me, and I lingered a moment, envying the world of sunny violence in which the good guys prevailed week after week . . . shooting accurately, too . . . the hundred-thousand-dollar car exploding with such vivid elegance I felt a twinge of contempt for myself, remembering how I'd stood there watching the taillights of the black van recede in the night. I watched the hunk snug his automatic into his shoulder holster, then I left the lobby and headed down to Ed's room. My room, now that I'd paid for it.

I didn't see Harry's white Olds in the lot, so I assumed he was still at George Washington University Hospital. I decided to call, see how he was doing, find out if Tim Cooney—Kinney—was still with him, tell them to stay put, that I'd meet them there. I'd have to lose Nick Kinney along the way, of course. I'd have to get a new pair of tires, first, call a garage . . . thinking along those lines when, with the key in the lock, I saw a black Ford Econoline van pull into the lot. It had an exterior visor, lots of chrome trim, chrome wheels, and little round windows in the aft panels of the cargo bay. It was backing into the space adjacent to the rear door of the lobby.

I pulled the key out of the lock, trotted over to the van and stood behind it, waiting. The door opened on the driver's side and Othman Mapes climbed out. He noticed me when I grabbed a fistful of his corduroy jacket. I said, "Where's Ed Quinn?"

"Let go me."

I yanked Mapes away from the door of the van and leaned inside. The dome light shone down on a bare mattress in the carpeted cargo bay. "Where is he?"

Mapes attempted to infect my hand with his sharp little teeth. I shook the fizz out of him, feeling none too proud of myself for breaking bad on a man half my size and thirty-five years my senior. I said, "They hauled Ed Quinn out of here in this van, Mr. Mapes. Where'd they take him?"

"Don't know what you talkin' 'bout, white man."

I increased the distance between Othman Mapes's shoes and the surface of the earth. "I'm going to drop you, Mr. Mapes, and on the way down you'll cave in the side of this vehicle."

"Fuck you."

What made it doubly difficult, this trashing of Othman Mapes, was not the possibility that he was innocent, but the certainty that my son, if he were watching me on TV—some slick cop show or other—would take me for the bad guy, twisting an old man's shirt, sticking my face in his. "Where's Ed Quinn?"

"Don't know no honky name Quinn."

"Who said he was a honky?"

"Fuck you' mama."

"Where'd you just come from, Mr. Mapes?"

"Home."

"Tell you what, you drive me to your home and show me around."

"Fuck you."

"That's not an option. Options are I get your address from the phone book and drive to your place with you creamed in the back of this van, or you drive me there uncreamed. Your choice."

Othman Mapes chose uncreamed.

As we pulled out onto New York Avenue I checked the sideview mirror. I couldn't say for sure, but it looked as if Nick Kinney's Taurus lurched out of the used-car lot after us. "Drive like the wind, Mr. Mapes."

Othman Mapes muttered colorfully.

10

It was a twenty-minute drive to Othman Mapes's house. We crossed the Potomac into Virginia and took the George Washington Parkway north into a suburb of D.C. called Alexandria. From what I could see of it at this hour of the night, Alexandria looked like Georgetown. From what I could see of the road behind us, I couldn't be sure we'd lost Nick Kinney. Othman Mapes certainly hadn't lost his inspiration. He kept up a nearly constant stream of barely audible imprecations. I ignored them for the most part, and concentrated on his route, which, north of downtown Alexandria, approached its end with a left onto Oronoco Street. Several blocks farther on, he hung a hard right onto a gloomy residential street the name of which I missed. He came to a rocking halt in front of a small white stucco house. There weren't any lights on inside, just a naked yellow bulb burning over the stoop. Mapes was staring out the windshield of the van, not looking at me or at the house. "Invite me in," I said.

Mapes shoved out of the van, stalked up to the door of the house and speared the lock with his key. He shouldered the door open, went in and flicked on a light. The house was quiet. I closed the door behind me and looked around. A Victorian sofa with a carved wood frame and feet shaped like claws dominated the living room. There were antimacassars on the sofa's armrests. One of the front windows had a Boston fern in it. The other window was lined with a collection of African violets, most of them in bloom. The faded wallpaper was flowery, and there were little flower patterns woven into the diaphanous curtains. An old hand-painted folding screen partitioned off one corner of the room. There was a small drop-leaf table behind it.

Mapes, watching me look over his house, was sullenly grinding his teeth. I nodded at a hallway that led toward the rear of the place. "What's back there?"

"Kitchen."

"Show me."

Mapes tossed his keys into a small ceramic dish, padded through an arch and down the hallway into a cramped kitchen. It was lit by a flickering fluorescent tube in an old Roper range. Dishes were drying on a rack, a towel spread over them. Telephone books were stacked neatly on top of the refrigerator.

"Where's that door go?" I said.

"Backyard."

"Open it."

Mapes opened the door and snapped on an outdoor light.

I saw two sawhorses and a battered garbage can, no lid. There was no alley behind the house, just a fence and what appeared to be railroad tracks in the distance.

"Is there a basement?"

"Crawl space. Check that out, too?"

"What else is on the first floor?"

"Baffroom. Broom closet."

The bathroom wasn't much bigger than the broom closet. The commode, the claw-foot tub, and the pedestal sink were all about six inches from one another. Everything was shipshape, though. The towels were precisely folded, and the soap dish, furnished with a fresh bar of Ivory, was immaculate. If soldiers wore faucets, the brightwork in the bathroom would have passed a change-of-command inspection. The kitchen and the living room were spotless, too. Old, but orderly. "Let's take a look upstairs," I said.

"Ain't nobody there."

"Prove it."

"I said they ain't no—"

I gave Mr. Mapes some physical encouragement and we lurched out into the living room and up a groaning staircase, Mapes's breath coming in harsh gasps.

Upstairs, the first door on the left was open. Mapes leaned in and turned on the light. It was a bedroom. The spread was stretched tight over the double bed, and two pairs of slippers sat side by side on the braided rug, pink pom-poms on one pair, leather piping on the other.

Mapes opened the door across the hall, snapped on the light and stood back. This was the media room: three vinyl-covered recliners, a TV, two metal TV tables, and another braided rug.

I turned off the light, keeping an eye on Mapes. He'd drifted down toward the end of the hall and was standing in front of a closed door. He looked as though he couldn't decide whether to pretend the room wasn't there or to fight to protect its sanctity.

I said, "Open it."

"Whoever you looking for, he ain't in here."

I elbowed Mapes out of the way and opened the door. Light from the hallway spilled into the room. I saw a figure lying on a bed, heard soft snoring, smelled stale air. I shook off Mapes's hand and started into the room, the floor creaking as I crossed it. "Ed?"

The figure stirred, reached for a bedside lamp and turned it on. I squinted at the old black woman who sat up in bed and squinted at me. She was thin and small. Like Mapes, she had large ears and prunelike bags beneath her eyes. She said, "Who are you?" This was not so much a question as it was an accusation, as if she knew who I was and was daring me to confess my identity.

I said, "I'm sorry to have bothered you, ma'am."

Mapes leaned in from the hallway. "Go back to sleep, Mama."

"Othman?"

"It ain't what you think. Go on to sleep."

I backed out of the room. Mapes gave his mother another comforting word and stepped into the hallway after me, closing the door. Just before it latched I had a last glimpse of the old woman. She was slumped against the towering headboard of her Victorian bed and was glaring at her son with what looked like shock and disgust.

"Now you seen everything," Mapes said in a whisper that verged on a shout.

He was ahead of me going down the stairs. He seemed in a panic. I had the feeling that in disturbing his mother I'd upset him more than if I'd actually found Ed. "Where's Quinn?" I said.

"Don't know who you talking 'bout, white man." Mapes reached for the front door.

I pulled him away from it. "Where did you go in your van earlier tonight?"

"I came here to check on my mama."

"Who are you?" It was Mapes's mother. She was standing at the top of the stairs, looking down at me as though her life suddenly made some kind of dreadful sense.

"It ain't nothing, Mama," Mapes said. "He goin'."

She said to me, "What is your name, sir?"

"Bodine."

She started down the stairs, clutching at her threadbare robe, a trembling hand on the banister. "What are you doing in my house?"

"Looking for a friend of mine. I'm sorry I woke you."

"Is this what it's come to, Othman, bringing them here in the middle of the night?"

"Mama, it ain't what you think."

Mrs. Mapes paused on the stairs and looked at her son as if she pitied him, or as if she were thinking of praying for him, of asking the Lord to let her boy lie a little more competently and quit insulting her intelligence. To me she said, "If your 'friend' pays me a call, I will tell him you were here tonight, Mr. Bodine." Her manner was elegant, and tinged with irony, as if she were too refined to display simple sarcasm or outright contempt.

"We'll be going," I said.

"Ain't going nowhere." Mapes had changed his mind about leaving and tried to jerk his arm free of my hand, but I held onto him and opened the door. Nick Kinney almost fell into the living room.

Mapes's mother said, "Ah, perhaps that's your friend now. Won't you come in, sir?"

Nick looked doubtful of the invitation, but he straightened his tie and stepped in, casing the room.

"I'll not ask for an introduction," said Mrs. Mapes. "I've heard far too many falsehoods for one night. In any case, you already know my son."

"Never seen neither of them before, Mama," Othman Mapes cried.

His mother ignored this and said to Nick, "No doubt you're familiar with this gentleman? He goes by the name of Bodine, but about that I'm sure you are more accurately informed than I."

Nick Kinney looked at me as though he'd been introduced to a post.

Mrs. Mapes extended her trembling hand toward the interior of her home and said to Nick, "Feel free to inspect the premises, too. I'm sure my son won't mind, will you, Othman?"

Without a word Nick edged down the hallway toward the kitchen, glancing at us over his shoulder.

"Mama," Othman Mapes whined, "it the stone truth I ain't never seen these white men before."

"And you, Mr. Bodine, you're going to tell me you have no idea who our young caller is?"

"I know him."

"Is he the friend you're looking for?"

I shook my head.

Nick Kinney came out of the kitchen and returned to the living room. He said politely, "Would you mind if I had a look at the second floor, ma'am?"

"So well-mannered, you young men. Please do."

Nick started up the stairs.

Mapes's mother stepped aside, and in the silence stared sadly at her son while fingering a wisp of gray hair. Her chin began to tremble.

"Mama."

"Don't speak to me, Othman."

"We'll be going," I said, tightening my grip on Mapes. "Good night, ma'am."

"Ain't going nowhere." Mapes swung at me and missed, and I wrestled him into the doorway.

I had him half through it when Nick Kinney came down the stairs, beeping. He had an electronic pager in his hand, one with an LCD readout of the number he had been alerted to call. He said, "May I use your phone, ma'am?"

"By all means. It's in the kitchen." Tears had formed in the old woman's eyes and were on the verge of spilling down her cheeks.

I had no idea what the trouble was between Mapes and his mother, but I'd obviously caused it to take a turn for the worse. I was eager to leave, but Mapes was hanging onto the doorframe, and Nick Kinney, talking into the phone while watching us from the end of the hallway, had motioned for me to stay.

He said into the phone, "I followed them to a house in Alexandria." He paused a second, then said, "Just an elderly woman." He nodded as if in response to instructions, then called out to Mapes's mother. "What's your name, ma'am?"

"Ain't none o' your business," shouted Othman Mapes, his fingernails digging into the doorjamb.

"I'll speak for myself," said his mother, her head thrown back, proudly defiant. "My name is Serena Mapes. M-A-P-E-S."

Nick Kinney frowned. "Mapes?"

"As if you didn't know."

"Her name is Mapes," Nick said into the phone. He paused, then blurted out, "But that's—" He glanced at me and checked himself, then whispered something urgent and perplexed into the receiver, pausing for a reply. "I'll try," he said, nodding. "Fifteen minutes."

I held onto Mapes as Nick hurried out into the living room and came up to me, adjusting the knot of his tie as he approached. The instant he touched the knot his expression became as blank as a smile button without a smile. It was as if the tie were wired to his brain. All he had to do was finger it and everything emotionally extraneous to his purpose was shut off. "Would you mind accompanying me downtown, Mr. Bodine?"

Othman Mapes had managed to work his way free of the door, but I had him pinned to the wall with my forearm. "Why?"

"The police want to talk to you. It's urgent."

"What happened?"

"I don't know any of the details, but I'm told it's very, very urgent. It involves my . . . a boy named Tim Cooney, and a man named Gibbs." Nick stepped through the door and held the screen for me. "Please, we've got to hurry." He gestured at his Taurus, which was parked at the curb.

"All right," I said, hauling Mapes out onto the stoop, "but Mr. Mapes, here, comes with me."

"Leave him," Nick said.

"He's a bird in hand, and I haven't finished plucking him."

Nick nodded at a car parked down the dim street, another nondescript Taurus. "I guarantee he'll be in hand, so to speak, even after you let him go."

I thought it over, then released Mapes and followed Nick Kinney to his car.

"And don't be coming back," Othman Mapes shouted after us. "Get my mama all upset. She eighty-two year' old."

The door slammed behind him.

"Mama?" he said. "Let me in. Mama, you locked the door!"

11

Nick Kinney swung left onto Washington Street and urged his automobile toward D.C. The Taurus was a pleasant change from Sweetser's cruiser. It smelled of new vinyl. Nick Kinney smelled of Old Spice. The setup, however, smelled of fish. If Harry Gibbs had returned to the motel, found Ed missing and called the cops, why had the cops called Nick Kinney? There was only one cop who knew Nick was watching me, and that was Sweetser. Maybe he'd staked out the motel, cornered Harry and intimidated him till he caved in and told Sweetser about Ed's answer to cancer. I rubbed my eyes, knowing Ed was right, that Harry was just a buff, but even so, I couldn't believe Harry would spill something like this to the police. Or maybe someone in a Ford Taurus had got to him. I glanced over at Nick Kinney. Despite the announced urgency of the moment, Nick seemed calm enough, one hand on the wheel, the other hand on his tie, shaping the knot.

"So you don't know what's going on," I said.

"Only that the police want to talk to you about the two people I mentioned."

"Who did you get the call from?"

"My father. I don't know what's going on because he didn't

want to go into the details over the phone. One thing I'd like to say, though, I'm sorry we got off on the wrong foot earlier tonight."

"Sure." I was keeping track of our route, watching road signs flash by. They told me we were nearing National Airport. Even with the Taurus's windows rolled up, I could hear the whine of jet engines in the near distance.

"Uh, do you mind if I call you Jack?" said Nick Kinney.

"I'd rather you didn't."

"Believe me, I feel bad I didn't admit to my father that I talked to you on the phone earlier tonight. He seemed so upset when I came into the foyer that I just didn't see the point of making things worse for . . . myself by conceding I'd mentioned his brother to you."

When I didn't reply, Nick said, "We're in the same business, the two of us, and I feel we ought to be able to establish a professional relationship here." As he spoke, he accelerated onto a wide, low bridge.

Off to the left the lights of Washington winked on the Potomac. Just a few hundred yards upriver the lights of a low-flying airliner, its blinking wing tips waggling queasily, were heading right for us. An instant later the jet shrieked over us low enough it must have scorched the finish on Nick's Taurus. Nick didn't flinch. I didn't, either, but that was because I had my skull jammed against the headrest. "My interest isn't in establishing professional relations," I shouted over the shriek of the plane. "What I want to establish are blood relations. You keep calling Ed Quinn your father's brother, but they don't resemble each other in the least."

"If you don't mind my saying so, Jack, it seems to me that the more significant relation is the one between your partner, Quinn, and this Tim, uh, Cooney. I'm told he's just a boy, whereas your partner's in his late sixties."

I said, "His real name's Tim Kinney. Your father says he's your brother, but he doesn't look any more like you than Ed Quinn looks like your father. Why is that?"

Nick motioned at the airliner. "I'm sorry, I didn't hear you." The plane was already a quarter mile downriver and about to touch tarmac at National. From my vantage point on the bridge, the airport looked like a mere polyp on Virginia's riverbank.

I said, "You want to know why your kid brother's been working for Ed Quinn, right?"

Nick palpated the knot of his tie. "I assure you this is the first any of us has heard of it."

"Well, this is the first I've heard of Ed adding a codicil to his will that benefits your brother Craig. He runs Kinfolk Realty, correct?"

"Yes, but—"

"You don't know anything about that, either."

"No. I'm in charge of Kintell, which is a separate corporate entity. I have no idea what's going on with Craig, but I do know it doesn't make sense for Quinn to have mentioned us in his will. Quinn hates us."

"Us?"

"My father."

"Why? I thought they were brothers."

Nick, fondling his four-in-hand, didn't reply. I waited, watching him, or trying to. My eye was drawn beyond him toward the Washington Monument. The towering spotlit obelisk, with a circle of American flags fluttering around its shank, was as impressive as a space shuttle before a predawn launch.

Finally Nick said, "My father's relationship to Ed Quinn is not the issue here. What's important . . . what's got my father upset, is Tim. He's worried that his association with Quinn may bring disrepute upon the family. Now, anything you could say that would put my father's mind at ease on that point would be greatly appreciated."

I sighed again. "You have to wonder why anyone would even want the job."

"What job?"

"*That* job."

Nick followed my finger. "I've been there several times on business," he said proudly. "Actually we met over there, in the EOB, but it's really the same as the White House."

"The EOB?"

"Executive Office Building."

The EOB looked like a rectangular wedding cake that had been frosted with gray icing. "Is there an SOB?"

"Sure. Senate Office Building. Listen, Jack, I told my father I'd have some answers by the time we arrived."

"No, you didn't. You said you'd try."

Nick Kinney gestured at the road ahead. "He's at my office on K Street." There was a trace of panic in Nick's voice.

"Kintell?"

"Yes."

"Are Kinfolk's offices there, too?"

"Kinfolk's on the floor below. Is Quinn deceased, by the way?"

"He's working on it," I said.

"If you were a little more frank with me, this drive might end productively for both of us."

"If your father and Ed Quinn are brothers, how come they don't look anything alike?"

"They grew up in the same house, but they're only step-brothers."

"That's a start," I said. "Maybe you and I could work out some kind of quid pro quo. You tell me about your father's relationship to my partner, and I tell you about my partner's relationship to your brother. You first."

Nick turned onto K Street. I saw banks, camera shops, and travel agencies on K Street. Plenty of restaurants, too, places that looked like they catered to the political palate: surf and turf, reef and beef, cod and cud. Nick was fingering his neckwear. I waited, suppressing the urge to tear the tie from his throat and feed it to him.

"All right," Nick said at last, "but I don't know much, just what little my father told me years ago."

"I'm listening."

"Well . . . after the war, my father inherited quite a bit of property from his father. He—"

"After which war?"

"World War Two."

"Where was this property?"

"Here in Washington."

"What kind of property?"

"Mostly rental. He had three or four skip tracers on his payroll at the time, and—"

"Your father or your grandfather?"

"My father. He inherited the skip tracers, too. The point is, they overcharged him for their time and skimmed the rents they collected. My father talked to Quinn about it. This was before there were any hard feelings between them. Quinn and my father were back from the war, and Quinn had taken a job with the D.C. police. He assured my father that with his police connections and his knowledge of the city, he could do the work of three skip tracers for half the cost. My father took him up on the boast. I guess Quinn was unhappy being a cop. He'd only been at it a few years. Anyway, they formed a partnership."

"In real estate or skip tracing?"

"Both, sort of. I'm not a hundred percent clear on it, but I gather that Quinn would often spot promising properties while he was out chasing skipped tenants, sites that might be ripe for development in years to come. He'd mention them to my father, who would hire a private detective to look into the situation, make a quiet investigation of the ownership without driving up prices. Before long, my father had several investigators working for him full-time. He was doing well enough he needed a tax write-off, so he incorporated an investigation agency and put Quinn in charge of the agents, the guys who were looking into the real estate deeds and so forth. My father expected the agency to lose money, but it gained a reputation with local realtors. They'd hire Quinn to check out suspected straws, and so forth."

"Doesn't sound like Ed's can of worms."

"It wasn't. The agents my father insisted on hiring were people he felt comfortable with, men he'd got to know in the OSS during the war. By then the OSS had become the CIA, and because of my father's connections at Langley, his investigation agency began doing domestic jobs for the Company, things the CIA didn't want the FBI to know about, investigations they're prohibited from undertaking because of the restrictions in their charter."

"What about the Pinkerton Law?"

"Nobody worries about that. Anyway, it became a sophisticated operation, but there were still a lot of bright guys doing little more than title searches. Quinn was one of them, and he got bored. He hated being a manager, too, and eventually he began working for a group of lawyers who'd broken away from the D.A.'s staff and formed a partnership of their own. They were doing high-volume divorce work at the time."

"That would be Ed's can of worms."

Nick nodded. "It was around then that they had a falling out, Quinn and my father."

Nick stopped at a light. He stopped talking, too, and stared at the light as if he were inspecting it for signs of wear and tear. I said, "A falling out over what?"

Nick cleared his unclogged throat. "My mother," he said. "She was the daughter of one of Quinn's divorce clients. Her mother was quite a prominent woman. Have you heard of the Wilkinsons? Anyway, according to the transcripts, my mother's father was an abusive type, and Quinn put a stop to it."

"Depend on Ed."

"She was very young, my mother, and . . . well, Quinn was a decorated war veteran. From the photographs I've seen, he was a handsome man. My mother was quite good-looking, and coming from a well-to-do family, she naturally interested Quinn."

There was a swell of pride in Nick's voice as he spoke of his mother's attractiveness. I knew how he felt. My mother, in her sixties now, had been a beautiful woman, too, and my father had been an indisputably handsome man. Whenever I gazed at the old photo portraits of the two of them—decked out in their forties duds, my mother's shoulder-length Ann Sheridan hair bang-rolled and glossy, my father's lieutenant's bars gleaming on his collar, his widow's peak more prominent than Robert Taylor's—I couldn't help wishing I'd been them.

"She had a lot of class," Nick continued, "but Quinn got the wrong idea. Or maybe she was impetuous, and Quinn got the right idea. I don't know. Anyway, he ended up in Korea and . . . my mother began seeing my father. Eventually she married him. She waited till Quinn came back from Korea, though."

Classy.

"I don't know all the details," Nick continued, "and I'm not sure I want to. I do know that my father helped Quinn to invest in real estate after his return from Europe. Thanks to my father's advice, Quinn had acquired a decent portfolio at the time of their falling out, after Korea. My father offered him a good deal more than the going rate for the properties, and Quinn sold him his holdings and left Washington for good."

"He sold him everything?"

"I'd have to ask Craig or my father to be absolutely certain."

"Either of them mention anything to you about Ed Quinn lately?"

"No."

"Is Craig an honest man?"

"Jack, I'm letting you jerk me around like this because my father's a demanding person who's demanded some answers and you've got them. Now—"

"I asked you if Craig was an honest man."

Nick clenched his teeth. "In all our business dealings, Craig and I handle ourselves with dignity and integrity. We run a family business with a family name. Our livelihood depends on our reputation. Which is why my father is so disturbed to find out that Tim has been involved in something that could become, you know, grist for the rumor mill. That's why he wants to talk to you before Sweetser does."

"I get to see Sweetser again?"

"Apparently he's on his way. My father has asked me to debrief you so I can fill him in when we arrive . . . which is now."

Nick braked and turned into a driveway that sloped down under a glass box of an office building. The attendant had gone home for the night and the gate had been lowered, but Nick had a card. He fed it into a slot in a box and the heavy meshwork grille rolled up with a grinding rattle. Nick let up on the brakes and his car rolled down into the garage. Except for a Taurus or two, and a silver Mercedes SEL, the cavern was mostly empty. Nick pulled beyond the Mercedes and parked next to a Baltic-blue Porsche 911 Carrera coupe with a slant-nose body, retractable headlights, and side air vents behind the doors. He turned toward me. "Now then, Jack, about that quid pro quo?"

"I was just bluffing," I said. "I don't speak Latin."

"Tell me about Tim."

"Well," I said, "there's a big difference in age between the two of you."

Nick nodded patiently. "Eleven years. He was unplanned. My mother was thirty-nine when he was born, and I guess it was too much for her. She died shortly after she delivered Timmy. Craig and I were in the waiting room. I remember my father talking to the doctor and then coming over to tell us . . . see, he holds it against Tim that she died. He's going to be very angry with my kid brother. Anything you can tell me that might reflect well on Tim, I'd like to be able to pass it on to Dad. For Tim's sake."

I held Nick Kinney's gaze, feeling not uncomfortable with the man. If it hadn't been for the Porsche, I might have divulged certain items of interest. But as it was, I couldn't imagine why the

District of Columbia Motor Vehicle Bureau would have issued duplicate tags to two different automobiles. Which meant the Porsche beside me was the same one I'd seen parked in front of the District Line Motel a couple hours ago when Sweetser and I set out for Georgetown.

Nick said, "What about it, Jack?"

I said, "Don't call me Jack, Nick."

12

Nick and I climbed out of the Taurus, and in testy silence headed for the parking-level entrance to the building, our footsteps echoing in the underground garage. Nick clanged open the metal fire door and held it for me. I stole one last look at the blue Porsche, then started up the stairwell. It smelled of damp concrete. There was a second fire door at the top of the stairs, and we went through it into a marble lobby. The lobby was deserted but for a black man in a guard's outfit who had his feet propped on a counter and was watching a portable TV. The lobby smelled of marijuana.

If Nick noticed the aroma, he didn't say anything, just printed his name in the sign-in log on the counter. He scrawled his signature in a box next to the block-letter version of his name, and entered the time. The red-eyed guard compared Nick's face to the photo on his laminated ID and nodded. I signed the book as Nick's guest, and we took an elevator up, Nick plumping the knot of his necktie as the elevator hummed. When the doors rolled open he was as placid as a Japanese garden.

He motioned for me to precede him out of the elevator, and the two of us, striding in sync, glided down a thickly-carpeted corridor. At the end of the corridor a heavy paneled door had a burnished brass plate screwed to it that said KINTELL. The doorknob was brass, too. There was a brass plate beneath the doorknob that had a slot in it. Nick took out the card he'd used to raise the grille downstairs and inserted it into the slot. The door buzzed, and we went in.

No one was behind the receptionist's desk at this hour on a Saturday night, and there weren't any clients sitting in the chrome-and-leather chairs that were clustered around a low glass-topped table. An assortment of magazines and newspapers had been fanned out on the table, *Forbes, Fortune, Barron's,* and *The Wall Street Journal. Gumshoe Gazette* did not appear to be among them.

Nick led me through a thriving copse of plastic ficus and into a bay in which adjoining chest-high cubicles had been deployed at angles to the surrounding walls. The exterior of each cubicle was upholstered in gray carpeting. The aisles between the cubicles were carpeted in the same neutral tone. Color was confined to the interiors of the cubicles: framed photographs of wives, sons, daughters; also the occasional calendar with a view of autumn leaves on a New England hillside. Not one centerfold in sight . . . just a center with folds: an old ex-jock with lappets of flesh festooning his collar and straining the stitching of his gray flannel vest. The cuffs of his white shirt had been rolled back to expose hairy thigh-thick forearms. His stumpy fingers, like fat Russians, were doing a Cossack stomp on the keyboard of an IBM PS/2 model 30. The big guy was saying "Um-hm" into a shouldered telephone receiver, nodding as the information he was gathering made its peristaltic advance through the coils of his mind and into the silicon brain of his machine. The nameplate on the outer wall of his cubicle said CAPARELLI. He appeared to be the only Kintell employee on the premises.

Nick Kinney, threading through the maze of cubicles, acknowledged Caparelli with a nod and continued angling toward a bank of offices on the far side of the bay. I tagged along behind him, pumping myself up for fun and games. My son and I were partial to *The Gong Show*, and what I had in mind here, if the Kinneys' act needed work, was to whack their gong. I might have to whack Caparelli, too. He was big enough he'd take two whacks.

Nick went up to a door with his name on it. He reached for the knob, hesitated, then knocked. After a moment the door was snapped open by a short thick-necked spiff wearing aviator glasses and a single-breasted leather sport coat over a nut-brown cashmere turtleneck. He was in his mid-thirties, maybe a couple years older than Nick. Like Nick, he had wavy dark-brown hair and a broadly handsome face. Unlike Nick, he had a kick-your-ass glint in his eye. It was the same guy I'd seen earlier in the evening talking to Othman Mapes at the desk of the District Line Motel. I'd even seen the glint before, flashing at me out of the portrait of the Marine private on the Chippendale side table in Douglas Kinney's Georgetown sitting room. This was Craig Kinney, son of the redoubtable Douglas, boss of the brusque Ms. Benedict, and ex-hubby of the well-bred divorcée who lived in contented if Porscheless estrangement somewhere out Connecticut Avenue.

Crooking a finger, Craig beckoned brother Nick into the office. He pointed the same finger at a secretary's desk just outside the office and told me to sit down on the chrome posture chair. "The cops," he said portentously, "will be along in a minute." He raised his eyebrows and shook his head as if to underscore the trouble I was in. His expression suggested, too, that my fate would be a lot worse if the cops weren't on their way. Then I'd have to deal with Cool Hand Craig himself, "and I am," said his glint, "a handful."

I had hands big enough that Craig Kinney's glint-show wasn't anything to me, a matter of aesthetics at best. I let him see as much, too, smiling around my contempt, saying, "So you're Craig Kinney."

"*Mister* Kinney, to you." *Glint, glint.*

I extended my hand. "Just call me Jack."

Humoring me, Craig stuck his mitt into mine, giving me a grip that—like the expression on his face—was trying. I clamped down on his small hand, grinding his phalanxes till the pain meter behind his eyes registered an imminent fracture. Then I stepped into the office, pumping and grinding and giving the decor a quick look . . . nothing I hadn't seen before, either: heavy drapes, brass fixtures, leather sofa, matching wing chairs, mahogany table desk. It was an office cloned from the sitting room in Douglas Kinney's Georgetown digs. All that was lacking here on K Street was a faux fireplace and a stuffed detective from Homicide.

I let go of Craig and turned toward his father, who was standing at the window, staring out at the lights in the buildings across the way. He had his hands clasped behind his back and was wriggling his fingers impatiently. When he swung around he seemed vaguely dismayed to see me heading in his direction. He said, "I'd like to speak to Nick alone, if you don't mind."

At that point it was only me with a glint, and I could see why Craig liked having one. All I had to do was flash it and Douglas ducked behind his desk, swallowing dryly. When Nick reached for his tie I turned the glint on him and froze his hand in mid-grasp. I pulled back one of the wing chairs and sank into it, checking brother Craig, who was still by the door, coddling his hand as if it were a sick hamster. I turned back to Douglas Kinney and encouraged him to have a seat, too. He hesitated. I gave him a low-grade glint and he sat down behind the desk and regarded me bleakly. "Now then," I said, "you tell me what it is Harry Gibbs found out about you people, and I'll tell you when to stop."

Douglas Kinney glanced down at a sheet of paper on the desk, cleared his throat and took a deep breath. "I'm sorry to have to inform you of this," he said, taking a deeper breath, "but, according to Detective Sweetser, the lawyer who supposedly hired you to investigate our realty agency has been taken to the D.C. Medical Examiner's office. Detective Sweetser is on his way here to discuss the matter with me, after which he wants you to make an interim identification of Mr. Gibbs's body."

I raised an eyebrow and scrutinized Douglas Kinney's narrow face for traces of fun he was undoubtedly having with me. But Kinney wasn't a kidder. Neither was Nick, who looked shocked and a little sick at the news. Craig, on the other hand, seemed to be enjoying the changes his father's bulletin was putting me through. I felt the sudden urge to douse Craig's glint for good, slam him against the wall, give him a dose of internal bleeding and a matching pair of hamsters.

I stood and Craig glinted, asking for it, but I forced myself to turn away from him. I was facing the window when I stopped turning, so I advanced on it and stared down at the lighted street. Traffic was thin, just a couple of cars, slow-moving and soundless. They always looked longer from above than they did at street level. Hearselike. One of them might be Sweetser's cruiser, coming to take me to the morgue. Where it would be cold.

I could see Douglas Kinney reflected in the window. I watched him, wanting to see a malicious little sneer cross his face, a look that would nullify the news he'd just given me, transform it into a threat. *Next time it'll be for real, Bodine, unless you and your buddy Gibbs blow town.* But Kinney was staring down at his desk, frowning at the sheet of paper he'd glanced at as he'd given me the news about Harry. Dead. Medical examiner. Interim identification. I repeated it all to myself, trying to accept it as fact, but my mind kept rejecting Kinney's news. I wanted Harry to be waiting for me in his Olds in the parking lot of the motel. I wanted him to jump out of the car the way he did when I pulled in earlier in the evening. I could see him running toward my car as I eased into a slot, opening my door and grabbing my hand, shaking it and telling me how glad he was I'd come, blurting random details of his journey, the mysterious asset, the oncologist who stuck needles up people's noses, talking a mile a minute, while Tim—

"Tim was with Harry," I said suddenly, still watching Kinney's reflection in the glass.

Kinney said morosely, "Nick, see if there's any coffee, please."

"Yes, sir." Nick opened an antique breakfront sideboard, found an insulated pitcher and left the office.

I said, "What about Tim?" I could hardly hear my own voice over the buzzing in my ears. My face felt hot.

Douglas Kinney leaned his elbows on the desk and pressed his palms together. He looked as if he were attempting to crush a nut. "The boy's been hospitalized."

" 'The' boy? You mean *your* boy, don't you?"

"Yes, *my* boy," snapped Kinney, glaring at me as if daring me to make something of it.

I said, "What happened?"

Kinney picked up the sheet of notepaper from the desk, took another deep breath, and began reading. "According to Detective Sweetser, a 911 operator logged an anonymous call instructing the police to investigate a late-model Oldsmobile that had been abandoned in an alley behind the District Line Motel on New York Avenue. The police opened the trunk of the vehicle and found my son, Timothy—who told them his name was Cooney—and the body of one Harold Gibbs. When Detective Sweetser heard about it, he recalled that 'Gibbs' was the name of the lawyer who allegedly hired you to investigate my company, Kinfolk Realty. He called me at home. We agreed to meet here. He asked me to have Nick escort you here as well. Detective Sweetser then went to the hospital where they'd taken Timothy and spoke to him. Timothy was in a state of shock, but Sweetser managed to get out of him that two black males had been lying in wait in the parking lot of the motel. According to Timothy, he was forced to drive into the alley behind the motel. At some point Mr. Gibbs resisted his assailants and died during a struggle, apparently by strangulation. The attack occurred at around seven-fifteen tonight. No arrests have been made."

Kinney's stilted presentation of the facts irritated me. It sounded too pat. Or maybe I was annoyed because I felt so unpat. This had to be some sort of ruse, or mistake. Or dream. But each time I tried to shake off the sense of unreality, one look at the numb faces of Nick Kinney and his father reaffirmed the fact of Harry's death. "Old lawyers never die," Harry used to joke, "they just lose their appeal, hee, hee, hee." Or get strangled . . . by the gunny? It was as hard to believe the gunny had choked Harry to death as it was to believe Harry was dead. The gunny was a cop, not a killer. His sidekick, the sport, was a hothead, but you don't choke someone as easily or as impulsively as you knock them into a TV set. The gunny would have pulled him off Harry. I shook my head. Either I was terribly wrong about the two of them or . . . the smirk on Craig Kinney's face explained everything. He'd been at the motel tonight.

"All right," I said to Douglas Kinney, "I want an explanation of what's going on between you and Ed Quinn."

Kinney, squirming in his chair, marshaled legions of indignation, his mouth moving long in advance of their arrival. "Now, just a—"

"Give it to me now," I said, "and I'll give you every consideration. If I have to work for it, though, I'm not going to spare you, your kids, or your reputation."

Craig Kinney drew back his leather sport coat, stuck the hand I hadn't crushed behind his back, and wrapped it around something that was clipped onto his belt. A short-barreled revolver was my guess. With his hand still behind his back, he said, "Dad?"

Douglas Kinney, his eyes hard on mine, his negligible chest heaving, shook his head.

"Just say the word, Dad, and he's out of here."

"It's all right, Craig. I'll talk to Mr. Bodine."

"But—"

"I said it's all right. We've done nothing wrong, therefore we have nothing to hide."

The door opened and Nick returned with the insulated pitcher and a sheet of paper. He sensed that things were revving in the red zone, but he went to his father and handed him the paper, pretending not to notice. "Dad, this is from Caparelli."

Kinney, with an effort a lot less taxing than he made it look, broke off our staring contest and glanced at the document Nick had given him, his gaze skimming the paper. After a moment he said sharply, "This material's almost a half-hour old. I told Caparelli I wanted updates instantly. The Metropolitan Police might consider a half hour from one desk to another instantaneous, but if that fat fuzz expects to continue working for Kintell, he'd better learn that instantly means instantly!" Kinney was half out of his seat, his rage having drained all color from his face.

Nick said calmingly, "I'll have a talk with him, Dad. Uh, would you like some coffee?"

Kinney slumped back into his leather executive's throne and said hoarsely, "Yes, thank you, Nick. Black. Use the china." He focused on the paper again, reading while Nick poured coffee into a fancy little cup that he'd found in the sideboard.

Nick glanced over at me. "You want some?"

I shook my head.

"Maybe," said Craig, "he only drinks it out of Styrofoam."

"Ease up," Nick said to his brother.

Craig's reply was interrupted by the phone. Douglas Kinney, having slid Caparelli's memo into a file folder, reached for the receiver and waved the folder at Craig. "Look this over." Into the phone he said, "What?"

Craig, drawing his hand out from behind his back, took the folder from his father. His eyes never left mine.

Kinney cradled the receiver. "That was the lobby guard. Detective Sweetser's on his way up. Craig, meet him at the elevator and brief him. Nick, stand by just outside the door. I'll buzz when I've finished with Mr. Bodine."

"Yes, sir."

Kinney got up and said to me, "I'll be right back." He turned

98

and opened a door behind the desk. It led to a private washroom. He went inside and locked the door behind him.

The brothers Kinney headed for the door that led out into the office bay. Nick knew nothing about making an exit. He just walked out of the room. But Craig, giving me a departing glint, left like MacArthur.

13

I was alone in Kintell's inner sanctum. My instinct was to toss the place, starting with the drawer in the mahogany table desk, but the sound of water hissing behind the washroom door ceased, and a moment later Douglas Kinney stepped out into the office. He'd toweled a rush of color into his cheeks, and had a bit of a bounce in his walk. He sat behind the desk again and motioned for me to sit opposite him in the wing chair.

I sat.

"Are you sure you don't want coffee, Mr. Bodine? You have a long night ahead of you."

I told him I was sure I didn't want coffee, which was a lie. I just didn't want his coffee.

Kinney shrugged, and refilled his fancy little cup. "Coffee always tastes best from china," he said. He raised the cup to his lips, arched his pinkie and blew on the surface of the steaming brew. There must have been a yard and a half of desk between us, but the sweet stench of bourbon on his breath was strong enough I almost slid my chair back a couple feet. "Now, then," said Kinney, sipping at the coffee, "I have no idea what Edward Quinn is up to. He's your partner. You're the one who should be telling me what's 'going on.' "

A long night, for sure, and Kinney had every intention of making it seem that way. I said, "Why did you deny knowing him earlier this evening?"

Kinney took a moment to perfect the placement of his cup on its saucer. "Because I had no wish to become involved with him in any way, shape, size, or form."

"Why? He's your stepbrother."

"Edward and I had a falling out. A long time ago. A very unpleasant falling out. I haven't seen him in over thirty years. Thirty-five to be exact. I had no idea he was ill, or that he mentioned Kinfolk in his will . . . if in fact he has."

"When Sweetser and I talked to you at your home no one mentioned Ed being sick or anything about a will. At least not in the foyer."

Kinney said nothing.

"Did Tim tell you about it after he delivered the codicil to Harry Gibbs?"

"That tone of yours, Mr. Bodine, what nuance is it striving to express?"

"My thirst for knowledge."

"Forgive me, but I think it suggests the hypothesis that I encouraged Timothy to ingratiate himself with Edward."

Ed Quinn hated for anyone to call him Edward, and I was beginning to understand why. I said, "*Did* you?"

"Whatever that boy has done has been without my knowledge or approval."

"Never had a clue to what your kid's been up to the past nine months?"

"I knew—or at least he told me—that he was in Ann Arbor, Michigan. That's all."

"What did you think he was doing there?"

"He was supposedly attending the University of Michigan, starting his sophomore year. That's where I've been sending his monthly allowance, his tuition checks, and so on."

"You never called him?"

Kinney squirmed in his chair. "Timothy knows where to contact me if he needs help."

"And he never said a word to you about working for Ed Quinn in Lansing?"

"No. Of course not. He knew I would have put a stop to it."

"Why do you think he took work with Ed?"

"I have no idea." Kinney fussed with a letter opener. "I suppose he was trying to make a point."

"What point?"

"That he could succeed as an investigator. I refused to let him work for Kintell during his summer break." Kinney said this as if it had been a difficult decision, but one he still stood by.

"According to Detective Sweetser, you run a first-rate investigation agency. Why deny your own kid a chance to learn from you?"

"Please understand that Timothy is not of the same . . . he's not like Nick or Craig. I've never expected as much from him as I have from them. I'm not saying he's a weak child. I never told him he was inferior. Overly sensitive, perhaps, but that's neither here nor there. The point is, I accept responsibility for his actions. But that is all."

"Not the blame?"

"No. I have done nothing underhanded." Kinney sat back in his chair, its lustrous leather squeaking as he gave me a satisfied stare.

I sat back in my chair, folded my arms, and gave him a patient smile. We were like two boxers who'd spent the early rounds feinting and had learned only that we both could feint. I said, "Nick told me you were in the OSS during the war."

"What does that have to do with what we're talking about?"

"Just that I would never think to characterize an ex-OSS agent as underhanded. Covert-handed, maybe, but—"

"Believe me, Mr. Bodine, if I were planning a covert operation, I never would have signed up a foolish boy like Timothy."

"From what I've seen of Tim, especially the last month or so, I'd say he's a pretty good kid."

"Good? At what?"

"I don't think you'd understand."

Kinney smiled coldly. "A moment ago you implied he'd insinuated himself into Edward's life as an undercover agent."

"Maybe he started out that way."

Kinney leaned forward, giving me a good look at the angry challenging iciness in his eyes. "Listen, my friend, how do I know it wasn't Edward who recruited Timothy and got him to move to Lansing, wherever the hell that is?"

"Why would Ed do that?"

"To annoy me."

"Has he tried to annoy you during the past thirty-five years?" I asked.

"No, but Edward is not a man to forgive and to forget."

"Yes, he is, that's just the kind of man he is."

"You know so much about him, do you?"

"I do," I said.

"I'll bet he never talked to you about me, did he?"

"I see now that it was an act of kindness."

"Just as mentioning one of my business operations in his will was an act of kindness? Listen, mister, Edward hates me. He's trying to get even. It's as simple as that. His method is obscure, but the malice behind it is plain."

"This falling out of yours, what was it over?"

"A woman," Kinney said, jabbing his chin at me as if he were proud of himself.

"It's hard to believe a person like you would be interested in Ed's type."

"You mean whores and hash-house floozies?"

"Working women."

"Eleanor was different. It's true, though, that they were totally mismatched and wouldn't have lasted in any case." Kinney's voice was full of righteous certainty, but there was a shade of wistful regret in it, too.

"What happened?" I said.

Kinney gestured impatiently. "Edward was twenty-seven years old and out of shape, but he reenlisted . . . volunteered to go to Korea. We tried everything to talk him out of it, Eleanor and I, but he went. He once told me he always saw the stark truth of things when he was in combat, and I think he wanted to get away from Eleanor for a time so he could come to terms with the challenge she presented."

"Challenge?"

"She wasn't a . . . floozy. He would have had to shape up, make something of himself."

"And?"

"He ran away. So I kept her company in his absence, at first as a favor, then as a necessity. I was a good deal older than Eleanor, and I tried very hard to maintain an avuncular distance, but Eleanor and I were . . . of the same temperament. We were meant for one another, and indeed, we had many fine years together, and two . . . three wonderful sons."

Kinney's fists were clenched, but he didn't look angry, guilty, or even worried. He looked like he needed another drink. "You 'had' many fine years together?" I said.

"Yes, *had*. Eleanor died in 1970."

"An accident?"

Kinney shot me a look. "In a manner of speaking. Timothy was born and . . . Eleanor was thirty-nine years old. She died of complications." Kinney opened his fists and stared at his empty hands as if the death of his wife had been foretold in the lines of his palms.

I'd been leading him away from his own turf—the high ground of social superiority—and luring him onto more treacherous terrain. Before I could set him up for a fall, though, he pleaded a "splitting headache" and headed for the washroom, locking the door behind him.

I leaned across the table desk and slid the drawer open. There wasn't anything inside the drawer but a tray of number-two pencils and a pad of lined paper on which nothing had been written. There wasn't much on top of the desk, either, just the cup of coffee, a colonial lamp with a brass base and a black shade, the hammered brass letter opener, a small battery-driven pencil sharpener, a phone with an intercom feature, and a calendar without any notes or appointments penciled in. Nick the Neat. I checked the wastebasket. It was empty. I gazed around the office. There weren't any file cabinets or bookcases, just the oriental rug, the two wing chairs, the sofa, and the sideboard with the coffee thermos on top of it. And the English hunting scenes on the walls . . . an office that showed no signs of ongoing effort. Nick had probably got the idea for it when he visited the White House. I sat down and waited.

A moment later Kinney turned off the water in the washroom and stepped back into the office. His color was high once again and his mood seemed to have gained a little altitude, too. But when he saw me sitting in the wing chair he seemed to falter, almost as if he'd forgotten I was waiting for him. If he had been a C-47 in a forties adventure flick, his engines would be making sputtering sounds, his fuel gauge trembling on empty.

Kinney drew his hand across his mouth, his eyes darting toward the sideboard as if a little voice had called to him from inside it. With a casualness meant to suggest he was satisfying nothing more than his curiosity, he went to the sideboard, opened the cabinet, reached in and came out with a fifth of Wild Turkey. He held the bottle up and frowned at it as though, being a coffee lover himself, he hardly knew one brand of booze from another. But what did it matter? He shrugged and escorted the fifth to the desk. He sat down, dribbled a dainty thimbleful of fire into the coffee cup, capped the bottle, and sucked up the sauce with his little finger arched. When he put the cup down he looked at it as though, if he lived to be a hundred, he'd never understand what people found so appealing about booze. To me he said, "Are you sure you wouldn't care for some coffee? Or perhaps a drink?"

I was visited by a sudden image of Kinney in the washroom, his head thrown back, Adam's apple jumping, eyes squeezed shut. Had his little finger been erect? Oh, yes. And he'd been nipping from an engraved silver flask, I was sure of it. Myself, I used to take a hit straight from the bottle, fist on the neck, *wham*, hot and hearty going down, get a good look at the ceiling as a bonus. "No, thanks," I said. "What I'd like is an account of Ed Quinn's past real estate holdings here in D.C."

Kinney's smile acquired a hint of cunning. "Would you, now?"

"Yes, and any properties he might still own."

The booze had fired Kinney's cheeks to a rosy glow. He reached for the bottle, refilled his cup, and stoked the blaze, watching me over the rim of the cup. "Just what kind of investigative work do you and Edward specialize in, Mr. Bodine?"

I opened my hand and swung my arm to include the whole of Kintell. "Nothing as sophisticated as this."

Kinney, holding the cup with both hands as if it were a communion chalice, smirked. "Divorces?"

"Ed's specialty, not mine."

"From the looks of you," Kinney said speculatively, "I'd say you specialize in . . . bodyguard work?"

"I don't guard bodies, Mr. Kinney. I explain them."

Kinney cocked an ear as if he hadn't heard. "Pardon?"

"I discover how human beings get turned into bodies. As in the case of Harry Gibbs."

Kinney blinked at me several times, working hard to hold his disdainful smile. "Really?"

I didn't grab Douglas Kinney's tie and twist it till his tongue stuck out and his eyes popped. Nor did I knock his china cup to the floor and crush it underfoot. That wouldn't help Harry. It might help me, but I had to help Ed. I was sure he was still here in Washington, alive, though not for long. When I found him, I'd have as a bonus the men who supposedly killed Harry. Through them, I would pressure Mapes into telling me what Craig Kinney said to him at the motel desk. When I knew how Craig fit in, I felt certain I would know the truth of Harry's death. This was all in the abstract, of course, a plan that would guide my actions over the coming hours, perhaps days. It was quite simple, as the best laid plans must be, its goal clear: to find Ed Quinn. I had a sense the Kinneys knew where he was, but I had learned all I was going to get from them: quite a bit from Nick, less from his father. Craig was hopeless. Sweetser was coming, though. It would be interesting to see the approach he took to the Kinneys. I nodded at the intercom. "Why don't you find out if Detective Sweetser's here?"

"Yes," Kinney said, "why don't I?" He parked his little cup on the wafer-thin saucer and pushed a button on the intercom. "Nick?"

"Yes, Dad?"

"Is Detective Sweetser out there?"

"Yes, he's waiting."

"Send him in." Kinney let up on the intercom and stood unsteadily. "I'd like to speak to him alone, if you don't mind."

I got up, too, not because I intended to leave, but because I didn't like Douglas Kinney looking down at me. As I stood, the door to the office opened and Sweetser entered, Nick Kinney holding the door for him. Sweetser paused a moment, looking back and forth between Kinney and me. He was breathing hard, and I could smell the odor of Venetian mints on his breath. Sweetser looked troubled, but only so long as it took him to spot the Wild Turkey on the table desk. Then he lighted up like a man catching sight of a friend in a roomful of strangers. "I . . . uh, just came from the hospital," he said to Douglas Kinney.

"I appreciate your consideration, Hank. Would you care for some coffee?"

Hank's face sagged. He was holding a white letter-size

envelope with a small bulge in it, and he began tapping the edge of the envelope against his palm, eyeing the bottle of bourbon.

"Or," said Kinney, gesturing at the booze, "maybe you'd prefer a drink?"

Sweetser, like a sail that had suddenly caught wind, said he thought it might be nice if he could have one mixed with the other, assuming it wouldn't be too much trouble.

"No trouble at all," said Kinney, reaching for the fifth.

Sweetser glanced at me, and said to Kinney, "Is he . . . in on this?"

"No," said Kinney. "Will you show Mr. Bodine out, Nick?"

Nick Kinney was still idling in the doorway. "This way, Mr. Bodine."

Sweetser said to me, "Don't leave the building."

"And miss a trip to the morgue?"

"Just wait outside."

"I'd like to hear your report," I said to Sweetser.

"You'll hear it when I'm done talking to Mr. Kinney. Go on, wait outside."

Sweetser was glint-proof, of course, so I went outside.

14

Nick Kinney followed me out of the office and closed the door behind me. Without a word he went to the secretary's desk and sat down, picked up the phone and tapped out a number on the keypad. He kept his back to me.

I scanned the office bay. Craig Kinney was jawing with the fat ex-cop, Caparelli, while thumbing through the file folder his father had asked him to read. Caparelli, craning over Craig's shoulder, wasn't reading the file so much as he was admiring it, smiling like a homicide dick who'd just smacked the game-winning hit against Sex Crimes.

I leaned back against the office door and stared absently at the empty tin of Venetian mints in the wastebasket beside the secretary's desk. I was trying to catch what was going on behind the door, but I couldn't hear anything Kinney and Sweetser were saying to one another. A fifth of bourbon was in there, and I couldn't even hear Sweetser slurp.

"Hi, honey," Nick Kinney said into the phone. "I know, and I'm really sorry. No, I won't be home for several hours yet."

I envied Nick. I wouldn't be home till I found Ed Quinn. Harry Gibbs wouldn't be home, ever. I thought of Harry's wife, Frieda. I knew her parents were dead. Harry's, too. They'd never had children, Harry and Frieda, and were devoted to one another, their expressions of affection cloying, but genuine. Each day was an exchange of endearments: kisses over the phone, a quick hike home for lunch, or a gift of flowers or sweets. Frieda once told me Harry had stopped at a shop in East Lansing that supplied party favors to sororities and fraternities and bought her a twenty-two-pound teddy bear with a pink ribbon. It hadn't been her birthday, or their anniversary, either. According to Frieda, it was the sort of thing Harry often did on a whim. At a party one time I got a glimpse of their bedroom. It was crammed with stuffed animals. They lived, as Harry once claimed, in a marital Eden. Then Ed Quinn "slithered" into the picture, and whenever Harry joined him on a stakeout, Frieda would worry about Harry the way a mother might fret over her little boy's involvement with an older, tougher kid. The second or third time after Joyce and I dined at Harry's home in White Hills, Frieda took me aside, saying she thought she could trust me . . . gazing up at me with a questioning arch to her eyebrows. After assuring her I was the epitome of prudence, she went on to express her disapproval of Harry's involvement with Ed and the "unseemly" business of spying on people whose marriages were unfortunate. What kind of work was that, after all? Why did Harry insist on being a part of it, of fraternizing with a man who enjoyed that sort of endeavor? Harry wasn't even a divorce lawyer. If, from time to time, he needed Mr. Quinn's help in the investigation of a civil case, or in locating missing heirs, that was one thing. But why did Mr. Quinn have to entice Harry into these all-night bouts of voyeurism? And why did Harry accept? I suggested to Frieda Gibbs that husbands and wives who abused or cheated on one another intrigued Harry because he'd never known anything but happiness in his own marriage. Frieda Gibbs—with *Psychology Today* on her living room coffee table, and romance novels spilling out of the bookcases in her den—did not dismiss my explanation. I assured her Harry would eventually grow bored with stakeouts. I almost said he would grow *out* of them, but I didn't. Nor did Harry lose interest in P.I. work. And now he was dead.

I took a half-dozen deep breaths, employing one of the "stress regulation methods" I'd read about in the Sunday magazine a couple weeks ago. Deep breathing wasn't anything a roundball player at the foul line didn't know about, or a woman giving birth. Or an ex-alky. It had the same relaxing effect whether you called it something fancy or just did it because it worked. Or because you thought it worked . . . like Ed with his heroin.

Across the bay Craig Kinney closed the file and winked at Caparelli. The fat cop's smile looked wider than his face. The two men spoke in low tones, glancing at me. Caparelli stifled a laugh. Craig reached up, slapped Caparelli on the back, and angled toward me through the maze of chest-high cubicles. Nick cradled the phone as Craig came up to him, and Craig, leaning down toward his brother, whispered, "Cappy's been off the force over a year now?"

"Something like that."

Craig shot a look at Caparelli and whispered even more softly to his brother, "The old fart still has a set of cuffs hooked to his belt."

"Did you talk to him about the delay on the bio?" Nick asked.

"Naw. Dad's just got a burr up his ass. I couldn't chew Cappy out when he'd done something as good as this on such short notice. Take a look." Craig handed the file folder to Nick.

I glanced at the folder and saw my name on the tab.

Craig noticed me noticing. He said, "Your life story, big guy."

"But not the authorized version."

"Grim reading," Craig said to his brother. "Cappy got it all from Bodine's ex-wife." Craig shook his head in mock dismay. "Being a happily married man, Nick, you wouldn't know about stuff like this, but let me tell you, an ex-wife with a load on is a mean beast. Check page three at the bottom. Almost makes you feel sorry for this poor fuck."

111

Nick flipped the pages and raised an eyebrow.

"Caparelli says talking to her was like listening to sharks feed."
Nick read on.

Craig said, "Toward the end she analyzes Bodine's relation-ship to his old man. He was a cop. Great little analyst, Bodine's ex. Says his old man got sick and disappeared. Word is he whacked himself. That true, Bodine, your old man sneak off to the old cops' burial ground and smoke his piece, or what?"

The problem with stress-regulation methods—breathing exer-cises, progressive relaxation techniques, visualization, biofeed-back, and so on—is that none of it's as satisfying as pounding your stressor to a pulp. "Yes," I said, "he did."

"I guess it'd be hard for a guy like you to face that," Craig said, "the father you idolized snuffing himself. That's what your ex says anyway. She also says it's a statistical fact that the sons of suicides are prone to whack themselves, too. What about it, Bodine? You ever consider slashing your wrists, or swallowing a megadose of vitamin A? Or a gallon of bourbon? Seems Bodine used to have a drinking problem, Nicky."

"Take it easy," Nick said.

"It's okay, Nick, Mr. Bodine and I are just talking."

I said to Craig, "I was just talking to your ex-wife earlier this evening, and she passed on a few tidbits about you, too."

Craig Kinney gazed at me with a frozen smirk. "Oh, yeah?"

"She blames the Marine Corps for turning you into a jerk," I said, "but I've got a feeling it was something you managed on your own."

Craig leaned close, rising up on the balls of his feet. "You ever seen combat?" he said, giving me a whiff of the bacterial warfare being waged in his mouth.

"I've been married twice," I said.

Craig's index finger stopped just short of my chest. "Let me tell you something, buddy—"

"Craig," said Nick Kinney, "give it a rest."

"I just want to tell him something, Nicky. I want him to know that my family—my father and my brothers—are everything to me."

The intercom buzzed and Nick reached for it.

"Especially my kid brother," Craig continued. "He's in a hospital tonight, and as far as I'm concerned, your pal Quinn and his lawyer, Gibbs, are responsible for putting him there. You hear me, Bodine? It's your guys' fault."

I doubted Craig Kinney was tough enough not to tell me what he was doing at the District Line Motel tonight, but Nick stepped between us and saved his brother from finding it out. "Dad wants us," he said to Craig.

Craig leaned around Nick. "If Timmy hadn't got mixed up with you squirrels, he'd be in school right now." Nick leaned around Craig, opened the door to the office and herded Craig inside. "So just remember, Bodine, you got some payback coming."

Nick, avoiding my gaze, closed the door. I stared at it a moment, acknowledging that Craig was right about the sons of suicides. It was indeed a statistical fact. I never assumed it applied to me, though, because my old man hadn't been a suicide in the strict sense. Suicide in the strict sense is an act of aggression, something one does not only to oneself, but to the people one leaves behind. They find you with your head in an oven or on a wall. They're the ones a suicide is aiming at when he pulls the trigger. But my father had done away with himself by literally doing away with himself, disappearing as only a cop would know how to disappear, vanishing so my mother wouldn't have to find him . . . splattered on the wall. I spent the better part of a year looking for him, but not looking for him. I knew what he'd done, and why, and as much as I wanted to find some trace of him—just to know he'd managed it all right—I didn't want to succeed. It would have been foiling his purpose. "I love you both," his note had said, "but don't come looking for me."

I picked up the phone on the secretary's desk. The receiver was still warm from Nick's ear. I tapped out my area code and number and listened to my phone ring, hoping I wouldn't have to listen to myself say, "This is Jack Bodine, leave your name and number and I'll get back to you."

"Hello?"

"Joyce, it's me."

"Hi, you. Sorry I missed you earlier."

I didn't hear any gun battles in the background, just the whirring of my wife's computer fan. "Eddie hit the sack?"

"Not without a struggle."

"You writing?" I said.

"Yep." She stifled a yawn.

"The case-study paper?"

"Groan."

After spending a full day managing the Bureau of Planning, Research, Evaluation, and Dissemination at the State of Michigan Department of Education, my wife wrote articles for academic journals. Recently she'd been working on "Generalizing from Single Cases." I wished she were here to generalize from Craig Kinney, see what she could come up with. "Hang in there," I said.

"It's lying here in a shambles around my ankles, Jack. The more I work on it, the worse it gets."

"Maybe you're pushing yourself too hard."

"Maybe you are, too. You sound bushed."

"Comes with the territory."

"Did you have trouble finding the motel from the directions Harry gave me?"

"No, I found it all right. I'm just wondering if you talked to him directly the first time he called you, or if you got his message off the machine?"

"I talked to him directly."

"Do you think you could repeat the message again," I said, "just in case I missed something when you gave it to me the first time?"

Joyce paused, thinking. "Let's see, Harry told me Ed left

114

town. I said I thought he was confined to a hospital, but Harry said no, that he went to Washington yesterday evening after making a change in his will. Then Harry said it was very important that you meet him in Washington at the District Line Motel on New York Avenue. I asked him why, and he said he thought someone was attempting to swindle Ed. I asked Harry for details, but he said it wasn't appropriate for him to discuss the situation. I told him you were looking for Ed, too, but that you were on the road. I told him I was sure you'd call in, and when you did that I'd give you his message."

"That's it?"

"Yes. He gave me the exact location of the motel, but that was all."

"Nothing about a will or a codicil, or who was trying to swindle Ed?"

"No. I would have remembered."

"Have you checked the answering machine lately?"

"No, not since yesterday."

"Would you mind giving it a listen, just in case?"

"He wasn't at the motel?"

"He was there."

"Are you all right?" Joyce asked

"I'm fine."

I could almost hear Joyce generalizing. "Jack, Harry's wife phoned me a while ago. She said someone's been pestering her about Harry and Ed Quinn."

"Did she say who?"

"A man named Caparelli. He asked questions about the kind of legal work Harry did for you and Ed. Frieda refused to give out any information, but she's worried because she hasn't heard from Harry all day, and you know how it bothers her when he gets involved with Ed. She phoned here thinking you might know something." Joyce waited for me to tell her what I knew.

I said, "Did Frieda mention anything about a codicil?"

"No. She said she didn't know what Harry was up to, just that he'd left town in a rush and called her from a pay phone on the road to tell her he was following someone, but not to worry, he could handle the situation."

I could almost hear Harry saying it. The hot, sickening fact of his death was on the line, too, a kind of buzzing sound, as if the circuits were overloading. For a moment I didn't know whether to hang up or to tell Joyce everything. I'd tell her eventually, but the identification of Harry's body ought to come first . . . though I had no doubt he was dead. "Joyce?"

"Yes?"

"Joyce, the real reason I called was just to . . . talk. I can check the tape remotely if you want to get back to work."

"No, I'm glad for the break. What's your number there?"

I gave her the number on the secretary's phone.

"I'll call you right back." She hung up.

I cradled the receiver and took in air. When I felt better, I raised up out of the secretary's chair and looked across the bay. Caparelli was on his phone again, nodding as he listened, his chubby digits dancing across his keyboard. Probably interviewing my high school guidance counselor.

He had his back to me, so I got up and pressed my ear to the office door, but I still couldn't hear anything that was going on behind it, just the barely audible murmur of voices. Hell of a door. I thought about kicking it in, but I sat down and forced myself to think about Frieda Gibbs and what I was going to say to her, searching for the right words.

I couldn't find any, and I ended up thinking about my first wife. It bothered me that she'd been boozily unburdening herself to a stranger, "analyzing" me for Cappy Caparelli. I hadn't talked to her in years, and it bothered me, too, that she was keeping up with the events of my life . . . the death of my father. Not surprising, though. She liked him a great deal despite the fact that his collar was far bluer than mine. My father liked her, too, and he took it hard when he found out we were splitting . . . about as hard as when I told him I didn't want to be a cop. In his mind, a cop's life was one of the noblest callings to which a man could pledge himself. Good and evil were real to him, and a cop was a soldier in the eternal war between them, fighting to protect his town and its families against the legions of the night. Whereas a P.I. was nothing but a mercenary who sold his skills to the highest bidder, who operated in a moral twilight, and was nothing more than a mere shadow of a cop, or a crook. For many years I was an embarrassment to my old man. And then, after he retired and began working with Ed and me, he was occasionally an embarrassment to us. But that's another story.

Joyce still hadn't called back when the door to Nick Kinney's office opened and Detective Henry Sweetser stepped out into the bay. He paused before closing the door and told the congregation of Kinneys—all of whom were out of my line of sight—not to worry, he'd get the job done. Then he closed the door and looked at me as if there were but one obstacle to overcome.

15

"How's Kinney's boy?" I said.

Sweetser studied me, his face taking on a succession of expressions as he tried to decide how to handle me. When finally he spoke, it was with something like grandfatherly disdain, as if more than my question amused him. "After two hours trapped in the trunk of a car?" he said. "After coming this close to suffocating? With just the fecal stench of a settling corpse keeping the kid company? Hey, he's doing great."

"Better than the corpse, anyway."

Sweetser reverted to a look my father used to give me after I became a P.I, as if he found nothing funny in Fate's warped sense of humor. "No thanks to you," he said.

"Is that your conclusion, or Craig Kinney's?"

Sweetser paused. "Which one's Craig?"

I said, "The pit bull in the leather sport coat." I almost added that Craig Kinney was the "spiffy" we'd seen at the desk of the District Line Motel earlier in the evening, but I invoked my rule of thumb, and said, "He holds me responsible for what happened to his kid brother."

Sweetser nodded as if this were a sensible conclusion for Craig to have reached. "I told him there's nothing we can charge you with, even though you okayed a shot for Quinn over Gibbs's objection. Depends on what the evidence techs find in your motel room, of course, but at this point there's nothing definite, just the fact you sided with the napheads who killed Gibbs. That's the thing that'll hurt you if it comes out."

"That they're 'napheads,' or that I sided with them?"

Sweetser cocked his head to one side and gazed down at me, his red-rimmed eyes locked onto mine. "Kinney's kid said at the hospital he thought Gibbs was married?"

I nodded.

Sweetser nodded with me. "As officer in charge of this case, I can take certain liberties in what I tell a murder victim's wife about the particulars of her husband's death, what I feel is appropriate, you understand? And I feel at this point there's no reason to let Mrs. Gibbs know the degree of blame that's yours in the death of her husband. There's other allowances I can make, too, depending on how you cooperate." Sweetser lifted his eyebrows, his expression an open invitation to accept the favor he was offering.

My impulse was to tell him to stuff his favor in his ear, but the phone rang before I could stuff my foot in my mouth. "That'll be my wife," I said.

"Your wife?"

"I left a message for her to call me here."

"About what?"

"I just wanted to let her know I was all right."

The phone rang again.

"You're not 'all right,' Bodine, so don't get her hopes up. And make it quick. We're due at the morgue." Sweetser motioned toward Caparelli's cubicle. "I'll be over there."

Sweetser ambled away, absently patting his trench coat where the corner of the white letter-size envelope peeked out of his pocket. I picked up the phone. "Joyce?"

"Sorry it took me so long," she said, "but Eddie heard me talking to you and he insists on asking you something."

119

"Sure." I heard the muffled sounds of the receiver changing hands, then the rasp of Eddie's breathing as he jammed the mouthpiece against his lips.

"Dad?"

"Yes, Eddie."

"I wanted to ask you something."

"Okay, ask."

"Um, where are you?"

"I'm in Washington, remember?" As I spoke, I watched Sweetser greet his corpulent crony, Caparelli, with a poke in the gut. Caparelli cuffed Sweetser on the chin, and the two of them began to yammer.

Eddie said, "Washington's where the president lives, right?"

"When he feels like it."

"Huh?"

"Nothing. Go on."

"Well," said Eddie, "you know his house, right?"

"Sure. It's the one with the paint peeling under the porch."

"What?"

"I saw it tonight," I said. "The paint's peeling under the porch."

"The White House?"

"Actually, it's green with pink trim."

"Really?"

"No, Eddie. It's so white it hurts your eyes to look at it, even at night."

"Really?"

"They've got spotlights on it."

"Well, what I was wondering is, could you stop there the next time you drive by and get me a model of it like the one Mom got me the last time she was in Washington?"

"That's the one you painted green with pink trim, correct?"

"No, that was the Michigan capitol. I painted the White House black 'cause I didn't have any red."

120

"Why did you want to paint it red?"

" 'Cause the Russians overtook it."

"Why don't you just repaint it white?"

"I would, but I can't find it."

"How about cleaning your room? It might turn up."

"I want to, but Mom says I got to go to bed."

"Well, I guess it might be easier if I just dropped in on the prez, huh?"

"You wouldn't have to do it tonight."

"All right, but just remember, this is the same guy you named that lilac after, the one you and your buddies pee on when you camp out in the backyard."

"You said we could."

"I didn't say you could name it George the Bush."

"Dad," whispered Eddie, "the phone could be tapped."

"That would be against the law."

"Not if they submit a affadavid to a magicstrate that says they got probable cause."

"Where'd you learn that?"

"TV. There was a two-hour *Miami Vice* tonight. I didn't get to see the end of it because Mom made me go to bed."

"I can tell you how it ends," I said. "The bad guy's making a getaway in his sports car, this white Lamborghini, and the good guy squeezes off a clip, gets lucky, and all of a sudden the Lamborghini's hamborgini. Now why don't you head back to bed like your mom wants you to?"

"Did you know who the bad guy was?" Eddie asked.

"No, I didn't recognize him."

"Well, you wouldn't say 'hamborgini' if you knew who he was."

"I'd like to talk to your mom again."

"He was a private detective, Dad."

"Oh? Well, just because a guy's a private eye doesn't mean he can't be bad."

"Dad?"

"What?"

"Don't get smart with President Bush, okay?"

"It's all right, he's got a sense of humor."

"You don't have to get me that model of the White House if you don't want to, either. Mom said she'll get me one when she goes to Washington. She says she's going next month."

"I'll see what I can do," I said.

"Dad?"

"What?"

"Have you ever done anything like what the P.I. on TV did tonight, the one they killed?"

"No," I said, not mentioning that several hours ago I'd conspired to commit euthanasia, lied to the cops about it, roughed up an old man, and let someone murder my lawyer. The evening was still young, too. "But you never know about people and what they're going to do," I added. "Sometimes even kids can be bad, thinking up reasons not to go to bed."

"There's something else I wanted to say," Eddie said, "but I'll let Mom tell you what Klutz did, okay?"

"Or you can tell me tomorrow. I'll be calling again."

"Okay. 'Bye."

" 'Bye."

I heard the receiver change hands. I listened to Joyce tell Eddie to hit the sack, then I heard Eddie ask Joyce to be sure to tell me that he went straight to bed. She came back on the line and said, "He's wound up tonight."

"How can you tell?"

"I didn't know he was watching *Miami Vice*."

"Make him watch two hours of *Mister Rogers* tomorrow morning and he'll be brain dead the rest of the day."

"A lot of it's because Halloween's coming up," Joyce said. "I promised him we'd work on his costume tomorrow. Did he tell you? He's decided to be the grim reaper. He smeared red paint all over the blade of the plastic scythe I bought him at Meijer's this morning."

"I thought he was going to be a mailbox."

"No. The grim reaper."

"I wish he'd be a mailbox."

"Jack, you sound strange."

"Did you come across anything from Harry on the tape?"

"No. I listened to all of it, too. Jack, did Ed Quinn finally pass away?"

"No. It's . . . Harry Gibbs."

"What about him?"

"He's dead."

"Harry?"

"They're making me look at a body in a few minutes. They're sure it's him."

"Oh, Jack, that's terrible."

"Yes."

"What happened?"

"Harry was . . . mugged."

"Oh, my God!"

I said, "What did the cat do?"

Joyce had a thousand things she wanted to ask, but she answered my question about Klutz instead, distractedly, knowing distraction was what I wanted. "Eddie was playing with his bug collection this afternoon, and Klutz ate his cicada."

"He *ate* it?"

"Jack, are you sure you're all right?"

"I'm better than Klutz."

We were silent a moment, then Joyce said, "Have they notified Frieda Gibbs?"

"I don't think so. They want me to make the interim ID first."

"How did it happen?"

I gave Joyce a condensed version of events at the motel and followed it up with what Douglas Kinney claimed to have got from Sweetser over the phone.

"Do you want me to come to Washington?" Joyce said. "It wouldn't hurt Eddie to miss a few days of school, and we could visit museums. We'd keep out of your way, but if you wanted us, we could help."

I felt like I'd been gone for six weeks and wouldn't be back for six more. I could use a visit from my family. I could use Joyce, too. She worked in Washington before she made the move to Michigan, and she knew her way around D.C. "No," I said. "I'll manage."

We were quiet. If Joyce were sitting right beside me, it would be the same . . . except that her hand would be squeezing mine.

"Jack?"

"Yes?"

Joyce hesitated. "I don't know. I just . . . that replica of the White House Eddie was asking about?"

This wasn't what she meant to say, but it would do. "Yes?"

"You can get one from any of the souvenir wagons along the mall."

"Thanks."

"Jack, I'm worried."

I told her not to worry. We said a few things of an intimate nature, edging nearer the inevitable disconnection. Finally I cradled the receiver. I didn't know of any breathing exercises that could alleviate the pang of loneliness, so I walked my ache over to Caparelli's cubicle.

Sweetser, his back to me, was listening to his old pal give an enthusiastic account of Kintell's "beaucoup bennies": the non-deductible cosmetic dental provision, the fifty thousand in employee life insurance, which, according to Caparelli, was a good thing, considering Kintell's receptionist. "That little fox bends over, I get chest pains." Caparelli saw me coming and cut off his pitch, alerting Sweetser to my approach with a nod of his head.

Sweetser turned toward me.

"I'm ready," I said.

"Catch you later, Cappy."

Sweetser and I started for the door.

124

"All aboard for the gravy train, Sweety." Cappy was making a hitchhiker's gesture with his thumb.

Sweetser pretended he hadn't heard. I did, too. Neither of us said anything on the way down to the lobby, but Caparelli's remark was as palpable as a third person in the elevator.

16

Sweetser's car was just down from the main entrance to Kinney's building, its emergency flashers blinking. We climbed in and Sweetser squealed through a U-turn, his headlights glaring off the plate-glass glitz of K Street. He called the dispatcher and said he was headed for the morgue, then hooked the mike. "It's a twenty-minute drive," he said to me. "By the time we get there, I want to know everything that happened in that motel room. I already know some of it, so don't get cute."

I gave it to him straight, everything as it occurred. I even told him I'd attended the gunny's seminar in techniques of heroin injection. I assumed Tim had told him about it, and even if he hadn't, I wanted Sweetser to know. It was clear now that Sweetser was playing the Kinneys' game, and my idea was to make it easy for him to force me to join in. It was the best way of finding out what the game was. I didn't tell him I'd seen Craig Kinney at the motel talking to Mapes, though. That was my ace.

When I finished my story, Sweetser muttered my name a few times, as if he hardly knew what to do with me, shaking his head, his breath coming in deep wistful sighs. "And you never heard any commotion out in the parking lot?" he said.

"After Tim helped Harry Gibbs outside, I went into the

bathroom and rinsed out the syringe. I closed the door so I wouldn't disturb Ed. I didn't hear anything."

We were stopped at a light. Sweetser, gazing up at it, said, "You're in an awkward position, taking lessons from a hit doctor, and all that. Could cost you your license, maybe even some time in the can . . . *if*," Sweetser added meaningfully, "it ever comes out." The light dropped to green. Sweetser's foot pounced on the accelerator and the car lurched through the gears.

"You mean it might not have to come out?" I said, trying not to sound as dumb as a parrot.

"Hey, Mr. Kinney handles security for some of the fanciest firms in the country. He finds out one of his kids is working under an assumed name for a gumshoe whose partner's feeding him heroin, he wants to keep it quiet. That can work to your advantage. Mine, too."

"Is this Kinney's idea, or yours?" I was straining my rule of thumb, of course, but not questioning cops was a rule that applied to honest officers only. With crooked fuzz, you could bend it a bit.

"What idea?" Sweetser said.

"Suborning a witness."

"People who put too fine a point on things, Bodine, sometimes end up sticking themselves."

Sweetser's face was plainly visible in the headlights of oncoming cars. Either he hadn't had the guts to bring the idea up with Kinney or the courage to kill it. Whichever, he was obviously ashamed of himself, but was pretending anger. And I didn't want to provoke him. I said, "I get your point."

Sweetser grunted, then brooded a moment. "So what about it?"

"I guess I don't want to stick myself any more than you want to stand guard in a Safeway."

"That's real fine," Sweetser said mockingly, "but pardon me if I think you're fixing to fuck me over."

"I wouldn't do that."

"You done it twice already. You let me waltz into Kinney's

127

house without telling me your partner was his stepbrother. You never told me Kinney's kid's been working for you and Quinn since last spring, either."

"I didn't know who the boy was," I said. "I'm sure Ed didn't, either."

"Come on," Sweetser said, "you guys had to know."

"No. Tim walked in off the street, told Ed his name was Cooney, said he was a college kid in need of a summer job. This was back in March. Ed had just begun to get sick, and he needed a legman right away. The boy signed on part time, and went full time the beginning of the summer."

"Quinn hired him just like that," Sweetser said, snapping his fingers, "and never even checked him out?"

"All he expected Tim to do was run film to the Motophoto, that kind of thing."

"Film?"

"Snapshots."

"Of what?"

"Bars, motels, parked cars, shadows behind window shades."

Sweetser dismissed this with a wave of his hand. "See, I wanna believe you, Bodine, but it's hard taking you straight up after you made a big point of asking Kinney about those pictures of his sons earlier tonight. You knew who the kid was then, and you didn't say. So why should I believe you didn't know who he was eight months ago?"

"Because if I'd known before tonight, I wouldn't have asked Kinney about him, would I?"

Sweetser, tugging on an incipient wattle, thought about this. "Kinney thinks Quinn recruited the kid in order to embarrass his family."

"He didn't."

Sweetser was silent for a good six blocks. Then he said, "You got a family of your own, Bodine, am I right?"

I was staring out the window, watching the bleak streets blur by, the sparkle of K Street having given way to block-long stands of nineteenth-century row houses. Even under the ugly orange glow of the sodium-vapor streetlamps, I could see that the row houses once had been grand homes. Now they looked as shabby and as forlorn as the black men I saw milling out front of the liquor stores that seemed to be on every other corner. I turned toward Sweetser. "What's my family have to do with the price of presidents?"

A traffic light jumped from orange to red and Sweetser hit the brakes. "Caparelli says he talked to an ex-wife of yours tonight."

"That's what I heard."

"So, this wife that called you at Kintell, she your second, third, what?"

"Who cares?"

"I do. I wanna know."

"She's my second and last."

"You two got any kids?"

"One."

"How old?"

"Nine."

"So you consider yourself a family man?"

"What does it matter?"

"See those guys?" Sweetser said, pointing at a sullen congregation of liquor store functionaries. "Washington's this year's murder capital because of those shitheads right there. Those street studs strut around like big men, bragging how many people they killed. With the same breath they'll tell you how many kids they've fathered, like notches on a gun."

"I still don't see your point."

Sweetser ignored the sudden static-garbled voice that squawked over the radio. "My point is I hate those guys, Bodine, hate 'em for what they're doing to their children. 'Cause I'm a family man." Sweetser was staring hard at the men on the corner.

The men were staring back.

"Just isn't any family life here anymore," Sweetser added sadly, his anger subsiding. "A town of families is a stable town,

129

a good place to live. Anything in life that's any good comes out of the family, right? Well, this town's fucked because the people that live here don't understand what I'm saying. Or don't care. You could figure it if they were on that corner hustling crack in order to help their families, but that ain't why. I mean, there's little girls getting themselves knocked up even before high school, don't want their friends thinking they're barren. Their mothers egg them on, too, proud of them 'cause they don't want any barren daughters. You know who raises the kids in this town, or tries to? The grandmothers." The red light dropped to green and Sweetser accelerated away from the malevolent stares of the men on the corner.

I didn't say anything, and after a moment Sweetser tried to tie up the strands of his argument. He spoke softly, with the oil of conspiracy in his voice. "See, if I help Mr. Kinney out on this investigation, it's not because I'm a creep like those bloods on the street back there, or like the slick punks killed your lawyer friend. I'm thinking of my family. My mother and my kid in college. I told you about them, right?"

"Right."

"Well, Douglas Kinney, he told me about his family there in that office. He don't run his businesses anymore, Kinfolk and Kintell. He retired. As of last month, his boys run them, and something like what happened tonight could fuck up their futures. Kinney don't want that happening to his sons. He wants to protect them. You can understand that, can't you?"

"I can."

" 'Cause you're a family man, right?"

"Right."

Sweetser said coyly, "You want to keep on being one, don't you?"

I looked at him.

"I ask 'cause there ain't nothing harder on a family man than having his wife and kid living in Lansing while he's doing time in . . . what is it, Jackson? That the state pen in Michigan?"

"Jacktown's one of them."

"So, this matter of cooperation we mentioned a while back, it pays. You get to keep your license, your freedom, and your family. In exchange, Mr. Kinney keeps his family business healthy, and I get a chance at a decent retirement opportunity so I can continue to provide for my family. Ain't none of us doing nothing here that wouldn't be a benefit to society, either. And in the end, the guys who did your pal Gibbs, they're the ones who pay. Just them and nobody else, not you, me, or Kinney. You see anything wrong with that?"

"Sounds fine. On paper."

Sweetser touched his thumb to his fingertips as if the essence of his point were balanced there. "That's all a homicide investigation ever is, Bodine. Nothing . . . but . . . paper." He flicked on his turn signal and swung into the parking lot of a building across from D.C. General Hospital. The building looked like one of the office structures on K Street. "The morgue," Sweetser said. "Here's where we start laying down the paper."

17

Sweetser spoke to a female morgue attendant, who showed us into a small room that had several plastic chairs and a dingy vinyl floor. The attendant left us, saying she'd be right back. Sweetser and I stood in silence, gazing at a window set into an interior wall. A drab curtain covered the other side of the window, a setup that reminded me of a movie-theater ticket booth. The last show was over and the curtain was drawn.

After a moment the curtain was opened. The attendant was on the other side of the glass, standing behind a gurney she'd rolled up to the sill. Someone was on the gurney, covered with a plastic sheet. Sweetser motioned me up to the window, and the attendant drew back the sheet. I looked at the person and nodded. Sweetser signaled the attendant, who folded the sheet over Harry Gibbs's face and closed the curtain.

We left the viewing room. I signed my name several times, and Sweetser and I quit the morgue. We didn't say anything on the way to the car. We got in and Sweetser started up and pulled into traffic. He belched once, but otherwise kept his thoughts to himself, driving hard and fast to a nearby bar and grill.

No surprise, the joint was jammed with cops. Not one uniform in sight, but I knew they were fuzz from the way it felt stepping through the door, as if I'd walked into a den of outlaws. Sweetser pointed through the swirling cigarette smoke at a free booth and said he'd join me after he used the phone.

"Are you going to call Gibbs's wife?" I said.

The phone was just inside the door. Sweetser had the receiver in his hand and was digging for change. "I don't make death notifications over the phone," he said. "I'll call the Lansing police later and have them send someone out to talk to her in the morning. I'm just checking in with my old lady. Go on, get that booth there."

I got the booth. It was just across from the bar, where a trio of detectives perched on stools was perusing a magazine layout on women weight lifters. ("She ain't nothing but Arnold Schwarzenegger with a pussy.") In the booth behind me a team of dirt-and-denim vice cops were pondering more philosophical matters. ("If girls are made of sugar and spice, how come they always taste like fish?")

One of the vice cops sought the expertise of a two-hundred-pound waitress, but she waddled by them and asked if I wanted to order. I told her I was waiting for the guy leaning into the telephone stall near the door. The waitress squinted at Sweetser and said she knew what he wanted, what did I want? I told her, and she grunted and turned away, lumbering past the detectives with the magazine. One of them asked her to make a muscle.

Sweetser had the right idea, of course. After a trip to the morgue, the best thing to do is head for home ground and try to forget what you've seen at the cold house.

The smell stayed with you, though, in memory if not in fact. It had overpowered the lingering reek of Sweetser's cruiser, and even now the cigarette stench of the bar wasn't foul enough to mask the dank clammy mix of chemicals and corruption. Or maybe I was imagining it, and there hadn't been any morgue smell at all. Either way, a jar of Vicks would have helped. I learned the Vicks trick from an old homicide-dick-turned-P.I. whom Ed Quinn had introduced me to years ago. He told me how, if he had to make a trip to the morgue, he always smeared a little Vicks VapoRub inside each nostril. I met him after he'd retired from the cops, but, like Caparelli at Kintell, he still carried cop gear wherever he went, mainly his detective's kit: a battered briefcase that held a tape measure, a pair of latex gloves, a clip-on penlight, a notebook, and a wedge of tailor's chalk for outlining bodies. He had evidence envelopes in there as well, and a pair of tweezers for collecting broken fingernails and strands of hair or thread. And always he had that little blue bottle of Vicks. His name was Smith. Everyone called him Smitty.

Behind me one of the vice cops explained the Polish lottery. ("Winner gets a buck a day for a million days.") I was desperate for a laugh, but the thought of old Smitty put the chill on my funny bone . . . something he'd said once, back when I'd met him for the first time. I was just a kid, Ed Quinn's gofer, in fact. Because I was so young, Smitty got a kick out of needling me. He told me about the morgue, how the M.E. conducted autopsies by digging into the body cavity and hefting the innards, squeezing them, weighing them, slicing them up, and sniffing them. It was important to me to show Ed Quinn how tough I was, so I passed off Smitty's tales of the M.E. with a shrug.

That's when he started in on the death technicians, the guys who dealt with you after the M.E. was done, when you weren't evidence anymore, just meat that had to be processed. According to Smitty, death techs worked you over with something called a vacuum trocar, a thick hollow steel spear with holes in its business end. *They stab that sucker into your stomach, poke it right through your liver and into your heart, suck, suck, all this tar-black blood blowing into the sink, this foul brown stuff coming next, see, 'cause they've turned that ol' trocar around and stuck it into your guts, spearing the coils again and again, grunting as they shove, ramming it all the way down, buddy, right into your scrotum, that ol' trocar making a slurping sound.* According to Smitty, not all death techs liked using the trocar. Some preferred to hook out your innards through your anus. I later learned that

Smitty had only read about these things in a book by a surgeon named Selzer, which somehow made it all seem worse.

I rubbed my eyes. The cigarette smoke made them burn. As I rubbed, I could see Harry Gibbs, an ardent nonsmoker, fanning the air, asking the bartender to open a window, insisting the vice cops quit blowing their fumes his way, all 130 pounds of him as irate as a vegetarian in a slaughterhouse. Then, like smoke drifting in front of a fan, the image of Harry was whisked away. All that remained was the knowledge that the death techs would soon have their way with him, and that they probably chain-smoked Camels. Harry was beyond caring, but there was little comfort in knowing that . . . or that the death techs would have their way with us all in the end. Me. Joyce. Even Eddie. Brooding on that, I felt as if someone were trying to hook out my heart through my throat.

The fat waitress, popping gum as if she were chewing firecrackers, heaved up to the table and clattered a plate of pancakes, eggs, hash browns, and sausage onto the Formica. She banged down a shot and a beer, too, and slid a sloshing cup of coffee in my direction. I sniffed the coffee. Like the waitress, it smelled sour.

As she turned away, Sweetser came up behind her and patted her on the fanny, whispering in her ear while shrugging out of his trench coat, making a grab for her. The waitress squirmed away, cursing and giggling.

Sweetser pegged his coat on the hook at the end of my bench and climbed into the booth, eyeing the eggs as if they promised more than satiety. He snatched up a triangle of buttered toast, speared a link of thick brown sausage with his fork and hesitated. "Hey, for what it's worth, I'm sorry about Gibbs." He said this with perfunctory solemnity, as if he were saying grace.

I said, "Sure." I could have said "amen" and it would have made as much sense.

Sweetser nodded and violated the egg yolk with the link of sausage and passed the dripping mess into his face, chewing and

135

shoveling, finishing off the food before the head on his beer had begun to settle. He lapped the buttershine from his fingers, knocked back the shot, and sucked down the beer, belching as he dug into his breast pocket and pulled out a crumpled pack of Winstons. He offered the pack to me.

I shook my head.

Sweetser shrugged, bummed a light from one of the vice cops, and sat back, gazing at me with the indifference of a lion that had just gorged on a kill. Finally he said, "Were you real buddies with Gibbs?"

"No," I said, "we weren't real buddies. Harry threw work my way from time to time, so I knew him, but it was mainly business between us." And it still was. This business of his death had the Quinn-Bodine Agency's full attention. The full force of the firm, from the man at the top to the gumshoe on the street, was committed to the case. Since Ed was on sick leave, that left just me. But I was enough. All I had for competition was Sweetser. If I couldn't market a better solution to the criminal justice system than this bent set of buttons, then I didn't deserve Harry's business. "I know his wife well enough, though, to know she's going to take his death very hard."

Sweetser grunted and sucked on his smoke. "Well, you can talk to her when she flies down. I want you to hang around for a couple days, be available when I need you." He eyed my untouched coffee. "Wanna trade that in on something sensible?"

"No."

Sweetser shrugged, twisted around on his bench and waved at the waitress. When he caught her attention he pointed at his empty beer glass, then turned back to me, sucking on a tooth . . . staring at me, the smoke from the cigarette twirling up from his hand. "You think I'm a kissass, don't you, Bodine?"

I didn't answer.

"Maybe I am," Sweetser said evenly. "If I thought it would help me get a job with Kinney, I'd kiss the ass of every one of those bloods we saw on that street corner tonight. I'd kiss your ugly ass, too. You might even say that's what I'm about to do, because I never been as intimate with a civilian as I'm gonna be with you." Sweetser paused and sized me up, squinting against the rising column of cigarette smoke. "I need your help, see? And you need mine. So I'm going to let my hair down, here, but not my guard. You understand?"

"Sure."

"Okay, here it is: Kinney's kid has never been printed." Sweetser paused again, watching me the way he had at the morgue when the attendant had drawn back the sheet covering Harry's face.

I said, "How do you know?"

Sweetser said cryptically, "I checked. He told the officer at the scene his name was Cooney. They never looked at his ID, so no one knows his name's Kinney."

"You weren't there when they opened the trunk?"

"No. I was in the comm room—this's after I dropped you off at the motel—and I caught the squeal: a corpse and a kid in the trunk of a car behind the District Line Motel. I didn't like the coincidence that I'd just dropped you off at the same motel, so I got on the net and talked to the scene. Uniform said the deceased's name was Gibbs. I recognized it from talking to you at the motel. Officer said the kid's name was Cooney, and that they were loading the kid into a meat wagon to take him to D.C. General. So I hauled over there. The boy wasn't squirtin' all over the interns, so they made him wait out in the hallway across from the E.R. He was there with the officer from the scene. He was in a daze, so the uniform hadn't got anything down in his notebook except what the kid said his name was: Cooney, Timothy Cooney."

"How did you make him as Kinney's kid?"

"I checked his ID. Driver's license, Social Security card, and a student ID from the University of Michigan: Timothy Kinney."

The waitress labored up to our booth with Sweetser's refill. She thunked the shell down on the table and picked up his empty, took a deep breath, and set out on the return trip to the bar. Sweetser caught the attention of the cops on the bar stools and pointed at the waitress. "Tell her to haul ass, she has to make two trips."

Ha, ha, ha, ha.

Sweetser saluted the laughter with the fresh beer, draining half the glass in two gulps, then sucking on his cigarette as if he were trying to see which he could finish first. "So I sent the uniform to the cafeteria for a coffee," he said to me, "and I had a talk with the kid, taking it nice and slow. I told him I knew who his father was, said I just talked to him. It takes a minute or two, but the kid finally tells me he's been working for his old man's stepbrother in Michigan and that his father don't know nothing about it, he's gonna kill him for being in the same trunk with poor Gibbs, eksetera, eksetera. We talk some more, and he tells me how he and Gibbs tailed two bloods to D.C. from Michigan last night, how you showed up at the motel this evening, what happened to Gibbs inside the motel, outside the motel, everything. You with me?"

"Yes."

Sweetser stubbed out his cigarette, pushed aside his empty glass and leaned toward me. "I got a team finishing up that motel room right now. Chances are the kid left a latent. You probably did, too, and about a thousand other people. Monday we'll print you and the kid and Gibbs and run a check on any latents that don't match. A lot of them are gonna connect to names. But not the kid's. There's no way, not through the prints, at least, that anyone can prove he's not Timothy Cooney. Anybody who comes into contact with him from now on—and if I can help it, there ain't gonna be nobody but me—they'll assume he's Timothy Cooney, college dropout. And the kid ain't gonna say nothing to correct them, neither. So there's no way anyone can tie him to his father or his brothers and their businesses. Except you. And I'm counting on you not to do that."

"You planning to tie a bag over the boy's head when he gets on the stand?"

"I told you, Bodine, this is the murder capital of the nation.

138

You think the *Washington Post* is gonna assign a photographer to snap some witness in a drug-related homicide? Anyway, nine-tenths of these cases are plea bargained. I doubt the kid'll ever have to testify."

"Then why have him lie about his name?"

"Because if his real name gets written down on a piece of paper, or entered into a computer, you never know what'll happen. The kid's sure the two boogies got no idea what his real name is, so they aren't going to be a problem when we pick them up."

"You sound confident of a bust."

"Cap gave me a dynamite lead."

"Caparelli?"

"Yeah, the big guy back at Kintell. See, soon as you and me left Kinney's place in Georgetown earlier tonight, Kinney called his office. Caparelli had the duty, and Kinney told him to find out what he could about his stepbrother, Quinn, what he's been up to recently, and so on. Caparelli makes a grand total of three calls and comes up with a kitchen worker at the hospital in Michigan where Quinn had his bladder removed. She says she saw Quinn leave in the company of a black male. Cappy makes a fourth call to one of your competitors in the Lansing area who tells him Quinn's tight with a black dude and his wife who go by the name of Bonnie and Clyde. Among other things, they're suspected of running a chain of chop shops between Lansing and the East Coast."

"Ed Quinn's not 'tight' with them," I said, "but I know the people you mean. I've spent the last thirty-six hours working that angle myself. I've tried to fence my heap in Toledo, Pittsburgh, Harrisburg, and Towson, Maryland. It's my opinion you'd do better to start locally with the desk clerk at the District Line Motel. His name is Othman Mapes."

"That the guy whose house you were at when Nick Kinney got the call from his old man to bring you in?"

I nodded. "Ed Quinn wasn't at Mapes's place," I said, "but I'm sure Mapes knows where he is. Nick Kinney said they've got somebody from Kintell watching Mapes, but you might want to assume control of that function yourself."

"Thanks," Sweetser said flatly, "for the suggestion."

If there's one thing a cop hates—especially a crooked cop—it's a private dick telling him how to handle his investigation. Knowing that, I knew Sweetser wouldn't care to hear my theory that Ed Quinn's "hit doctor" was a crooked cop, too. So I just let him cow me with his bloodshot stare, not mentioning the red Escort that had darted out of the motel parking lot right behind Othman Mapes's black van, either. "I just thought you'd want to know," I said.

Sweetser sniffed with annoyance, sat back and raised his empty glass, tipping it high to hurry the dregs, watching me over the rim. When he lowered the glass he said, blandly, "By the way, Gibbs have any hobbies?"

"Hobbies?"

"Yeah. You know, fishing? Tennis?"

As far as I knew, Harry's sole hobby was tagging along with Ed Quinn on divorce cases, but I was sure that wasn't what Sweetser had in mind. "What does it matter if Harry had any hobbies?"

"He swim? Jog?"

"Not that I know of."

"Any reason he avoided that kinda thing?"

"You mean physical exercise?"

"Yeah."

"I don't know that he avoided it. Why?"

"In a case like this, you want to go to the prosecutors and tell them it's clean, no possibility the victim had some kinda condition that might queer a conviction."

"A condition?"

"Yeah, like if he was epileptic, or something, and swallowed his tongue in the struggle."

I thought back to the morgue and what I'd glimpsed on the gurney behind the viewing glass: Harry's eyes wide open, bulging slightly; his tongue, thick and gray, protruding from lips as blue

140

as his opaque eyes. "Have you got a reason to think that's what happened?" I said.

Sweetser lifted an eyebrow in a facial shrug. "You never know what the M.E.'s going to find, Bodine. And like I said, something of that kind could fuck up an airtight case."

The pay phone by the front door rang. It was barely audible over the din in the bar, but a vice cop who'd been yanking on the cigarette machine next to it pulled the receiver off the hook. He glanced in our direction and covered the mouthpiece. "Hey, Sweety," he shouted, "it's for you."

Sweetser turned and waved. "I'll be right back," he said to me, easing himself out of the booth and hulking over to the phone. He took the receiver from the vice cop and turned his back toward the bar as if to sequester the conversation. Even in the dim light of the bar I could see that the seat of his pants was shiny. I could see it was shiny because he wasn't wearing his trench coat. It was hanging next to me, the white corner of the envelope peeking out of his coat pocket. It was a simple white letter-size envelope, the kind old Smitty used to carry in his evidence case.

I checked the pay phone. Sweetser still had his back to me. The vice cop who'd handed him the phone was busy committing police brutality on the cigarette machine. His buddies in the booth behind me had climbed out and were aiming themselves at the head. The detectives at the bar had tears in their eyes (something about the lieutenant being as busy as a one-legged man in an ass-kicking contest) . . . laughing a little myself, I tugged the envelope out of Sweetser's raincoat and opened the unglued flap. There was a small brown pill bottle inside. I didn't touch the bottle, just shook it till I could read the label. It said: HANE'S DRUGS INC., FRANDOR SHOPPING CENTER, LANSING, MI., 517–555–1861, 113579, 08/03/89, DR. CONSTABLE, FOR GIBBS, HAROLD. NITROGLYCERIN 1/150. DISSOLVE 1 TABLET SUBLINGUALLY IN CASE OF CHEST PAIN EVERY FIVE MINUTES. MAY REPEAT 2 TIMES. IF NO RELIEF IN 15 MINUTES, CALL DR.

I closed the envelope, stuffed it back into Sweetser's coat pocket and gazed around the bar . . . taking in the mounted Redskins helmet—complete with face mask and battle scars—the pennant from the '88 Super Bowl, the team pictures, and the autographed publicity stills of individual players—a choice shot of Sonny Jurgenson hanging over the bar, his belly bulging—the cops at the bar wheezing with glee at the thought of "an erection as hard as woodpecker lips," Sweetser hanging up the phone, his lips pursed hard in thought as he trudged back to the booth with that rolling-shoulders shuffle of his . . . a tired old cop on the make, worn out from suborning and suppressing and God knew what else . . . not to mention the beating his liver was taking. I wanted to feel sorry for him, but I couldn't do that anymore than I could ask him about those pills in the pocket of his trench coat.

When he reached the booth he snagged his coat off the hook and shoved his arm into a sleeve. "They're through with the room," he said, "and they're towing Gibbs's car downtown. I got to head back to the station. Let's get outta here."

We did.

18

IF YOU CAN READ THIS, said the bumper sticker on the Safeway semi just ahead of us, YOU'RE TOO CLOSE. Sweetser accelerated into the eerie sucking silence of the semi's slipstream. There was a second truck behind us, and its lights threw a stark, jolting shadow of Sweetser's head on the tailgate of the truck in front of us. I could see my head, too.

I closed my eyes and saw Harry Gibbs laid out on the morgue gurney. I wondered if MacDonell Magna Jet Black Fingerprint Powder had made the dark smudges on his throat. Evidence techs, if they still used powder these days, like to dust human flesh before it's refrigerated. They don't close the corpse's eyes or tuck its tongue away before the M.E. has a chance to look at it, either, though possibly the M.E. had made a preliminary examination of Harry and had pulled back the lids of his eyes looking for burst blood vessels as evidence of strangulation. While inspecting Harry's "oral cavity," he might have given his tongue a tug, too. Though maybe not. Maybe no one had touched Harry but the person who strangled him. And maybe what looked like fingerprint powder was a massive contusion, Harry's eyes having been popped and his tongue squeezed from his throat by strong, unyielding hands. But what about the pills in Sweetser's coat pocket? They suggested Harry had died not of strangulation, but of a heart attack. Joyce's father had described his coronary in terms of suffocation, said it felt as if someone were sitting on his chest. But would a heart attack, no matter how sudden and severe, make a man's eyes pop and his tongue protrude? I had no idea. And there wasn't any use speculating till the M.E. wrote his report. All I knew from having seen Harry Gibbs on that gurney was that death looked as if it had come to him as the surprise of his life, a shock of such proportions he seemed to have choked on it.

A sudden gust of wind buffeted Sweetser's cruiser and I opened my eyes. The Safeway trucks had peeled off onto New York Avenue. A moment later a sign for the Baltimore-Washington Parkway flashed by and Sweetser accelerated onto the parkway, heading north. Four hours earlier I'd driven south on the same road from Towson, veering west onto New York Avenue toward the District Line Motel. My car was still at the District Line, my travel bag in the trunk. Wherever Sweetser was taking me, it was not toward my toothbrush.

For a moment I indulged the fantasy that I was leaving Washington for good, that I had the Pennsylvania Turnpike behind me, Toledo, too, Brighton, Williamston, Okemos, and finally the side door of my house. I saw myself locking it, shedding my clothes and climbing into bed with Joyce. She rolled toward me. I told her to go back to sleep, but she couldn't, and I got up and fetched her a tall glass of milk and told her all about it, everything but what Harry had looked like on that gurney. She wouldn't want to know about that, nor would I be capable of describing his odd expression, that look of ghastly profundity mixed with goofy petulance, his eyes telling me he knew something astounding, while his out-sticking tongue ridiculed my need to know what it was. I would not describe Harry to Joyce.

Sweetser, though, would be easy. I watched him squint against the light from oncoming cars, creases, jowls, and wattles stark in the headlamps, his broad broken-veined beak and bourbon bags purplish in the glare. I saw Victor McLaughlin sitting next to me, gruff, rude, and solid, his broad mouth—with its expressive, almost prehensile lips—manifesting a ready corruptibility.

"You're looking at me like you got something on your mind," Sweetser said.

What I had on my mind—homesickness aside—was what I wasn't looking at: mug shots of the black men who'd ambushed Harry and Tim. Sweetser hadn't even asked for a description of them. Maybe he was satisfied with Tim Kinney's description, or maybe he already knew what they looked like. The one who'd shown me how to stick Ed was a cop, I was sure of it. He'd known the exact location of the Fifth District station, the very station Sweetser worked out of, "just up the road" from the motel. Probably Sweetser owed the gunny a favor, which was why a homicide dick had shown up at the motel earlier tonight, and not a uniform in a prowl car. Maybe the gunny was Sweetser's partner. And the existence of the nitro tablets, if the prescription were genuine, would obviate an investigation: no one choked Harry Gibbs to death. He died of a heart attack. It was entirely possible Tim Kinney's version of Harry's death had by now changed radically from the one his father had read to me at Kintell's offices. *Honest, Mr. Bodine, he had a heart attack. No one ever touched him.* "Yes," I said, "there is something on my mind."

"Don't let it turn green," Sweetser said, swerving off the parkway and onto an exit ramp.

"Where are we going?"

"There." Sweetser flew through an intersection and cornered into the parking lot of an upscale motel called the Inn Deluxe. "Nice place to spend the weekend. You'll like it."

"I've already got a room back at the District Line Motel," I said.

Sweetser knocked his car out of gear and turned toward me. "Now you got one here."

"My clothes and my shaving kit are there, too."

"This one's got a valet service. There's also a restaurant, a bar, a band, a pool, and a workout room, whatever you need. There's even a shop where you can buy a toothbrush and some underwear."

"I could use a new ascot, too, but I'm not working on an expense account."

"Kinney said he'd pick up the tab. So enjoy yourself. Monday morning, hit the lobby ready to go. I'll give you a lift to the station and you can dictate your statement to a stenographer. Nine sharp."

"This is Saturday night," I said. "The prosecutor's office isn't going to wonder about the delay?"

Sweetser laughed. "With the shit that's going down in D.C. these days? Just don't worry about it, Bodine. Take a swim. See you Monday morning."

"At nine."

"Right."

"To tell a stenographer—"

"You heard me."

"—that I think the Kinneys are feeding Ed Quinn heroin in exchange for the item he left them in his will?"

"You don't have to tell what you think, Bodine, just what happened."

"If I was you," I said, "I'd be nicking the Kinneys for a good deal more than a cubicle next to Caparelli."

"You let me worry about that."

"All right, but there's something else you ought to be worrying about, just a minor implausibility that might occur to someone from the Fifth District who isn't angling for a cubicle next to Caparelli."

"Yeah? What?"

"The problem of why Harry Gibbs is dead, and Tim Kinney isn't."

"I already thought that through," Sweetser said. "The kid isn't

146

lying next to Gibbs in the morgue for the same reason you aren't."

"And why is that?"

"Hey, you think those two bloods couldn't have done you if they'd wanted to? Kinney's kid says they were heeled. One of them screwed a piece into his ear."

"What kind of piece?"

"He don't know, but he's got the bloody ear."

"What's that prove?"

"Maybe nothing. But the way I got it figured, you're still alive because you're Quinn's buddy. After all, you fixed it so he'd get his shot. The kid's alive because he's tight with Quinn, too, said Quinn treated him like a son. But Gibbs, he's dead because he wanted to cut Quinn off, and send him back to a hospital."

I wouldn't gain anything by arguing the issue with Sweetser. I just wanted to establish that as a coconspirator, I was not without qualms. Or curiosity. "Did you find any legal papers on Harry's body?" I said.

"I don't know what they came up with. If I can ever get rid of you, I'll be heading back to the station to check the evidence sheets. I hope for your sake they didn't turn up any dope in that motel room."

"Seems like you could fix it if they did. For my sake."

"No way, Ofay. If it was there, they got it tagged and bagged. I couldn't help you."

"On the other hand, I suppose you could have fixed it so they'd find a stash. For your sake."

"You mean tell an evidence tech to plant drugs at a crime scene so I could hold it over your head?" Sweetser laughed again. "You don't understand those guys, Bodine. I even hinted at something like that, Internal Affairs'd be on me like sweat. If they found dope in your room, it's because you left it there. If they didn't, you skate. I can't do nothing about it. All I can do is tell you to get outta the car and get a good night's sleep. You look beat."

I got outta the car. "Monday," I said.

"Sweet dreams."

I slammed the door and walked to the lobby. As I pushed through the entrance I heard Sweetser's tires snapping gravel. I glanced back and saw him cut into traffic. I didn't see anyone watching from the parking lot, but I went up to the desk anyway and asked the clerk the price of a single. He told me they only had doubles. I said I'd take one. I filled out the form, then glanced around the lobby. It was deserted. I told the clerk I changed my mind and wanted to make a phone call before registering. He said the phones were down from the desk and around the corner, gesturing to his right. I pointed, too, so if Sweetser or the Kinneys had anyone staking me with a pair of binoculars, it would look as if I were confirming the clerk's directions to my room. I thanked the clerk and walked to the end of the desk and turned the corner. The phones were in an alcove opposite the rest rooms, out of sight of the parking lot. I looked for a rear exit, found one off a conference room and walked back to the phones. I dialed the same cab company I'd called earlier from the District Line Motel and told them I was at the Inn Deluxe north of New York Avenue, just off the B-W Parkway. The dispatcher knew the place. I told him where I wanted the cab to meet me, and he said it would be there in ten, fifteen minutes.

I headed for the rear entrance. The cab showed in twelve minutes, pulling up just outside the door I was waiting behind. I snaked through the door and slid into the hack. The driver looked like the Afghan who'd come for me at the District Line. He seemed to know how to get there from the Inn Deluxe, too, nodding yes, yes as I told him to take the parkway south and head west on New York Avenue.

"Noo Yoork same Roote Feefty?"

"Same."

He reached for his flag, and we were off. I kept low in the backseat, watching out the rear window. No one pulled out of the lot of the Inn Deluxe as we left it, and no one pulled into the lot

148

of the District Line after we arrived. I hadn't taken my eyes off the road the entire distance, and I felt very sure we hadn't been tailed.

I leaned over the seat and paid the driver. If he was an Afghan, and if Afghans fought as hard as they drove, the Russians had made a smart move quitting Kabul. I gave the driver a decent tip and he thanked me with grave intensity, as if he knew what I was up against and didn't think much of my chances.

I got out of the cab, eyeing Othman Mapes behind the desk of the District Line. He was alone, standing with his back to me, leaning against the counter. I scanned the parking lot. Mapes's van wasn't in sight, and my car still had two flat tires. I thought about having the Afghan stand by while I wrestled Mapes into the cab, but somehow I didn't think the Afghan would hang around for that. Also, I didn't want any witnesses. I decided Mapes had parked his van behind the lobby again, which was why I couldn't see it. I slammed the door of the cab. The Afghan clanked his vehicle into reverse, and I headed for the motel lobby. Having suppressed the impulse to cream Douglas Kinney—not to mention Craig—I was one pent-up P.I. This time around, Othman Mapes definitely was going to deliver me to Ed, and without any jive on the drive. No lip on the trip.

I pushed into the lobby and advanced on the desk, but the clerk behind it wasn't Othman Mapes. He was wearing Mapes's smock, but he was older than Mapes, darker, with a pleasant smile and eyes whose whites were as yellow as his teeth. "Yes, sir?" he said warmly, his dentures clacking.

It was an effort to unclench my jaws. "Where's Mapes?" I said.

"Offman? He gone for the night. Don't know where he at, neither. Called him 'bout somethin' jus' five minute' ago, but his mama don't know where he at herself, don't 'spect him back tonight, maybe never. They havin' a hard time, them two. You a frien' o' Offman's?"

I said I was, and the clerk said he didn't know Othman very

well, had never had a chance to work with him even though Othman had been employed by the owners of the District Line three, four years now, which was nothing when you considered the clerk had twenty-two years standing the desk, midnight to eight. He rattled on, garrulous less from senility than loneliness. There aren't many things lonelier than manning a motel after midnight, unless it's checking into one, which I decided to do. Sweetser was right. I was tired, so suddenly and completely beat I could have curled up on the counter and fallen asleep with the old man chewing on my ear. "I'd like a single," I said when he paused for a breath.

"They all double."

"Double's fine."

The old clerk pushed the form pad at me, and I registered under another phony name, paying another thirty-six bucks, plus tax. As I took the key, I said offhandedly, "What's the problem with Othman and his mother?"

The old man shrugged. "Don't know. Offman, he don't tell me nuffin'. His mama, she a fine woman, though. Hate to see 'em feudin' like they is. You get to my time o' life, you don't wants to be feudin' wiff you' family, you understand what I'm saying? They's jus' some things a man—"

"I'll take your word for it."

"Say, you a frien' o' Offman's?"

I'd already answered that question, and I didn't want to let him get started on the story of his life again. "Yes," I said, turning away, "but don't take my word for it."

The old man gave me a phlegmy chuckle.

I paused, risking another soliloquy. "When's Othman due on the desk again?"

"Oh, he got the four-to-midnight tomorrow."

"Thanks."

"Ain't no trouble," said the old-timer, his cuspids clacking as if he had a mouthful of castanets.

I fled the lobby by the rear door, bypassing the room the clerk

150

had just assigned to me. I cased the parking lot as I walked, noticing nothing unusual except for the tires on the left side of my Chrysler. They were as flat as my Michigan accent.

I stopped in front of Ed's room. They'd taped a yellow crime-scene ribbon across it, and I pulled the tape away from the door. I still had the key to the room, and I stuck it into the lock, gave the key a twist, pushed, and went in without touching the knob. If there were prints on it, they were probably mine, but we'd see.

I leaned the door shut behind me and flicked on the light with a fingernail. Sweetser's evidence technicians had dusted the switch. They'd dusted everything. The room looked as if it had been vandalized with a dirty powder puff: gray smudges on dark surfaces, black smudges on light surfaces. I inspected a sampling. They'd found some first-rate latents on the bedside table, the TV, the ice bucket, and the folding luggage bench outside the bathroom. They'd dusted the bathroom, too. There were fresh prints on the vanity, the faucets, the flush lever, and the light switch. Again, they were probably all mine, but it was possible the sport and the gunny had removed their gloves to cook a hit and had got careless.

I rubbed my eyes and yawned. I wasn't eager to shoot the room. Sweetser's evidence techs appeared to have done a credible job, but their work would pass through the detective's hands, and there was a good chance his fingers would leave fewer prints on file than those his evidence techs submitted. My camera was in the trunk; a ninety-millimeter lens, too, but I couldn't remember if I had the tripod. I held out my hands. Steady as a rock. And if the flash was home with the tripod, I could use a table lamp to illuminate the latents. I was sure I had several rolls of black-and-white Plus X in the—

I heard the scuff of a shoe outside the room. As I turned toward the door, someone tapped on it.

19

The knock was tentative, almost apologetic. "Mr. Bodine?"

The voice was as diffident as the knock. I eased up to the door. It was still ajar, and I nudged it open with the toe of my shoe, not wanting to disturb the prints on the knob.

"Can I come in, Mr. Bodine?" Tim Kinney stood just off the threshold, wan as a wraith, wearing his trench coat like a shroud. I stepped back from the door. "Sure. Just don't touch anything."

Tim took a quick look over his shoulder at the parking lot, then slipped inside. "I don't think anyone followed me."

I didn't think so, either. If the Kinneys had tailed him here, they would have snatched him before he got to the door. Unless they wanted him to be here. I stepped out into the dimly lit parking lot and looked it over. Maybe twelve of twenty rooms had cars parked in front of them. On the far side of the lot I saw a half-dozen more vehicles, but none that I recognized, no red Escorts, black Ford Econolines, nondescript Tauruses, unmarked Chevrolets, or Baltic-blue Porsches. I went back into the room and leaned the door shut.

Tim, standing at the foot of the bed in which Ed Quinn had writhed and groaned, was staring at the blankets. He looked as rumpled as the bedding. His hair was matted and his thin face was creased, as if he'd been sleeping on a rough surface. Finally he turned toward me, but didn't say anything. I didn't, either. It was easy making it hard on the boy, who looked more than a little disappointed in himself. "I'm sorry," he said at last. As he spoke his gaze fell to his wing tips. Ed always wore wing tips.

"Why are you sorry?" I said.

Tim shrugged. His chin was trembling.

I said, "How did you get here?"

"Took a cab."

"From the hospital?"

He nodded. "I hid in your car. I assumed you'd come for it eventually. I was lying down, and I just happened to wake up in time to see you."

"The doctors said it was all right for you to check out?"

"Not exactly. The policeman who was with me had to leave, and the nurses kept saying they were going to admit me, but they never did. It was really crowded. People in the emergency room were drunk, or crazy on crack. There was a lot of arguing, and I didn't like the way everyone looked at me. They were all black. I wanted to get out of there, so I just left."

"How come you didn't go to your father's house?"

Tim's chin started trembling again. "Nick wanted to take me there, but Dad said if I was old enough to sneak around with Mr. Quinn, then I was old enough to spend a night in D.C. General."

I had no trouble visualizing Douglas Kinney turning his back on his son, not even a hitch in his stride as he walked out of the waiting room.

Tim forced his gaze to meet mine, his shadowed eyes full of self-reproach. "You want me to go?"

"I'd like to talk to you, but I want to shoot some latents first. Did Ed show you how to do that?"

"Once."

"I could use your help."

"Okay." Tim seemed eager to be of service.

"Don't touch anything." I left the room and gathered my photographic gear from the trunk of my car, just the lens, camera, film, and flash. The tripod was there, but with Tim's help, I wouldn't need it.

Back in the room, I loaded the Canon and mated it with the telephoto. I had Tim hold the flash at a forty-five-degree angle to the plane of each latent while I photographed the prints. We worked in silence, talking only to set up the shots. It took us fifteen minutes to shoot the entire room. It would have taken a lot longer if I'd had to dust the prints myself and snap a series of protection shots, but I'd done this often enough, I was sure of my f-stop. I didn't shoot any latents on their objects, either, nor the object in relation to the room. I doubted my photos would be used in court, or that I'd be lucky enough to snap a print belonging to the gunny or the sport. Still, tired as I was, it was worth fifteen minutes of my time, even if the Kinneys had planted Tim. He'd tell them I'd shot the room, they'd wonder why, and I'd have that much leverage. Between a rock and a hard place, leverage could make the difference.

I stuffed the camera back into its case, shut off the lights, reapplied the crime-scene tape, and stowed the gear in the trunk of the Chrysler. I pulled out my travel bag while I was at it, and carried it down to the room I'd just rented from the old desk clerk. It was a duplicate of the one Tim and I had just left. Even the art on the walls was the same, cheap watercolor prints of Washington real estate: the White House, the Capitol, the Supreme Court. EQUAL JUSTICE UNDER LAW, said the inscription above the court's columns. No sense asking what justice there was in a law that denied a dying man a vein full of heroin. Wouldn't want a junkie nurse to be tempted, or a pol to lose a vote or two among the righteous. So the terminally ill all died equal. "Sit down, Tim."

Tim sat stiffly in a chair like the one in which the sport had slouched in room 133. I sat on the end of the bed just across from Tim and let the silence collect around us like an audience. Or a jury. "Want to tell me what happened?" I said.

Tim looked as if I'd asked him to relive a nightmare, which I had. I couldn't blame him for balking. "My father said he already explained to you what happened," he said.

"He explained. A detective named Sweetser explained, too, but I want to hear it from you. You were there, they weren't."

Tim vented a sigh of dejection. "For all the good I did."

"Start at the beginning. You left the room with Mr. Gibbs. Then what?"

Tim squirmed beneath the wrinkled panels of his coat. "They were waiting for us, the two black men who'd been taking care of Mr. Quinn."

"Waiting where?"

"I'm not sure. I helped Mr. Gibbs into his car and got him settled. Then I walked around the front of the car and got behind the wheel. As I was pulling the door shut, they jumped into the backseat. The one who showed you how to give Mr. Quinn the heroin stuck a gun in my ear." Tim touched his ear as if it were infected. It looked red and a little swollen. "The other one jumped in behind Mr. Gibbs, the one who knocked him into the television. I recognized them by their voices."

"Do you remember if they called each other by name?"

"No. I mean, they might have, but I can't remember. I was scared."

"Go on."

"Well, Mr. Gibbs tried to get back out of the car, but the guy hooked his arm around his neck and yanked on him till he was halfway into the backseat."

"The young one did this, the one in the leather jacket?"

"Yes. Mr. Gibbs was gagging and kicking. I wanted to do something, but . . . I just did like he said and drove behind the motel."

"Like who said?"

"The one who gave Mr. Quinn the shot. He kept poking me in the ear with a gun saying, 'Drive,' and 'Turn here.' The other one, the one who had Mr. Gibbs by the neck, he said, 'How's it, white man? How's it?' Poor Mr. Gibbs's arms were flopping and his feet were kicking the dashboard. I didn't know what to do, so I just drove into the alley."

"What do you think you should have done?"

Tim shrugged. "Something."

I tried to visualize Tim doing "something," but I couldn't see him doing any more than what he said he'd done. I wasn't sure I'd have done anything different myself. I might even have permitted my assailants' names to pass in one ear and out the other, worrying about a bullet doing the same. "What happened in the alley?" I said.

Tim rubbed his ear, pretending he hadn't heard me.

"I said what happened in the alley?"

The boy hung his head and dropped his hands between his knees. "They pushed me into the trunk," he said listlessly, "and threw Mr. Gibbs in after me. Then they slammed it down. The air pressure hurt my ear. I must have cried out, because they banged on the trunk and told us not to make any more noise or they'd open the trunk and shut us up for good."

"Us or you?"

"What?"

"Were they talking to you, or to you and Mr. Gibbs?"

Tim thought about this. "Both of us, I guess. Except that Mr. Gibbs, when I whispered to him, he didn't answer. I nudged him, but he was . . . dead." Tim shuddered, his eyes roving left and right, his breath ragged.

"Go on."

"It was dark and . . . crowded in there. And Mr. Gibbs, I don't like to say this, but he . . ."

"There was a smell."

Tim nodded.

"Has anyone explained it to you?" I said.

"Explained it?"

"When people become very frightened," I said, "they some-times lose control of themselves. Also, in death, muscles relax, and there are unpleasant odors, particularly if the dead person has been strangled."

Tim drew a deep breath and let it out unsteadily. "I just keep telling myself I should have done something."

"Did anyone open the trunk before the police arrived?"

"What? No. No one. What do you mean?"

I stared hard at the boy, giving him a Raymond Burr special, two laser beams of skepticism.

Tim held my stare, then his gaze faltered and fell to his lap. "I don't think so. Actually, I have a hard time remembering what happened after I realized that Mr. Gibbs was, you know. I've tried, but I . . . I remember the hospital, and the detective who talked to me there. I told him what I could recall, everything I just told you. He left, and later my father and my brothers came, and I told them, too. It's just that, I mean, I was in there with Mr. Gibbs for a long while, but I must have fainted and . . . I don't know. It's like a dream that I can't quite remember well enough to explain?"

Tim ended his speech in a questioning tone, as if he were asking me if his amnesia made sense. "You've spent a lot of time with Mr. Gibbs the past two days," I said. "Did you notice him taking any medication during that period?"

"Medication?"

"Pills." I considered telling Tim they were the size of Venetian mints, but he wouldn't have any idea what I was talking about unless Sweetser had perfumed his mouth while interviewing the kid. I said, "Tiny tablets in a small brown glass bottle."

Tim shook his head. "I never saw him take any pills. But we weren't together every minute. All day today Mr. Gibbs was gone. As soon as it was light, and we were pretty sure Mr. Quinn and the black men were going to stay at this motel, Mr. Gibbs called a cab and—"

"I know, he researched the case while you watched the place. But how about when you were driving down here from Lansing? It's a long trip."

Tim looked off to one side, searching his memory. "No, he never took any medicine. Although he might have taken something when we stopped."

"When did you stop?"

"Whenever the men driving the van stopped. It only happened twice, once on the Ohio Turnpike and once on the Pennsylvania Turnpike. And again in a place called Breezewood. They'd get gas or something to eat. We worried they'd spot us, but we had to get gas, too, so we'd wait till they'd drive away, and we'd pull in and I'd jump out and fill the tank and we'd drive real fast to catch up to them. Mr. Gibbs said he always wanted to tail someone on his own, you know, working on a real case, just like you or Mr. Quinn. He really thought it was great, following that van."

"Was it a black van?"

"Yes."

"Did you make the tag?"

"What?"

"Did you write down the number on the license plate?"

Tim shook his head sheepishly. "We never thought of it. I'm pretty sure they were out-of-state plates, though."

"From which state?"

"Virginia. Or Maryland. They look a lot alike from a distance." Tim frowned. "When you met us tonight outside the motel, we never told you they drove Mr. Quinn here in a van, did we?"

"No."

"I guess we were just too excited by everything that was happening."

"Harry never got so excited, though, that he had to take a pill?"

"No, sir. But like I said, he could have taken one when we stopped. There was one time, now that I think about it, when he ran into the service plaza to get us something to eat, some potato chips and candy from a machine. He brought me some burgers this afternoon when he came back to the car, too. I thought I was going to die of hunger." Tim paused and a look of bitter dejection came over him. "Now I don't care if I ever eat again."

"When your father and brothers talked to you at the hospital, did they happen to mention what it was Ed changed in his will at the last minute?"

"No. My father asked me about it, but I couldn't tell him anything. That's what really made him angry. He . . . well, never mind."

"What?"

Tim swallowed. "He said he didn't think Mr. Quinn had taught me very much about being an investigator."

"Did he know you were working under Ed's license the past six months?"

"No." Tim hesitated, then said, "I'm sorry I lied to you and Mr. Quinn about who I was."

"Why did you misrepresent yourself?"

"I knew my father and Mr. Quinn didn't get along. When I asked Mr. Quinn for a job, I figured he would kick me out of his office if I told him my name was Kinney, so I made up a false name."

"If you knew Ed and your father didn't get along, why did you come to Ed for a job?"

Tim tried to sit erect, but invisible hands seemed to be holding him down. "I don't know."

"Sure you do."

"Well, I . . . actually I wanted to work for my father at Kintell during the summer break. Kintell's an investigation agency that my father—"

"I know. Go on."

"He said no. He said I wasn't, you know, qualified to do the work. I said I could learn, but he ended up yelling at me. That's when I got the idea of working for Mr. Quinn."

"Is that why you went to college in Michigan?"

"Oh, no. My great-grandfather attended the University of

Michigan, and everyone in our family has gone there ever since. I completed my freshman year in Ann Arbor."

I intended to check that out, of course, which was why I asked Tim what college he was in.

"Arts and Letters. I was an English major." He said this as if he were admitting he still had training wheels on his bicycle.

"And you never told anyone in your family—not even Nick or Craig—that you'd quit studying Spenser?"

"You mean the detective?"

"The poet."

"Oh. No, sir. When my father said I couldn't work for him in the summer, well, that's when I got the idea to work for his stepbrother. I didn't say anything to my father because I knew he wouldn't let me do it. I wasn't even supposed to know he had a stepbrother."

"How did you find out about Ed?"

"Craig told me about him once. He said he was somewhere in Michigan and that he was a private detective. I made an actual investigation out of it, Mr. Bodine. I found out where Mr. Quinn was, then I told my father I had a friend from school who'd helped me get a summer job in Lansing working at the Oldsmobile plant. My father said fine. I think he was glad not to have me around all summer."

"Why?"

"I don't know. I guess I remind him of my mother. I don't look like her. Nick and Craig take after her, but I'm the one who reminds him of her." Tim's voice trailed off. He didn't seem bitter, just hurt and confused.

"So you got a job with Ed to prove to your father that you could learn the private investigation business?"

Tim nodded.

"Maybe you wanted to irk your father, too?"

The boy looked away, his mouth crimped and petulant. "No. I mean, all I'm sure of is that after I got to know Mr. Quinn, I really liked working for him. I didn't want to brag to my father about it because I was sure he'd make me quit. So I just let him think I was back at school in Ann Arbor. I thought about transferring to Michigan State and working for Mr. Quinn part-time, but then he had his operation and I ended up spending every day at the hospital. I never told anyone in my family that Mr. Quinn made a change in his will, either. I know you think I did, but I didn't."

"I believe you," I said.

The boy seemed surprised. "You do?"

"Sure. Ed left everything he had to you when he changed his will the first time, didn't he?"

Tim looked properly modest. "Yes, but he really doesn't have anything valuable. I mean, nothing anybody else would care about. Just his war medals, and things like that. He had a pair of binoculars, too, and some camera things. It was all pretty old equipment, though. I mean, I was thankful he left it to me, but—"

"My point is, if you had ingratiated yourself with Ed on your father's orders and had got him to will you the works, then why would your father engineer a last-minute change in the will?"

"That's right," Tim said, gazing at me as though I made perfect if unsatisfying sense.

"Then again," I said, "your father would have had to do some last-minute scrambling if you suddenly told him you didn't want to play his game. That would have been the ultimate irk, wouldn't it?"

"I never told him I was working for Mr. Quinn. He didn't know about it until tonight. Truly."

Tim fixed his eyes on mine. If the need to be believed were gravity, Tim Kinney would have been a black hole. I said, "What else did your father say to you at the hospital?"

"He said they were going to handle things so no one would know I was related to him. Also, I'm supposed to tell anyone who asks me about Mr. Gibbs that my name is Cooney, and not Kinney." Tim made this sound as if he'd been disowned.

I said, "They?"

161

"What?"

"You said 'they' were going to handle things. Who do you mean?"

"My father and Nick and Craig. And the police."

"Detective Sweetser?"

Tim looked at his wing tips as if they worried him. "My father said I'm not supposed to talk about it."

"But here you are, talking about it."

Tim nodded, staring hard at his shoes.

I said "Why?"

"I . . . you're going to look for him, aren't you?"

"Ed?"

"Yes."

"You want to help me do that?"

"Yes."

"Are you still trying to irk your father?"

"No, I—"

"You want to live your whole life that way, Timmy, trying to get his attention?"

"I don't care about him anymore. Not after what he said at the hospital."

"What did he say?"

"I don't remember exactly."

"Then why is your resentment so exact?"

Tim folded his arms, burying his hands in his armpits. To his lap he said, "My father told me I'd . . . never amount to anything."

Douglas Kinney had spent the past couple decades browbeating his son into an ineffectual milksop. I didn't expect to undermine Kinney's effort overnight, but I couldn't help making a stab at it. "How old are you, Tim?"

"Nineteen."

"What had your father amounted to at nineteen?"

"When he was my age," Tim said, sounding both jealous and proud, "my father parachuted into Germany. He was twenty-

162

two, actually, but he was one of the youngest men in the OSS. He has this Luger he took from a Nazi officer. And Nick was in the Naval Security Group. He never told me where they stationed him because it's top secret. And Craig was with the Marines in Vietnam." Tim said this as if he'd just explained the world, and had also delivered the world's explanation of Tim Kinney, who hadn't parachuted into Germany, or served in Vietnam, or with the Naval Security Group.

Being a NavSecGru veteran myself, I could understand Tim's admiration of Nick. But Craig and his father were another matter. "Listen," I said, "nobody knows if they're going to amount to anything at the age of nineteen or twenty-two. I know of a twenty-two-year-old kid who parachuted into Germany and amounted to a drunk."

"My father's not a drunk!" Tim said heatedly. Then he paused and reconsidered. "Anyway, it's not his fault. He drinks because of my mother. She died when I—"

"I know," I said.

"You want me to go away, don't you?"

"Did you plan on staying?"

"I could help you."

"You could get in the way, too."

"I know the city."

"I've got a map."

Tim filled his lungs. "I want to be there when you find Mr. Quinn."

"Why?"

With a cracking voice, Tim said, "He's all I've got."

True enough. There'd been a time when Ed was all I had, too, so I knew what he meant to Tim. "When I find him," I said, "I'll find those black men, too, the ones who crammed Harry Gibbs into that trunk with you."

"I'm not afraid."

Tim looked terrified, but I gave him credit for the lie. I said, "Ed doesn't want to go to a hospital, you know."

"I know."

"And I'm not going to make him go to one."

"I know that, too. That's why I came. That's how I can help you, Mr. Bodine."

"In what way?"

"Well, after you find him, I could take care of him. We could go someplace, him and me. No one would know. And you could take those two men to the police without having to worry about Mr. Quinn."

Tim had a point. He had his chute hooked to the static line, too, and I was too tired to argue him out of jumping. I nodded at the second bed. "You can have that one. We'll find Ed in the morning."

"Thank you, Mr. Bodine."

I didn't say he was welcome.

20

A while after the traffic noise on New York Avenue began to build, the TV, the dresser, and the mirror took shape in the room. Soon it was light enough that I could see Tim Kinney lying at an angle across his bed, his face half buried beneath the pillows, one bony white foot sticking out from under the frayed bedspread. He'd awakened me with his mumbling several hours ago. Then he'd drifted deeper into his dreams, crying out from time to time, his words garbled, his sleep troubled. He never woke, and I couldn't sleep, but I didn't envy him his rest.

I rolled out at eight-thirty, grabbed my overnight bag and padded into the bathroom. My eyes were red, my back stiff, my bladder a Hindenburg of urgency. I took care of first things first, then lathered with motel soap, tugged a razor across my face, and showered.

The last of my clean clothes consisted of a pair of wrinkled khaki slacks, a rumpled cotton sweater, and a faded green polo shirt. I pulled them on. Preppie was the preferred disguise when working the East Coast north of New York. In the city itself I liked the Oxbridge look, black round-rimmed spectacles, pegged wool slacks with an unconstructed tweed sport coat and a mud-colored scarf. And a pair of pointy Italian shoes.

Black neighborhoods in any city were always a challenge, though. You could usually get by wearing dark blue pants and a blue chambray work shirt with your name embroidered on the pocket, rub a little bootblack under your nails. But my preppie duds would have to do for D.C. After all, I wasn't expecting to work the neighborhoods I'd cruised with Sweetser last night. I was after Othman Mapes, and from what I'd seen of Alexandria, my preppie apparel was not inappropriate.

I slipped into my Timberland loafers and treated myself to a moment in the mirror, toying with cover stories as I combed my hair, imagining I was down from Cambridge, avoiding a conference at NIH on new directions in analgesics: Dilaudid-HP, schnapps up the schnoz, that kind of thing, segue into . . . sailing. Quite a chop on the Chesapeake yesterday, but three Bloody Marys at the Annapolis Hilton's dockside bar and it was a smooth cruise all the way back to town. Say, is this Georgetown, or am I lost?

Or play it straight, Hal Heartland here, happy as a clam to have found a reasonably-priced motel in the nation's capital, a bit run-down and a little out of the way, but you can't beat the District Line at thirty-six a night, not when you've got the whole darn family with you. I've got to meet them down at the Smithsonian, by the way. That's near the mall, right?

I yawned, but not with fatigue. The mental patter was a sign, too. I'd been running on adrenaline last night. Now it was a matter of doing a difficult job on too little sleep. I had a trunk full of gear, though. I'd inventoried it last night when I put the camera away. I had Tim Kinney for a sidekick, too, though maybe that's why I was uneasy.

I stepped out into the room. Tim was up and dressed, wearing his trench coat over the same black jeans and striped button-down shirt he'd worn last night. He was sitting on the edge of his bed, staring at the blank TV screen, hands limp in his lap. Despite my disguise, he seemed to recognize me. "Good morning, Mr. Bodine."

"How are you feeling?" I said.

"Okay."

Tim didn't look okay. He looked paler than he had last night. His lips were almost blue, as if the cold light of day had given him a permanent chill.

He said, "Your wife called while you were in the shower."

"What did she want?"

"I don't know. She said she'd try to get in touch with you later."

"All right. Here." I tossed my car keys to Tim. He made an effort to catch them, but he had stone hands, and the keys bounced off his palm and dropped to the floor. "I'm going to call for a tow," I said. "Take off the front tire they slashed last night and replace it with the spare. That way the truck can hitch to the rear axle and we'll be ready to roll as soon as I can get someone here."

"All right." Tim picked up the keys and stood. His face was so drawn he looked as if he'd lost ten pounds in his sleep.

"You sure you want to help me find Ed Quinn?" I asked.

Tim nodded. Once. It looked like the best he could do.

"All right, get the car ready."

He went out, his coat sagging off his shoulders the way it had last night when he'd left the bathroom after woofing his Wendy's. As he was closing the door I caught a look at the sky. It was as overcast as Tim's face. I'd planned to walk him around back of the motel and have him show me the spot where they'd thrown him into the trunk of Harry's car, but seeing the mood he was in, I decided against it.

I glanced at my watch. Nine, Sunday morning. Sweetser wouldn't be looking for me till nine, Monday morning . . . unless Douglas Kinney had discovered his son was missing from D.C. General and had loosed the dogs. He might not look in on the boy right away, though, might even prefer to let his kid sweat it out till Monday morning, and have Sweetser transport him to the Fifth District station when they were ready for Tim to give the police stenographer his version of events. Then they'd want to tuck Tim away somewhere. Maybe, after I'd given my statement to the stenographer, they'd give him to me to return to the Water Wonderland. And why not? The Kinneys had bought a controlling interest in a cop, and the cop had subcontracted my cooperation. Which made me the Kinneys' man . . . till I found Ed Quinn.

I settled down at the telephone and hefted volume two of the D.C. yellow pages—L through Z—walking my fingers through the towing ads. The second service station I tried stocked radials big enough to fit my Chrysler. They had a truck and a driver on duty. I gave them the location of the District Line Motel and they told me I could expect help in twenty minutes.

I moved to the window and pulled aside the curtain. Tim seemed to be having a hard time distinguishing the front end of my car from the rear. I went out, jacked up the Chrysler, told him how to change a tire, returned to the room, and called Joyce.

Eddie answered and told me his mother had gone out to visit a lady named Gibbs. I could hear the television in the background. It sounded as if Bugs Bunny had his hands full. Bugs Bodine told Eddie to cut the juice to the junkbox. When Eddie came back on the line he was in a state of high miff, but he answered my questions as best he could, saying he didn't know exactly what had happened, but it was something bad, because the police came to the door early this morning and asked Mom some questions. After they left she said she'd be back as soon as she talked to a lady to see if there was anything she could do for her. It was about her husband being sick or hurt or something.

"I see. Well thanks, Eddie."

"Can I turn the cartoons back on?"

I felt a twinge of irritation. "No," I said. "I'm not done talking to you."

"What else do you want to say?"

"I want to know how you're doing."

"I'm doing okay."

"Good."

"Can I go now?" Eddie asked.

"No."

"Why not?"

"Because I want to talk a little more," I said.

"Why?"

"Because I *miss* you. I'm sitting here alone in a crummy motel six hundred miles from home and I want to talk to somebody who'll cheer me up."

"Oh." The line was silent. After a moment Eddie said, "I can't think of any jokes."

I couldn't either . . . just the one about the private dicks watching a mongrel lick its pecker. I said, "How about telling me what you've been doing?"

"I been watching *Bugs Bunny*."

"Besides that," I said.

"Nothing. I just got up."

"How about yesterday? What did you do?"

More silence

"Were you alive yesterday?" I said.

"Sure."

"Well, what did you do?"

"I don't remember."

"Life isn't being wasted on you, is it, Eddie?"

"No."

"How can you be sure if you can't remember what you did with a whole day?"

"I don't know."

"Name one thing you did so I'll know you weren't dead yesterday."

"I told you, I can't remember."

"Yesterday was Saturday, right? I'll bet you watched cartoons in the morning."

"Yeah, I guess."

"You aren't sure?"

"Yeah, I'm sure."

"Which ones?"

"Um . . . I don't remember."

"See? Watching cartoons is the same as being dead."

"No, it's not. I like cartoons."

I liked cartoons, too. I was grilling Eddie because I was in a grilling mood, warming up for Othman Mapes. Also, I was raw around the edges because of Harry. I felt as if some part of me had been hacked off. It was true what I told Sweetser last night, that I wasn't close to Harry Gibbs. I wasn't close to my foot, either, but I'd sure miss it if I woke up one morning without it. "I'm sorry I've been giving you a hard time," I said to Eddie. "I'll call you back when I'm in a better mood."

"I remember something I did yesterday," Eddie said.

"Good, but you don't have to tell me now."

"We rode bikes down the new people's driveway."

"Tell your mom I called, all right?"

"Wait, Dad, this is awesome. Me and Tory and Howard made this bike jump down the new people's driveway. You know how their driveway goes downhill toward the back of their house? There's this pile of dirt at the bottom and some old boards and if you hit them just right, you can really grab air."

"That sounds like fun," I said, imagining the new people watching a trio of ruffians tear up their backyard. "Have they moved in yet?" I said.

"Who?"

"The new people."

"No, nobody was around."

"You guys weren't wrecking things, were you?"

"No, we were just making these really sweet jumps. You know what?"

"What?"

"I could jump farther than Tory or Howard, and they both got twenty-one-speed mountain bikes. And Tory weighs ninety-two pounds. See, I figured out how if I did a rabbit hop when I came off the top of the dirt pile, I could grab max air."

"Sounds dangerous."

"We were careful. We didn't land where the nails and glass were. We're going to do it again today."

"What if the new people don't want you guys grabbing air in their backyard?"

"They don't care."

"How do you know?"

"They haven't even moved in yet."

"Yes, but they own the property, and I'm sure they don't want anyone mistreating it even if they haven't moved in."

"But—"

"When you own a house, Eddie, it becomes special, almost like a part of yourself. I don't think you should be riding down their driveway anymore."

"But—"

"You hear me?"

"Okay."

Eddie's excitement had subsided. His voice was dull with disappointment and defeat. I was right to put a stop to the bike jumping, but it felt all wrong. And I knew why. "Eddie?"

"What?"

"I'm proud of you for jumping the farthest."

"Thanks."

"I mean it."

After a moment Eddie said, "Tory's always bragging about everything."

"Feels good to excel, doesn't it?"

"What's 'excel'?"

"It's what you do when you grab max air."

"I guess it's no big thing."

"Yes and no," I said. "You can't do the big things if you haven't succeeded with the little ones first."

"Huh?"

"Listen, buddy, I'm going to call your mom over at the lady's house, but if I miss her, tell her I'll phone later. All right?"

"Okay."

"It was nice talking to you."

"Dad?"

"What?"

"Did you get me a White House yet?"

"No," I said, "but I'm working on it."

"Okay."

" 'Bye."

" 'Bye."

"Eddie?"

The line was dead. I'd said everything I wanted to say to my son, but somehow it didn't feel like enough . . . probably because I'd been spending too much time with Tim Kinney. Tim was so praise-starved, even six months under Ed Quinn's wing hadn't done much for his moxie.

I checked my address book and dialed Frieda Gibbs's number, waiting. I tried to imagine her in tears, but I couldn't. I saw her as she always was, cheerful, rosy-cheeked, chattering about her roses. During those Saturday night dinners at her home, Harry and Joyce would discuss legal approaches to evaluating evidence, while Frieda and I would trade tips on how to fight canker, gall, powdery mildew, anthracnose, rust, and black spot. We had—

"Hello?"

I was hoping Joyce would answer the phone, but it was Frieda who picked it up. She sounded anesthetized. I said, "Frieda, this is Jack Bodine."

She didn't reply.

I sensed she wanted to hang up on me. "Frieda?"

Another long pause. I waited for her to break the connection, but she said, "It happened because of this business with Ed Quinn, didn't it?"

I sighed. "Yes."

"Are you still in Washington?"

"Yes, Frieda. I . . . is Joyce with you?"

"Would you like to speak to her?"

I wanted to, but it didn't seem fair to Frieda, who would never speak to her spouse again. "No," I said. "I just wanted to make sure someone was with you." I felt sorry for Joyce, too. Frieda was my responsibility, not hers.

"Were you with Harry when it happened?" Frieda said.

"No. I'm very sorry, Frieda. I—"

"Did they tell you how it happened?"

I hesitated. "Not exactly," I said, telling myself this was not exactly a lie.

"Was it his heart?"

"I'm not sure." I wanted to ask her about Harry's condition, but she was suddenly crying. I could hear Joyce in the background, comforting her.

I heard the sound of the mouthpiece rustling over clothing, then Joyce came on the line. "Jack, it's me."

"I'm sorry you got mixed up in this."

"I don't mind."

"I know, but I'm going to call Will Cuyler and ask him to get over there."

"He's Harry's law partner?"

"Yes."

"I can call him," Joyce said.

"Thanks, but I want to talk to him about something."

"All right."

"Frieda's taking it hard, isn't she?" I said lamely.

"Very."

I pictured Frieda at her dining room table, staring out at the sere bloomless canes of her roses. "I talked to Eddie," I said. "He told me the police came to the house this morning."

"Yes," Joyce said. "When they broke the news to Frieda she told them Harry had been looking for Ed, and that you were his partner. They came to question you. I told them you were out of town."

"I'll call Cuyler. If I'm not able to get back to you . . ." I trailed off, not certain of what I would do if I couldn't get back to her.

"Just leave a message on the machine," she said.

"All right."

"And take care."

"I will." I broke the connection, dialed Lansing information, and asked for the home number of Wilfred Cuyler. I'd done some work for Cuyler in the past, but the two of us had never developed much of a liking for one another. He'd been to Saturday night dinners at Harry's place the few times I'd been there, and in each instance he left early on the excuse that he did his brief writing Sunday mornings. I found it hard to believe he always had a brief to write on Sunday morning, but I could hardly blame him for wanting to leave Harry's early. After all, you had to love roses to hate black spot, and Cuyler didn't care one way or the other. Nor was he interested in the philosophy of evidence. He was strictly shoptalk. In my own way, I was, too. Discussing black spot with Frieda Gibbs wasn't a whole lot different from talking crime with cops. But Cuyler was literal minded. When he talked shop he talked the brief he intended to write Sunday morning. Unfortunately, his briefs never sounded very interesting. He answered my call in the middle of the first ring, barking his name into my ear.

"Mr. Cuyler," I said, "this is Jack Bodine of the Quinn-Bodine Investigation Agency."

It took Cuyler a second to place me. "Yes." His tone was curt. Whatever I wanted, it better not have anything to do with black spot.

"I'm calling from Washington, D.C. Harry Gibbs died here last night."

"What?"

"I just talked to Frieda Gibbs. She needs help making arrangements."

"What happened?"

174

Cuyler sounded irritated. He did not want to stop writing his brief. This did not irritate me. Cuyler was dedicated to his work, and I liked that, even though I didn't particularly like him. I said, "Harry was mugged."

"Good God!"

"You think God is good, Mr. Cuyler?"

"I didn't mean it literally."

"Well, Frieda Gibbs believes He's good. She told me once that her roses are proof of His goodness. At the moment, however, her roses are dormant and her husband is dead."

I could almost hear Cuyler rubbing his temples. "I'll drive over there at once."

"Good, Mr. Cuyler."

"How did it happen?" Cuyler asked.

"According to a witness, Harry was strangled during a struggle."

"Strangled? Are you sure it was a mugging?"

"I'm going to find out," I said. "And you can help."

"How?"

"Harry recently prepared a will for my partner, Ed Quinn."

"Yes, he mentioned something about that."

"What exactly?" I said.

"Nothing specific, just that Quinn was ill."

"The specifics are that Ed changed his will several days ago, then disappeared from the hospital where he was dying of cancer. He ended up here in Washington. Something bothered Harry about the change Ed made in the will, so Harry followed him here to D.C. and tried to tell him the people who benefited from the change were defrauding him."

"If that's true," said Cuyler, "it would nullify the codicil."

"I'd like to know what's in that document," I said. "Harry wouldn't tell me because it was privileged information."

"And well he shouldn't," Cuyler said primly.

"I don't know if he physically brought the codicil with him," I continued. "He probably did. If not, then I assume it's at your

175

office. Or maybe there's a copy there. Would you check Harry's files?"

Cuyler said, "Is Mr. Quinn deceased?"

"I don't know. He disappeared again."

"I'm sorry, but unless I have a death certificate, and unless you are mentioned in either the will or the codicil, you have no—"

"I would keep the information strictly confidential."

"Yes, but if it became known . . . you see, we have a fiduciary responsibility to a testator—"

"Mr. Cuyler, your partner's dead and mine's dying. I need to know what's written on that piece of paper."

"I'd be breaking the law," Cuyler said stiffly.

"What do you think Harry's killer did?"

"That is not the point. If the police ask to examine the codicil, that's one thing. But I can't just—"

"All right. Will you call Frieda Gibbs and tell her you're on your way?"

"Yes," Cuyler said solemnly. "I'll be there in fifteen minutes."

"I haven't mentioned anything to Frieda about the exact nature of Harry's death. She believes it was his heart. I think the fewer the details the better, at least at this point."

"I agree."

"Did you know he had a heart condition, by the way?"

"Yes. He carried medication with him wherever he went. He always insisted his health was nothing to worry about, though."

"What did the medication look like?"

"Pills, I think. They were in a little brown bottle."

"I see. One last thing. They probably told Frieda she's to come to Washington to identify Harry and claim his body. If so, could you help her set up a flight?"

"I'll make the trip with her."

"Good. That's very good, Mr. Cuyler." I gave him the number of the District Line Motel. "When you get the flight arrangements worked out, leave a message for me here at the desk. I'm registered under my wife's name: O'Connell. I'll try to meet you at the airport, but if I can't make it, the District of Columbia Medical Examiner's Office is on Nineteenth Street at Massachusetts Avenue, Southeast."

"I see."

Cuyler did not sound happy to know the location of the morgue, and I couldn't blame him. The only advice I could offer was to pack a jar of Vicks, but Wilfred Cuyler wasn't the kind of man to whom you gave advice. I said, "If you change your mind about the codicil—"

"I can't do that," he said resolutely.

"The police handling the case will want to look at it. You could save some time if you brought a copy of it along with you."

"Well, I suppose."

"Fine. Also, please don't return to Lansing till I've had a chance to speak to you."

He said he wouldn't.

I called the lobby and told the young woman on duty that I'd be staying another night. Then I went out into the parking lot and gave Tim a hand with the tire.

The tow truck pulled into the lot just as we finished. I helped the driver hitch the car, and Tim and I hopped into the cab of the truck. The garage was out New York Avenue toward Maryland. I watched for a tail, but we were clean. The drive looked like it would be uneventful, but we passed a cemetery and I thought I saw Othman Mapes placing a pot of yellow chrysanthemums on a grave. The headstone was near the road and I was almost certain it was him.

I told the driver to turn around. I'd never tailed anyone from a tow truck before and was looking forward to the experience. But by the time the driver made his U-turn and cruised the cemetery, Mapes—if that's who it had been—was gone. So were the flowers.

We turned around again and continued to the garage. While the mechanics mounted a pair of new tires, Tim and I crossed the street to a Slurp 'n' Burp and had breakfast. The boy was mostly uncommunicative, so I browsed through a discarded *Washington Post* while I ate. Local area news was in the Metro section, but there wasn't anything on Harry. I noticed an ad, though. It was for a funeral home that billed itself as one of the largest undertakers in the world. "In case of death," said the ad, "there are now five places you can go, Silver Spring, Riverdale, Capitol Hill, Rockville, and Spring Valley." I'd always been told that in case of death there were only two places you could go.

But that's how life is these days, so many more choices, and none of them any good.

21

I finished my food. Tim abandoned his, and we walked back to the gas station in continuing silence. The boy's mood was a match for mine, and it was all right with me if he didn't say anything for the rest of the day. It might even be something to look forward to, the silence. There wasn't much else. I wasn't eager to work in the rain that would soon be falling, nor was the certainty that I'd find Ed—if not sooner, then later—doing anything for my morale. When I found him, I'd be back to square one. Minus Harry Gibbs.

They'd finished mounting the P225/75R14 all-weather radials, so I had Tim wait in the car while I paid with my plastic. I signed the charge slip, then described for the mechanic the route Othman Mapes had taken to his house last night. The mechanic told me I could get there again by threading through the District and crossing the Fourteenth Street Bridge, or by retracing last night's route south through Maryland, which, he thought, was probably easier. I thanked him and left the station.

The new tires had a blue protective coating that almost matched the color of my car. It was the sort of thing that might stick in a mark's mind—blue whitewalls—so I made a mental note to watch for a car wash. I got in and started up. It was good to have the Chrysler rolling again. I pulled into traffic and hit the gas.

Tim fidgeted as I drove, but I kept my pennies in my pocket and the boy kept his thoughts to himself. It wasn't till we crossed the Potomac and exited north into Alexandria that he finally asked me where we were going. I told him we were looking for the clerk who'd been standing the desk at the District Line Motel last night. "His place is just up the road," I said.

"But this is Old Town," Tim said, sounding surprised that a motel clerk could afford the neighborhood.

Glancing left and right down the side streets, I saw row after row of fastidiously maintained colonial-era town houses. I hadn't noticed them last night, nor had I paid much attention to the general level of affluence signified by the merchandise displayed in shops along Washington Street itself. I'd been aware of a Georgetown ambience, but "Old Town," as Tim called it, went beyond that. It possessed the subdued elegance of a fine antique. Granted, the patina was marred in places. Several of the art galleries showed abstract paintings in Williamsburg windows, and the BMWs looked garish on the quaint cobblestone streets. There were a few homes that seemed ready to fall down, too, and others of the same style that were as new as my blue-tinted radials. But not to quibble. Old Town, with its architectural integrity and its ubiquitous Beemers, was prime yuppie territory, a community of smart-money people. Even their homes, wearing historical-society plaques like Phi Beta Kappa keys, looked smart. "The clerk's place isn't quite old enough for Old Town," I said to Tim. "But even if it were, I doubt George Washington would have slept there."

"I didn't know there were any redlined areas left in the vicinity," Tim said. He sounded as if he knew what he was talking about. And he should. If I were to believe Sweetser, Tim's old man was D.C.'s answer to Donald Trump.

I wheeled left where Mapes had turned last night. We didn't cross any red lines as we entered his neighborhood, but the change in tone was marked. No ornate brass door knockers or carriage lamps with genteel gas flames on these homes. They were humble dwellings of shingle or stucco, and were set on diminutive lots bordered with rusted chain-link fencing. There were a hundred neighborhoods like this in Lansing. I felt right at home.

"I get it," Tim said. "This is one of the old black neighborhoods from after the Civil War. I guess the clerk could afford it."

A mental alarm sounded. "You think he's black?" I said.

"I know he is. I saw him visit Mr. Quinn at the motel yesterday while I was watching the room."

"What's he look like?" I said.

"He's . . . I don't know, kind of short, maybe sixty-five, medium complexion. He's got heavy bags under his eyes. His hair is combed back, kind of ripply. He had a name tag pinned to his jacket, but I couldn't read it from where I was—" Tim stopped as if he'd just remembered something important. "I guess I should have mentioned him to you last night, but it slipped my mind when you pulled into the motel parking lot. I was really glad to see you after what Mr. Gibbs said about you not—" Tim cut himself off again.

"What did Mr. Gibbs say?"

"Well . . . when it got late, he wanted to go into the room without waiting for you."

"You told me that."

"Yes, but . . . see, he didn't think you'd be coming even though your wife said you were on your way."

"Why didn't he think I'd be coming?"

"I'm not sure."

I was sure Tim was sure, but I'd turned onto Mapes's street and I was busy watching for his van while keeping an eye out for Ford Tauruses. This was easy to do because there weren't any vehicles on Mapes's street, not one. I parked opposite his house, cut my engine, and noticed something else I hadn't taken in last night: Mapes's home was the only occupied dwelling on the block. The windows on all the neighboring homes were boarded up. Their gutters sagged and their yards were littered with discarded tires, shattered liquor bottles, beer cans, broken furniture, and yellowing wads of newspaper trapped beneath spindly shrubbery.

Tim said, "This looks like a changing neighborhood."

Indeed. Across the street from Mapes's white stucco home stood a development of nearly-completed three-story brick town houses. They did not appear to be occupied yet, but construction was far enough along that each house sported the requisite brass knocker, portico lanterns, and working shutters, the façades mimicking the two-hundred-year-old specimens ten blocks distant. Being so freshly cloned, however, the town houses here lacked the patina of the originals. They had built-in garages for BMWs, though.

"Mr. Bodine?"

"What?"

"You think the desk clerk knows where Mr. Quinn is?"

"Yep."

"Is that his house?"

"Actually, I think it's his mother's house." As I said this the curtains parted and the wizened face of Mapes's mother peered out at us.

"Was that him?" Tim asked.

"No. I don't think he's home. His van's not around."

"Maybe he parked it in back."

"No alley in back."

"Do you think Mr. Quinn's inside?"

I shook my head. "This may turn out to be a long day, Timmy. Unless . . . did the men you followed from Lansing stop anywhere in the Washington area before ending up at the motel?"

"No, sir."

"You're sure there were only two black men accompanying Ed on the trip?"

"Yes, it was just them the whole time, even after they got here to Washington . . . except for when the desk clerk went to the room yesterday. And he didn't stay long."

"Did you mention the clerk to your father when he talked to you at the hospital last night?"

"No."

"Why not?"

"My father was too busy yelling at me."

I turned toward the boy. "What do you think he's going to do when he finds out you've been tagging along with me?"

Tim shrugged.

"You like having him yell at you?"

Tim swallowed so hard he made a gulping sound. "No. I just . . . see, all the time I worked for Mr. Quinn, he treated me with respect, and—"

"That's because you treated him with respect. You have to keep in mind, though, that he's not your father."

Staring down at his lap, Tim said, "He's more like a father than my father."

"Ed's going to die, Timmy. He'll be gone, and your old man won't understand why you disobeyed him for Ed's sake. You run the risk of alienating your father permanently. Then what?" I wasn't trying to get rid of Tim, but we'd reached the point of no return, and I wanted him to be sure he knew what he was doing.

Tim gave me a sidelong look and said, "You did. You took the risk. Your father wanted you to be a policeman, but you went to work for Mr. Quinn as a private investigator. Mr. Quinn told me about it."

"Listen, Timmy, any man who respects himself wants his son to grow up to be just like him. But there's a difference between what a person is and what he does, and we often confuse the two. My old man did. When I told him I didn't want to be a cop, it hurt him. It shouldn't have, because I respected what he was. I just didn't care for what he did."

"My father doesn't."

183

"Doesn't what?"

"Want me to be what he is. He doesn't think I'm good enough."

"No, Tim. It's just that he doesn't respect himself."

A glimmer of denial and indignation crossed Tim's face. "How can you . . . you don't know him."

"I know he's a drunk."

"*You* were," Tim said. "Mr. Quinn told me that, too."

"I don't know if I was a drunk, Tim. I certainly drank too much. But here's the point: I drank because I didn't respect myself."

Tim looked me full in the face. I could see he was interested in knowing about this tributary of my past, but his curiosity seemed to be undercut by the suspicion that whatever I told him, it wouldn't be the truth. Or maybe he couldn't believe I had let the conversation get this far. I didn't mind. I knew I'd have to explain these things to my own son some day, so explaining them now to Tim was something of a dry run. Tim said, "I know it's none of my business, Mr. Bodine, but you're saying stuff about my . . . I mean, it seems like you did the same thing to your father that you're telling me not to do to mine, and yet, oh, I don't know."

I said, "My drinking got serious because getting divorced was the worst thing that ever happened to me, and I didn't handle it very well."

"She left you?"

"I told her to leave." Which was true. It wasn't the whole truth, but it was as much as I ever told anyone, even Joyce.

Tim, with an air of if-you're-so-smart beneath the innocence of his query, said, "Why did you marry her in the first place?"

"Because," I said, "she was intelligent and beautiful, and every man who met her wanted her. And because they wanted her, I figured she must be worth having. And I got her. But it turned out she wasn't what I wanted at all."

This was also true, and Tim knew it. But he knew, too, it

wasn't something he could learn from, at least at this stage of his life: nineteen years old and still trying to figure out if he deserved to be his father's son. He stared at me for a moment, then turned away with a look of dissatisfaction, his eyes glazing over . . . maybe because my eyes were glazing over. I was thinking about the first time I saw Christine. I was nineteen, too, having a good time at a mixer in the MUG, the Michigan Union Grill. If I'd known a little more about women I . . . but I didn't, and Christine turned out to be an education, though not the kind the university was charging me tuition for, modest as it was in those days . . . which was why Christine was at Michigan instead of at Harvard. They'd sent her a letter of acceptance, Harvard had, but all her folks could afford was the U of M. Myself, I thought I was doing pretty well, attending classes at the "Harvard of the Midwest," but Michigan wasn't good enough for Christine, not by half. She lived every day with the feeling that she'd missed out on something acutely important. It grew worse, and toward the end, when we were married and living in Lansing, she talked as if she were drowning in a sink of provincial oblivion. If she'd been an actress, or a painter, or a writer, and wanted to go East to make her mark, I would have understood. But Christine didn't want to go East for anything so simple as the acceleration of her career. She didn't have a career, and didn't want one, smart as she was. It would have been demeaning, having to work. It took her a long time, most of our marriage, to understand that what she really wanted out of life was a baby with blue blood in its veins. If she'd known this early on, she could have saved us both a lot of grief, but Christine married me for the same reasons I married her. We were two people who'd got what everyone else wanted, and we were unhappy as hell with our success.

It turned out all right for Christine, though. Acting on her theory of the superiority of "aged gene pools"—a locution that always made me think of stagnant water—she ended up in Boston, figuring the best place to find a pool of aged genes was

Back Bay. The last I heard, she managed to marry a Beantown Brahmin. Remembering, though, what Caparelli had told Craig Kinney about his talk with Christine, I hoped for her sake there was more to being a blue blood than getting sloshed on a Saturday night. She could have done that in Lansing.

Tim caught my eye again, looking at me out of the corner of his own. "If you didn't want her," he said, still a hint of a challenge in his voice, "then what *did* you want?"

I was in a bar when I figured it out, sitting on a stool trying to pretend I was having as much fun as the assholes in a Miller Lite commercial, pickling my cortex in the company of swilling failures who were to a man divorced and done with marriage, one of the boys, watching the woman who was playing electric bass on the stage behind the bar. The band was new in town, and in those days a female bass player was an absolute first. I'd never seen a woman in a band except on the Spartan Stadium football field. She wasn't as good-looking as Christine—had a little gap between her front teeth—but the longer I watched her, the more she intrigued me. Between sets I talked to her, and was disappointed to find out she was not an intriguing woman. But when she stepped up onto the stage and began playing her bass, the magic was there again. At that moment I understood, however dimly, that what I wanted was a woman who could *do* something. I knew it wouldn't be worth the effort to tell Tim about Joyce, though. What he needed to know was what I learned after I married her, the real reason I searched hard for a woman I could love. "I wanted a family, Tim. And I finally got one, and it's the most important thing in the world to me, as important as my work. Can you understand that?"

Tim couldn't seem to get enough air into his lungs to answer. He only nodded. Dejectedly.

Watching him, I had a premonition. Somehow I knew he would never find the right woman, or have kids of his own. No dogs or cats or a lawn to mow. All the family Tim Kinney would ever have was Nick and Craig and Douglas Kinney. I could almost hear the irritated contempt in his old man's voice, and suddenly I felt as sorry for Tim as I once felt for the dumped wives whose settlement cases Ed and I used to accept, sitting on our bar stools, shaking our heads at their poor plight, drowning our sorrows and theirs in beer and club soda . . . the soda for me. I said, "I've met your father, Timmy, so I know what he's like. But he's the only father you'll ever have. Things worked out okay for my father and me, so there's still a chance for you, no matter what decision you make. If I were you, though, I'd tell your old man what I'm up to. It would be an easy way to get back in his good graces."

Tim chewed his lips, and in a small voice said, "I want to help Mr. Quinn."

"All right," I said, "but let's be sure we're both clear on one thing. Ed doesn't want to return to a hospital, and we're not going to take him to one, right?"

"Yes. Right."

"Do you understand what that means?"

Tim frowned. "Yes. I think so."

"What it means is, we're helping him die. Are you sure you want that on your conscience?"

Tim looked at me again out of the corner of his eye. "What about you?"

"It will be hard for me. In many ways, Mr. Quinn has been like a father to me, too."

Tim's brows drew together. "Mr. Bodine?"

A peach-colored Sedan de Ville had pulled up to the curb at the far end of the block. I said, "What?"

Again the boy hesitated, gathering his thoughts. "I talked to this old friend of his. He came to visit Mr. Quinn at the hospital a week or so ago and . . . I don't know, maybe I shouldn't mention this, either."

The driver of the de Ville, a short plump man in a dark suit, got out of his car and opened the trunk. "What was this old friend's name?" I said.

"I think it was Smith. He said to call him Smitty." Tim chanced eye contact with me. "Do you know him?"

I nodded. "What did he say?"

"Well, when he was done talking to Mr. Quinn he came out into the hallway and asked me some questions. He was trying to figure out who I was, and I told him I worked for Mr. Quinn. He sort of joked about it, how young I was and everything, and then he asked me how you were taking it, Mr. Quinn being sick and all."

"And?"

"I said I didn't really know."

"And?"

"Well, he told me that when your father was sick, you . . . sort of helped him along?"

"What do you think Smitty meant by that?" I said.

"He said he thought your father wanted to commit suicide, and that you sort of, you know, helped him do it? In order to put him out of his misery?"

Good old Smitty.

"He told me everyone knew about it," Tim hurried on. "I mentioned it to Mr. Gibbs when we were following Mr. Quinn here to Washington, and he said he heard the same thing. That was why he kind of doubted you'd show up at the motel last night, because he suspected you were the one who hired the black men to get Mr. Quinn out of the hospital in the first place."

I looked Tim Kinney in the eye. "I didn't kill my father."

"Then . . . it's not true?"

"No, it's not true."

Tim seemed relieved, but a little disappointed, too. "You must think I'm . . . I don't know." Tim shrugged, and trailed off.

Through the accumulation of raindrops gathering on my windshield, I watched the man in the dark suit pound a real estate sign into the berm between the sidewalk and the curb. The sign said OPEN and there was an arrow on it that pointed in our direction. I said to Tim, "I think you're doing the best you can."

Tim hung his head as if his best weren't good enough. "I even thought of asking Mr. Quinn if he wanted me to do something, you know, because of the pain he was in. But I didn't, because I knew I couldn't."

"That's understandable," I said.

"See, Mr. Bodine, I don't think I can even give him a shot for the pain. Last night I said I would, but—"

"I'll do it."

"Yes, but when we find him, you'll take the black men to the police, and then I'll be alone with Mr. Quinn, and I'll have to give him his shots, and . . . I just don't think I can."

The realtor had finished setting up his sign and was walking back to the open trunk of his car. He tossed the hammer inside and slammed the trunk. "You'll manage," I said.

"I'll try," Tim said, "but when I watched the man do it last night, the one who shoved the gun in my ear, I . . . when he sucked Mr. Quinn's blood into that needle I almost ran back into the bathroom."

"But you didn't."

"No, but . . . I don't know, Mr. Bodine. I just don't know."

I didn't, either, but if I'd known the day was going to be as long as this, I would have eaten six breakfasts. Trouble was, the first one felt like it wanted to get another look at its plate. I reached for the door handle. "I know this much, Tim, it's always better to act than to worry about acting. So let's see if our desk clerk's mother knows where her boy hangs out, okay?"

"Okay."

22

I climbed out of the Chrysler and hunched my shoulders against the cold drizzle. Tim turned up the collar of his trench coat and followed me up the steps to Mapes's door. I knocked and waited, watching the realtor as he gunned his Cadillac toward us and pulled into the driveway of one of the newly-minted town houses across the street. He got out, slammed the door of the de Ville, and gave my rust-pocked Chrysler a look of sour disapproval.

I knuckled Mapes's rickety screen door again. The realtor heard the clatter and caught sight of us. He froze, and gave Tim and me a look of angry curiosity. At this range I could see that he had an olive complexion and dark soulful eyes that gave off something more than anger and curiosity. If a gumshoe develops anything over the years, it's a sense for anxiety in others, and the realtor's apprehension was almost palpable. I had the feeling that if I crossed the street and approached him, he would have turned and fled, or attacked me. I was about to see which it would be, when Mrs. Mapes opened up and peered at me through her screen door.

She was wearing a dark green dress made of heavy feltlike cloth and a black pillbox hat with a pinned-up veil. She looked as if she had just come in, or was on her way out. She looked as

190

if she remembered me, too. The recognition did not appear to be a pleasant one. "Good morning, ma'am," I said. "I'd like a word with your son."

"He is not here."

"Do you know where we might find him?"

"If he's not at the motel," she said, "I wouldn't know where to tell you." As she spoke, her eyes wandered to the realtor across the street.

"Maybe Othman mentioned something after I left last night," I said, "that would give me an idea of where to look for him?"

Mapes's mother brought her gaze to bear on mine. "My son did not reenter this house after you left. I haven't spoken to him since I shut him out. And if I knew where he was, I wouldn't tell you." The screen door was ajar. Mrs. Mapes pulled it closed.

I said, "I see."

"But if you find him," she added, her voice softening, "tell him I accept the apology he tendered while I was out this morning."

"He was here?"

"He left a gift with a note."

"Did the note give any indication where he is?"

"No. I do not wish to be rude again, but Othman must have explained how I feel about you people." She said this to me, but it seemed to include the realtor across the street. I looked at him. He was tapping an ABAJAN REALTY sign into the sodded front lawn of the new town house, glancing at us as we talked.

I said to Mrs. Mapes, "You think I'm a realtor?"

Mapes's mother tilted her head slightly and fixed me with a knowing stare. "Let's be clear, sir. You managed to turn out my neighbors and my friends, but you won't do the same to me. This is where my husband died. This is where I raised his son, and where Othman raised his own sons. I will not leave. Not ever. Not alive." She glared at me, defiance dancing in her eyes.

"I'm not a realtor, ma'am."

Mrs. Mapes merely smiled at me.

191

"But from what I've seen of the neighborhood," I said, "it's my guess they've offered you a pretty price for your house."

"They have, but the attractiveness of the offer is not the point." She said this patiently, as if she were explaining a rule of grammar to a slow student.

"Why have you decided to hold onto your home?" I asked.

"I am attempting to thwart an injustice. Now, if you will excuse me." She moved to close the door.

"Will you tell me about it?"

Mrs. Mapes paused, looking at Tim as though his function in all this was vaguely troubling. To me she said, "Your technique is somewhat clinical. Perhaps you are a psychiatrist?"

"No, ma'am."

"Is that your ploy? Declare me incompetent so Othman can commit me to a nursing home?"

"I haven't any ploy," I said.

"These days, when a wealthy white man comes knocking on my door, he has a ploy."

Sometimes, when you disguise yourself as a preppie, you have to live it down. "If I'm your idea of a wealthy white man," I said, "you'll be easier to commit than you think." Mrs. Mapes didn't smile, but she didn't slam the door in my face, either. I had the feeling she found me a bit of a challenge. I said, "Do you think we could begin again?"

She sighed. "All right, Mr. Bodine. Let's see, last night you were searching for your 'friend.' This morning you are searching for Othman. I presume they are not one and the same?"

It surprised me that she recalled my name. "You have an excellent memory."

"I am not senile, if that's what you're implying."

"Of course not. I was just wondering if you remember your son mentioning someone named Ed Quinn? He's the man I'm looking for."

Mrs. Mapes stepped closer to the screen door. "Quinn? You mean Eddie Quinn?"

192

"Yes, ma'am."

Mrs. Mapes appraised me intently. "How is it you know Eddie?"

"I'm his business partner." I turned to Tim, who was standing at parade rest, listening to our conversation. "And this is my associate, Mr. Cooney."

Tim nodded, almost managing a smile.

Mrs. Mapes said craftily, "Are you a private detective, young man?"

Tim said proudly, "Yes, I am."

Mrs. Mapes said to me, "I presume you have some form of identification, Mr. Bodine?"

I produced my license and my business card and held them up to the screen for her examination.

Mrs. Mapes adjusted her wire-rimmed bifocals and compared my photograph with my face. Then she peered at my card. "Quinn and Bodine, private investigations," she muttered to herself. She gave me a skeptical once-over and said, "How long have you known Eddie Quinn?"

I told her, and asked the same question of her.

"Why, I've known Eddie since he was a boy," Mrs. Mapes said. "I did more to raise him than his own mother. He used to call me Nanny. He meant it as a high-toned joke, but it was true. I was his nanny."

Try as I might, I could not picture Ed Quinn with a nanny. I said, "Where was this? When?"

Mrs. Mapes sensed the trouble I was having with her information. She drew herself up as if presenting testimony to a jury, and said, "In the District. I started in 1927, and every morning for over forty years I arose before dawn, crossed the river, and labored in the house of Judson Kinney. When he died I continued with his son Douglas. I was a good many years with him, too. Eddie Quinn was the best of them, the one bright memory . . . perhaps because he wasn't a Kinney. They treated Othman like a little monkey, but Eddie was good to him."

"Ed knew Othman?"

"Of course. Othman would come with me to the Kinney house. He grew up with Eddie Quinn and Judson's boy, Douglas. Douglas had six years on Othman. He had his own circle of friends, too, all white boys, but there was only three years between Othman and Eddie, and the two of them were as close as brothers, always looking out for one another, even after they grew up. Why, Eddie saved Othman's life in Korea."

"I didn't know that."

"After the war, Eddie left Washington. We haven't heard from him for quite a while."

"Othman hasn't talked to Ed lately?"

"No."

There were details of Ed's connection to Othman Mapes that I wanted to explore, but the old woman looked tired and I didn't know how long she'd last. I said, "Does a company named Kinfolk Realty mean anything to you?"

Mrs. Mapes stiffened. "Why do you ask?"

"I'm trying to find out if Ed owns property here in Washington and if Kinfo—"

"Are you talking about my home?"

"I don't know. Am I?"

"I thought you weren't interested in it?"

"I am if it has something to do with Ed Quinn."

Mrs. Mapes evaluated me once again. I did not pass with flying colors, but my association with Ed earned me a gentleman's C. She said, "In 1954, Eddie Quinn sold this home to me for six thousand dollars."

Six thousand didn't sound like a lot, but in '54 it would have been a sizable sum of money for a nanny. "Did you pay cash?"

"I put down what Eddie asked," Mrs. Mapes said coolly.

"Is there a mortgage?"

Mrs. Mapes raised her chin defensively. "Eddie told me not to bother about the mortgage, but over the years I've managed to send him something in excess of six hundred dollars."

"Six hundred."

"It isn't much, I know, but he always said the payments weren't important. All these years, he never once bothered me about them. It's been his way of showing his appreciation for all I did, raising him. As I said, I was more of a mother to him than his own. I don't know if you're aware of this, but she was a woman of considerable beauty, an actress, who married into the Kinney family for status. She shunned Eddie afterward because he reminded her of her first husband, who was a notorious pugilist. Some said he had black blood in his veins, but that was because he once called himself black Irish, and the papers blew it up into a scandal, and Eddie's mother left him. Eddie was only a baby at the time."

The wind picked at the collar of my polo shirt and the drizzle stung my ear. "Would you mind if we came in, ma'am? Or perhaps I could give you a ride somewhere if you were about to go out? We could talk on the way."

"I have just returned from church. It was my intention to lie down."

"We wouldn't keep you long. Just a few questions."

"About Eddie Quinn?"

"Yes."

"Is he in trouble?"

"He's disappeared, and my associate and I are worried about him."

"You still think he's here, in my house?"

"No. I see now that this is the last place he'd be."

"But you believe Othman knows where he is?"

"I do."

"If Eddie Quinn's your partner and friend, why is it he chose to 'disappear' without telling you anything about it?"

"He was kidnapped."

Mapes's mother studied me, thinking and frowning, shivering in a sudden gust of wind. "Othman would not threaten Eddie in order to get my house. That's absurd."

"A moment ago you were ready to believe Othman was conspiring with me to have you committed."

"That was a facetious remark, and you know it."

"I know more than that." I gestured up and down the street, noticing, as I did, that the realtor had gone inside his town house. "I understand what's going on here."

Mrs. Mapes gave me a patronizing smile. "To understand is hardly sufficient, Mr. Bodine. Anyone with an ounce of sense can understand what's happening here. They even wrote it up in the *Washington Post*, spelled it out in black and white so everyone would understand. But it hasn't made a bit of difference."

"Tomorrow's *Post* will headline my death on your doorstep."

"I beg your pardon?"

" 'Freezing Rain Puts Bite on Wealthy White Man's Ploy.' "

Mapes's mother subjected me to another moment's scrutiny, then pushed open the screen door.

We went in. Mrs. Mapes said she would make some instant coffee. I said that wasn't necessary, but she said it was. She told us to sit on her claw-foot sofa, and we sat. Before she went into the kitchen, she produced a newspaper clipping and said I should read it. "I'll be right back."

When she was gone I turned to Tim. "Let me do the talking. And remember, your name is Cooney."

"But Mr. Bodine, she said her son's name is Othman?"

"Yes."

"And he's the clerk at the motel?"

"Yes."

"Well, I've heard that name before. Our maid's husband is named Othman."

"What's her last name?"

"Mapes."

"We're making progress, Tim."

"Do you think I could ask the old lady some questions?"

"I'd rather you let me do the talking."

196

"But—"

"Give me a minute, Tim, I want to read this." I turned to Mrs. Mapes's article, which had been clipped from the *Washington Post* in early August. It said:

> From the vantage point of her white stucco house in Alexandria's Parker-Gray Community, Serena Mapes has seen many neighborhood homes and institutions demolished in the last 54 years in the name of urban progress.
>
> The structures of an earlier era have been replaced by streets, office complexes and, most recently, the King Street and Braddock Road Metro stations. "Everything has come into the black community and moved us out," says Mapes, 82. Today, according to Mapes and many others in the predominantly black neighborhood of about 1,500 on the edge of fashionable Old Town, long-time residents are threatened more than ever, but not just by the encroachment of brick and cement. Expensive renovations are being made and stately town houses are rising on lots where the homes of the working class once stood. Many Parker-Gray residents fear they will be forced from their homes by speculators and young professionals recently lured to the area by its location and the new Metro stations.

The remainder of the article dealt mostly with the strained relationship between city officials and Parker-Gray residents. One Garry Abajan, a local real estate agent, was quoted as saying that when the King Street and Braddock Metros were opened they assured the influx of professionals and upper-income people who could afford Old Town's higher-priced housing. According to Abajan, spillover into Parker-Gray was "inevitable."

I handed the article to Tim and told him to read it. As he did, I listened to teaspoons clinking on cups in the kitchen and water growling to a boil.

Tim was still reading the clipping when Mrs. Mapes teetered

into the living room carrying a black lacquered serving tray. There were two cups of coffee on the tray, a cut glass creamer, and a matching bowl of sugar. She set the tray on the coffee table in front of us and eased herself into a straight-backed chair near the screen that separated the dining area from the living room. She folded her hands in her lap and crossed her legs at the ankles. The bones of her ankles were the size of knobs on a four-poster bed. She said, "Now then, exactly what is it you want to talk to me about, Mr. Bodine?"

I reached for my coffee. Mrs. Mapes had poured it into a simple white cup with brown trim that had probably cost seventy-nine cents with a ten-dollar purchase at her local Safeway. It was the same pattern they'd offered at the Meijer store back home several years ago. I had a complete set, four place settings plus serving bowls, cups and saucers. Mine were trimmed in blue. I sipped the coffee and said, "Have you ever heard of Kinfolk Realty?"

"Yes, I have. Eddie Quinn's stepbrother, Douglas Kinney, owns it. I mentioned him a moment ago."

Tim interrupted me. "Were you his nanny, too?" he said.

Mrs. Mapes seemed faintly provoked by Tim's curiosity. "Not exactly," she said. "Douglas never thought of me in that way. He was seven going on eight when I started with the Kinneys in 'twenty-seven, and he treated me strictly as a cook and a maid."

"What else can you tell me about him?" Tim asked.

"I can tell you that he never knew his mother. I didn't either, but I heard she was weakened by the influenza of 'eighteen, and died at Douglas's birth two years later. His father remarried in 'twenty-five. Eddie was only two or three at the time, but Douglas's father never formally adopted him, which is why his last name is different. Douglas was always the favorite. Even Eddie's mother indulged Douglas. He had a spoiled, bullying nature, and lorded it over Eddie." Mrs. Mapes rattled off these facts as if it gave her pleasure to exercise her memory. She also seemed to take grim satisfaction in recounting Douglas Kinney's shortcomings. "When Douglas married and had children of his own, I did my best to keep his older boy, Craig, from abusing his little brother, Nicky, the way Douglas Kinney abused Eddie. There were three years between the boys, just as there'd been between Douglas and Eddie. But it's bred in the bone, I suppose, and Craig turned out a mean one. He gave his brother the devil of a time. And they were full-blooded siblings, too, unlike Douglas and Eddie. It was the same pattern repeating itself."

Tim said, "You don't like Mr. Kinney very much, do you?"

"I do not like the Douglas Kinneys of this world, nor their women."

"Why?"

"Because we black women must spend our days working for them, raising their children, cooking their meals, and cleaning their homes. By night, we clean our own homes and raise our own children. But our homes and our sons and daughters don't belong to us any more than the white woman's children belong to us. It is the drug pusher who holds deed to the black woman's offspring, just as the white man holds deed to their homes. That is the truth of Washington, and of this nation. Is something the matter, young man?"

Tim, his face flushed, looked down at the newspaper clipping in his hand. "No."

"Even as we speak," said Mrs. Mapes, "my daughter-in-law is cooking and cleaning for Douglas Kinney, the same pattern repeating itself. I suppose I am to blame. I recommended her for the job when I turned in my resignation. She's been there a good while herself, ever since my grandson, Bernard, was killed in Vietnam. Nineteen seventy. That's twenty years Wilma has worked for Douglas. She complains, but she has been at it only half as long as I, and has had to clean up the messes of only half as many Kinneys. Just one, as a matter of fact. Timothy, I believe his name was. I never had the pleasure of meeting him." Mrs. Mapes's eyes lingered on Tim.

Tim shifted uncomfortably, then glanced at me.

Mrs. Mapes said, "What do you suppose your associate finds so disconcerting, Mr. Bodine?"

I said, "I believe he just realized he knows a man who worked with your son when Othman was on the police force. His name is Sweetser?"

"I have heard the name, but not in any favorable connection."

"Am I right," I said, "that Othman used to be a police officer?"

"A dangerous, thankless job, particularly for a black man. I was never so relieved as on the day he retired. It must be three or four years now." Mrs. Mapes sagged a little, as if the weight of the recollected years were tiring her, but then she straightened her shoulders, and said, "You were asking me about Douglas Kinney and his real estate company, were you not, Mr. Bodine?"

I sat forward. "Yes, ma'am. Do you know if they own the property on either side of you?"

"No, I don't. You would have to ask Mr. Abajan about that." She nodded toward the window.

"You're referring to the man who was watching us from across the street?"

"Yes. I'm sure he would know. He—"

Tim said abruptly, "Did you know Douglas Kinney's wife?"

Mrs. Mapes adjusted her glasses and studied Tim with the same care she'd given my ID. "I knew her very well. Why do you ask?"

"I was . . . just wondering what she was like."

"Eleanor Kinney was an intelligent, attractive woman, though a bit frail." Mrs. Mapes paused, and Tim waited expectantly.

"Is that all you remember?" he said.

"I remember that Douglas was thirty-four years old when he stole Eleanor from Eddie Quinn. Everyone thought Douglas was a confirmed bachelor, but Eleanor sparked something in him, perhaps memories of his stepmother. After her death, poor Douglas used to spend hours studying her photographs. Eleanor

200

had his stepmother's cheerful, robust nature. Douglas's stepmother was an outdoor girl, you see. She had beautiful brown hair that would fly in the wind as she rode her horses. I knew her briefly before she took the fall that killed her. Snapped her neck. Eleanor conveyed the same sense of fresh air and fun. She cared nothing for horses, though. What is your name again, young man?"

"Cooney."

"Cooney. You bear a striking resemblance to Douglas Kinney when he was your age."

"I do?"

"Remarkable. In any case, Douglas's wife, like his mother, was doomed. Eleanor had two children in her youth, and became pregnant again late in life. Despite Douglas, she carried the child to term and had a normal delivery. Then she died a day later. Massive hemorrhage, they said. She was thirty-nine. I fell ill myself, and retired not long after."

Tim nodded, not wanting the old woman's reminiscence to end, but not quite knowing what to say to keep it going. Then the significance of her remark hit him. "What did you mean, 'despite Douglas'?"

Mrs. Mapes thought about Tim's question, then about Tim, leaning toward him as she answered. "What do you think I meant?"

"I . . . don't know."

Mrs. Mapes hesitated, weighing her response, then said coolly, "Douglas wanted her to abort the baby. He pleaded with Eleanor to have it terminated."

Tim blinked.

I blinked.

Mrs. Mapes leaned a little nearer. "Douglas seemed to sense something would go wrong."

"How do you know he pleaded with her?" Tim asked plaintively.

"She told me so. I was at the hospital with her when she died. Douglas had business, and was gone for the afternoon. Mrs.

Kinney screamed. There was blood. The doctor rushed in, but Eleanor faded as fast as the sun behind a cloud. Just at the end she told me about Douglas not wanting the baby. She said I should apologize to him for her, and tell him not to blame the child. Then she died. When Douglas arrived at the hospital I told him what she said. He wept. They brought the baby to him, thinking it would help, but he wouldn't touch it. I don't believe he ever held that child, not according to Wilma."

Tim looked as if he'd been kicked between the eyes.

Mrs. Mapes turned to me and said, "To continue what I was saying about Mr. Abajan, his current strategy is to lobby the city to raise the assessment on my property to the point where I will be unable to pay the taxes."

I said, "I assume this Mr. Abajan has approached you about selling your home?"

"I should think that would have been obvious from the article I showed you."

"Has he been the only realtor to contact you?"

"You want to know if the Kinneys have been after me?"

"Yes."

"To their credit, they haven't. There have been others, though, many others. Hardly a day goes by. There was one here yesterday, a rather tiresome bald-headed little man."

"Was his name Harry Gibbs?"

"Names were not exchanged. Nor were pleasantries."

"Would you mind telling me what this man said to you?"

"He wanted to talk to me about my house. I told him I did not wish to discuss it."

"Nothing more was said?"

Mrs. Mapes hesitated a moment, looking off to one side. "He said he hated to pry, but that he wanted to ask a few questions. I said if he hated to do something, then he shouldn't do it. But of course he went right ahead and asked me who held the mortgage on my house. I told him it wasn't any of his business. He said he knew who it was. I said if he knew, then why ask? He was wearing a very nice coat, dark blue cashmere. I closed the door in his face."

"Was Othman here when you talked to the man?"

"No. Othman has been putting in a considerable amount of time at the motel these past few days. Is there anything else, Mr. Bodine? I would like to lie down."

"You've been very helpful, Mrs. Mapes."

"That's because I have been very frank." She glanced at Tim, who appeared to be chasing his thoughts among the arabesques of Mrs. Mapes's faded oriental rug. "Perhaps I have been brutally frank," she added, "but I am too old to bother with lies, and too tired to mince words. And I want you to return the favor."

"If I can."

"Do you have any evidence that suggests Othman is working against me?"

I hesitated.

"Tell me," insisted Mrs. Mapes.

"I can't say for certain. My investigation isn't complete."

"Then what is your suspicion?" Mrs. Mapes said tartly.

I didn't want to lie to her, but I couldn't bring myself to tell her my suspicion, either. Resisting the urge to squirm in my seat, I said, "At considerable risk to himself, Othman has been helping Ed Quinn through a difficult time. I suppose you could call it a measure of Othman's loyalty to Ed that he's made it so difficult for me to find my partner."

Mrs. Mapes loosed a troubled sigh. "I see. But what is this 'difficult time' all about?"

"It's a complicated matter. Perhaps, after you've napped, I could return?"

"All right," she said wearily. "But you must promise."

"I promise." I stood. "I promise to do what I can for you, too. Thank you for the coffee, Mrs. Mapes."

"And thank you for being honest with me about Othman," she said. "He's been acting odd lately, and I'm worried it has something to do with the house. The gift he left this morning is small comfort, I suppose, but when one gets old, one lives on a smaller scale, and it makes Othman's apology for last night all the more appreciated. Let me show you it." She rose stiffly, went to the other side of the screen, and returned with a cluster of potted chrysanthemums. The mums were bright yellow. "I found these on my doorstep when I returned from church. Othman's note says, 'I'm sorry, Mama.' Aren't they pretty?"

"Yes," I said. "Very."

23

"I'm going to take a shot at that realtor across the street," I said to Tim. We were outside Mrs. Mapes's house, drifting down the walk toward the curb. Tim didn't seem to be listening. "I've got a hunch about him," I said. "You want to come along, or wait in the car?"

"I'd like to go for a walk, Mr. Bodine."

It wasn't the best time for a walk, what with the drizzle building toward a steady downpour. But I couldn't blame the boy. After what Mrs. Mapes had said about his father, he had a lot to think through. And he was wearing a raincoat.

"Twenty minutes," I said. "Be back here at the car."

"All right."

"If you don't show, I'll assume you ended up at one of those Metro stations mentioned in that article we read."

Tim nodded and walked off, his shoulders stooped, the wind teasing the tails of his trench coat.

I crossed the street, skirted my car, and headed for the town house Mr. Abajan had planted the sign in front of, realizing for the first time since I'd arrived in D.C. that I almost felt good. Not good, exactly, but eager to tell Ed what I suspected about the Kinneys. There'd be something Ed would see, some angle from which to analyze the situation, that hadn't occurred to me yet. I wanted his advice, in other words. Maybe even his approval.

I was halfway up the walk to the town house when I noticed Mr. Abajan watching me from one of the narrow side windows that flanked the front door. I mounted the stoop and waved at him benignly. Abajan hesitated, glaring at me through the pane. A gust of wind snapped the rain against my neck, but I did not permit myself to flinch or frown.

When he opened the door, he said, "What?"

I smiled at him, but he didn't smile back. Standing in the door with his fists at his sides, his hot eyes glaring at me, he was roiling with suspicion and worry. I said, "I'm a private investigator, Mr. Abajan," giving it to him straight, not wanting him to mistake me for a psychiatrist. I showed him my license and my card. He glanced impatiently at both of them, then took a closer look at the card, his hostility modulating into wary curiosity. He said, "Quinn and Bodine? You work with Quinn?"

"Ed Quinn. The name's familiar?"

"Yes. I spoke to someone yesterday who claimed to be his lawyer."

"A small bald man who wore a dark blue overcoat?"

Abajan nodded. "He said his name was Gibbs. May I see your identification again?"

I took it out of my wallet and handed it to him. He studied the license at length, then the card, the rain filling my ear as I waited. "You're Quinn's partner?" he said at last.

"Yes."

"I see. I'm sorry I snapped at you." Abajan's manner had improved considerably. It was even a shade more ingratiating than mine. He returned the license and asked to keep the card. I let him have it, and he tucked it into his plump wallet and invited me inside.

The town house, empty of furniture, smelled of fresh paint. The wall with the fireplace was finished in raw brick, but the rest of the interior was off-white, with an inexpensive grade of taupe-colored carpeting underfoot. Abajan nodded at a card table and several folding chairs that had been set up in the dining area, and invited me to sit. "I'll be right with you," he said. "I've got to make a call."

I sat. The table was piled with stacks of fact sheets, Fairfax County estimated closing-costs work sheets, contracts, addenda, and financial information sheets . . . oh so many dotted lines. I scanned them while Abajan phoned someone named Max from the kitchen and told him to hurry over, explaining impatiently that he needed "a body" to cover his appointments. He hung up without saying good-bye and sat down opposite me at the table. "Actually, I was expecting Mr. Gibbs," he said. "Has he been detained?"

"Permanently."

"What do you mean?"

"Mr. Gibbs is dead."

Abajan's mouth dropped open. "Oh, no!"

I counted three gold molars before he buried his face in his hands, his breath hissing out of him as if he'd sprung a leak. I said, "Are you all right?"

"I'm just so worn down by this thing," he said, his voice muffled by his hands.

"What thing?"

He raised his head and gazed at me listlessly. "This whole affair. I'm sick to death of it."

"It might help," I said soothingly, "if you told me about your conversation with Mr. Gibbs. I'm investigating his death."

A ray of hope shone through Abajan's bleak expression. "I was counting on him, you see. He seemed so certain he could deliver the mortgage. We were going to talk to the old woman, break it to her gently. He *promised* me the mortgage."

"The mortgage on the house across the street?"

"Yes. I told him I was willing to pay top dollar to his client, this partner of yours, this Quinn who holds the paper. I told Gibbs I'd go as high as seventy thousand."

"Back up a minute. How did Mr. Gibbs happen to come to you?"

"He walked into my office yesterday and said he talked to someone at the real estate desk at the *Post* who told him about my development venture here in Parker-Gray. He said his client held the mortgage to a certain property that I might be interested—" Abajan stopped short and said, "How did Gibbs die?"

"We're waiting for word from the Medical Examiner."

"Surely the police have some idea?"

"I'm sure they do."

"Are you working with them?"

"I'm working instead of them."

"I don't understand."

"I don't, either, although I'm learning fast. That's why I'm here talking to you about the conversation you had with Mr. Gibbs yesterday."

"Yes, well, as I mentioned, this Gibbs fellow stopped by my office—it must have been around one—and said he represented the man who held the mortgage on the Mapes property. I've been trying to buy it for months now. The old woman has refused every offer I've made. She must be ninety. Dotty as a duck. Honest to God, she sneaks out at night and upends my signs. Or scribbles the damnedest things on them."

"Do you own the other houses on the block?"

Abajan shifted in his seat as if his shorts were too tight. Then his hands began playing over the stacks of forms on the table. He squared the corners and riffled them with his thumbs. Finally he said, "Let's say I know the people who own them."

"Straws?"

"Silent partners. Friends, actually." He sighed and drew a hand down over his face. "I told them they could expect a one-hundred-percent return on their investment in two months. Well, it's going on six months now and these people are making some terrible phone calls, friends of mine! And the builder, if I don't come through with that parcel soon, he's going to commit himself to another project. I explained all this to Gibbs yesterday. I mean, to have him walk in off the street like that and tell me the old woman's mortgage was in default and that I could buy it! My God, I would have offered him a hundred thou—" Abajan swallowed, and narrowed his eyes. "He *is* dead, isn't he? You're not trying to fuck me over, are you?"

"Is that real estate talk?"

The door bell rang.

Abajan got up and admitted a young couple who were dressed like me—sweaters and slacks—except their sweaters were draped casually over their shoulders, with the sleeves tied loosely around their necks. Both the man and the woman wore Top-Siders. And wedding rings.

Abajan shook hands with them. After a brief round of pleasantries, he launched into a spiel about the house.

I got up, drifted over to them and cleared my throat.

Abajan glanced guardedly at me and told the kids to feel free to inspect the premises on their own, he'd get back to the two of them shortly. The youngsters bounced up the stairs, chattering excitedly.

As soon as they were out of sight, Abajan asked me to excuse him for a moment. He hurried into the kitchen and called information, asking for the number of the morgue. He got hold of someone there, talked briefly, then hung up, satisfied that Harry Gibbs was indeed dead.

"I'm sorry," he said, returning to the living room, "but one can't be too careful."

As he said this, the front door opened and a woman entered. She was middle-aged and rather handsome, with half-inch nails that had been painted the same color as the bright green scarf with which she'd tied back her glossy black hair. Abajan went over to her and they conferred in low tones.

The young home-buyers were drifting down the stairs. Abajan introduced the woman to the kids as Maxine Armitage. He assured them "Max" would give them a proper tour of the place, and delivered them into her hands. Max, guiding them through the dining room and into the kitchen, began the same speech Abajan had started a moment ago, regaling them with a list of the "features" they were about to behold: the side-by-side frost-free energy-saver refrigerator, the over-under convection "slash" microwave combo, the solid-state five-cycle super-quiet dishwasher, the heat pump, the central air-conditioning, the energy-efficient water heater with programmable shutoff, and the Acrylon carpeting throughout . . . Max spewing it at the kids with a kind of breathy secrecy, as if she were divulging the choicest gossip.

The young man told Max that he and his wife had already looked around and rather liked what they had seen, and were prepared to discuss financing options. Immediately Max aborted the tour, sat them down at the card table and began to talk turkey.

Abajan drew me to a far corner of the living room. "Believe me," he said, "I'm sorry about Mr. Gibbs. As I told you, I was counting on him to bail me out. But now . . ."

"Did he mention an outfit called Kinfolk Realty?"

Abajan tensed and stepped away from me, frowning with alarm. "No, why?"

"Are you sure?"

"Those sharks? Believe me, I would have remembered. Have they got their teeth into the old girl?"

"My partner, Mr. Quinn, made a change in his will recently. It's my guess Kinfolk Realty gets the mortgage on the Mapes house when Quinn dies. He's got cancer."

"Oh, my God!" Abajan swayed, threw out a hand, caught himself on the mantel and started gasping.

Max's prospects craned in their seats, but Max tapped her pencil and brought their attention back to the closing-costs work sheet, saying to the young man, "A street-money loan might cost you anywhere up to three points. Depending. But let's assume you qualify for our one-year adjustable-rate mortgage and you put down, say, forty thousand. We're also offering a three-year ARM at a slightly higher rate, but let's look at the one year for now, just to keep the monthly payments down at the start." Max's pencil began spilling numbers onto the work sheet. ●

Abajan, meanwhile, was staring into the fireplace as if the ashes of his career were cold on the grate. He put a hand to his brow and muttered, "Excuse me, I'll be all right, I just, it's . . . oh, my God, what am I going to do?"

"With principal and interest plus one-twelfth annual taxes and insurance," chattered Max, "you're looking at a total estimated monthly payment of twelve hundred thirteen dollars." She glanced up smiling at the young man as if this was a remarkable bit of good news.

Her mark, however, was gazing out the window and across the street at Serena Mapes's last stand. He said, "Doesn't that seem a bit high, Mrs. Armitage, considering the situation over there?"

"Oh, don't bother about those old things," Max said. "They're scheduled to be razed any day. The entire block is going to be redeveloped by the same people who did such a lovely job on this property."

A morbid, slightly manic smile had formed on Abajan's face. Suddenly the smile turned down, and for a moment I thought he was going to be sick. He said to me, "What did the Kinneys offer your partner?"

"A way to die."

"What do you mean?"

"They're pumping him full of heroin."

"The Kinneys?"

"Not them personally."

"How can you be sure they're involved?"

I nodded toward Mrs. Mapes's house. "Last night I saw the old woman's son talking to Craig Kinney."

"There at the house?"

"No, at the motel where Mapes works."

Abajan clenched his fists. "That lying little prick!"

Maxine Armitage scowled at us.

I edged Abajan into what was probably a den or a small family room. It was just off the living room and had a set of French doors that faced onto a diminutive backyard enclosed by a stockade fence. Like the front yards of the homes across the street, the rear of the town house was littered with refuse, though of a different kind. I saw a spray of roofing shingles, scraps of plywood underlayment, empty cardboard boxes, short lengths of two-by-four, and puddles of hardened cement that looked like gray cow flops. "You had some kind of arrangement with Othman Mapes?" I said.

"He assured me he was going to have her committed," Abajan said through clenched teeth. "We had it all worked out. This week at the latest. Excuse me, I'm going to get to the bottom of this." Abajan stormed out of the den and into the kitchen.

In the dining room Max was telling the kids that the value of their purchase would appreciate a good twenty percent the day they bulldozed those "old things" across the street. "It's the leverage of a lifetime," she assured them.

Abajan punched a number into a phone on the kitchen counter, waited, and said, "Mrs. Mapes? This is Garry Abajan. Is Roland there? Well, where is he? When do you expect him back? All right, forget it. I just want to get in touch with Othman. Well, have him call me. Yes, it's urgent. Tell him I want to hear from him right away. Yes, he's got my office number. They can page me wherever I am. You just tell him I've got to speak to him at once. That's right, Garry Abajan." Abajan slammed the receiver onto the cradle and wiped his brow.

I closed the kitchen door. "Were you talking to Mapes's mother?"

"No, but that's a good idea, tell the old bitch what that little prick of hers has been up to." Abajan reached for the phone.

I grabbed his wrist. "Don't do that."

"What? Why not?"

"Because I'll break your arm."

In the silence I could hear the rain pattering on the sill. Abajan cleared his throat. "All right. Please, let go of me."

I increased the pressure on his wrist. "Who did you just talk to?"

"Othman Mapes's daughter-in-law. *Ouch!*"

"Why?"

"Because it's too early for him to be at the motel, and I'm not supposed to call him at home. He doesn't want his mother to know about our deal, so I route my calls through his kid so Roland can pass it on and have his old man get back to me. Now, please, let go of me."

I let go of Abajan. I felt as if I'd just released an eel. I wanted to wipe my hand, and did, saying, "The son's name is Roland?"

"Yes."

"What's he look like?"

"I don't know. I've only talked to him on the phone."

"How old is he?"

Abajan shrugged. "In his thirties, early forties."

"Where does he live?"

"I don't know."

"What's the number you just called?"

Abajan reeled it off, and I wrote it down in my note pad. "Have you got a telephone book here?"

"No. Just the phone. I brought it from the office."

I opened the kitchen door. Abajan followed me through the living room and into the foyer. "This partner of yours," he said, "this Quinn fellow? Tell him I'll go as high as a hundred and fifty thousand. Tell him."

I paused at the door. "Money doesn't mean much to him at this point."

Abajan leaned close to me. "He can use it to get all the heroin he wants. He can use the master bedroom in this house, too. I'll leave the back door open. Tell him."

I didn't say I wouldn't.

213

24

Tim Kinney wasn't in the Chrysler waiting for me. I checked up and down Mapes's street, but he wasn't around. I watched for him as I drove over to Washington Street, but I didn't see any stoop-shouldered kids in trench coats along the way. The rain was coming down hard enough now that most everyone was off the sidewalks, so if he was still wandering around, I probably would have caught sight of him. Deciding to let him go was not difficult. As my "associate," he wasn't fooling anyone, and both of us knew he wouldn't be of much use when I found Ed Quinn. I rather hoped he'd gone to his father. When all the cards were dealt, Tim would be in his father's hand, where he belonged. Till then, it was a matter of filling out my hand, and of playing my cards with care.

I pulled into an upscale Chinese restaurant that had opened early to attract the Sunday morning dim sum crowd. They had a phone and a set of books inside the door. I found Mapes, Roland F. listed in the Virginia Metropolitan Area book at 3016 Foreman Lane, Alexandria.

The map I'd purchased from Othman Mapes last night didn't have an index of Virginia streets, so I tried a gas station across from the restaurant, and asked directions of the attendant. He didn't have any idea where Foreman Lane was, but he was happy to sell me a map.

I studied it, got back into my car and headed south on Washington, cutting over to Route 1. About two miles south of the Beltway, I turned onto Foreman Lane, which turned out to be an access road into the Queen's Gardens Apartments complex. Number 3016, a brick three-story building of maybe six apartments, was at the far end of the complex. Residents parked head-on outside their buildings. In front of 3016 I spotted a red Ford Escort with a Fairfax County Police Association decal on the rear window.

I backed into a parking space across the street and down a little ways from the Escort. It was raining hard now, and the first thing I pulled out of my trunk was a raincoat with eleven layers of Kevlar-29 packed into the zip-out lining. The raincoat was good for anything up to and including a .38. I struggled into the coat, grabbed my Samsonite briefcase and got back into the car. The briefcase, according to the ads on TV, was good for anything up to and including a gorilla.

I set the briefcase beside me on the front seat, opened it, and took out my father's service revolver: a .38 Police Special with a two-inch barrel. I'd once fired the gun at the raincoat, so I knew they both worked. I checked the revolver's load, and stuffed it into the right outside pocket of the raincoat.

Next, I took a two-by-three-inch adhesive label out of the briefcase. On it I wrote: Mr. Roland F. Mapes, 3016 Foreman Lane, Alexandria, VA. I applied the label to an envelope that bore a canceled special-delivery stamp.

Then I got back out of the car and took a quick walk through the slanting rain over to building 3016. I went in and checked the mailboxes just inside the door. R. Mapes lived in apartment 301.

I started up. The stairwell smelled of cat spritzel. On the third-floor landing I paused and listened. I heard my heart thumping. All was quiet behind the door to apartment 301, though. I pulled out the gun and tried the knob, but the door was locked. Crouching down, I slid the envelope under the door, holding onto the corner where my mother's return address was. Still on my haunches, I tapped the butt of the revolver on the door, keeping well below the peephole.

After a second or two I heard the soft sloppy sounds of slippers coming near. Whoever was wearing them paused on the other side of the door. I waited, then felt a tug on the envelope. I held on.

The security chain rattled and the dead bolt clunked. As the door started to open I pulled the envelope out from under it, stood up and shouldered into the apartment, pinning between the door and the wall what sounded like a surprised female.

I held her there while I took in the layout. The living room was straight ahead with a dining area off to the left. The kitchen was out of my line of sight. To my immediate left and down at the end of a hallway was the bathroom, its door open, the light off. There were two doors along the left-hand wall of the hallway. They would lead to the bedrooms. No one came out of them. By this time, considering all the noise she was making, I was reasonably sure it was just me in the apartment, and the woman I'd sandwiched against the wall. I took a look behind the door.

She was black, about five-two, thirtyish, wearing a café-au-lait-colored robe that was a shade lighter than her skin. I stuffed the envelope into my pocket and the gun, too, then closed the door behind me. "I won't hurt you," I said.

She swung at me, lunged down the hallway and disappeared into the room adjacent to the bathroom, slamming the door. I let her go, passed through the living room and leaned into the kitchen. An automatic coffee-maker was dribbling into a squat carafe, and the refrigerator was thrumming. I took a quick look through the sliding glass door that opened onto the balcony and saw a pair of folding lawn chairs glistening in the rain. I backtracked to the hallway and headed down it and into the first of the two bedrooms. It was being used as a den. There was a sewing basket on the floor beside the sofa. Books and newspapers were lying around and a *TV Guide* was open on top of the television.

On a bookshelf next to the TV I found a photo portrait of the man who had given the heroin injection to Ed at the District Line Motel last night, "the gunny," as I'd thought of him then. It looked like a graduation portrait, but not one taken to commemorate academic accomplishment. The gunny, aka Roland Mapes, was wearing a set of policeman's blues.

He was in another picture, too, a framed snapshot of a family gathering. He was anchoring the left end of a line of Mapeses, including "the sport," who was standing between Roland Mapes and Othman Mapes, his arms around both of them. The genetic resemblances between the three men—now that I saw them posed cheek by jowl—were as plain as the ribs sizzling on the Weber grill in front of them. Old Mrs. Mapes was in the picture, too, as was the woman who'd just fled into the adjacent room. On the far right I picked out the Kinneys' maid, Wilma, called "Willie" by Detective Henry Sweetser. They were a handsome clan, the Mapeses, and I stole their picture, sliding it into the lining of my coat. Then I went into the hallway and paused outside the door the woman had slammed. She sounded as if she were pleading with someone. I listened for a moment, and decided she had called 911.

I tried the knob, but the door was locked. I stood back and kicked it open. She was on the far side of the room, standing between an empty bed and a set of partially closed venetian blinds, a phone to her face, her eyes huge with fright. "He's coming into the bedroom!" she shouted. "That's right, my name is Tanalya Mapes, and I'm at Queen's Gardens Apartments, building 3016, number 301. Hurry." She had the receiver in her left hand. Her right hand was full of revolver, which she pointed at my head. Cops taught their wives how to shoot, and I didn't have any Kevlar between my eyes, so I stepped clear of the doorway.

"I just want to talk to you, ma'am," I said from around the corner. "I'm sorry if I frightened you."

Into the phone she shouted, "Yes, that's him talking. He's right here peeking at me, a big white man. What? Brown hair, brown eyes, green raincoat—"

"It's olive," I said, "and my name's Bodine, B-O-D-I-N-E."

"He . . . he says his name is Bodine."

I lowered my voice and said, "Tell them I'm a private investigator and that I'm here to talk to you about Roland Mapes, who's wanted for the murder of Harold Gibbs at the District Line Motel last night."

Tanalya Mapes lowered the phone. She lowered the gun, too, an Airweight with a shrouded hammer. The 911 call taker's tinny voice was squeaking out of the receiver, asking Tanalya if she was all right. Tanalya looked down at the receiver as if she couldn't remember having picked it up. Then she pressed the mouthpiece against her shoulder and said to me, "Roland didn't do it."

"I'm relieved to hear that, Tanalya. There's just one other thing, then. Where is he holding Ed Quinn?"

She licked her lips and said into the phone, "Hello? Yes, this is Mrs. Mapes. I'm all right, now. Yes. I . . . made a mistake. Yes. No, I'm okay. Just . . . never mind. Yes. Thank you." She dropped the receiver onto its cradle and the Airweight into the pocket of her robe and drew a deep, shaky breath. The look of terror was gone. A dull foreboding replaced it. "I don't know anyone named Quinn," she said.

She looked as if she didn't. She looked like someone who might not even know how to lie. Lots of cops marry women who are profoundly innocent of evil. Cops see so much of it on the streets that when they come home they want sweetness and light, and the bad stuff is never mentioned. Ever. Then again, there are cops who tell their wives everything. "Why don't you come out into the living room and sit down?" I said.

"I tell you I don't know anything."

I nodded down the hall. "Come on."

With a little quiet coaxing I got her out of the bedroom and into the living room. She chose an armchair in the corner by the sliding glass doors. Remembering the Airweight in her robe pocket, I sat as far away from her as I could get and still be in the same room, which was sensibly furnished with inexpensive but solid furniture. There was a large, well-executed pastel on the wall behind the couch, a framed combination portrait of four black musicians, one of whom, blowing on a peculiar upturned horn, looked as if his cheeks were about to burst. "Dizzy and Dexter and 'Trane," I said. "Who's the one on the right?"

"Clifford Brown."

"Died young." I stared at her. "I assume you're Roland's wife?"

"Yes." She clutched at the lapels of her robe.

I said, "I met Roland last night at the motel where his father works. He had another man with him who wore a leather jacket and running shoes. He had one of those stylish flat-top haircuts like the football players wear. Do you have any idea who that might have been?"

"Roland's brother, Jerome." Tanalya Mapes said this as if Jerome had a lot of nerve being Roland's brother.

"Where are they?"

"I don't know," she said. "Really, I don't."

Tanalya had beautiful caramel-colored eyes. When they weren't full of anguish they would probably be sensitive, warm, trusting, and gullible. "You want Roland to die young, too, Mrs. Mapes?"

"What do you mean?"

"I mean if the D.C. cops find him before I do, he's going to die young, so you'd better tell me where he is."

"I don't know what you're saying," she cried.

I didn't, either, except that it wouldn't hurt to have her more afraid of the cops than of me. I knew I could dream up a good scenario, too, but I had to wear her down a little first. I said, "Where did Roland get the drugs?"

"I don't have to tell you anything."

"I suppose a police officer could find a supply of heroin without any difficulty if he wanted to." It took something out of her that I knew Roland was a cop, but she didn't reply. "What kind of job does he have with Fairfax?" I said. "Is he a narc, or what?"

"Who are you?"

"I told you, I'm a private investigator."

She couldn't seem to decide if that was good or bad. "I honest and truly don't know where they are," she repeated, pulling a trembling hand across her eyes. "I just know Othman shouldn't have got Roland messed up in it."

"What's done is done. The thing now is to fix it so Roland won't get into worse trouble."

Tanalya looked as though she might begin to cry. "Please go."

I heard a siren. It was a mile or two off, whooping. "Sounds like the police are going to be here shortly," I said.

"They'll arrest you." The thought seemed to arrest Tanalya's tears.

"That depends," I said. "If I tell them I'm here looking for the Mapes brothers who are feeding a sick man heroin and are wanted by the D.C. police for the murder of another man, the cops will turn to you, and you will have some explaining to do. But if I tell them I've made an embarrassing mistake, that I barged in on you thinking that the Mapeses who lived here were the ones who owed a client of mine six months back rent, the pressure will be on me, and not on you. It won't be anything I can't handle, though, assuming you don't press charges."

Tanalya thought it over.

"All I want to do is find Roland and Jerome," I said, "so I can have a word with them about what happened last night, get their side of it."

"They didn't hurt that little bald man."

"Of course not."

"All they did, they just . . . when him and the boy come out

220

the motel, they just made them drive around behind it and get in the trunk. That's all. They didn't hurt no one. Roland said he could hear that little bald man in there scrabbling around, yelling and saying how he's going to fix him good. He was alive!"

"What did Roland do after he put the bald man and the boy into the trunk?"

Tanalya's eyes roved left and right in her hopelessly honest face. "Him and Jerome went back into the lobby, and their father fixed it so they could get into the room and get the sick man out. They put him in his father's van and drove it 'round to the back of the motel, next to the car. Then Roland drove Jerome back to his girlfriend's place. When they left the alley they could still hear that little man in the trunk, fussing. Roland heard him. He . . . was . . . alive."

"What happened to the sick man?"

"Roland's father drove him someplace."

"Where?"

"I don't know."

"Where did Othman take the sick man, Tanalya?"

"Please, I don't know."

"Roland told you everything but that?"

"He didn't tell me none of it. He came home and went to bed. I could see he was worried sick, but he wouldn't say what it was bothering him. Then late, maybe two o'clock, he got a call from his father. Roland whispered to him over the phone so I couldn't hear. Then he called Jerome and I heard him say they had to go away, the two of them, and he left. Wouldn't tell me anything."

"What did he tell Fairfax?"

"Nothing. He took a leave of absence before he went to Michigan."

"How come his car is still out front?"

"They took Jerome's, left me the Escort."

"What kind of car does Jerome drive?"

"I don't know."

"Sure you do."

221

"I . . . it's a 'seventy-six Grand Prix. Bronze color. Or copper."

"Tell me where they went, Tanalya."

She shook her head. "I kept asking Roland, but he said it was nothing I should know about."

The police siren was growling down over the sounds of car doors slamming. I said, "If Roland told you it wasn't something you should know about, how come you're able to tell me what happened last night at the motel?"

"I called his mother. She told me."

"Roland's mother?"

"He always telling her things he don't tell me. But I made her. I said I would tell Roland's grandma what they was up to, her and Othman."

"You're referring to their plan to get the house away from the old woman?"

It surprised Tanalya that I knew about Othman's plan, but the shock barely registered against the jealousy that had suddenly filled her at the mention of her mother-in-law. "Yes."

"Does Roland's mother know where the sick man is?"

"I don't know. I didn't ask."

"They call her Willie, don't they?"

Tanalya's mouth twisted into a smile of bitter resentment. "Her friends do, but you can believe I don't."

25

Tanalya Mapes refused to press charges. The Fairfax County cops had to release me, and it killed them. I understood how they felt. When one of their own takes a leave of absence, and a private investigator breaks in on his wife a few days later, the boys at the station don't buy "it was a mistake." If they had been D.C. cops, they might have connected me to Harry's case, but they weren't, and didn't, and after seven hours of strenuous stonewalling, I walked.

Rode, actually. A cop in a Fairfax County cruiser dropped me off at my car. Night had fallen and the drizzle had become a cold, unrelenting downpour, the kind of rain that invigorates viruses, strips the leaves from the trees, and beats the mums to death.

I drove out of the Queen's Gardens Apartments and stopped at a McDonald's. It was warm and dry and familiar, a home away from home. Even the grease smelled friendly. I ordered a bag of bloat, took a trough near the phone, and called the District Line Motel. Othman Mapes answered. I said my name was O'Connell and asked if there were any messages for me. Mapes recognized my voice, and the ensuing silence was steely. I repeated myself. Mapes's desire to hang up was almost tangible, but he gritted his teeth and informed me that a Mr. Cuyler had called with a message that he and Mrs. Gibbs wouldn't be arriving in Washington till Monday morning, something about snow closing down the Lansing airport. Mapes gave me the number of the flight they expected to arrive on tomorrow, and I wrote it down, telling him as I did that the Mrs. Gibbs in question was a new widow, that her husband had died the night before. Mapes said nothing, so I added that her dead husband was all she had in the world. Mapes asked me if there was anything else I wanted. I told him yes, and that I was going to get it, too.

I hung up, inhaled my Quarter Pounder, and called Douglas Kinney's number to see if Willie was there. When she answered I broke the connection.

Then I sat down, finished my fries and studied my map, routing myself up the George Washington Parkway to the Key Bridge and into Georgetown via M Street and Wisconsin Avenue, something that turned out to be easier than it looked, despite the rain.

Of course, there weren't any parking places in front of Douglas Kinney's house, so I nosed into his driveway and set the brake. Kinney's garage door was open and his Mercedes was inside, next to a Taurus that looked like the one Nick had used to tail me last night. I also saw an ice-blue Porsche parked beneath a streetlight just down from the garage.

I killed my headlamps and noticed in the sudden darkness a dim light deep inside the garage. I climbed out of the Chrysler and hustled through the rain and into the garage, which smelled faintly of oil, rubber, and grease: a Ford smell. Surely it wasn't the Mercedes, on whose glossy flanks fell a shaft of subdued kitchen light. It filtered through a door with a nine-pane window. The caulking on the lower panes was loose, and the lock, a dead bolt, was equipped with a thumb bolt. As a deterrent, the door and its hardware ranked with Nancy Reagan's "Just Say No" campaign against drugs, not at all what one would have expected from the CEO of the Brooks Brothers of security services.

I pressed my nose to the middle pane and cupped my eyes with my hands. I saw a mud room just inside the door, and beyond that, another door. The inner door was open and I could see a rack of copper cookware hanging above the butcher-block work stand where Wilma Mapes was sitting, alone, with her head in her hands. I tried the door, but it was locked.

"Who's there?" Wilma said.

"Nevermore."

Wilma crept warily toward the inner door and turned on the garage light. The moment she recognized me, she reached for the shade, yanked it down, and turned off the light.

So much for poetry. I felt for a door bell, but I couldn't find anything except my way out of the garage. I turned up the collar on my coat and trotted through the rain to the lamplit corner, turned, splattered through the puddles, and ran up the steps to Kinney's front door. I banged the lion's head knocker. On either side of me the feathery blue flames in the porch lanterns fluttered innocently. I hammered again.

Wilma Mapes inched open the door and peered out at me. "What you want?" she said.

"Ed Quinn."

"Don't know any Quinn," she said.

"He's with Roland."

"Don't know any Roland."

"He's not *any* Roland," I said. "He's your son, and he's married to a woman named Tanalya, and he lives at 3016 Foreman Lane, apartment 301. Also, he's an officer of the law in Fairfax County, Virginia. Here's a picture of him with you and Othman and Jerome." I fished out the photograph I'd hidden in the lining of my raincoat where the Fairfax cops wouldn't find it. They'd found my father's gun, of course. I had a license to carry his piece, but the cops were holding it pending a trace of the serial number. They should have been able to trace it in a matter of seconds using their computer, but I wasn't going to get the gun back till tomorrow. It was the "best" they could do. The best

Wilma could do was make a grab for the snapshot out of my hand, but I snatched it back and tucked it away. She tried to slam the door in my face, but I shouldered into it.

"Get off!" she grunted.

We traded lunges. "I'm coming in, Mrs. Mapes."

"Ain't."

I proved her wrong, but not without effort. Being a poor sport, she tried to sock me in the groin, but I deflected her fist and slapped her hard enough that tears welled in her eyes. "Where is he?"

Wilma shook her head, dabbing at the tears with her striped apron.

I shut the door against the rain, and heard voices shouting within the house. They were muffled, but nearby, coming from behind the French doors of Kinney's sitting room. "Is that them?" I said.

Wilma knew who I meant, and nodded.

"What's their problem?"

"Don't know."

"Do they know about Roland?"

"No. I mean, they don't know any Roland."

I said, "Tanalya told me all about it, Willie, so let's quit dancing."

Wilma's face hardened. "Say I could trust her."

"She had no choice but to tell me. You don't, either."

"It weren't Roland hurt that little bald man," Wilma said.

"Tim told me it was Jerome."

"The man alive they close' the trunk."

"I already heard that version from Tanalya."

"Jerome my baby!"

He'd probably been a cute kid, too, all the women at the market clucking at him. "Tim says he's a murderer."

"Wasn't *Jerome* done it." Wilma's emphasis implied Jerome hadn't done it because she knew better, knew precisely who'd done it.

"Then who did?" I waited, listening to the heavy rasp of her lungs, watching her bite her lip and twist her apron with her large nicked hands. She was on the verge of a decision. The Kinneys' argument was on the verge of an eruption. Wilma glanced at the sitting room doors, then faced me again, this time squarely. I saw something ancient in her eyes. I'd seen it earlier in the day, in old Serena Mapes's face as she'd fretted over Othman's duplicity, wanting to believe in his innocence, knowing better but not admitting it, not even to herself, fearing the worst from her son.

"Come 'round to the back," she said. "We can talk."

"We talk here," I said. "And now."

"But they—"

The sitting room doors burst open. Nick Kinney, resplendent in a charcoal three-piece pinstriped suit with a claret-colored foulard knotted neatly at his neck, stormed into the hall. He started up the staircase, saw me and stopped, holding his pose as rigidly as a clothing store mannequin. Craig Kinney surged out of the sitting room in pursuit of his brother, glanced in my direction and froze at the foot of the stairs, one hand on the newel post. He wore a gray herringbone sport coat, a burgundy crew-neck sweater, pleated wool slacks, and tassel loafers. Douglas Kinney showed next, nattily casual in an open-collared white shirt under a pale green cardigan, a pair of dark brown wool slacks completing the ensemble. With a little work on their expressions, the three Kinneys could have posed for a Brooks Brothers ad. As it was, Douglas Kinney's face had an alcoholic flush and Craig's eyes were glinting fire. As for Nick, he touched his tie and stepped forward as the family spokesman, cool as a squirt of Right Guard.

"What do you want, Mr. Bodine?"

"Ed Quinn."

Nick forced a laugh. "You act as if he's here."

I had a peripheral fix on Nick and his father. Craig I kept in full view. He'd taken a step toward me, but Nick Kinney edged between us, raising his hands in a placating gesture. "Please, Mr. Bodine, just go."

Craig said mockingly, "Please, Nicky, just get out of the way."

Nick stiffened. "Don't go into a routine, Craig."

"A routine?"

"He's right, Craig," I said. "Better laid back than laid out."

Nick plumped his tie, exuding composure. "Mr. Bodine, the truth is, we're having a family discussion. We'd be glad to talk to you later, but now is not a good time."

"Willie," said Craig Kinney, "open the door. I'm going to toss him."

Wilma did as she was told, and the sound of eaves water splattering on the porch suddenly filled the foyer. The Kinney clan glanced toward the door and kept looking at it as if rain were a phenomenon new to them.

I turned, too.

Detective Sweetser stood in the doorway.

26

Sweetser showed surprise and anger at finding me with the Kinneys, but beneath his surface irritation I sensed anxiety and suspicion. He did a better job of masking it than the realtor had, but the same fear was eating at him, and for the same reason. He was worried I'd cut a deal that left him out in the rain.

His gaze skittered away from mine and sought explanation from the Kinneys, but Douglas and his sons had turned toward one another, the three of them exchanging perturbed, uneasy looks as they whispered among themselves. The crease between Sweetser's eyebrows deepened. He gave Wilma a questioning glance, but she averted her eyes.

For most of a minute, with the rain dancing on his head, Sweetser stood in the open door, waiting for Douglas Kinney to ask him in. But the Captain of Kintell, when he stopped whispering to his sons and addressed the old dick, only glared at him, his gun-muzzle eyes narrowing with impatience. Or maybe he was having a hard time keeping Sweetser in focus.

Sweetser said, "Can I come in, Doug?"

Kinney flared at the use of his first name. "You're here at a bad time, Detective Sweetser."

"Yeah, but this is about our, uh, conversation of last night.

I've got some papers to show you." Sweetser tapped the lapel of his trench coat.

Douglas Kinney motioned at the small table standing beneath the pier mirror. "Leave them."

Sweetser made a diffident entrance, water dribbling off his shoulders onto the oriental runner. "I'm sorry if I interrupted something," he said, "but I promised I'd get this stuff to you as soon as—"

Kinney cut him off. "Just leave them."

Flushing with embarrassment, Sweetser opened his coat, twisting the buttons as if he were snapping the necks of small birds. He pulled out a folded sheaf of documents and laid them on the table. "I hope you get a chance to look at these soon," Sweetser said.

"I'll ring you in the morning," Kinney said. "Now, if you don't mind?" Kinney gestured with the back of his hand as if he were shooing a goose out the door. Wilma was still holding the door open.

Sweetser gave the situation one last look, his eyes darting from face to face, calculating the vectors. He turned to leave, then paused. "What is this? You got a problem here, Mr. Kinney?"

"Yes," Kinney sneered, "despite your assurances that I wouldn't."

"Hey, I dropped Bodine at a motel and told him to stay put, just like you sa—"

"I'm not interested in excuses," Kinney said. "I care only about your ability to carry out an action without botching it."

"All right. You want I should get rid of him?"

"No, I want you should leave him here so we can play charades by the fire." Kinney's long thin face was on fire, but his eyes looked like two dead coals.

Nick Kinney leaned over the banister and laid a hand on his father's shoulder. "Dad? Take it easy."

"Take it easy?" Kinney barked, his voice shrill with sarcasm. "You mean like Detective Sweetser's been taking it easy? No, that's not the way we do things at Kintell, Nick. Maybe the D.C. police let their men take it easy, but at Kintell taking it easy gets a man fired. Assuming," Kinney added portentously, "he manages to get himself hired."

"Dad, please." Nick turned and said to both Sweetser and me, "Gentlemen, my father has a lot on his mind tonight. I'm sure he'd be happy to talk to both of you in the morning."

Sweetser pulled his coat back and exposed the butt of his revolver and the jut of his paunch. "Let's go, Bodine." He cupped his hand and beckoned.

I looked over at the Kinneys. Douglas was making a stern appraisal of Sweetser's performance. Craig, leaning against the newel post, was giving me a sly grin, his eyebrows raised expectantly.

I turned toward the door. Sweetser looked relieved that I hadn't made him reach for the iron on his belt. I gave Wilma a wink of solidarity and stepped into the rain. Sweetser followed me out, and Wilma put her hip to the door and shut it behind us.

"Hold it, Bodine." Sweetser was glaring at me. It's hard to glare in a driving rain, water dribbling off your nose. "Just what the hell are you doing here?" he said.

I shrugged. "Old man Kinney called me at the motel and said he wanted me to come over and discuss a certain matter."

"Kinney asked you to come *here*? What the hell for? Come on, let's hear it or I haul your ass to the Fifth for interfering with a homicide investigation."

I took a deep breath and let it balloon my cheeks as I exhaled. "Well, Kintell's got a branch office in Detroit. They handle special security jobs for G.M. Or maybe it's Ford. Anyway, Kinney said I'd be stepping in at a middle management level."

"Stepping in . . . what the hell do you mean?"

"I mean they offered me a job."

Sweetser gaped at me a good five seconds, squinting against the cold rain, the downpour chattering on his epaulets. "You?" he said at last. "Work for Kintell?"

231

"As a reward."

"For doing what?"

"You."

Sweetser cocked his head. "What did you say?"

"You know too much, Henry."

"What the fuck are you talking about?" Sweetser bellowed.

"I'm talking about Othman Mapes's kids. One's named Roland. The other's Jerome. We know you got a make on them."

Sweetser's mouth looked like a hole in a doughnut. "I don't know who you're talking about."

"We also know you saw Craig Kinney at the motel last night. That's got us worried."

Every muscle in Sweetser's face went to work dissembling his astonishment. He shook his head and the water flew left and right off his nose. "I never saw Craig there."

"Sure you did. He was the 'spiffy' wearing the leather jacket. Had the blue Porsche idling out front of the lobby. Remember?"

"No."

"He was jawing with Othman Mapes, your old pal from the Second District. They were trying to decide on a place to stash Ed Quinn where no one would find him."

"What the fu—"

"Mapes called you at the station, had you come sit on me while Craig Kinney helped him figure out what to do with Ed. But you decided to ingratiate yourself with Douglas Kinney instead. That wasn't part of the plan, Hank."

Our eyes locked, the rain working us over.

"I don't know what you're talking about," Sweetser said at last.

"Sure you do. And the Kinneys know you do. They know you found out about the other stuff, too."

"What other stuff?"

"Their plan to cheat Mapes's mother out of her house." I winked at him. "Some big bucks in that, huh?"

Sweetser looked stunned. "They told *you*?"

"Don't break simple on me, Henry, I've been working for the

Kinneys all along. I'm the one who okayed the shot for Ed Quinn, remember? You think I'd do that if I wasn't in on it? The Kinneys bought me months ago. I've been baby-sitting Tim without him knowing it. I've been baby-sitting you, too. And in case you're interested, I told Kinney I thought you were an okay guy, so don't blame me."

"This is bullshit."

"Yeah, but you heard what Kinney said. He as much as called you a schmuck. You're out. I'm in."

"Oh yeah?" said Sweetser. "Then how come you're standing here in the rain with me?"

"They don't want me to do you inside."

Sweetser stepped back.

"By the way," I said, "they want the pills."

"What pills?"

"Harry Gibbs's nitroglycerin." I held out my left hand and slid my right hand inside my coat.

Sweetser snapped his .38 off his belt and pointed it at me. "You fuckers."

I smiled. "Hey, Hank, you think I was going for a gun? Just a joke, buddy. We want the pills, though."

If Sweetser's face hadn't been wet from rain it would have been wet from tears. "Fuckers," he cried again, backing down the steps. He backed all the way to his car, the gun trained on me the whole distance. The car was double parked, flashers blinking, the rain boiling on its roof and fenders. I watched Sweetser lay into it, slam the door and hit the gas. His rear tires, spinning on the slick pavement, gave off a human cry as the car slid around the corner and fishtailed into the night.

I was alone.

I turned and faced Douglas Kinney's big red door. I leaned against it and gently tried the latch, but it was locked. I stepped back. I knew I couldn't blow the door down no matter how hard I huffed and puffed, so I left the porch, made my way to the corner and walked down the street to where Craig Kinney's

Porsche was parked beneath a light. I knelt down, unscrewed the caps on the Porsche's valve stems, and let the air out of its street-side tires. I locked it, stole into Kinney's garage, dug my penlight out of my breast pocket, and let the Michelins on the Mercedes exhale. I gave the Taurus's Firestones a breather, too.

There was a can of Rain Dance paste wax on a shelf. I hid my car keys under the can's concave bottom, then stuck the butt of my penlight into my mouth, wrapped the tail of my raincoat around my fist, and punched out the lower left pane of glass in the door that led to the mud room. The shattering of the glass was barely audible over the downpour. As far as I knew, the house wasn't equipped with an alarm system, but if I'd just triggered one, then *c'est la vie*.

I reached through the jagged opening and felt for the thumb bolt, gave it a twist and eased into the mud room. It was dark. The lights in the kitchen were out, too. I played my penlight over the floor in front of me and saw a bucket, a pair of rubber boots, an umbrella, and three mops. A corduroy gardening smock was hanging on a hook. The shelving held miscellaneous tools, gloves, insecticides, scrub brushes, paper towels, ammonia, and cleanser.

The inner door was closed. Its hinges squeaked as I stepped through it. The kitchen was dark, and smelled vaguely of bacon and Top Job. I could hear the muffled voices of the Kinneys. They were shouting again. I angled my penlight into the shadows. The beam glared off implements of stainless steel, copper, enamel, and high-impact plastic. It illuminated the burnished black face of Wilma Mapes, too.

She was standing behind the door, flashing a fifteen-inch chef's knife by Sabatier.

27

Wilma Mapes raised the knife. "Should kill you," she said. Her breathing was heavy and fast.

I aimed the penlight at her eyes. "No, you shouldn't," I said. This wasn't much of a rebuttal. Nor was my penlight mightier than her sword.

"You the only one knows 'bout Roland and Jerome," she said.

I could hear the muffled voices of the Kinneys arguing in the depths of the house. "The Kinneys know."

Wilma shook her head.

"You're saying Tim Kinney didn't recognize Roland and Jerome last night at the motel?"

Wilma kept shaking her head. "Kinneys and Mapeses don't circle with the same peoples. You the only one knows."

"How can you be sure?"

"Don't got to tell you what I sure of."

"Be a good idea."

"Be better I cut you, say it a burglar."

"The police would find the photograph of you Mapeses."

"I take the picture off you, throw it away."

"I locked it in the trunk of my car."

"Take your keys, open the trunk."

"I hid the keys before I came in."

"Think you so smart."

"You stick me, Mrs. Mapes, and you're doing Douglas Kinney's dirty work. Seems like you'd've had enough of that over the years, cleaning his house, cooking his food. Raising his kids."

Othman's mother could have put it better, but I said it well enough that Wilma lowered the knife a notch. It was only heart high now. "Be a foo' to trust you," she said.

"You were a fool to trust Sweety. The Kinneys bought him."

"Bought?"

"They promised him a job working for them when he retires."

Wilma considered this. "So?"

"So I'd hate to have my sons' fate in Sweety's hands, a white man on the make, I don't care how close Othman and Sweety used to be."

"I tol' you, Sweety don't know it was Roland and Jerome."

"He knows, Mrs. Mapes. I told him on the porch."

"Damn you."

"He already knew."

"Never said nothing."

"That's why you ought to be worried. He's got to pin Harry Gibbs's death on someone."

"Roland and Jerome didn't hurt the man."

"If they're innocent, I'll prove it."

"You tol' Sweety, maybe you tol' somebody else."

"I could have told the Fairfax County cops. They spent the afternoon using me for wit practice, but I never mentioned Roland or Jerome being at Othman's motel last night. That's the deal I cut—pardon the expression—with your daughter-in-law, and I held to it. Call her and ask."

Wilma Mapes looked as if she'd sooner call Barbara Bush and ask to kiss her toes. "Skinny peola with her blow hair," she said resentfully. "Got no grandchildren 'cause of that skinny-hipped Miss Anne. Never worked a day in her life, neither. Ought to stick her sometime, too."

236

"You aren't going to stick anyone, Wilma."

"Makes you so sure?"

"We wouldn't be having this tedious conversation if you meant to."

"Maybe I'm tired of talking."

"You're just looking for a good reason to do what's right."

"Ain't going to hear it from you." Wilma's voice was constricted, and there were tears of frustration glittering in her eyes.

"How about this?" I said. "The codicil Ed Quinn made out before he left Lansing isn't any good. It was procured under fraudulent conditions, and the court will toss it. Also, it was written by hand, and holographic codicils aren't honored in Michigan."

Wilma's eyes narrowed as she thought about this. "The house'd go to Timmy, then," she said. "Othman say Quinn lef' it all to Timmy in the will."

"But Tim's a Kinney. A good lawyer could easily convince the court Tim set Ed up. So the same fraudulent conditions would apply, and everything would revert."

"Revert? To who?"

"Me. I'm Ed Quinn's partner. His original will stated that all his assets became mine at his death. If you carve me up, the mortgage goes into probate along with the rest of Ed's estate, and you'll never get anything out of your mother-in-law's house." I had no idea if this was true, but I was giving Wilma something better than truth, and I could tell it was hitting home. "The best thing to do is keep on my good side. I won't forget it when I take control of the old woman's place."

Wilma lowered the knife to her side. "Okay," she said at last. "But I ain't saying where Roland and Jerome is. I ain't telling no one, not even you."

I thought of Eddie, imagined my own kid in a jam as bad as this, and knew I wouldn't rat on him, either, no matter what he'd done. "You'd better tell me," I said.

"They good boys. All my boys good, but they only two of 'em left. Othman, Junior, killed in the riot, and Bernard in Vietnam, and I ain't losing Roland and Jerome. Even if they been bad, I don't care, 'cause being good don't mean nothing in this world, or I'd have four sons 'stead of two."

"Just tell me this," I said, "are they upstairs with Ed Quinn?"

"Say what?" said Wilma, still squinting into the waning beam of my penlight.

"Ed's here, and if Roland and Jerome are up there with him, I'd appreciate it if you'd have them give me a hand carrying him down the stairs. If we hurry, we can do it before the Kinneys finish their spat."

"Don't know what you talking 'bout."

"Why do you think I snuck back into this house, Wilma? I came for my partner, and I'm not leaving without him."

"He ain't here."

"Sure he is."

"Ain't."

"There was a breeze blowing down the stairs when you were holding the front door open a minute ago. They probably have a window raised in his room, and I smelled something you're not supposed to smell in a house with Persian rugs and French ceilings. He's up there."

A long sigh broke from Wilma Mapes's chest. "Hell," she muttered, turning away and tossing the knife aside. It clattered on the counter and fell to the floor. "They ain't with him, Roland and Jerome. Timmy's there, is all. The Kinneys, Nick and Craig, they arguing 'bout moving Quinn somewheres else." She sighed again and leaned her weight on the counter. She looked like a baker lost in thought, the heels of her hands deep in dough.

I almost felt for her, but I reached for a switch instead, and happened to turn on the light in the garage. There was a second switch, probably a three-way controlling the kitchen's overhead fixture, but I left it alone. I clicked off my penlight and watched

Wilma in the indirect glow from the garage, a light that would fall less harshly on the truth. "Wilma?"

She looked at me over her shoulder. "What?"

"Tim says the man was dead when the lid of that trunk came down."

"He was alive when they close' it. Roland say so."

"Tim says otherwise."

"Timmy lyin'."

"Why would he lie?"

Wilma turned toward me. "I raised that boy to be a honest soul," she said. "I was his mama ever' way but bearing him from my body. Even take his side when his father get on him. Raised him like my own, but he ain't really mine, see? He theirs, and he saying it to protect his own. If Timmy would tell the truth, you would see it ain't Jerome or Roland hurt that man."

"If it wasn't them, who was it?"

We were back where we'd begun, Wilma and I, and she had to make up her mind all over again. The muted sounds of the rain and of the Kinneys' distant feud seemed to deepen the silence between us.

I said, "Understand that in court I can't repeat anything you tell me here. That would be hearsay. You know what hearsay is?"

"I watch TV."

"Okay, then give me some hearsay, or one of these nights you're going to be watching Roland and Jerome on the eleven o'clock news."

Another long moment. I was beginning to envy the quarreling Kinneys. "Just start from the beginning," I said. "Tell me how you and Othman got involved in this mess."

Wilma folded her arms as if she were cold, clasping her elbows and holding them tightly to her torso. "It start the day after that little fat man make his last offer to Othman's mama, say he pay her twenty-nine thousand for the house." Wilma shuddered as if the thought of all that cold cash gave her a chill.

239

"A man named Abajan?"

"Yeah. Othman's mama run him off the property. Next day I come to work, and Craig, he's here for breakfast. Always eat here since he get divorced. He axed me what's wrong. I tol' him 'bout Othman's mama's house. He got real interested, axed if she owned the place outright. I said no, she ain't paid nothing on it for years, but she acting like she buy it with her sweat and blood. She full o' pride and big words, but we the ones got to pay the taxes, Othman and me. Don't care if she did get me this job." Wilma fixed me with a look of acute bewilderment. "Why she want to keep that house, anyhow? Ain't nobody want to live with white peoples all 'round."

"What did Craig say?"

"He axed why ain't the bank take it away from her, and I told him it was Othman's friend hold the paper."

"Ed Quinn?"

"Yeah. Craig say get the friend to foreclose the mortgage."

"And?"

"I tol' Othman that night what Craig say. Made him call Quinn. That when Othman found out Quinn was sick and dyin'. Othman tol' Quinn he sorry to hear it, axed if they's anything he can do. Quinn say, 'Yeah, get me out this hospital and set me up with a needle and some dope.' He jus' talking, but Othman say maybe he could work something out. He told Quinn his mama going senile, say he need money to take care of her, had a good offer on her house, but she wouldn't sell. Quinn say he'll think 'bout changing his will, leave the house to Othman. Othman say he don't know 'bout that. When Othman told me, I axed him why he didn't say yes right then. Othman say it because he be the one making his mama leave, and he just couldn't do it. I told him I do it, have Quinn leave me the house." Wilma hung her head. "Me and Othman ain't get much sleep that night, fighting 'bout his mama."

"Did it ever occur to you to just pay off the mortgage?"

Wilma looked vaguely pleased not to have dulled her blade

sticking someone as thick as me. "Where we goin' to get the money for that?"

"You and Othman are hard-working people. You've got nothing saved?"

"Not with his mama sick the last twenty years."

"The mortgage is something less than six thousand. That van Othman drives is worth twice that."

"Ain't his van," Wilma said. "Borrowed it from Sweety to get Quinn from Michigan. Sweety 'bout to lose it hisself. Can't make the payments. Othman tol' him he'd help out when he get the money from the house. That why he let Othman borrow it."

"How's Othman get to work without a car?"

"Usually Jerome drive him to the motel. Sometime Othman take a Metro and a bus. Anyhow, them house papers all got his mama's name written in, and she ain't never signing it over to us, no matter who it is paying the bills."

"What happened after Othman talked to Ed?"

"I come to work next day, told Craig about it, and he say for Quinn to leave the house to the Kinfolk 'stead of Othman or me. Say he evict Othman's mama out, she never know Othman have anything doing with it. Then, when he get her out, he could sell the house and give Othman the money for it, a lot more than the other man, too. So Othman call Quinn, and Quinn say okay, he's gonna leave the mortgage to the Kinfolk."

"Does Ed know who owns Kinfolk?"

"He don't care it's Mr. Kinney. He want the drug. He leave that mortgage to the devil, he have to."

"Did Craig know about the heroin?"

Wilma shook her head. "He just say for Othman to tell Quinn to change his will so Craig's company get the house when Quinn die. Craig say he take care of the rest, soon's it happen. So Othman have Roland and Jerome drive to Michigan and get Quinn out the hospital. They figurin' on stayin' with him there, but the lawyer find them somehow. So they drive all the way back here 'fore they feel safe, bring him to the motel. I s'posed to

241

stay with Quinn last night, but Mr. Kinney say he have some people coming for dinner. Then Othman, his boss change the shift, say he have to stand the desk. So Roland and Jerome, they end up takin' care of Quinn again."

"Why did Craig Kinney go to the motel last night?"

"Middle of dinner Othman called me here to the house, say there some trouble with Quinn at the motel, say he have Roland and Jerome lock Quinn's lawyer in a car trunk. He say he have to leave town with Quinn. I tell him don't do that. Po-lice figure he's behind it, he do. He keep saying he have to run, but I'm tellin' him we have to stick it out, find a place to keep Quinn. I tell Othman when the lawyer get out the trunk he should say he don't know nothing 'bout nothing. I'm talkin' on the phone, and Craig, he come into the kitchen, axed why I ain't bring the soup out, and who am I telling not to know nothing? I figure Craig got to be told 'bout it anyhow, so I say there some trouble at the motel. He talk to Othman on the phone, say Othman should stay put, say he be there soon's he can. That when Craig find out 'bout the heroin, when he get to the motel."

"And?"

"He mad. He get madder when Othman tell him 'bout the mens stashed in the trunk of that car."

"Did Craig ask who put them there?"

"Sure, but Othman just say it was two friend' of Quinn's did it. He say he didn't know who they was. Tol' Craig they drove the car 'round back of the motel and lef' it there. He tell him Quinn's in the van in the alley, too, say he didn't know what to do with him, couldn't take Quinn home 'cause of his mama." Wilma shook her head. "Craig tol' Othman he a foo'."

"What did Craig do?"

"Went to the alley."

"Did Othman go with him?"

"He had to stay on the desk. But he got a boy comes to the motel every night to clean the lobby baffrooms, run cash to the drop box, things like that, and when he show, Othman say to watch the desk, he be right back. Gets to the alley and there's Craig standing by the car, next to the trunk, and Othman could just tell he done something."

"Was the trunk closed?"

"Yeah, but—"

"And Othman didn't see what Craig did?"

"Could guess. We know Craig got some big plans for that house, time he get it. And the man in the trunk, that lawyer, he trying to mess up the deal. Craig knew he was in there, too, 'cause Othman told him before he went to the alley."

"What did Craig say to Othman?"

"In the alley? Say Othman should follow him in the van to his father's house, say I can take care of Quinn here till he die. Othman did like Craig say, even helped carry Quinn upstairs. Then he head back to the motel."

"Did Othman ask Sweetser to come to the motel last night?"

"Ax?" Wilma shook her head. "Sweety always droppin' by and runnin' off his mouth to Othman on the night shif'. Last night he come in and Othman ax Sweety to go to one of the rooms, take a man to the station awhile, hold him there so Othman can run a errand without the man seeing him do it."

"Why didn't Othman have Roland and Jerome stuff the man into the trunk with the others?"

"Roland didn't want to risk it. He was thinking the man had a gun."

"How much did Othman tell Sweetser?"

"Told him 'bout Quinn and the heroin."

"But not what Roland and Jerome did to the lawyer?"

"Didn't do nothing to him!"

"They crammed him into the trunk of his car with Tim Kinney."

"Keep tellin' you he was still alive when they left the alley. Could hear him in there!"

A dark thought crossed my mind. "Did Sweetser go into the alley before he went to see the man in the motel room?"

"Willie?"

The voice was Nick Kinney's. He was on the other side of the kitchen door, pushing through it. I ducked down behind the counter.

"Willie," Nick said, "We'd like to see you a minute."

"Yes, sir." Wilma shuffled away. I heard the door swing closed. I waited a few seconds, then eased over to it and listened. Nick and Wilma were talking, but not about me. Their voices grew fainter, and I heard a door click shut down the hall. Several seconds later I caught the muffled sounds of a renewed dispute.

I pushed through the kitchen door and into the hallway.

28

The hallway leading from the kitchen toward the front of the house was lit by a flame-shaped bulb in a brass sconce. As I crept past the light, my shadow darted courageously ahead of me. It could afford to be bold. I was the one making the tongues in the grooves of the old oak flooring cry out with every step.

As I neared the closed French doors of the sitting room, I paused and listened. I could hear Craig arguing with Nick. He said he thought Nick was panicking. I pressed my ear to the door.

"I am not panicking," Nick replied flatly. "Do I look like I'm panicking?"

"You look like you always do," Craig snapped, "like you got a broomstick up your corporate ass."

Nick said calmly, "Wilma—"

"Hey, Nicky," Craig interrupted, "what happens if they find Quinn before he croaks, huh? What if he tells them where he's been and why? Hey? You take him out of this house and he's a loose cannon on your corporate deck."

"Oh?" Nick said. "And what if Bodine had realized he was here? Then what?"

"Wouldn't have been a problem, Nicky. I had it all figured how to handle him."

"I don't want to hear it," Nick said. "What I want is for Willie to call her husband and have him drive over here with the van. Quinn's leaving this house, and he's going back where he came from. And I don't believe you need another drink, Dad."

I eased away from the door and crept toward the pier table. Sweetser's documents were still lying on it, ignored or forgotten by the Kinneys. I picked them up. There were two sets of papers, both photocopies. One set was a summary of the District of Columbia Deputy Medical Examiner's autopsy report on Harry Gibbs. The other set, stapled to the autopsy report, was a copy of pages nine and ten of the police report on Harry's death. On the autopsy report, certain passages of medicalese had been underlined in red ink. These emphases called attention to the absence of signs of trauma to the deceased's neck or throat. The cricoid cartilage was intact, and there was a complete absence of asphyxial hemorrhages of the eyelids, thus ruling out the possibility of strangulation as a cause of death. Nor was blood loss from the cranial laceration deemed sufficient to have resulted in the subject's demise. Rather, it was the examining pathologist's opinion that the subject had died of a myocardial infarction. This judgment was based on the freshly scarred heart and the abnormally high levels of the enzymes CPK, SGOT, and LDH in the subject's blood. Finally, as requested by the investigating officer, toxicological analyses had proved negative. No traces of pentaerythritol tetranitrate, nitroglycerin, digitoxin, or any other such drugs were found in the subject's system. Nor did the oral cavity, esophagus, or stomach contain any dissolved or particulate evidence of such drugs.

I flipped to the attached pages from the police report. They contained a vouchered listing of all the items gathered at the crime scene. Someone had underlined in red ink the fact that the list contained *all* the articles removed from the interior of a 1989 Oldsmobile Delta 88, the trunk of said vehicle, and the body of the deceased. According to the report, the glove compartment had yielded an owner's manual, a motor vehicle registration form, proof of insurance, an ice scraper, and several ballpoint pens. Miscellaneous wrappers and cartons from a fast food chain were found on the floor in the front and back of the car. A bloody washcloth was found on the front seat. The trunk contained nothing but a spare tire, a jack, a tire iron, and a set of keys belonging to the deceased. A search of the deceased himself yielded a wallet, a dozen credit cards, several business cards, $122.39 in cash, a ballpoint pen, a pocket notebook, a pocket calculator, a handkerchief, a pair of tinted glasses, and a leather glasses case. None of the articles listed were underlined in red ink, just the word ALL at the top of the list.

I put Sweetser's papers down on the table and started up the stairs. Beneath the thin oriental runner the varnished boards emitted shrieks of alarm, but Nick and Craig Kinney were too busy bickering to mark my ascent. I heard Wilma's deep voice, too. She sounded as if she were talking to someone on a telephone, her tone one of uninspired persuasiveness edging toward frustration.

As I reached the top of the stairs I became aware of the odor I had smelled earlier in the foyer downstairs. It reminded me of boiled Brussels sprouts, and it intensified as I crept down the hallway toward the first room on the right. The door was open. I paused outside it, listening, then leaned around the doorframe and looked in. No one was in the room, which was furnished with a tuxedo sofa, a pair of wing chairs, and a rolltop desk.

There was an open door next to the desk, and it led to a bedroom. I tiptoed over to the door and leaned in. A window across from the door was raised, and I could hear the rain. The damp breeze that spilled over the sill was strong enough to billow the heavy maroon curtains that hung floor to ceiling.

Tim Kinney was next to the window, dozing in an antique rocking chair. The rocker had a rolled headrest, and Tim was lying back against it, his trench coat wrapped around him for warmth. He still hadn't shaved and a wispy blond beard blurred his gaunt cheeks and the jut of his delicate jaw.

Ed was in the room, too, lying in an Empire bed under a down comforter. He was staring at a nineteenth-century ceramic chandelier. The chandelier held delicate, flame-shaped bulbs like the one in the sconce downstairs. The fixture was controlled by a dimmer. The voltage was low enough that I could make out the intricate shapes of the filaments inside the bulbs. They gave off a diminished orange glow, like the last embers of a dying fire.

Ed's eyes rolled in my direction. "Jack." His voice was a hoarse whisper.

"Hi," I said.

"How'd you find me?"

"I tagged you with a microwave homing device, routed it through Pentagon computers, and parafoiled onto the roof as soon as Vegas posted the odds on my getting past the Kinneys."

Ed seemed to smile, but I knew it was a grimace.

I glanced at the needles and at the lone half-empty packet of white powder on the bedside table. "Need a shot?"

"Need to talk."

"Sure."

Tim, waking, blinked several times. Then he clamped his hands onto the rocker's armrests and pulled himself forward, his mouth falling open. "Mr. Bodine!"

"Sorry I didn't wait for you earlier this afternoon, Tim."

"Oh. Oh, that's all right. I took the Metro to Rosslyn and walked here and . . . see, I was going to talk to my father about what the old woman said, but . . . Mr. Bodine?"

"What?"

"I didn't know Mr. Quinn was here. Honest."

"How'd it go, the talk with your father?"

"Well, he . . . we didn't actually get around to the part about . . . what the old lady said . . . but at least he didn't yell at me for leaving the hospital."

"Tim, buddy?" breathed Ed. "Mind giving me a minute alone with Jack?"

"Oh. Of course not. I'll wait out there." Tim got up and

stepped into the sitting room, rubbing his eyes. I laid a hand on his arm as he passed me. "Your brother Nick wants Ed to leave."

Tim gave me a look of concern. "Why?"

"He doesn't like the risk Craig took in bringing him here."

"But—"

"By the way," I whispered, "does Ed know what happened to Harry Gibbs?"

Tim shook his head. "Nobody wanted him to feel, you know, responsible."

"Sure."

"Are you going to tell him?" Tim asked.

"We'll see. Just give us a minute, then we'll have a talk with your family about what to do."

"All right." Tim went out.

I closed the door behind him and sat down in the rocker next to Ed, wondering if Tim would blow the whistle on me. I suppose it would be a kind of test. I looked down at Ed and said, "So?"

"Problem, Jack."

"The crudités aren't fresh, or you don't like the decor?"

"It's Tim's old man, Dougy. He's my stepbrother."

I nodded.

"You know about that?"

"My partner disappears," I said, "and I start asking questions."

"They didn't give me time to leave you a note or anything."

"Roland and Jerome?"

Ed held my gaze. "Don't let Harry make trouble for them, okay? They're way out on a limb because of me."

"He won't make any trouble."

Ed glanced toward the closed door. "He out there?"

"No."

"Where is he, still at the hospital?"

"They're keeping him under observation."

Ed said, "Jerome, the guy who shoved him into the TV? He feels bad about knocking him down. He's just a hot-tempered blood."

249

"Is he around?"

"Here? Naw. Just been me and Dougy since last night. I call him Dougy 'cause it eats at him."

"You two are enjoying your reunion, I take it?"

Ed clamped his eyes shut. "I sure made a mistake doing this bit with the dope, Jack. Your old man was a hell of a guy. He didn't screw it up like this when it got too much for him. Went over the wall, and all the king's horses and all the king's men couldn't find him again, me and you included. No muss, no fuss."

"Take it easy."

"Easy, hell. Harry's in a hospital, and Tim and me are here under Dougy's roof. Of the two of us, I feel sorriest for the kid. Says he wants to give it one last shot, work things out with his old man, but—"

"Might be best."

"Know what he told me? Says he thinks his old man's always been hard on him 'cause they're so much alike, Dougy and him." Ed gave out a derisive laugh. It sounded as if he were gargling tar. "I told him maybe they looked a little alike, but if he really had anything in common with Dougy, I'd have noticed it. Hell, Jack, the kid's worked for me for over six months now, and he's not nothing like Dougy. He's . . . he's a good kid." Ed's voice lowered. "I don't know, I guess only a son could love a jerk like Dougy."

Beneath Ed's pain and fatigue I detected a layer of jealousy. "All the time Tim worked for us," I said, "you never had any idea he was Kinney's boy?"

"No, not till he walked in here earlier today." Ed glanced at me. "He don't know nothing about it, Jack, so don't be too hard on him."

"It?"

"That business with the will."

I leaned closer, braving Ed's breath. "I'd like to talk to you about the will."

"No big secret. I left the mortgage on an old house to Dougy's kid, Craig. Actually to some realty company he runs. Favor to another guy."

"Name of Mapes?"

Ed stared at me. "Gonna wear the gum right off your shoes."

"I didn't want to get rusty while I was enjoying the nation's capital."

"Right."

"Did you know Kinney owned the company when you changed the will?"

"No, but I'd have done it anyway. See, Othman's mother—you know about her?—well, he says she should be in a nursing home, so he needed whatever he could get for the house. And I had to get outta that hospital. I—" Ed sucked in his breath, clenched his teeth and clamped his eyes shut. He stayed like that a good thirty seconds. When the pain eased he said, "I ain't gonna last much longer, Jack. Thing is, I don't want to die in Dougy's house. I don't want him looking at me when I'm dead, you know what I mean? That's why your old man took off. Didn't want anybody looking at him."

"Sure you won't try a hospital?"

"Room somewhere. Dougy'll let me go. His middle kid, Nick, he's been working on him to get rid of me ever since he found out I was here. I can hear them down there arguing. I think he's about got Dougy convinced."

"You remember what Harry said about there being a doctor here in D.C. who could—"

"No."

"Ed—"

"Please, Jack, don't."

I worked my thumbs over the knotted muscles at the hinges of my jaw.

"Listen," Ed gasped, "you can forget me, if you want, but take the kid with you. And take care of him. He wants to be a P.I. Make him a good one. Hell, he's your partner now."

251

"You're my partner."

"Jesus, Jack, you know I left him my agency. He's a good kid. Hey, I never asked you for a favor since that time."

This was a reference to some trouble Ed once had with a bookie. I bailed him out by borrowing against the cash value of my life insurance. The money saved Ed a broken hand, and later on, when it was obvious he wasn't going to pay off the loan, he offered me an interest in his agency. Ever since that time he treated me as his partner and not his surrogate son. "It's me who owes you," I said.

"Awww, fuck this stuff. Let's get outta here, okay?"

"One thing. You ever work with a guy named Sweetser when you were a cop here in D.C.?"

"No, never heard of him."

I stood up, stuffing the pockets of my raincoat with the needles, the dope, the filters, and the rest of it. "I'll talk to Tim, see what he wants to do."

"Thanks, Jack."

"You're looking flabby," I said. "Do some sit-ups or something. I'll be right back." I stepped into the sitting room. Tim was perched on the edge of the tuxedo sofa, the tails of his trench coat folded over his knees. I closed the bedroom door. I closed the door to the hallway, too, and leaned back against it. "I'm taking Mr. Quinn, Timmy. You want to come with us, or do you want to stay here with your father and your brothers?"

Tim stood up. "Where are you taking him?"

"Not to a hospital."

"Well . . . does he want to leave?"

"He says he'd feel more comfortable somewhere else."

"Away from my father?"

"How about you?"

Tim looked down at the rug, his sallow face pinched with indecision. "I . . . don't know."

"Ed wants you to come."

Tim started to speak, but a voice rising from the hallway

downstairs distracted him. "If Mapes won't come get him," Nick Kinney cried, "I'll take him there myself."

I heard Craig and his father shouting after Nick. Nick answered with a curse, and I could feel the floor shudder as he pounded up the stairs. I stepped away from the door.

29

The door flew open and slammed against the wall. Nick Kinney lunged into the room. Craig was on his heels, snatching at his brother's sleeve. Douglas Kinney was a step or two behind Nick and Craig, just as he'd been downstairs in the little scene I'd witnessed earlier. They were shouting at one another, then all at once, seeing me, they fell silent, three jaws dropping with the realization that the jig was up.

After a moment of dumbstruck silence, Nick Kinney said, "I can explain everything."

"That's the spirit," I said.

"What are you doing here?" Douglas Kinney demanded.

"Just be glad I didn't find any pirated VCR tapes, or you'd be looking at a visit from the FBI on top of everything else."

Kinney turned to Tim. "What's he doing here?"

"He's taking Mr. Quinn away," Tim said meekly.

Craig Kinney shook his head. "No, he isn't."

"He wants to take care of Mr. Quinn himself," Tim said.

"No way," Craig said.

"It's the perfect solution," Nick insisted. "If Bodine wants the responsibility, then let him have—"

"He wants Quinn to change his will, asshole."

"Let him," Nick answered. "Then we're free of this mess."

"I told you, Nicky, I got plans for this guy."

Nick Kinney opened his hands to his brother. "Craig, except for harboring Quinn, we haven't done anything illegal. So if Bodine wants him, he can have him. Forget Parker-Gray."

Craig said softly, "Don't you want to hear what happened last night, Nicky?"

"I *know* what happened. You made the mistake of bringing Quinn here, and Dad made the mistake of letting him stay."

"No," Craig said softly, "I never brought Quinn here."

"All right, Mapes brought him here, but you told him to."

"No, I didn't. I was never at the motel. But Bodine was. Bodine brought Quinn to D.C. and the lawyer followed them—"

"Craig."

"—and Bodine killed Gibbs."

"What are you saying?"

"You heard me, Nicky. Bodine did Gibbs. Mapes wasn't involved. It's just a coincidence Bodine stashed Quinn at the District Line Motel. Bodine did everything on his own. He's been supplying Quinn with dope to get him to change his will, write him into it."

Nick Kinney looked to see if I was enjoying Craig's scenario. I indicated I was taking it with a grain of salt.

Nick turned back to his brother. "I don't want to hear any more of this, Craig."

"Picture it, Nicky. Bodine's using drugs as leverage, but Quinn's lawyer figures out what's going on. He tracks Bodine from the motel in Lansing to the motel outside Baltimore, the one in Towson Bodine checked into yesterday afternoon before he came to D.C. The lawyer asks what's going on. Bodine gets rid of him and sneaks away with Quinn again, checks into the District Line. But Gibbs finds him and gives him a hard time. Finally Bodine gets fed up and puts Gibbs away. Tim sees it. Bodine decks Tim, shoves him into the trunk of the car along with Gibbs's body. They find Tim and Gibbs, but Tim's so scared of Bodine he blames Gibbs's death on some black guys who were never there."

"For God's sake, Craig—"

"Just listen, Nicky. After he does Gibbs, Bodine takes Quinn back to his room in Baltimore. But he runs out of dope. So Bodine tells Quinn he won't get more unless Quinn cancels the codicil, writes Tim out of the will, and puts Bodine back in. But Quinn, sick as he is, refuses. Bodine loses his temper and threatens him. Quinn says, 'Go ahead, kill me, do me a favor.' So Bodine does him a favor."

"Craig—"

"Wait. Bodine smothers Quinn. Then he comes to D.C., figuring to take a crack at Tim. He knows sooner or later Tim's going to tell the cops the truth: that Bodine wasted Gibbs, so Bodine shows up here, but we scare him off. Sweetser's a witness. He testifies Bodine was acting weird, says he told him to get out of town. Bodine just drives around, getting depressed. He knows that wasting Quinn has cost him his chance at Mapes's house. He knows he's up to his ears in a double murder. First the lawyer, now Quinn. He doesn't know what to do. He's scared. So he decides to bag it. He . . . what the hell, he jumps off a bridge."

"Craig, what is the *matter* with you?"

"Once we get our version between Sweetser's ears, he won't see it any other way, not if he expects a job at Kintell."

"This is preposterous."

"No it's not, Nicky. It's sad. Bodine kills Gibbs, then Quinn, then himself. It's a very sad story."

I said, "Thin on characterization, though."

"I'm taking no more lip off you, Bodine." Craig Kinney stuck his hand under his herringbone sport coat and snatched a revolver off his belt. Two-inch barrel. It was a quick, practiced motion, one he'd probably perfected nights in front of a mirror, twenty draws before saying his prayers.

Douglas Kinney took a look at the gun and skittered into the hallway. Tim Kinney stepped backward, stumbled against the sofa and sat down, cringing at the sight of the weapon. It was just like Dodge City, the citizens running for cover. Nick Kinney, to his credit, stood fast. "Put that away, Craig."

"When I'm done with it."

"Craig!"

"Here's what we do," Craig said. "We tie his ass up, find his car and pull it into the garage. Then we haul him downstairs, dump him into the trunk and stuff Quinn into Dad's car, which you, Nicky, drive over to the embassy side of the Q Street Bridge."

"Craig, please!"

"You park by the Turkish Embassy, wherever you can find a place. You work your way down onto Rock Creek Parkway and wait under the bridge. There's a grassy area, lot of rocks? That's the drop zone. You wait there. I follow you five minutes behind. In rain like this on a Sunday night there won't be any walkers. Not much traffic on the parkway after dark, either. I wait on the Georgetown side of the bridge, make sure no one's coming. Then I drive Bodine's crate onto the bridge, make the drop and you take it from there. You cut his restraints, arrange him a little so it doesn't look like he was tied up when he hit. Then you come up to the top of the bridge. I'm waiting for you in the bushes. Bodine's car is still on the bridge. You and me take the Mercedes and drive up to Baltimore, unload Quinn at the motel Bodine checked into, do him, come back here and pop a beer. How about it?"

Nick Kinney turned to his father. "For God's sake, Dad, *say* something."

"Craig," said Douglas Kinney from the hallway, "Tim would have to change his statement, and in the chain of events you've just described, he's the weak link. Don't you agree?" Kinney said this speculatively, as if he were playing devil's advocate. He took a quick look at me and I noticed a trace of a glint in the old man's eye.

"You a weak link, Timmy?" Craig said, winking at his kid brother.

Tim had flattened himself against the back of the sofa as if he were trying to blend in with the upholstery. "What?"

"You want to spend your life being a weak link, Tim?"

"No," Tim said uncertainly.

Douglas Kinney shot a scornful look at the boy and shook his head disgustedly. He said, "What's more, Craig, if you carry Edward into Bodine's Baltimore motel yourself, you risk being identified later. There's the problem of the maids, too. They would have cleaned the room today and would testify that Edward wasn't there at the time."

"Good point, Dad. The plan needs a little work, and Tim needs a little coaching, that's all."

Nick Kinney emitted a slightly manic laugh. "I don't believe you two."

Douglas Kinney, his cheeks on fire, said, "What do you think Bodine will do if we let him walk out of here, Nick?"

"Yeah," said Craig, "what about that?"

"It depends on the deal we strike with him," Nick replied. "I assume he's not taking Quinn to a hospital, in which case he'll be into us for our silence, just as we'll be into him on the same grounds. We can work something out, Craig. Just put the gun away before someone gets hurt."

"You know, Nicky, you got a tendency to hang back. Why don't you—just once—be bold?"

Nick Kinney stared at his brother with an air of cold calculation, nodding to himself, his eyes narrowing with contempt. "Like when you were a wild man in Vietnam?" he said softly.

"What?"

Seeing the look of ugly menace that came over Craig's face, Nick seemed to regret his remark. "Never mind. Just put the gun away."

"Never mind *what?*"

Nick went over it again in his mind, then decided to play his ace. He said, "Just never mind that the only time you set foot in

Vietnam, you did it standing guard for some NavSecGru squids in Da Nang."

Craig scowled at his brother. "Who told you that?"

"After which you did six months sea duty defending the admirals' coffee cups."

"Where'd you get that?"

"A guy named Stokes. Dropped into the office a couple months ago, looking for you. You were out in Vegas getting your divorce. Stokes and me got to talking. He told me everything."

"He told you pucky."

"Everything he said, Craig, I checked it through BuPers at my last Reserve meeting."

"I don't give a fuck what you checked, you nosy little shit."

"You spent the rest of your tour on Guam. So let's just forget about Bodine."

"You don't think I can waste him?"

"Waste him? You mean 'shoot' him?"

"The hell you think?"

"What about the plan?" Nick said sarcastically.

"We change the plan. Waste him for a prowler. He's in our house and we got a right to do him."

"Craig!"

"Fuck you, Nicky."

Without further discussion, Craig Kinney shot me in the chest. I was lunging for him when the round slammed into me, and the impact took a little off my punch. So I hit Craig again, and broke his nose for sure.

He went down in a heap under the rolltop desk. I bent over him, rubbing my chest. He wasn't out, but he wasn't in, either. He still had the gun in his hand, so I stood on his wrist till his fingers opened, and took the piece away from him. I turned toward Nick and his father. They weren't coming at me. Douglas Kinney had turned fish-belly white. I was reminded of Tim back at the motel room, flat against the door, paralyzed and ghostly pale. I glanced at the boy. He was gawking at me, too, giving me a look of stunned disbelief. No one said anything. The only sound in the room was the remembered *pop!* of the gun, which was fading fast beneath the rattle of the rain on the window.

Tim said, "Mr. Bodine, Craig *shot* you!"

"Right."

"But—"

"Timmy, when I spend four hundred bucks on a raincoat, it does more than repel water."

30

I used Craig's gun to wave old man Kinney into the room. He hesitated, pondering defiance, but even as he was examining the notion, his feet brought him inside. I said, "Sit right there, Doug."

Kinney slouched moodily next to Tim.

"You too, Nick. There."

Nick sat down on the other side of Tim. The three of them kept a close eye on my gun hand. They also kept as much distance between themselves as they could, which wasn't easy for three men on a love seat.

Under the rolltop desk Craig started to come around. His legs, bent at the knees, were lolling from side to side.

I edged over to the door and called down the stairs. "You there, Wilma?"

No answer.

"Wilma?"

I heard the steps creak. "What you want?"

"I want you to come up here."

"What that noise? A gun?"

I glanced down at the revolver in my hand. "A .38 Smith and Wesson. Come on up."

"You been shot?" she said.

"Technically."

"Say what?"

"Wilma, I'd like you to help me get Mr. Quinn down the stairs."

Douglas Kinney cupped his hands around his mouth. "Stay where you are, Wilma." Kinney was yelling at her from the far limits of his authority, and his voice had that shrill quality I'd heard a few moments ago when he'd railed Sweetser downstairs in the foyer.

I said, "I need your help, Wilma."

"I'll help you," Tim said, his eyes wide with brave intentions.

"Shut up," snapped his father.

"Thanks, Tim," I said, "but you sit tight." Over my shoulder I shouted, "You there, Wilma?"

"Goin' home."

"Help me with Ed, and I'll give you a ride."

"Takin' a bus."

I heard the shuffle of feet, the opening of a door, and the splattering of rain on the steps in front of the house. I heard the *whoosh-thump* of a spring-loaded umbrella, and then the heavy thud of the front door closing.

Craig Kinney groaned, straightened one leg, then the other. He was flat on his back, his legs fully extended, the toes of his shoes pointing outward. They drew together, then flopped outward again as his fists squeezed and relaxed.

"You don't need to point that gun at us," Nick Kinney said. "No one will try to stop you if you take Quinn yourself. I guarantee it."

Douglas Kinney shot Nick a cold glance.

Nick ignored his father. "Go on, Bodine. Get Quinn out of here."

I had the half packet of dope, the needles, the cotton filters, the lighter, and the spoon. All I needed was Ed.

"You can trust us," Nick said.

Nick and Tim, yes. Doug and Craig, no. There was a phone on the table beside me, but I couldn't think of anybody to call for help. It was a lonely feeling, almost as acute as the throb where the bullet had struck me. "Okay," I said to Nick. "You carry him down. Tim, you stay here and keep your father company."

As I reached for the door to the bedroom, the knob was pulled out of my grasp. Ed Quinn, one hand clutching his bladder bag, peered out at me. "I heard a shot," he said, his voice as ragged as his pajamas.

"It's checkout time," I said.

"I heard a shot," Ed insisted.

I pointed to the dent in my left lapel. "See that?"

Ed noticed the gun in my hand and Craig Kinney moaning on the floor. "He popped you?"

"Remember how you used to kid me about this coat?"

Ed managed a smile. "Yeah," he said. "Now that you finally got to use it, was it worth four hundred bucks?"

Craig drew his knees up, rolled to his side and spat onto the rug.

I said, "So far."

Ed started to chuckle, but his laughter sounded like a series of yelps, as if every rib in his body were cracked and shards of bone were piercing his lungs.

"Nick'll carry you," I said.

"Hell, I'll do it myself." Ed nodded at the Kinneys. "You watch them. I'll holler when I get downstairs." He shuffled out of the bedroom, holding his bladder bag to his body, taking short, slow steps, his breath coming in short, shaky gasps. Then he stopped and looked back into the room, his eyes on Tim. " 'Bye, Timmy," he said.

"Can I come with you?"

Ed didn't say no, but his face closed down.

"Please, Mr. Quinn." Tim started to get up, but Douglas Kinney grabbed his son by the neck and pulled him back onto the love seat.

I'd had enough of the Kinneys for one night. "You work things out with your father," I said to Tim. "We'll talk later." I reached for the door, pulled it shut, and offered an arm to Ed. "Come on."

We wobbled along the hall to the stairs and started down. With each step Ed cursed his guts, fate, Jesus, and me, apologizing with one breath, cursing with the next. It seemed we were fifteen minutes getting down the stairs, though it probably wasn't more than one.

When we made the ground floor, Ed reached for the newel post and said he needed to rest. I kept an eye on the head of the stairs. The Kinneys weren't coming after us, but I could hear them up there arguing the matter. I turned back to Ed. He was holding his bladder pouch like a woman with a clutch bag. The bag was translucent, and a dribble of yellow urine was wetting the front of his twisted pajama bottoms.

I said, "I'm going to carry you." I pocketed Craig's weapon and gathered Ed into my arms. Ed stood six-two and once weighed 210 pounds, but he didn't seem any heavier than my son. I carried him down the hall and into the kitchen and eased him onto the padded stool at the butcher-block island in the center of the room. In the mud room leading to the garage, I found a pair of large rubber boots. I slipped the boots onto Ed's stark white feet and wrapped him in the old corduroy gardening jacket I snagged off a hook. I picked him up again and carried him through the garage and out into the rain. The downpour hadn't let up. If anything, it was raining harder now than it had all day. The temperature was falling, too. By the time I got the Chrysler's rear door open and Ed laid out on the backseat, he was shivering uncontrollably.

I ran back into the garage and snatched my keys from under the can of Rain Dance, splashed outside again, opened the trunk of the car and found a blanket. I covered Ed with the blanket, then got behind the wheel and started up. As I backed into the street I took a last look at the Kinney house. I'd left the light in the garage on, and I saw Tim Kinney, still wearing his trench coat, standing between the Mercedes and the Taurus. The cars, with their tires flat, were leaning toward him as if bowing to royalty. I levered the Chrysler into drive, but kept my foot on the brake, waiting. If Tim wanted to come, I'd take him. We stared at one another through the silver wall of rain. Finally he waved good-bye. I waved back, then snapped on the wipers and the heater and urged the Chrysler through the rain. I drove with soft hands and a softer foot, not wanting to bounce Ed around, wherever it was we were going.

My first thought was to leave town and head back to the motel outside Baltimore where I'd taken a room before I'd got the call from Joyce to come to D.C. The Kinneys knew of that room, though. The best thing would be to try another town, maybe Harrisburg, some two hours off.

I hadn't gone two blocks when I realized I'd gone far enough. Every bump in the road made Ed cry out as if the backseat were a bed of nails. He needed a shot, and I needed to find a place to give it to him, and soon.

I had enough dope to cook a single dose. After I gave it to him, I'd have to try the 1700 block of Harvard Street, Northwest. A night like this was tough on pushers, though. And even if I found one, I wasn't sure I'd be able to score . . . although not many narcs posed as preppies. Still, the dealers would be skittish. Meanwhile, Ed would be alone with his pain.

I remembered Abajan's offer to let us use a room in the house across the street from old Mrs. Mapes, but who would watch Ed while I shopped for sugar?

I thought of Othman's mother, saw myself standing in the icy autumn rain beneath her yellow porch light, waiting for her to answer her door. Hers would be the only light on the block. But if I took Ed to her, I'd have to explain what Othman had been up to, and it would be the same as turning off her light for good. I told myself it was the price she had to pay for having lived in Ed's house all these years, but I knew I couldn't do it.

Which left Othman. According to old Mrs. Mapes, he owed Ed his life. He also owed Ed for having lived in his house the past thirty-five years. Most important, he owed Ed a new supply of white stuff. As a black ex–D.C. cop, he'd know how and where to get it, too.

I saw a gas station ahead. It was closed, but I pulled into it anyway, and stopped under the self-service awning. I opened the map I'd bought from Mapes, spread it out on the seat beside me, snapped on my penlight and looked for New York Avenue.

"Jack?"

"What?"

"Where are we?"

The awning prevented the rain from thrumming on the roof of the car, but I still had to strain to hear Ed. "I'm checking a map."

"What?"

I turned off the blower. "We'll be there soon."

"Where we going?"

"I'm taking you back to the motel Mapes works at."

"Jack?"

"What?"

"Dougy isn't following us, is he?"

"No."

"You won't let him get me again, will you?"

"You're safe."

"I mean afterward. I don't want him looking at me when I'm a cold cut."

"I won't let him."

"Thanks."

"Sure."

"Jack?"

"What?"

"I been thinking."

"No wonder you hurt."

"Let me out right here."

266

I wiped condensation off my window. Thick sheets of orange rain slanted through the ugly light from the sodium vapor lamps, the rain falling with enough force to churn the water in the overflowing gutters. "No," I said. "We're going to Mapes's motel."

"Leave Othman out of it, Jack."

"He owes you."

"No, he don't."

"He didn't keep his part of the deal. He gave you over to Kinney."

"It wasn't his fault. It was Dougy's boy, Craig, made him. We were standing there in the alley and Craig told Othman how it was going to be. Othman didn't—"

"*You* were standing in the alley?"

"Yeah."

I cut the engine and slung my arm over the seat. "You got out of the van?"

"Yeah. I heard someone shouting for help, but it was muffled, weird."

"Who was it?"

"Harry. His car was parked right next to Othman's van. He was in the trunk hollering."

"Are you sure it was Harry's voice you heard?"

"Yeah."

"How can you be sure?"

"I talked to him. He asked me to let him out of the trunk. I said I didn't have the keys. Then Timmy says—he's in there, too—Timmy says he's got the keys. I asked Harry if the car had a trunk release in the glove compartment, but he says no, I'd have to pry it open. I told him I didn't have the strength to do that. I could hardly stand up. Anyway, I didn't have a tire iron or anything. It was inside the trunk of the car. I didn't know if the van had one, or where it was. I told Harry he'd have to pry it open himself from the inside, but he said he already tried and couldn't get any leverage. He said to find somebody that could get him out. I'm thinking if I do, then what about me? I asked Harry about it, and he says he's gonna take care of me, get me the best treatment, all the same stuff he said in the motel. I told him I didn't want no hospital. He starts crying, he's really freaked in there. Me, I was about ready to pass out . . ."

Ed's voice trailed off. For a moment I thought he'd slipped away, but then he said, "That's when Dougy's kid turned up."

"Craig?"

"Yeah. I didn't know who he was at the time, but he acts like he knows me, asks me how I'm doing. I'm standing there in my pajamas, dribbling piss. I tell him I'm doing fine, been to the Smithsonian, the National Gallery, and the White House. Hope to climb all five hundred feet to the top of the Washington Monument tomorrow. That's great, pop, he says, why don't you get back into the van? I asked him to let Harry out of the trunk first, but he says soon as he gets me away from the alley they'll call the cops about the guy in the trunk, not to worry, they'll take him to a hospital."

"Did he know Tim was in there, too?"

"No. I don't think so. He didn't act like he cared one way or another who it was in the trunk. That's when Othman shows, and the two of them help me back into the van. Craig says he'll see to it someone takes care of me where we're going. I says, wait a minute, who? Craig says everything's cool, we're going where Othman's wife, Wilma, can do the job. I wouldn't have gone with him if I'd known he was taking me to Dougy's place."

"Who drove you there?"

"Othman."

"Did Craig stay behind?"

"No. He had Othman drive him around front of the motel in the van. Then Craig got out and said for Othman to follow him. I guess he had his own car around front."

"Was Craig waiting for you when you arrived at Kinney's place?"

"Yeah. Othman followed him all the way. Jack?"

"Yes?"

"I feel bad."

Ed sounded worse than bad. I reached for the ignition and started up, flicked on the heater, the wipers, and the lights, and pulled back out into the rain. "Hang on," I said. "I'll make you feel better."

31

The closer I got to the motel, the harder the rain beat down. It slanted into my windshield as if it were trying to change my mind about taking Ed to Mapes. I kept heading for New York Avenue, though, pulling over now and again to check the street signs against my map. It was hard to read the signs because of the greasy condensation filming the inner surface of the windshield. I wiped it once or twice with the heel of my hand, but all that did was resmear the glare pattern created by oncoming cars. The beams of my own headlamps slowed me down, too, atomizing the solid sheet of rain into a million points of light. George Bush might have found it inspiring, but all it gave me was a headache.

It was a good twenty minutes before I saw the motel's flickering sign through the rain and pumped to a gentle stop just down from the driveway. Traffic sluiced around me as I squinted at the car parked in front of the lobby. It sat where Craig Kinney had parked his Porsche last night, but this wasn't any Porsche. It was Henry Sweetser's unmarked cruiser. I could just make him out, standing at the desk, talking to Othman Mapes. Sweetser had his back to me, but I knew it was him by the way he stood, hands on his hips, soggy trench coat pulled back from his barrel body.

Ed moaned in the backseat. I nudged the accelerator and turned into the motel driveway. At the same instant a tour bus, air horns braying, roared past me in a boiling fog of rain spray. I checked the lobby and saw Sweetser glance in my direction, but he returned to his discussion with Mapes, and I rolled past them toward the room I'd rented from the old man with the clacking dentures, number 143. I had the key in my pocket.

I parked as close as I could to the room and told Ed we'd arrived. He answered, but the rain was so loud on the roof I couldn't catch what he said. I told him I was going to unlock the door to the room first, then come back for him. I didn't hear what he said, just saw him raise his hand in acknowledgment. I got out of the car and splashed over to the room, slid the key into the lock and pushed. The door swung inward, then caught against the security chain. A woman cried out and a man growled a profane warning.

I pulled the door shut and hurried back to the car. Ed was trying to sit up. He looked like something rising from the grave. I opened the car door and leaned in. "Someone's in my room," I said. "I'll have to get another. Hold on, okay?"

Ed gave me a stricken stare, as if he didn't recognize me. "Jack?"

"It's me. I'll be right back."

"Wait. I . . . thanks, partner."

"I'll have us a room in a minute. But just remember, you start snoring and you sleep in the car. Now lie down and take it easy. Everything will be all right."

Ed lowered himself back down onto the seat. I closed the door without slamming it, and headed for the lobby. I passed the room with the crime-scene tape, but I didn't consider using it. Criminals never return to the scene of a crime, but cops always do. There was a two-foot eaves over the walkway fronting the doors to the rooms, and I stayed under it all the way to the rear entrance to the lobby. I eased the door open and paused next to the throbbing ice machine, listening to Sweetser and Mapes.

". . . telling me he ain't . . . nothing to do with it?" Mapes said.

". . . never touched him."

The rattle of the ice machine covered my entrance, but it was covering their voices, too. I crept closer, my back flat against the wall.

". . . Craig out there three, four minutes . . . didn't do nothing? I saw the look in his eye, Sweety."

"Whatever. I just . . . for a little help. A favor for a favor."

"Favor?"

"Yeah."

"What I owe you a favor for?" Othman Mapes said.

"Are you forgetting last night?"

"Trying to."

"Hey, I did everything you asked, Othman."

"Don't remember askin' you to suck up to old man Kinney."

"Hey—"

"Don't remember askin' you to take that Bodine dude to Georgetown, neither."

"You said to get him out of your hair."

"What you take him to Kinney for?"

"It was a chance to meet him."

"And a chance to fuck me over?"

"Come off it, Othman."

"You do the lawyer, Sweet?"

"What?"

"You deaf? Somebody squeezed him off, and if it ain't Craig, or the dudes was takin' care of Quinn, who the fuck do it?"

"Wait a minute. You think I—"

"You knew he was in the trunk of the car. I tol' you."

"I never went into the alley."

"How 'bout after you brought Bodine back here from Kinney's place?"

"Othman, buddy, I never went to the alley, not even after it was a crime scene."

"You in charge of a homicide, but you never been to the damn scene? Come on, Sweet, I used to be your partner."

"You can ask anyone who was there. You can ask—"

"See me doing that?"

"—Meevis, you know him?"

"Fuck no, I don't know Meevis. Don't think I know you, neither."

"Othman, I went to the private dick's room, and I took him for a ride so you could figure out what to do with Quinn. I did everything you asked."

"Everything Kinney ask, too?"

"Hey, he didn't know nothing about them two in the trunk."

"Craig knew! I told him on the phone. Way I see it, Craig told his old man 'bout it before he left to come here, then his old man tol' you what to do when you was in Georgetown with the peeper."

"Kinney never said nothing about no car trunk."

"Willie say he took you aside, tol' you something, and you started jumpin' up and down, asking, 'This high enough, Mr. K?' "

"All I did," said Sweetser, "was dog it so Nick could tail us here."

"And then?"

"And then *what*?"

"What'd you do?"

"I went back to the station. I walked into the comm room and caught Meevis's squeal, turned around and met him and Kinney's kid at D.C. General."

"Roland tol' me they still got him down as 'Cooney.' How'd you know his name was Kinney, standing in the communications room?"

"I recognized the stiff's name, the lawyer, from talking to Bodine. I went to the hospital expecting the kid to fill me in is all.

Turns out he's Kinney's son working for Bodine's partner under a phony name. I figure if I can keep the kid's ID privileged, I'm on the inside with his old man. I sent Meevis back to the scene, and called Kinney. Kinney says to meet him at his office on K Street. I'm there toot sweet, never checked the alley."

"Well, if you so tight with Kinney, how come you here pissing about him?"

"Bodine says Kinney crossed me. I don't buy it, but I gotta be sure. Willie's at Kinney's place every day. I'm thinking maybe she's heard something, or can find out."

"One thing she find out, Sweet. Ain't nobody choke that lawyer like the kid say."

"What do you mean?"

"Willie called me a while back, say the lawyer's pump blew."

"What?"

"Willie took a look at them papers you lef' with Kinney. Say the lawyer had the big one. Now, how come you been here all this time and ain't said nothing 'bout no heart attack?"

"Okay, Othman. Just let me ask you something. Why ain't I heard you say it was Roland and Jerome stuffed the lawyer into the motherfucking trunk in the first place?"

Mapes said stiffly, "Don't know what you talking about."

"Bodine told me it was them."

"You wired, Sweet?"

"You think I'd come here wearing a wire?"

"I think you'd shove one up your ass to save it."

"You know I'm no rat, Othman."

"Don't know what you is no more."

"Ain't no different from you, bro, just getting over."

"Try getting the fuck out."

"One thing," Sweetser said sadly. "When we were partners you talked better than me. Now you sound like the sorriest nigger in the tank. Why is that?"

"Because I'm ashamed to talk like you."

"Jesus Christ, Othman—"

"Get out of my motel."

"Aw . . ."

"And don't be coming back."

"Thanks 'partner.' Thanks . . ."

Sweetser moved off. I heard the downpour swell and subside as the door opened and closed. I could hear Mapes muttering as I watched the plate-glass pane to the right of the plywood insert. I couldn't spot Sweetser's car from my position, but after several seconds I saw headlights flare and swing away from the building, silver needles of rain slanting through the beams.

I waited a few seconds more, then stepped into the lobby.

Othman Mapes, his hands gripping the edge of the counter, was glaring angrily at the window opposite the desk. All he could see was himself reflected in the glass, but maybe he didn't like what he saw. When he noticed me he looked even angrier, his body stiffening as I approached the counter and leaned toward him. His gray smock was almost the same color as his face. The swollen purplish flesh beneath his eyes twitched, both bags, different rhythms.

We held each other's gaze for a good ten seconds, neither of us speaking. Then Mapes said, "You don't look so good."

I almost reached for his neck. "You booked my room," I said.

"Damn right."

I threw the key on the counter. "Give me another."

Mapes shook his head.

I said, "Ed Quinn's outside in my car and he needs a room."

Mapes's eyes enlarged. "I told Nick Kinney when he had Wilma call, and I'm tellin' you, Quinn ain't stayin' here. Anyhow, I ain't got no rooms."

I pointed at the vacancy sign outside. "It says you do."

Mapes reached down under the counter, flicked a switch, and the sign said, NO VACANCY. "Now, get out."

"You owe him."

"We're even."

"Never. You owe him your life. The least you can do is give

275

him room and board for the rest of his. After all, that was the deal you struck with Ed. I know you've got rooms, and I'm betting you can get the board. It's bought and sold down on Harvard Street, Northwest . . . according to your boy, Roland."

"Roland?"

"Your son, Roland Mapes. Wilma must have told you I know about Roland and Jerome."

"Don't know what you talkin' 'bout."

"Last chance, Othman. Either you take Ed in or I take him to your mother and tell her what's going to happen when he dies and the Kinneys end up with the mortgage on her place."

Mapes opened his mouth, but his words were drowned out by the blare of an air horn and the mushy sound of large tires skidding on wet pavement.

Somehow I knew what had happened. I didn't want to look, but I went to the window and shaded my eyes against the glare of the lobby's fluorescent lights. Out on the street, just down from the motel, I saw a silver-sided tour bus like the one that had honked me over a few minutes earlier. It had slid sideways to a stop, and was several hundred feet beyond the man in the corduroy work jacket and garden boots who was sprawled near the motel driveway.

I slammed through the lobby doors and splashed to Ed's side, squinting against the downpour. He was lying on his stomach with his legs crossed at the knees, his left cheek hard on the pavement, one arm under him, the other flung wide. The garden coat and the rubber boots were tinged red by the bus's taillights. Ed didn't move.

The driver ran up to me insisting he hadn't hit Ed, at least not head-on. He swore Ed had purposely staggered into the side of the bus as it had gone sliding by him.

I told the driver to turn on his emergency flashers and set out his flares. He ran back to the bus and I waved traffic around Ed. When the driver got his flares going I knelt down beside Ed and tried to catch what he was saying, but his mouth never moved and I knew I'd imagined hearing his voice. I couldn't possibly have heard anything over the roar of the rain and the bus's idling engine and the traffic hissing in the other lanes. What I could hear, though, was a distant siren shifting into a tremolo each time the ambulance came up on another intersection. Then it would switch back to a steady scream as it accelerated nearer and nearer.

A small crowd had formed and someone offered me an umbrella. I held it over Ed. It was a quiet crowd. The only voice I heard was the driver's, pleading for someone, anyone, to verify that the accident wasn't his fault.

A moment later the ambulance showed up, followed by a white Metropolitan Police scout car with a light blue stripe along its side, its siren purring down. In the cross-glare of the flashers the EMTs examined Ed on the street, then moved him to a stretcher and eased him into the wagon.

"Where are you taking him?" I asked the driver of the ambulance.

"Morgue."

A cop in a slicker stepped up to me. "You know the guy?"

"Out by D.C. General?" I asked the EMT.

"Yep."

"You know the guy?" the cop said again.

"No," I said.

"You okay, buddy?"

"Yes."

"You see what happened?"

"No. I was in the motel lobby, checking in. I didn't see anything."

The cop turned away and approached the driver of the bus. Other cops were working the crowd, asking if anyone had seen what had happened.

The EMTs slammed the ambulance door, climbed into the cab, and drove away with Ed Quinn's body. I watched the lights of the ambulance recede in the rain.

When the EMTs got where they were going, they would roll Ed into the same wall with Harry Gibbs. I didn't know it for sure, but it seemed likely. I stood there quite a while before I decided that part of it wasn't important.

Then I got into my car and headed for Georgetown.

32

The rain let up as I drove. By the time I reached the awnings and embassies of Massachusetts Avenue, it had stopped altogether. The street, washed clean, glistened in the glare of my headlights. People were venturing out of the upscale bars and foreign restaurants in the area. Quite a few of the patrons, chatting in pairs and foursomes as they headed toward their cars, looked like businessmen, or Washington's version of businessmen: late-dining lobbyists. Others were single males, many of whom were walking exotic dogs. I saw a few tourists with maps and cameras in hand, and several strolling couples with their hands full of nothing but each other, pausing to gaze at the oriental rugs, books, jewelry, and audio equipment displayed in the lighted windows of the shops.

I double-parked just south of Dupont Circle, jumped a rain-swollen gutter and entered an all-night drugstore. It was between a vegetarian restaurant and a lingerie boutique, but the pharmacist standing behind his counter at the rear of the shop looked like a regular guy. I gave him a regular-guy smile as I approached his window and told him what I wanted.

He was hesitant at first to help me out, but when I showed him my license and explained the reason for my request, he typed up a label and glued it to a little brown bottle. As he gave me the empty bottle he said with a wink that he just *had* to know the outcome of "our" ruse, and invited me to his place later for a drink. He said he'd be off duty at eleven-thirty. With a face as straight as a regular-guy's libido, I told him I was sorry, but I'd probably be with the police all night. On my way out I stopped at the register by the door and paid for a box of letter-size business envelopes and a roll of paper towels. You can find anything in a drugstore these days, even a paramour.

Back in the car I dried my head with a length of paper toweling and combed my hair. Then I tucked the little brown bottle into one of the envelopes I'd bought, and stuffed the envelope into the pocket of my Kevlar raincoat, the pocket without Craig's gun. I felt ready, and knew that as long as I did not allow myself to feel anything at all about Ed, I would continue to feel ready. I had the rest of my life to miss him. The next few minutes were for Harry Gibbs. And me.

I fired up the Chrysler and continued out Massachusetts Avenue, leaning the heavy car into the puddles on Dupont Circle. I veered off onto Mass. Ave. at the other side of the circle, turned onto Q Street, and drove two short blocks to the Q Street Bridge. I knew the name of the bridge this time across. I'd heard Craig Kinney mention it in his suicide scenario, the one in which I was scripted to take a dive onto the boulders of Rock Creek Park. It curved like a dam, the Q Street Bridge, and as I swung through the arc for the third time tonight, my headlights swept over the low brick retaining wall and illuminated the spray-painted graffito I'd first noticed last night with Sweetser: RICH PIGS WILL FALL. I hadn't taken the big fall. Maybe it was the Kinneys' turn.

As I swung into their street, I let up on the accelerator and cruised their place. The upstairs windows were dark, but the gas-fed porch lamps were still flickering. There was also a light burning in the room where I'd first noticed the photographs of Kinney's sons, the room where Craig and Nick and Douglas had been arguing earlier this evening.

I didn't waste time looking for a parking place. I drove around to the side of the house and pulled into the driveway. The garage door was down. I nudged the Chrysler into park, snatched the key from the ignition, and inventoried my raincoat. I had Craig Kinney's piece in one pocket—five rounds remaining—and the envelope with the bottle of pills in the other. I'd dumped the needle and the dope in a trash barrel outside the drugstore on Dupont Circle. I reached for the glove box, found my Sony M 200 microcassette recorder, inserted a fresh tape, and pushed the record button. Into the built-in condensor mike I said, "This is Jack Bodine in the case of Bodine versus Kinney. The date is October fifteenth. Time is 10:37 P.M. I'm about to initiate contact with the occupants of 5912 P Street, Northwest, Washington, D.C. The home is owned by Douglas Kinney." I hit the stop button, rewound the cassette, and listened to my initialization of the tape to make sure the batteries were juiced. Then I tucked the recorder into the loop of cloth I'd sewn behind the double-breasted lapel of my Kevlar coat. When I folded the lapel back into place, the recorder was hidden and the condensor mike was even with the buttonhole.

I got out of the car, hopped the puddles on the uneven sidewalk, rounded the corner and headed up the walk to Kinney's red front door. A frontal assault. I climbed the steps, took a deep breath, and hammered on the lion-head escutcheon. When I heard someone coming to the door, I pushed the record button on my machine and smoothed my lapel.

Tim Kinney answered, yanking on the door with a frantic urgency. A look of confusion and uncertainty flashed across his thin face at the sight of me, but a sigh of relief followed this reaction. "I was expecting Nick and Craig," he said in a whisper, "but I'm glad it's you. Come in."

"Your brothers aren't here?"

"No. Nick took Craig to the emergency room at G.W. to see about his nose. It wouldn't stop bleeding. They think it's broken."

I flexed the hand I'd used to pop Craig. My knuckles were swollen, but Tim's news eased the ache. I stepped into the foyer and the boy closed the door behind me. I nodded toward the interior of the house. "Your father still here?"

"Yes." Tim drew a wavering breath and eyed the sitting room. "He's in there. I tried to talk to him about, you know, what that old black woman said, but he just told me to go away. Then a few minutes ago I saw him get his gun out of the display case, the gun he took from a German officer during the war. He's had an awful lot to drink, Mr. Bodine. I think he wants to kill himself."

I slid my hand into my coat pocket and mated my palm to the knurled grips of Craig Kinney's .38. I laid my thumb on the hammer of the .38 so it wouldn't catch on my pocket when I drew the gun. Then I walked over to the sitting room and stepped through the French doors.

Douglas Kinney sat behind the Queen Anne table desk. The gun Tim had mentioned—the Luger I'd seen in the memento case last night—was resting on the leather surface of the desk, midway between Kinney's hands. Kinney was studying his hands as if he'd measured the distance between them and was concentrating on equalizing their position, making sure each hand was six inches from the pistol. There was a bottle of Wild Turkey on the desk, three-quarters down. The glass beside it, a short tumbler, was empty.

After a moment Kinney looked up at me, his head lolling back, then forward, his eyes focusing on me with difficulty. Earlier in the evening his cheeks had been flushed, but now his face had a pale greenish tint that was almost the color of his cardigan. He looked as if he were seasick. His unfocused gun-muzzle eyes had a sheen, though, that made him seem almost feverish. He appeared ill, yet excited, like a man whose ailment is an inspiration to him. When he spoke his words were slurred. "What d'you want?" he said.

I edged into the room, my hand damp on the grips of the gun in my pocket. The hammer was resting on the empty chamber.

If I drew the piece, I intended to squeeze off three rounds, double action, straight into Douglas Kinney's chest: *pop, pop, pop*. I imagined him flying backward, slamming into the mahogany sideboard behind him, his body sliding beneath the table desk and collapsing in a twitching heap. Having thus shot him in my mind, it would be easier to do it for real, without hesitation. "I know what happened," I said.

"Leave me—"

"And so do you."

"—alone, or I'll call th' p'lice."

Kinney, his hands still flat on the desk, watched me with a growing steadiness, as if his rising anger were sobering him up. I couldn't be sure about the gun in front of him, but I could see that his brain was full of bullets. His eyes, like machine pistols on full automatic, were suddenly blazing. "You want to call the police," I said, "that's fine with me."

"Shoot you for a trespasser first."

"Old gun. Hard to find ammo for it?"

"Nine mill'meter. Ver' common."

Kinney had me zeroed in now. I moved away from the door, wondering whether a nine-millimeter slug had more penetrating power than a .38, trying to remember the specs on my Kevlar coat. Kinney, tracking me across the room, turned his head in a series of lurching swoops. When I stopped, his eyes recalculated my range again, but his head wouldn't hold steady. I was peripherally aware of Tim. He'd entered the room and was standing several steps inside the door. He was still wearing his trench coat. It wasn't wet, so he hadn't been outside. It wasn't buttoned or belted, either, so he hadn't been about to leave. He was simply wearing the coat. He had his hands driven deep into its pockets as if he were cold. I said, "Tim's worried about what you intend to do with the gun, Mr. Kinney."

Kinney's head jerked toward Tim, his eyes narrowing suspiciously. "What'd you tell him?"

"Nothing," Tim said hoarsely. "I mean, he just got here."

Kinney's head waggled as he tried to refocus his gaze on me. When he got me narrowed down to a pair of Bodines, he treated me to a smile of confident superiority. "Your frien', the lawyer. He died of a heart attack. Nobody kill' him. So jus' get out."

"He was murdered, Mr. Kinney."

"Liar."

"I can prove it." I couldn't, of course, not to a jury's satisfaction. But I was betting Douglas Kinney was too drunk to know that, or to care. With my free hand I reached slowly into my coat pocket and brought out the envelope containing the little brown bottle. I opened the unglued flap with my thumb, showing Kinney what was inside.

Kinney gave the pill bottle a look of bleary alarm. "Where' you get that?"

"Sweetser's bailing out, Doug."

"Wha' d'you mean?"

"He gave the pills to me."

"Why in hell would he do tha'?"

"Because they didn't show up on the police report," I said, "which means the evidence techs didn't find them on Harry Gibbs's body, or in the trunk of his car. Yet according to his law partner, Harry always carried them. So, in order to explain the fact that the pills weren't found where they should have been found, I made a deal with Sweetser. I'm going to say I had them all along."

"Why?"

"So Sweetser won't be canned from the D.C. cops and lose his pension for suppressing evidence in a homicide investigation."

"So you kill' the lawyer," drawled Kinney cleverly.

"Why do you say that?"

" 'Cause you took his pills 'way."

"No. I got Harry's nitroglycerin tablets from the same person Sweetser did."

Kinney looked at Tim.

Out of the corner of my eye I could see Tim shaking his head. He said, "I . . . don't understa—"

"Shut up!" screamed Kinney.

"But Dad, you just . . . why did you *say* that about the pills?"

Kinney realized he'd been too clever, but his mood was one of drunken defiance, and he wasn't about to admit his blunder. "I'll handle this, Tim'thy. Jus' shut up." Tim lapsed into silence. His father, eyeing me with a look of sullen hatred, said, "Leave. No more talk."

With my eyes on Kinney I said to Tim, "Did you have to pry the pills out of Harry's hand, Timmy?"

Tim stepped back, shaking his head. "I . . . don't know what you're saying, Mr. Bodine."

"I'm saying that when Harry Gibbs had his heart attack you took his pills away from him, the pills here in this envelope."

"No."

"You had them in your hand when the police jimmied open the trunk of Harry's car, which is why they never showed up on the police report. They never searched you, not till Sweetser came to the hospital. He found them, and figured out what you'd done. He got the truth out of you, went straight to your father and struck a deal."

"No, he didn't get the pills from me."

"Sure he did. It's the only way he could have ended up with them. Anyway, he told me so."

"No."

"He never went into the alley," I said. "He was never at the crime scene last night. He got them from you. At the hospital."

"He didn't get those pills from me," Tim said. "He must have got them afterward, after he left me at the hospital and went to the police station. Or something."

"That's what he intended to say in court, Tim, assuming your father came through with a job at Kintell. That's why he brought the pills and the papers to your father's house earlier tonight, to clinch the deal. He's been waiting for the M.E.'s report to verify that Harry Gibbs died of a heart attack and not, as you said, strangulation. He brought a copy of the police report, too, to prove to your father that the pills weren't found on Harry's body. It was his hold over your father."

"I never saw those pills before in my life," Tim cried.

"This bottle of tablets was Sweetser's first-class ticket on the gravy train, Tim. That's why he placed them in this evidence envelope. Your fingerprints are all over the bottle."

Tim took another step back. "Wait . . . I remember. Mr. Gibbs dropped that bottle when we pulled into a rest stop. We were following Mr. Quinn and those black men to Washington. It was on the Pennsylvania Turnpike. The pills fell out of his pocket and I picked them up and handed them back to him. That's why my fingerpr—"

"Last night at the motel you insisted you knew nothing about Harry having a heart condition. You swore you never saw him take any pills, never saw this little brown bottle. You killed him, Timmy."

"You're crazy, Mr. Bodine. Why would I do that to Mr. Gibbs?"

"Because he wanted to take Ed Quinn to a hospital."

"Yes, but . . . I wouldn't . . . let Mr. Gibbs die because of that. I—"

"Or because you heard him mention that 'Kinfolk outfit' to Ed in the motel room last night."

Tim was suddenly silent.

"As soon as you knew your father was ripping off Ed, you were afraid. You threw up thinking about it, Timmy, and when Harry Gibbs got those pains in his chest, you saw a chance to save your old man."

Tim said nothing. He did not deny my accusation, nor did he shake his head. He was frozen, his eyes fixed on his father, looking to him for help, solace, guidance. Or forgiveness. But what he got from Douglas Kinney was a sneer, and the slurred order to get out of his sight. "You ruined my life once," Kinney groaned, "killed your own mother, killed her sure's you killed Gibbs. Now you're killing me . . . what's left of me. An' my business. Ruined. Go on," Kinney cried at me, "get ri' of him, take him away."

Tim, his eyes welling with tears, backed up against the doorjamb. His chin was trembling, and his face crumbled as sobs, unchecked, racked his slender chest. "I'll go to prison," Tim gasped. His throat was so constricted with tension and pain that he sounded as if he had laryngitis.

"Good," roared his father. "An' good ridd'nce, too. Teach you something. Be a man. Go on, get out of my sight, you . . . you *Edward* lover."

"Dad?"

"Don't 'Dad' me," Kinney mimicked. "Edward Quinn's your 'dad.' Why don't you run to him? Let Edward clean up your mess."

"But—"

"I don't want to hear. You did it for him, not for me. Him!"

"No," Tim cried. His spine was flat against the doorjamb, but he was reaching back as if for support, one hand gripping the jamb, the other clenching one of the muntins on the folded-back French door. He'd turned his face aside and tears were raining down his cheeks. "For you, Dad," he hiccupped. "I did it for you."

Kinney, his face twisted into a grotesque knot of anger and humiliation, bared his teeth. "Get out, God damn you. Go 'way!"

"Come on, Tim," I said. "Let's leave your father to his bottle."

"No!" squealed Tim. It was the cry of a two-year-old refusing to leave home for its first morning of day care, the anxiety of separation and loss flaring into panic and terror. "I don't want to leave you, Dad. Please don't let him take me."

Douglas Kinney's chair slammed into the buffet behind him as he jumped up, snatching the Luger as he rose. He did it in one motion, raising the gun to his head and digging the muzzle into the soft flesh beneath his jaw, pushing against his neck with such force his head was driven back, the whites of his eyes stark against his gray-green face. He gaped at Tim, tensing his index finger against the trigger. "Get out of here you cowar'ly little murderer! Get out, or I'll kill myself!"

I had drawn my gun . . . Craig's gun. I was ready. If Kinney turned toward me with the Luger, I would shoot him, three times, double action. But if he wanted to pop himself instead, I saw no reason to do his dirty work for him.

"Dad, don't!" screamed Tim.

I said, "Leave the room, Tim."

"Get out, you scrawny failure!" Kinney shrieked. "Get out of my life or I'll do it, I swear I will. It'll be on your head, Tim'thy. Yours!"

"But, Dad," Tim sobbed, "I *love* you."

"Ooooh," groaned Douglas Kinney, "oh, no you don't."

"I do."

"Shut up!" Kinney cried, pointing the Luger at Tim.

I shot Douglas Kinney then . . . not to kill, but to thwart. My bullet struck him in the upper arm and knocked the Luger out of his hand. The impact spun him around and threw him against the buffet. Bottles and glasses crashed inside the cupboard as Kinney slammed into it. He didn't go down, though, but caught himself, and reached for the Luger with his left hand. It was lying on the top of the buffet, and he grabbed it and straightened up, his right arm hanging limply, his left hand shoving the muzzle of the Luger under his chin again.

I aimed for his ear this time, but I didn't shoot. Kinney didn't, either. He just held the Luger under his chin, wheezing, his eyes shut tight against the force of the bullet he wanted to fire into his brain. I said, "Get out, Tim." But Tim stood fast against the doorjamb.

I waited.

Kinney tried harder to squeeze off the round, but he didn't have the strength to do the job.

I waited some more.

Eventually Kinney knew he had failed, and he threw the Luger down on the desk and slumped into his chair, his eyelids fluttering, his left hand rising to his mouth.

I edged over to him and grabbed the Luger. The barrel was hot. I hadn't seen the Luger recoil, nor kick any brass. Nor had I heard a report. But Kinney had discharged the gun. His round must have been fired the same instant as mine. I looked over at Tim. He was still standing against the doorjamb, but as I watched him he began to slide down the jamb to the floor. He ended up in a sitting position, his wing tips straight out in front of him. He was looking at his father, but his eyes expressed neither love nor disbelief nor shock, nor anything.

I slid the heavy Luger into my coat pocket and went over to the boy. I knelt and probed his neck, digging my finger into the hollow beneath his jawline, searching for a pulse. As I felt for it, I gazed around the room. Everything, even the knickknacks on the desk, seemed to pulse with energy and life, everything but the carotid artery in Tim Kinney's neck.

I looked down at the boy. The round from the Luger had pierced the left lapel of his trench coat. I lifted the lapel and looked at his chest. There was very little blood. My eye traveled up the doorjamb. The bullet had lodged in the wood about four-and-a-half feet above the floor. There was a trace of blood and tissue surrounding the bullet hole, but no blood trailing down the jamb from the hole to where Tim was sitting. Tim had died instantly, shot through the heart.

I stood up. The muscles in my gun hand felt hot with the strain of squeezing the grips. I forced myself to relax, to take in a deep lungful of air . . . which smelled of gun smoke. And vomit.

Douglas Kinney had spilled his stomach onto the desk, and was presently filling his lap. The sweet-sour stench of bile and booze was sickening.

I did not want to go near him, but I followed the revolver in my hand, and reached out for the phone on his desk. It was flecked with vomit. With two fingers I lifted the receiver from the cradle and tapped out 911 on the keypad with the barrel of my gun.

As I reported to the cops, Douglas Kinney dropped to the floor and began soiling his oriental carpet. The 911 call taker said she could hear him.

33

Othman Mapes stepped out of his mother's house with a half-dozen clothes hangers slung over his shoulder. They were hung with pants, shirts, sweaters, and a navy-blue blazer. The blazer was covered with a clear plastic bag. Mapes carried a battered brown suitcase, too, and had a bowling trophy tucked under his arm. He trudged down the walk in a weary stoop, as if he were bearing not only his own burden, but the white man's as well.

When he reached Sweetser's van I killed my engine and walked over to him. The rear doors of the van were open and he was loading his belongings inside. He didn't look up as I approached, just hefted the suitcase onto the bumper and nudged it between a houseplant and a small microwave oven. There were a half-dozen grocery bags in the van, too. They were stuffed with bedding, shoes, music tapes, and kitchen utensils. Mapes continued to ignore me, looking for a place to set his brass memento. Now that I had a closer look at it, I could see it wasn't a bowling trophy, but a marksmanship award. The navy-blue jacket wasn't a blazer, either. It was the uniform blouse of a police officer.

"This a sentimental journey?" I said.

Mapes answered without turning around. "Sweetser called

and said what happened at Kinney's, everything but what you wanted to talk about. So just get on with it." Mapes's breath plumed in the cold autumn air. It was six A.M., and the temperature had dropped into the low forties during the night.

"Where you off to?" I said.

Mapes hung the uniform from a chrome hook on the wall of the van. "Moving out, Wilma and me. We'll be staying at the motel till we find a place."

I looked over at the house and saw Wilma Mapes backing through the screen door with an armload of clothes. I saw, too, the yellow chrysanthemums that Mrs. Mapes had shown me yesterday, the ones Othman had swiped from the cemetery. The pot was lying on its side in the middle of the yard. The plant and its root ball had been dislodged from the pot, which looked as if it had been thrown into the yard from the stoop. As the screen door slapped shut, I saw a curtain move in an upstairs window. Old Mrs. Mapes was peeking out at us. I said to Othman, "Why?"

Mapes straightened up and turned toward me. "I told my mother what I've been doing behind her back with the Kinneys, all of it." He said this with a sigh that was empty of everything but exhaustion.

"I see."

Mapes continued to meet my gaze. It was easy for him. He had nothing left to dissemble, nothing more to hide. The puffy flesh beneath his eyes no longer twitched, and his syntax was as white as the soles of my feet. Maybe it was easier for him to lay bare his offenses in the white man's dialect than in his own.

"Coming clean seems to have bleached your speech," I said.

"You here to do the dozens, or what?"

I sensed a cynical curiosity stirring in Mapes. The longer he stared at me, the more he looked like a man who'd heard it all and didn't expect to hear anything new from me. If he listened, it was only because it was his habit. Dressed as he was—a brown flannel sport jacket over a white shirt that was turning gray, and a gray tie that was fading toward white—he looked as I imagined he did in the days when he was a homicide dick: Henry Sweetser's partner. According to the uniforms that had been the first to arrive at Douglas Kinney's house last night, they'd been quite a pair, Sweety and Othman. I told the responding officers I was working with Sweetser on a case that involved the Kinneys, and they called Sweetser to Georgetown, telling me as we waited that Sweety and Othman had worked out of the Second District maybe five, six years ago. Between the two of them they'd earned over a half-dozen commendations before Othman retired and Sweetser transferred to the Fifth. Neither of the uniforms remembered Ed Quinn, though. I said to Mapes, "Did you tell your mother about Ed?"

"About him being sick?"

"About him stepping in front of a bus."

Mapes nodded. "When Wilma got home she told her what you said last night in the Kinneys' kitchen, too. 'Procured under fraud.' She have that right?"

I nodded. "I didn't know it for sure last night, but just before I came here I talked to a lawyer named Cuyler, the man who left the message for me at the motel yesterday evening? He said he went over Ed's papers last night. Kinfolk Realty won't inherit the mortgage. Obviously, Tim Kinney won't, either."

Wilma Mapes, standing a few feet away, listened apathetically to our conversation. Othman looked to her for sympathy, or maybe encouragement, but all he got was a tired shrug that said, "I told you so, but I'm too tired to tell you again."

I was pretty tired, myself, having played my tape for Sweetser before spending the wee hours with the brothers Kinney and their father. After the docs at George Washington had tended his wounded arm, the cops had brought him back to his house, and the five of us—Sweetser, Nick, Craig, Douglas, and I—drank instant coffee around the kitchen counter, thinking it all through. Douglas spent most of the time sobering up. Craig didn't say much, either. With his nose packed and taped, and his eyes black and unglinting, he'd been a pleasure to work with.

"What's going to happen to old man Kinney?" Mapes said.

"His liver will fail."

"Is he going downriver?"

"You mean prison?"

"Yeah, Lorton."

"He was cleaning his gun," I said. "It went off and killed his boy. When he realized what he'd done, he tried to shoot himself, an act of drunken despair. I was there and winged him, saved his life."

Mapes's mouth became a gash of cynical irony. "I knew it. The Kinneys skate."

"Ice's a little thin," I said, "but everybody skates, including you."

"Kinney's a killer."

"There's only one human being he's any danger to now," I said, "and he's drinking him to death."

"It'll make the papers," Mapes said.

"Not the worst of it. That's what matters to his sons."

"What do you care about them?" Mapes asked.

"Nothing at all. But if I help the two of them keep their old man out of jail and the affair with Ed Quinn out of the papers, then they sign over Ed's estate without making me fight for it."

"I thought you said the codicil isn't any good."

"It isn't, but I'd have to prove it in court. This way, the Kinneys and I spend ten minutes in a lawyer's office, sign some papers, and it's all over."

Mapes glanced at Wilma, who was still standing to one side, the bodices of her dresses flowing over her thick arms. "You going to call the mortgage in?" she said to me.

"Depends on Othman."

Mapes greeted this with another cold smile, as if too much had been dependent on him for too long. "Depends on me doing what?"

"Nothing. No deals with Mr. Abajan. No tricks to get your

mother out of her house. And no moving out on her, either. She needs you."

Mapes looked at the sky, then down at the cracks in the pavement. He didn't say anything.

"What about Roland and Jerome?" said Wilma.

"I never heard of them. You let Othman abandon his mother, though, and I'll make them famous."

"I'm *not* abandoning her," Othman said sharply. "I'm not. I just . . . can't face her." His voice was throttled with shame and grief.

I glanced over his shoulder. Behind us the sun had edged up over Abajan's town houses. Its first rays were working their way down the humble façade of Mrs. Mapes's home, lighting up the weathered white stucco with the promise of a new day. In the shadows below, I could see the old woman standing behind the screen door, wrapped in a robe. "Is that you, Mr. Bodine?" she called out.

I raised my hand and waved.

"Don't you hurt Othman," she cried.

"No, ma'am."

"You hear me? Don't you hurt him."

"I won't." I leaned close to Mapes and lowered my voice. "Will I?"

Mapes drew a deep breath, turned on his heels and walked back to the house, head down, hands clenched at his sides. I could see him as a little boy, heading home to ask forgiveness for some childhood transgression, his mother waiting for him behind the door, knowing what to say. Halfway up the walk Othman stopped, picked up the fallen mums, and stuffed them back into the pot.

"What you even care?" Wilma Mapes said to me.

I was already heading for my car, though, and I pretended I hadn't heard her question. It was easy enough to fake. I had a lot on my mind, mainly Frieda Gibbs and Wilfred Cuyler. They were due at National Airport at nine-thirty, and I'd be driving them to the morgue so Frieda could claim Harry's body and I could claim Ed's. Afterward I wanted to see about burying him at Arlington Cemetery. I had to meet with a police stenographer later in the day, too, and tell my tale for the record. And, of course, I couldn't forget to buy my kid a memento of the District of Columbia, a replica of the White House.

As I drove across the Fourteenth Street Bridge, I thought about buying a White House for myself as well. As the most preeminent parcel of real estate in town, it would be just the thing to memorialize my trip to D.C.

But I realized I didn't need one. I owned old Mrs. Mapes's white house—Ed's house—and it would do.

I ended up buying myself a T-shirt instead. It said, LIFE IS HARD, THEN YOU DIE.